4-in-1 Mystery Collection

Camp Club Girls
Alexis

Erica Rodgers

BARBOUR BOOKS
An Imprint of Barbour Publishing, Inc.

Print ISBN 978-1-68322-991-9

eBook Editions:
Adobe Digital Edition (.epub) 978-1-64352-125-1
Kindle and MobiPocket Edition (.prc) 978-1-64352-126-8

Published by Barbour Books, an imprint of Barbour Publishing, Inc., 1810 Barbour Drive, Uhrichsville, Ohio 44683, www.barbourbooks.com

Our mission is to inspire the world with the life-changing message of the Bible.

Member of the
Evangelical Christian
Publishers Association

Printed in the United States of America.
006538 0519 BP

Camp Club Girls:
Alexis and the Sacramento Surprise

A Problem at the Park

SLAM!

Alexis Howell jolted up in bed. She sat for a moment while her shocked heart slowed down.

Who on earth is banging doors this early in the morning? she thought. *It's only—*

She looked at the clock on her wall.

"Nine thirty!" Alexis exclaimed.

She knew she had set her alarm for eight o'clock, but she reached over and saw that someone had unplugged it. Alexis threw the covers off and flew out of bed. Why did her little brothers always mess with her on important days? She didn't want to be late!

She yanked on a pair of shorts, slipped on a pair of flip-flops, and scurried toward the door. Alexis passed her desk and reached out, but her hand closed on thin air.

"Where's my paper?" she yelled.

"You mean this one?" her brother asked. He was standing at the top of the stairs waving a paper airplane. The boys were twins, and at first glance she sometimes couldn't tell them apart, which made them even more annoying.

"You made it into an airplane?" cried Alexis. "Give it to me!"

"You should have said *please*," her brother said. He drew his arm back and flung the airplane down the stairs.

"No!" cried Alexis. She bounded toward the stairs.

She could see the important paper circling toward the living room. Here, like everywhere else in her house, were countless stacks of paper. Her mother and father were both lawyers. They worked in the same office, and since that office was being renovated, all of their work had migrated to the Howell house. If that tiny paper airplane landed in the middle of that mess, she would never find it!

Alexis leaped down the first three stairs. On the fourth, however, her foot landed on a remote-control race car and flew out from beneath her. Alexis crashed down the rest of the stairs and slammed into the closest pile of files. It was a paper explosion.

"What on earth?" cried Mrs. Howell. She ran in from the kitchen and found Alexis knee-deep in paper, searching. More paper still fell like rain from the ceiling.

"Oh no!" said Alexis. "Where is it? Where is it?"

"Calm down, Alexis," said Mrs. Howell. "Where is what?"

"The emails! I printed out Kate's email and wrote her flight information on the back. If I can't find it, we won't know when to get her! And I'm running late!"

Her mom placed a hand on her shoulder.

"Calm down," she said. "We have plenty of time. Here, I'll help." Alexis's mom began stacking her files. In no time she uncovered a small, crumpled airplane. Alexis flattened it out and took a deep breath.

"Thanks, Mom." Alexis read the page again just to be sure it was the right paper airplane.

Camp Club Update
From: Alexis Howell

Hey, girls! How is everyone? I'm great, but things have been boring since I got home from camp. I have two more weeks until cheerleading starts, so I'm at home with my brothers way too often! The only investigating I've done lately involves a missing Spiderman sock and the cat from next door. Isn't that sad?

Oh! I almost forgot! A lady at my church could use your prayers. Her name is Miss Maria, and she runs a nature park outside the city. It's a great place to see the local plants and animals, but lately not many people have been visiting. If Miss Maria can't get some big business, she's going to have to close the park. The park is all she has. It would be awful if she had to sell it. She rented some fake dinosaurs that look real and really move, like the animals at Disneyland. Maybe this will bring more business! Pray that it does!

 Kisses, Alex

Alex,

 It was so good to get your update! I'm sorry to hear about Miss Maria. Is she really getting mechanical dinosaurs? That is so awesome! Are you up for a visitor? Sounds like you could use a little excitement, and I can get there easily. My grandpa is a pilot and gets me great deals to fly all over the country. That really comes in handy when I get the urge to visit California! LOL!

 I would love to see you, and besides, I've never seen animatronics that close up before! Do you think Miss Maria would let me touch them? Let me know what your mom says!

 Love, Kate

Alexis must have read Kate's email forty-three times, but her heart was still racing. She had thought she wouldn't see any of the other Camp Club Girls until next summer, but in less than an hour Kate would be there! Alexis was sure this week would be amazing. How could it not be? They would find some crazy case to solve—maybe a stolen piece of art or a break-in at the Governor's Mansion. Whatever they did would be ten times better than doing nothing—as she had done for the last month.

On her way to the kitchen, Alexis poked her head into the bathroom to glance in the mirror. She pulled her loose brown curls into a quick ponytail and wiped the sleep from her eyes. They were an electric blue, and Alexis knew they clashed with her hair, but she liked being a little different.

She stepped back and scrunched her face. If only she could make her freckles disappear! They stood out on her pale skin like spots on a snow leopard, and she could never decide if she liked them or not. She had tried once to cover them with her mom's makeup, but it had been the wrong color and waterproof so she couldn't remove it easily with water. She hadn't known that her mother had special makeup remover. That day she had gone to school looking like a pumpkin.

Oh well. Sometimes she was proud of her freckles. They measured how good her summer had been. The more fun she had in the sun, the darker they got.

"*Lots* of fun in the sun this year, I guess," she said, then she spun out of the bathroom. Her toasted blueberry waffles were waiting for her in the kitchen.

"Thanks, Mom," Alexis said as she ate.

"You're welcome, but do you really need to say it with your mouth full?"

Alexis swallowed. "Sorry."

Her twin brothers, who were seven, had freckles just like Alexis but had also inherited the red hair from her mother's side of the family. The boys finished eating and began playing hide-and-seek among the towering files in the living room. Alexis ignored the possibility of disaster and ate quickly. She was counting down the minutes until she would see Kate at the airport.

Twenty minutes until they left.

Forty minutes until they parked.

Forty-five minutes until—

The television caught her eye. She usually ignored the news, but the anchorwoman with big hair was showing a shot of her friend, Miss Maria, standing in front of the nature park. Alexis grabbed the remote and turned up the volume just in time to hear the introduction to the story.

"Let's go to Channel 13 reporter Thad Swotter for more about this story."

"Thank you, Nicky," said the newsman. He flashed the camera a cheesy smile. "Yesterday one more company refused to sponsor Aspen Heights Conservation Park. That makes them number ten on the list of people who have denied the park money this year. You may ask, *Thad, who's counting?* And I would say no one—except the park's owner."

Thad Swotter laughed into the camera, his mouth still stretched into a wide, fake smile.

"As a last-ditch effort to revive the park," he continued, "Maria Santos has scattered a stampede of mechanical dinosaurs throughout the park. The exhibit opens to the public today and will be there through the end of this month."

"Well, Thad," said the woman with the big hair, "do you think this will bring in more visitors?"

"I know Miss Santos hopes so," said the reporter. "It looks like she's spent her life's savings on the project. It certainly is creative, but I think it will take more than a bunch of toy dinosaurs to keep that park from becoming extinct!"

"Thanks, Thad. Now over to Chris for last night's sports report."

Alexis had forgotten about her waffles. None of her friends had ever been on the news before, but she wasn't excited. She was worried. Had Miss Maria really spent the last of her savings on those dinosaurs? If so, things must be pretty bad.

Alexis whipped out her bright pink notebook and scribbled:

Mission: Find a way to help Miss Maria.

Step One: Visit park with Kate and ask how we can help.

Going to the park was a great idea. It seemed like the perfect place to find an adventure. Kate really wanted to see the dinosaurs, and maybe they could help Miss Maria while they were there. Alexis shoved her notebook into her pink camouflage backpack. She never left home without it. Taking notes was one of the most important things an investigator could do, and Alexis considered herself an investigator. After all, the Camp Club Girls were regularly finding cases to solve.

Half an hour later Alexis and her mom were at the airport, waiting for Kate to pop through the exit gate of the security checkpoint. Mrs. Howell said that she used to be able to meet people at the door of the plane. Alexis couldn't imagine that. For as long as she could remember, she had waited for visitors here— next to the gift shop and at a safe distance from the burly security guards. It would have been fun to meet Kate at her gate—they would already be having a blast. But Alexis was stuck waiting near a rack of overpriced California coffee mugs.

The first thing Alexis noticed was Kate's new pair of glasses flashing through the crowd. They were bright green and came to a point at the sides. They made Alexis think of the Riddler, one of the best Batman villains. She laughed at the thought and met her friend with a hug.

"It's so good to see you!" said Alexis. "How was your flight?"

"Long, and they wouldn't let Biscuit sit with me! He had to go *under the plane*! Do you have any idea how *cold* it gets down there?"

Alexis caught her breath and stopped abruptly. She'd forgotten about Biscuit! How many times when the boys begged for a dog had Mrs. Howell firmly told them their house, especially now, with all its stacks of paper, was no place for a dog! Alexis suspected the real issue was that her mom didn't like dogs. At all. She frowned when people walking their dogs didn't clean up their droppings in the yard. She'd also opposed a neighborhood park being turned into a dog park.

What will Mom do? Alexis thought. *Will she make Kate send Biscuit back home? Will she make Biscuit stay in the garage? But then Biscuit will cry all night.*

"Alexis!" Mrs. Howell called. Kate realized that her mother and friend were far ahead of her. She glanced at her mother's face. Mrs. Howell looked cheerful and friendly. Apparently she either hadn't heard Kate's words clearly or didn't know that Biscuit was a dog.

Lord, please help Mom be nice about Biscuit! Alexis prayed silently.

Alexis's mom led the girls to the baggage claim. They picked up a neat little suitcase and a not-so-neat black and white puppy. At the sight of Biscuit, Mrs. Howell's smile faltered.

"Don't worry, Mom," said Alexis. "Biscuit can stay in my room— away from your files." Mrs. Howell said that she wasn't worried, but her face relaxed only a bit. Alexis knew that she had been thinking of the endless stacks of paper that could easily become chew toys and chaos.

Thank You, God! Alexis mentally murmured. She knew if Mom didn't say anything now, she never would. Now, if only Alexis and Kate could make *sure* Biscuit didn't get in Mom's way or cause trouble!

"We're going straight to the park," Alexis said to Kate as they arrived at the family's green Durango. They buckled themselves into the backseat, and Mrs. Howell dug around in her purse for some cash to pay for parking.

"The dinosaur exhibit opens today, so tons of people should be there," Alexis added as her mom pulled onto the highway.

Alexis was wrong. A half hour later Mrs. Howell drove through the two towering redwoods at the entrance to Aspen Heights and frowned. Theirs was only the second car in the parking lot.

"I don't understand!" said Alexis. "Where is everyone? It was on the news and everything!"

"Don't worry, sweetheart," said her mother. "I'm sure more people will come. It's not even lunchtime yet."

Lunchtime came and went, though, and only a handful of people were enjoying the park. Alexis and Kate walked the shade-speckled trails with Biscuit on his leash.

"Wow!" said Kate. "There are so many plants here!"

"I know," said Alexis. "Miss Maria tries to keep a little of everything. She especially likes the endangered ones."

"Oh look! Another dinosaur!" Kate ran up to a Triceratops that looked like it was eating the fuzzy leaves of a mule ear. A miniature Triceratops was feet away near an evergreen bush. Alexis figured it must be the baby.

Miss Marie had certainly arranged the dinosaurs well. Alexis and Kate had to look hard to see the electrical cords and power boxes hidden among the plants, feeding power to the animatrons.

Alexis had never been easily able to imagine what dinosaurs looked like. But these animatrons were full-sized. They had been meticulously fashioned to resemble the original animals as closely as possible. Alexis began to understand the fascination some people felt for the extinct creatures.

"They're a lot different than in the *Jurassic Park* movies," Alexis noted. "I thought they'd be taller than this. Some of them aren't too much bigger than a large man."

Kate laughed. "Alexis, you're the one from California! You should be the first to know that movies aren't always true to life!"

Alex grinned. "Actually, most of the movie stuff goes on around Los Angeles, and that's quite a ways down the coast. We see movie crews around shooting sometimes. But other than that, we don't have much more to do with the entertainment industry than you probably do in Philadelphia."

"Well, most of the dinosaurs were actually probably smaller than the ones in those movies. And sometimes the movies weren't accurate in re-creating the dinosaurs.

"Like these Velociraptors," Kate said, pointing at the herd of creatures with their waving arms. "See how they're kind of feathery looking? This is more accurate than the portrayals that show them with scaly, lizard-like skin. Just a couple of years ago some paleontologists found a preserved Raptor forearm in Mongolia that proved it had feathers."

"How in the world do you know all that?" Alexis asked.

"Discovery Channel," Kate said with a grin. "And a teacher who spends her summer looking for dinosaur footprints!"

The girls walked along the pathway to the next creature, a Dromaeosaurus lurking near a nest of eggs that looked like they came from a much larger beast.

"This one is even better than the Raptor!" said Kate. "Look! Its eyes blink!"

"Actually, Kate, I think it's *winking*! The other eye is stuck!"

The girls' laughter was cut short. They jumped in alarm as another dinosaur nearby, a Dilophosaurus, raised its head and bellowed. As the animatron swung its head around, Alex gasped.

"It spit at me!" she cried. "I've been assaulted by dinosaur spit! That must have sent out a gallon of water, and all on me! My shirt is soaked!"

Kate clutched her sides, laughing. "Well, at least they used water instead of adding more components to make the expectorant more realistic!"

"What?" Alexis asked.

"At least they didn't make it slimy and mucusy like real spit might have been!"

"Oh, I'm sorry I asked," Alex said. "Wait a minute while I throw up at that thought—and it wouldn't be water either!"

The rest of the animatron trail passed uneventfully. More bellows and eye blinks and movements, but thankfully, no more assaults by spitting dinosaurs.

As Alex's shirt started to dry in the hot sun, the girls started giggling again about the spitting dinosaur.

"Sounds like a rock band," Alex said. "The Spitting Dinosaurs."

"Yeah, or maybe a little kids' T-ball team!" Kate added.

The girls laughed all the way back to the visitors' center. The entrance from the walking trails looked like an old log cabin with a green roof. That led into another larger building with the same log design. The larger building housed more exhibits and displays about nature and animals.

Alexis noticed that more cars were now in the parking lot, and her smile stretched even wider. It would be horrible if the dinosaurs turned out to be a waste of Miss Maria's money.

When they walked into the visitors' center, a lanky teenager greeted them from behind the desk.

"Hey, Alex, who's your friend?" he called out.

"Hi, Jerry. This is Kate." Jerry was tall and a little thin, as if the summer between eighth and ninth grade had stretched him out. His dark hair had light streaks from spending plenty of time in the sun. Between that, his flip-flops, and his tan, he looked as if he'd stepped right out of a surfing movie.

"Hi, Kate," said Jerry. "It's good to meet you!"

"You too," said Kate, looking at her shoes shyly.

Bam! The door to the visitors' center flew open and Miss Maria stormed in.

"That newsman from Channel 13 just got here," she said. "Try to ignore him." She stopped to hug Alexis with her wiry, suntanned arms and shook hands with Kate.

"But Miss Maria," said Jerry, "don't you want to be on the news? It might get more people to come to the park."

"Yes, it might, but that young reporter isn't very pleasant." Miss Maria tucked a piece of short salt-and-pepper hair behind her ear. "More than toy dinosaurs, huh?"

Miss Maria grumbled to herself until a visitor stuck his head through the open door and called to her.

"Hey, Maria! Good job with the Triceratops and Raptor footprints. They're so realistic! And I'm glad you put a Raptor by the fountain. He looks good there. I'll be back with my family, and I'll encourage my students to come!"

Miss Maria thanked the man, who introduced himself as a biology professor from one of the local colleges. "But I've always longed to be a paleontologist!" he confessed.

As the professor waved goodbye, Alexis noticed that Miss Maria didn't look too happy.

"He liked the dinosaurs!" Alexis said. "What's wrong, Miss Maria? Didn't you hear? He's bringing his whole family! And he's sending his students over!"

Miss Maria looked out the window and tapped a finger on the sill.

"Yes, I heard him," said Miss Maria. "The question is, did *you*? He said he liked the footprints—what footprints is he talking about? Alexis, did you and your friend notice any footprints this morning?"

Alexis shook her head. "But we weren't looking that closely," she said.

"And there shouldn't be a Raptor near the fountain at all," said Maria. "I put them all in the dogwood grove."

"Someone must have moved him," said Alexis.

"But why would they do that?" asked Kate.

"Why would anyone dig up my pansies, or carve their initials in a hundred-year-old redwood tree?" said Maria. "Sometimes they do it because they have no respect for God's creation. Sometimes they do it to cause trouble. And sometimes they do it to show off to their friends. Who knows why else they do it! But moving around some of those dinosaurs isn't easy, and they're liable to mess up the wires—to even get electrocuted. Let's go take a look."

Miss Maria had placed the six Raptors together in a little herd. Sure enough, when they rounded the corner to the dogwood grove, the smallest one was missing. Little footprints led away through the trees. They had three toes, like a bird had made them, with two of the toes being longer than the third. The group followed the tracks along the trail until they reached the fountain. Then they saw him.

The diminutive dinosaur was posed on the edge of the fountain. Fortunately, he was one of the models that wasn't animated or electric. He was about two feet tall and bright green. His long tail kept him balanced on his back legs as he leaned toward the water. He looked as if he'd simply left the herd to get a drink.

"Weird!" said Jerry.

"Yeah," Alexis agreed.

She walked carefully around the fountain. She and Alexis had been laughing too hard earlier to notice the footprints if they'd been there. And this Raptor hadn't stood out when they'd seen it earlier—they didn't know Miss Maria hadn't put it by the water. Her mind kicked into overdrive just like it always did when she found something strange or out of place.

How did he get there? she wondered. *If someone moved him, why are there only dinosaur footprints in the mud? Shouldn't there be human prints too?* Alexis pulled her notebook out of her backpack and instinctively began writing things down.

"Interesting *and* irritating," said Miss Maria. She scooped up the Raptor and walked back toward the path holding him beneath her elbow. "You all go back to the visitors' center to greet people as they arrive," she said. "I'm going to go check around."

When they reached the center, Jerry's younger sister, Megan Smith, ran out to greet them. She was going into the seventh grade, like Alexis, and looked just like her brother, only with longer hair.

"Hi, guys!" Megan said. She pointed toward the parking lot. "Did you see the news crew?"

"Yeah," said Alexis.

"Maria wants us to stay away from them," said Jerry. Was Alexis imagining it, or was Jerry irritated?

"Oops. . . ," said Megan. "I gave the guy with the funny hair a tour. He said he was interested in seeing all of the dinosaurs."

"That's okay, Meg," said Alexis. "A tour couldn't have done any harm. Maybe he liked the park enough to do a big story for the evening news."

Kate pushed her glasses up on the bridge of her nose and pointed toward the parking lot.

"I wonder why he's coming back," she said.

Sure enough, the reporter was striding across the parking lot. The wind tossed his bright blue tie around and lifted his hair up at an odd angle. Alexis wondered if he was wearing a wig. She would have thought he was too young for that, but then again, she also knew teachers and men at church who were way younger than her dad and hardly had any hair.

"Hi, kids!" he said. "I'm Thad. Thad Swotter—investigative reporter for Channel 13."

Not quite as impressive as he is on TV, thought Alexis.

"Some place you guys have here," Swotter said, looking around. His tone reminded Alexis of how her father greeted her great-aunt Gertrude. They visited her in Phoenix sometimes for Thanksgiving. He always *said* he was glad to be there, but Alexis didn't think he meant it.

"Miss Maria has worked very hard to share California's indigenous plants with our community," said Alexis. Thad Swotter smiled, and Alexis thought his perfect teeth might be a little big for his mouth.

"Indigenous, huh?" said Swotter. "That's quite a big word for such a little girl. You know, I was sure I saw some specimens that were *definitely* not native to California."

"Well, yes," said Megan. "On the tour, I showed you the olive and the fig tree. Miss Maria works very hard to keep those alive through the winter. She likes to give people glimpses of other parts of the country and even the world too."

"Yes, I remember," said Swotter. "And the thorns were creepy. I'm glad we don't really have those in the foothills of the Sierra Nevada Mountains!"

"Thorns?" asked Kate.

"Yes," said Alexis. "Miss Maria's favorite plant is the Christ's-thorn in her greenhouse. It's planted next to a replica of the crown of thorns Jesus wore."

"Cool!"

"*Cool* it may be," said the reporter. "But I don't see how those thorns have anything to do with us. They're out of place."

"That's not true," said Megan. "God created all of it, so everything belongs."

"*God* created?" Swotter lifted his eyebrows in amusement. "You kids are almost as bad as the bat that runs this place!"

Alexis reared up, ready to defend Miss Maria, but she took a deep breath instead. She knew it would be disrespectful to argue with Mr. Swotter. She even resisted the urge to roll her eyes—which was not easy when she was annoyed.

"This is exactly why nobody comes here!" Swotter laughed. "No one wants to come to a park to get preached at!"

"No one's preaching, sir," said Jerry respectfully. "People don't have to believe in God or Jesus to appreciate the plants. If it really bothers them, they can stick to the other parts of the park."

"They could," said Swotter, "but it'd be easier for them not to come at all. Look, kids, California has enough theme parks. If I want to hear a fairy tale, I'll go to Disneyland." He snickered again and walked off to examine a clump of poppies.

"He's rude," said Kate. "Good thing he doesn't act that rude on TV."

"He practically does," said Alexis. She looked around the empty park entrance. Where was Miss Maria? She had been gone for a long time.

"Those footprints were weird, weren't they?" Jerry laughed. "It's like the dinosaurs just woke up and decided to explore the park!"

Thad Swotter stood up and scribbled furiously in his notebook. He headed toward his van, almost stomping on the poppies as he went. Alexis heard him yell something at his cameraman, who had fallen asleep on the steering wheel.

"What's up with him?" asked Megan.

"Maybe he's late," said Alexis. The group turned back toward the visitors' center. "I think we should check on Miss Maria." Before anyone could agree with her, a scream ripped through the trees.

Then all was silent.

"It came from over there." Jerry pointed toward the trail that led to the Triceratops.

"Oh no! Miss Maria!" Alexis tore off through the trees and the others followed.

When they came around the last corner, Alexis almost screamed herself. Miss Maria was lying on her back in the mud, next to the mother Triceratops. She wasn't moving.

Her large eyes stared unblinking into the cloudless sky.

The Footprints

Hospitals had never bothered Alexis. Her grandma was a nurse, so she had grown up visiting them. But this—this was different. Alexis had never visited someone who was actually *hurt*. She hated to admit it, but she was more than a little scared.

For the first time, Alexis noticed the smells of a hospital. Grandma's strong perfume had apparently masked all the hospital odors the other times she'd been in them. Alexis noticed that the hospital smelled like a mixture of cafeteria food and cleaning supplies.

Kate reached over and looped her arm through Alexis's.

"Don't worry," she said. "It could have been a lot worse."

Alexis tried to smile, but it didn't quite work.

Miss Maria was in a room on the fourth floor. The door was slightly open, and Alexis and Kate stopped just outside. A deep male voice drifted out into the hall. Apparently a doctor was talking to her.

"Your back's not broken, Miss Santos, but you pulled some muscles pretty bad. If you're not careful, you could end up in a brace for months. I'd like to keep you here for observation. If everything goes well, you can go home in a couple of days."

"Thank you, Doctor," said Miss Maria. The strength in her voice calmed Alexis a little bit. Alex's racing heart slowed. The doctor swept out into the hallway, nearly knocking into the girls. Alexis heard the *click, click* of high heels behind her and turned to see her mom.

"That parking garage is a nightmare! Be glad I dropped you girls off at the doors!" She stepped forward and knocked lightly on the door. "Miss Maria?"

"Oh! Visitors!" chimed the older woman.

The girls filed into the room and sat down in the mauve chairs next to Miss Maria's white bed. She looked cheerful. Her mood was contagious, and Alexis smiled.

"How are you feeling?" she asked.

"Oh, just fine," said Miss Maria. "It doesn't hurt too badly right now."

They talked for a while, mostly about Miss Maria's injury and the attractive male nurse who kept coming in to check on her. Apparently Miss Maria had climbed up onto the Triceratops to get a better look at the footprints that were also leading from it to the distance. When it moved unexpectedly, she fell off.

"Serves me right for thinking I needed a bird's-eye view!" she said.

After twenty minutes, Mrs. Howell's phone rang. She dug it out of her purse and stepped outside to take the call. Her irritated voice drifted through the closing door. "No, Amanda, they don't owe anything. I told you that case was pro bono. . . . Yes. . .the hearing is next Friday. . . ."

After the door was shut, Miss Maria smiled conspiratorially. She crooked her finger and beckoned Alexis and Kate to come closer.

"Just grab a seat on the bed here," she said, patting the blanket on either side of her skinny legs. "I have a favor to ask."

Alexis sat down. She knew Miss Maria would need help now that her back was hurt. She probably wanted someone to feed her cat while she was in the hospital.

"It's about the park," Miss Maria said. "The doctor says I can't work for a while. I was wondering if you might be able to help me out a little." Alexis was puzzled. Why was Miss Maria whispering? It wasn't really a secret that the park would need a few extra hands, was it?

"Of course we'll help at the park, Miss Maria," said Alexis.

"Yeah," said Kate. "We can do whatever you need. It will be fun to see more of the dinosaurs."

"Well, that's just it. I hope you'll see a *lot* more of the dinosaurs," said Miss Maria. Her mouth stretched into a secret smile, and she leaned toward them, wincing as her back was strained.

"My friend Gretchen told me that you found her kitten, Poncho, when no one else could. And your mother has mentioned the mysteries that you girls have already worked on. I would love the Camp Club Girls to investigate."

The word *investigate* made Alexis's heart race. She was really interested in the footprints and the little Raptor, but she also didn't want to make something out of nothing. Just the other day her father had accused her of seeing a mystery in everything. He had been joking, but she knew there was truth in what he said.

For instance, every time she went to the grocery store with her mother she couldn't help but ask herself crazy questions. Why could you pull an apple from the bottom of a pyramid without the others rolling to the floor? Why did Fred, the baker, constantly move the cakes around in his display case?

"I want you to find out what is happening," Maria said. Alexis turned her attention back to the hospital bed. "Find out where those footprints are coming from, and how the dinosaur got from one place to the other. I don't like the idea of someone fiddling around in my park. If those dinosaurs are ruined, I'll have to pay for them. And if a visitor gets hurt, I could never forgive myself. Could I bother you girls with this?"

"Bother us? Miss Maria, it wouldn't bother us at all!" said Alexis.

"Really!" said Kate. "This is what we do best."

"Good," said Miss Maria. She sighed and slumped back in her bed. "It feels good to leave this in the hands of detectives I can trust. The police would just laugh at me."

Alexis dug out her notebook.

"Miss Maria, do you feel well enough to answer a few questions?" she asked. Alexis wanted to start the investigation right away. It felt like so long since she had helped someone. Miss Maria nodded, and Alexis launched her first question.

"When was the last time you visited the Triceratops and the

Raptor? Before this afternoon, I mean."

"Last night as I closed the park," said Miss Maria. "I always walk a complete loop after I close the gates."

"And did everything seem normal?" asked Kate.

"Yes. Everything was just as I left it. I don't think anyone could have been hanging around and changed things after I left. I'm pretty sure no stragglers were there at the time. Not many people had been there in the first place. I paid extra close attention, since the dinosaur exhibit was opening today. I wanted everything to be perfect."

Alexis scribbled onto her paper.

"And do you recall seeing the footprints then?" she asked.

"No, I do not. But it was getting dark, so I could have overlooked them. I know the park like the back of my hand, so I never take a flashlight. It only attracts the bugs, and I must be sweet, because they bite me like crazy."

Mrs. Howell stuck her head back into the room. Her cell phone was still attached to her ear.

"Hey girls, I think we should let Miss Maria get some rest," she said.

The girls each grabbed a sun-wrinkled hand and squeezed.

"Get better," said Alexis. "And don't worry about a thing. The Camp Club Girls have this covered."

The girls went swimming in the neighborhood pool the next morning. Then promptly at 1:00 they sat at the Howells' computer. Earlier, Kate had texted the Camp Club Girls who were available to meet them online for chat at 1 p.m. California time.

Promptly at 1:00, Alexis started the computer, while Kate pulled open her tiny battery-run notebook computer. "This is a new prototype one of my dad's students is working on for Dell," she explained. "Dad let me bring it as long as I'm careful. He even thought a road trial might be good for it," Kate explained. "It's even waterproof and is the smallest in existence."

"Wow!" Alexis exclaimed. "It must be cool to have a dad who works with technology!"

"Well, it can't do everything a full-sized computer can do," Kate

admitted. "But it can handle more functions than an iPhone."
A subdued *ding* let the girls know a message was waiting.

Elizabeth: *Hey y'all. How are things in sunny Calif? I hear
we have a new mystery on our hands.*

McKenzie: *I don't think I've recovered from the last
mystery yet! Can this one beat our missing horse
problem? Any more animals involved?*

Kate: *None so far. Unless you count Biscuit. . .who's here
and is barking that he loves you.*

Biscuit yipped as if he could read the girls' notes!

Alexis: *But we are dealing with animatronics.*

Elizabeth: *What in the world are those?*

Kate: *Animated dinosaurs. They're built to be the size of
real dinosaurs and are electronically wired to show the
mannerisms of real dinosaurs. Almost like movie props.*

Bailey: *Movie props? What are you guys involved in? Wish
I could be there. I'd love to be in movies.*

Alexis: *Not movies! At a local park.*

Sydney: *They had those at a park in Virginia once
when my aunt was filling in there for the park ranger
department. They're cool.*

Bailey: *Sounds like a good movie to me. We'll call you
Queen of the Dinosaurs, Alex. Maybe one will chase
you up a tree.*

Alexis: *Just like that lady in* King Kong *got chased up a
building, right?*

Bailey: *Something like that.*

Kate: *Anyway. . .no movies involved, Bailey. But there is a
news anchor who's a real dog.*

Sydney: *I hope you're covering Biscuit's ears.*

Kate: *Oops, no offense, Biscuit!*

Alexis: *Well, here's what's happening. . . .*

Alex filled the girls in on what was going on so far.

Elizabeth: *So if Miss Maria saw everything right, the park was perfectly normal when it closed. So whatever happened occurred after dark but before lunchtime yesterday when you were there.*

Kate: *Right.*

Sydney: *Did you see anything strange in the park?*

Alex: *Well, at the fountain I noticed that there was only one set of footprints. Just those tiny Raptor ones. If a person had moved him, shouldn't there have been human prints too? Boots or shoes or something?*

McKenzie: *But wouldn't there be a lot of ways someone could erase tracks? Sometimes when I'm out in the woods on my horse, even in the mud we don't leave tracks because the wind will blow leaves over the tracks.*

Sydney: *Or could someone have put down leaves or grass to start with so they wouldn't leave tracks?*

Bailey: *They could have even used stilts or something so they didn't leave prints. Did you see any holes in the ground?*

Alex: *I guess those things could have happened. I think if they had stilts that would have been too noticeable; you know, their bringing them into the center and taking them out.*

McKenzie: *Perhaps the first thing we need to do is figure out the motive. Why would anyone move the dinosaurs or decorate the park with footprints?*

Bailey: *Do you think someone is just trying to be mean? Do people dislike Miss Maria?*

Alex: *I think everyone likes her but the rude news anchor. Everyone at church loves Miss Maria. And if someone was hanging around the park bothering her, Jerry would have told us.*

Elizabeth: *Didn't you say Miss Maria has some Christian stuff in the park? Maybe someone doesn't like that.*

Kate: *Alex and I wonder if it's a joke.*

Alexis: *After all, most kids would think it would be pretty funny to move a lady's dinosaurs around and make them come to life!*

Kate: *Of course, they might get electrocuted in the process!*

McKenzie: *You know the area, Alex. Any bored kids around who might do this?*

Alex: *Thousands. Especially after that news anchor's rude report. They might do it thinking it's a joke, not to hurt Miss Maria.*

Kate: *By the way, I'll send you the link to the news story. The local channel has a video of it on their website.*

Elizabeth: *What's the plan of action?*

Alex: *We need more information. We'll have to investigate the scenes—the fountain and the Triceratops area.*

After a little bit more chat, the girls signed off.

"We can look harder for clues and do some interviews," Kate reassured Alex. "Maybe someone saw something."

"Yeah. Jerry and Megan live just outside the park, near Miss Maria. They might have noticed someone suspicious sneaking around," Alexis said.

•—•—•

At the dinner table that night, Alexis's thoughts turned to Miss Maria's money problems. How could the park raise enough to stay open? She prodded her family for ideas, but no one thought of anything original.

"She should charge a small fee to get in," said Mr. Howell.

"She does, but it's certainly not enough to cover all the bills, Rich," said Mrs. Howell as she dished salad onto the plates. "And I know she hates doing that. I told her before that she should raise the rates, but she won't agree to that."

"I hate this stuff!" said one of the twins, poking at his salad.

"Yeah! We're not rabbits!" said the other. But they both wolfed down the food in seconds.

"Mom's right," said Alexis, ignoring her brothers. "Miss Maria would never make people pay."

"What about extra donations?" asked Kate. "Would she accept

gifts from people who *wanted* to give?"

"Kate, that's it!" said Alexis. "We could put a box at the entrance for donations. If visitors want to help, they can!"

"Oooh!" said one of the twins. "Put one by the bathroom and make people pay for their toilet paper!"

Mr. Howell was caught off guard. He burst out laughing, and a piece of lettuce flapped out of his mouth and onto his chin. Mrs. Howell shot a killer glance at the boys and then at her husband. The twins piled mashed potatoes onto their plates in silence. Alexis had a feeling that her dad sometimes got into more trouble than her brothers.

"Mom," said Alexis quietly, "can we turn on the TV?"

"You know I hate having that thing on while we eat," Mrs. Howell said. She put the chicken on the table and dashed off to get the rolls out of the oven.

"I know," Alexis called after her, "but there's supposed to be another story about the park!"

"Okay, but just for a few minutes."

Alexis got the remote off the TV and pressed a button. Thad Swotter's face appeared on the screen. His neon purple tie with blue stripes clashed horribly with his yellow hair.

"The reopening of Aspen Heights today was shrouded in mystery," the reporter said. "Maria Santos put mechanical dinosaurs in her nature park to draw in visitors. But it seems that the animatrons have begun wreaking havoc instead."

A picture of the Triceratops jumped onto the screen. The scene clipped away to show footprints. Swotter's voice broke in to explain.

"It seems that these footprints were not part of the original display. They just appeared. In fact, Maria Santos was injured today while inspecting them. Also, a small Raptor was found this afternoon a long way from his herd."

Now a picture of the fountain sprang onto the screen.

"He was found here, at the edge of the water, taking a drink. One park volunteer said that the dinosaurs may have simply come to life. I laughed at first, but that was before my camera captured *this*."

Another series of pictures ran across the television. Dinosaurs and footprints were scattered all over the park, where none had been earlier. All the small, nonmechanical Raptors were huddled around the entrance sign as if they were reading it. The baby Triceratops was in the middle of the bridge that crossed the creek. But the last picture was the scariest one of all: Tyrannosaurus Rex tracks. They led to the outer fence and back, as if the giant carnivore had been looking for a way out of the park.

"This is *way* too science fiction," said Alexis. She jumped out of her chair and ran to the phone.

"Alexis, please finish your dinner," said her mother as Alex dialed. Alexis held up a finger and begged silently for "just one minute." The phone on the other end of the line began to ring.

"Hello?" said a voice.

"Jerry! Are you watching this?" said Alexis.

"The news? Yeah! Isn't it cool?"

"It's crazy!" said Alexis. "Why didn't you tell me the dinosaurs had moved again?"

"How was I supposed to know?" said Jerry. "We closed the park after Miss Maria got hurt. I walked around the park before I closed it to make sure no stragglers were still in it. Everything was fine then. Then Megan and I cleaned the concession stand. I sure didn't hear or see anything. Miss Maria called a little later, asking us to let the news crew in to film some shots. I didn't stay with them; I had paperwork to do."

"Okay," said Alexis. "I was just shocked, that's all. I guess I'll see you tomorrow."

Alexis hung up the phone and crossed her arms. On the television, Thad Swotter was still rambling about dinosaurs coming to life.

"I don't know what's going on," Alexis explained as she sat back down at the table. "Jerry practically lives at the park and didn't know about the dinosaurs moving again. So how did the *reporter* know?"

"Yeah, Thad Swotter doesn't even like the park, so it's not like he'll hang around there for hours waiting for something to happen," Kate added.

"Wait!" Alexis exclaimed. "Thad Swotter doesn't like the park!" Kate's eyes widened.

"How did he know the dinosaurs had moved again?" she murmured. "Wasn't the park already closed?"

"Yeah," said Alexis. "It had been closed for hours." She leaned forward and quietly continued, "He knew because he was there, Kate. I bet he took the pictures after he moved the dinosaurs *himself!*"

The girls watched the screen as the camera zoomed in. Thad Swotter's goofy grin was more than a little suspicious. He was enjoying Miss Maria's troubles way too much.

"Enjoy it while you can, Mr. Swotter," Alexis said. "The Camp Club Girls are on to you now."

CHAPTER 3

Jurassic Jaws

TO: Camp Club Girls
SUBJECT: Mystery Suspect
Suspect: Thad Swotter
Possible Motives: 1. Dislike of the park and Miss Maria. (He called her a "bat" yesterday and complained about the plants related to Christian history.)
2. Just to get a story—he is a young reporter who wants to be the best. A huge story, like dinosaurs coming to life, would give him quite a boost.
Evidence: Dinosaur positions found changed after news crew had been there.

Alexis hit the SEND key on her email and picked up Biscuit's leash. She would take him for a walk around the block while Kate was getting dressed. It would give her some quiet time away from her little brothers.

Alexis stepped outside and stood on the front porch for a moment, breathing in the dewy Sacramento morning.

Her cell phone suddenly buzzed with a text.

HI! BETH HERE. YOU'RE UP EARLY. GOT YOUR EMAIL.

Alexis: LUV THIS TIME OF DAY. REMINDS ME THAT EVERY DAY IS A NEW BEGINNING. NO MTR HOW BAD ONE DAY IS, THE NEXT IS ALWAYS NEW AND DIFF.

Elizabeth: MAYBE THAT'S WHAT GOD MEANS WHEN HE SAYS

HIS MERCIES ARE NEW EVERY MORNING. READ LAMENTATIONS 3:22-23. CuL8r.

Alexis stumbled as Biscuit pulled her onto the sidewalk.

"Okay, I'm coming! Want to help me figure out this case while you're sniffing around?" Biscuit looked back at her as if puzzled. Then he dove headfirst into a clump of orange honeysuckle.

"Gotta tell you, Biscuit," said Alexis. "I think you're letting the Camp Club Girls down!"

Alexis thought about the mystery. She knew they could connect Thad Swotter to the mysterious movements of the dinosaurs. The question was, *how*?

At first it sounded strange. Why would a grown man resort to such silly tricks? Was Swotter just playing a joke on Miss Maria?

Possibly, but if he was, he was going to a lot of work just to annoy someone he barely knew. The second motive made more sense. If Swotter was the only reporter able to get pictures of the dinosaurs, it might give him a boost at his job. He *had* been sent to cover the opening of the dinosaur exhibit. While this was a big deal for Miss Maria, Alexis knew that a couple of robots at a nature park weren't really big news in California's capital.

In fact, Alexis couldn't remember seeing Thad Swotter before yesterday. He was probably the new guy—the new guy who wanted to make it to the top as fast as he could.

That reminded Alexis of a movie she had seen. The main character was a reporter who had to cover the worst stories ever, like cat fashion shows. Maybe Thad Swotter was like that guy and wanted a more dramatic story. Maybe he wanted one so much, he was making it happen.

Too bad he's not as funny as the guy in the movie, thought Alexis.

Would it really be that bad if Swotter wanted a good story? Alexis didn't think so, but moving the dinosaurs around did more than draw attention—it put people at risk. Miss Maria said between the weight of the dinosaurs and the sensitivity of their electrical setup—the hidden generators—someone could get hurt tampering with them.

Not only that, but if one of the *dinosaurs* got damaged, Maria would have to pay for it. That would be expensive, and Maria certainly couldn't handle an expense like that.

Thad Swotter must be using the park to catapult his way into stardom, no matter what it costs anyone else, Alex thought.

Alexis Howell was not about to let him succeed. She started jogging back to the house to discuss her thoughts with Kate.

●—●—●

After breakfast Mrs. Howell dropped the girls off at the park. It looked like a completely different place. The little Raptors were still huddled around the entry sign, but that was not what made Alexis gasp. The parking lot was *full*.

Hundreds of people were entering the park. After five minutes of pushing through the crowd, Alexis and Kate found Elena Smith, the woman who helped Miss Maria run the park. She was also Jerry and Megan's mother. In her late thirties, she had a wonderful sense of humor. The thick, dark hair that usually fell to the middle of her back was pulled up in a ponytail.

"Wow, Mrs. Smith!" called Alexis. "This must be a record! I've never seen so many people here before!" But Mrs. Smith looked anything but happy.

"This is crazy! Only three of us are here to answer questions! We ran out of maps fifteen minutes after opening too. Megan is inside making black and white copies to hand out."

"But this is good, right?" asked Kate. "More visitors are what Miss Maria needed, right?"

"Yes," said Mrs. Smith, "but not like this. These people don't really care about the park. They only want to see the dinosaurs that 'come to life.' Hey!" Mrs. Smith yelled over the crowd to a pair of girls who had left the path. "You're not allowed to walk over there!"

"We're not walking!" one of the teens answered. "We're *skipping*!" And they were. They were skipping right through the Jeffrey Pine saplings that had been planted by the church preschool class.

"You see?" said Mrs. Smith. "This has been happening all morning. Don't they realize they could kill those trees? They're delicate!" Mrs. Smith stomped off to make sure the trees were okay.

Alexis and Kate turned toward the visitors' center. Jerry met them in the doorway.

"Did you get up early?" asked Alexis. She noticed that Jerry's eyes were all red and puffy. He didn't answer her question.

"Isn't this great!?" he said, pointing to the teeming crowd.

"I don't know," said Alex. "It seems a little out of control." A tangle of loud kids rushed by, knocking into her without excusing themselves.

"Yeah," said Megan. "But we'll fix that." She handed Alex, Kate, and Jerry each a stack of maps.

"We're going to start giving guided tours!" said Jerry. "We can each lead one. Some people will still wander around on their own, but this will help us spread out and keep an eye on things."

"That's a good idea," said Alexis. "Someone's already rearranging the park at night. The last thing we need is visitors doing the same thing during the day!"

Alexis and Kate paused near the entrance sign. The little herd of Raptors was examining it, rocking their heads back and forth as if the writing confused them.

"They're turned on!" said Alexis. "The Raptor that was moved yesterday wasn't plugged back in. It was just sitting on the fountain."

Kate found the cord that powered the Raptors and followed it across the path to a large bush. A deep *humm hummm* came from behind its leaves.

"It's a generator!" Kate said. She ran back to where Alexis stood near the sign. "Not only did the suspect move the dinosaurs, he moved the generator too. Then he plugged them back in!"

Whoever did this had put a lot of effort into it. Generators were heavy, Alexis knew, but a full-grown man—or reporter—would have been able to do it easily.

Alexis examined the dinosaurs one more time.

"These do look pretty funny," she admitted to Kate.

"Yeah, they're cute, standing and reading the park rules," Kate admitted. "Whoever did it has a sense of humor. But look at this ground!"

Kate pointed to the trampled grass. "I was hoping we'd find some clues."

"You're right. We'll never be able to find clues around here," Alex said, thinking of the hundreds of hiking boots, sneakers, and flip-flops that had already passed through that morning. "Maybe we'll have more luck inside."

"Come on, time for the tours!" Jerry announced.

Jerry directed a large group of people to Alexis. Alex's group took off ahead of Kate's group, and Alex led the visitors through the park. She pointed out interesting features but otherwise let them explore on their own. The most important thing was to make sure no one left the path. Already a first-grader had fallen into a bed of California thistle. A few of the green barbs were still visible in the seat of her khaki Bermuda shorts as the group continued.

Alexis was excited. Guiding a tour group was the perfect way to investigate the mystery sites. She could poke around and no one would even suspect that she was gathering evidence. It would just look like she was examining the plants.

When they reached the stream, the group had to wriggle its way around the baby Triceratops. The small dinosaur was still standing in the middle of the bridge, just as it had been shown on the news the night before. A science teacher from the local middle school reached out to touch him.

"Wow," he said. "It feels so real!"

"Please don't touch him, Mr. Bell," said Alexis politely. "I think they're very expensive and very delicate."

"Sure, Alexis. He's amazing! I could almost believe the rumors that the dinosaurs come to life! May I take a picture?"

"Of course," said Alexis. "Take as many as you want."

The crowd moved ahead to study the wildflower meadow, but Alexis lingered to look for clues on the bridge.

Nothing. Alexis knew she shouldn't be surprised. Hundreds of visitors were trampling this area, just as they'd done at the entrance. The suspect could have left absolutely anything, and she would never know.

Alexis guided her group farther down the trail. At least she could still study the Tyrannosaurus Rex. His area was more secluded than the busy footbridge.

Alex knew that it had taken ten people and one huge crane to place the Tyrannosaurus Rex among the aspens and dogwoods on the other side of the meadow. The slender trunks of the trees made him seem taller than his thirty feet. Alexis knew that although the Tyrannosaurus Rex didn't weigh anywhere near what a real Tyrannosaurus Rex would weigh, it was still well over a thousand pounds. There was no way Thad Swotter, or any other human, would be able to move this guy.

While the crowd stared at the mammoth creature, Alexis found the footprints that had been on the news. They were huge. She could even see the marks where the six-inch claws had scarred the earth.

She followed the tracks about a hundred yards. She looked back now and then to make sure no one from the group followed her. The footprints went all the way to the outer edge of Aspen Heights, where a chain-link fence marked the end of Miss Maria's property. Alexis gasped.

A hole gaped in the middle of the fence, right where the footprints ended.

"What could have done that?" she whispered. Fence cutters? Maybe, but how hard was it to break through metal? It must have taken a lot of strength.

Alexis was supposed to follow the evidence, but now the evidence was starting to scare her. She saw no trace of humans here either—just dinosaur footprints and a fence that looked as if a pair of Jurassic jaws had torn right through it.

Impossible. She refused to believe that the dinosaurs were actually coming to life.

Alexis heard someone call her name. It sounded like Mr. Bell. The tour was probably ready to move on.

"Coming!" she cried, and she weaved her way back through the trees.

At the Tyrannosaurus Rex, the group was busy taking pictures of the dinosaur staged so beautifully among the aspen trees. Alexis saw that Kate's group had caught up and was milling around the glade as well. One visitor was taking a video of the Tyrannosaurus Rex with his cell phone.

Alexis edged toward the dinosaur, just in case any clues were hiding in its monstrous shadow.

The dinosaur stood on its strong back legs. Its thighs were as thick as redwood trunks. Its arms, on the other hand, were tiny—hardly long enough to allow the creature to grasp his own hands. Alexis wondered if God might have given the Tyrannosaurus Rex monstrous teeth so the other dinosaurs wouldn't laugh at his silly proportions.

His head moved proudly through the air, looking over the forest and their little tour. Alexis knew a hidden generator hummed, although the noise of the tourists masked its gentle noise.

Kate joined Alex and started snapping pictures. "As soon as this tour is over, wait before you start the next one," Alex told Kate. "I have something to tell you!"

Kate gave Alexis a searching look. "Okay, sounds like you found a clue."

"Well, not a clue, but certainly something strange," Alex said. "But we don't have time to go into it now."

"Okay," Kate said, going back to her photography. "Stand by the Tyrannosaurus Rex and let me get a picture of you with it."

Alex got near the animatron and dodged the thick tail as it swung back and forth. Alexis was looking for clues as to where the footprints began when she heard a loud *crack* and an angry *roar*! She looked up and didn't have time to scream.

The Tyrannosaurus's head plummeted toward her, hundreds of sharp teeth gleaming in the sun.

The tour group fled the aspen grove, some screaming and some laughing. Children were scared out of their minds, crying and hiding their heads in their mothers' necks. Needless to say, the tour was over.

"Did you see that?" called one girl to her friend. "It almost bit that girl's head off!"

Kate ran over to Alex. "Are you okay?"

Alex weakly nodded. She was still shaking.

"Come on. I think you need a Coke," Kate said. "You need to sit down inside the visitors' center and relax a minute."

Alexis and Kate were following the crowd back to the visitors' center at a slow walk. Alexis glanced back and saw the slumping dinosaur. He was bent over the spot where Alexis had been standing, and he wasn't moving anymore.

Alexis didn't think the Tyrannosaurus Rex had really attacked her, but she was shaken up. It was hard not to be scared when a head full of teeth came at you out of nowhere. On the other hand, it *wasn't* hard to imagine what the Channel 13 guy would say about the park tonight.

Alexis could already hear it. *"A young girl was attacked today by an animal that has been extinct for thousands of years. . . ."*

Alexis didn't notice when they crossed back over the bridge, but Kate grabbed her arm and spun her around.

"Alexis!" she whispered. "The baby Triceratops—it stuck its tongue out at me!"

"I guess its mother needs to teach it some manners," joked Alexis.

But Kate didn't laugh.

"Alexis, look at the power cord. . .it isn't plugged in."

Puzzling Pictures

The panic caused by the Tyrannosaurus Rex spread through the park faster than fire. At the end of the afternoon, Mrs. Smith and Megan pushed the gates closed. Jerry had already been on the phone with Miss Maria and called the electrician who had helped set up the animatrons. Hopefully, he could figure out what was wrong with the dinosaur.

Alexis and Kate decided to use the free afternoon to sleuth. They decided it wasn't enough to wait until something else happened. They had to get ahead and catch him in the act.

So now Alexis and Kate were dragging Jerry and Megan around the park with a handful of cameras.

"Hey, Alex," said Jerry. "Why are we doing this?"

"We're trying to find out how the dinosaurs are moving around at night," said Alexis.

"Why does it matter?" asked Megan. "They're bringing in a lot of business, aren't they? Why don't we just leave it alone?"

"Because Miss Maria says that moving them is dangerous. Someone could get hurt. And I know it sounds crazy, but if they really *are* coming to life. . .someone could get torn apart." The memory of a murderous mouth full of teeth flashed through Alexis's mind. She shivered.

"Yeah," said Kate. "People today get mad over a cold cup of coffee. What do you think they would do if their kid got eaten by a park display?"

Alexis laughed nervously. She knew that Kate was right. Last week one of her mom's clients wanted to sue a fast-food restaurant because the ice in his drink melted too fast. Mrs. Howell had refused to pursue the lawsuit, of course, but it made Alexis think. The smallest, silliest things could make people so angry. A real dinosaur attack would make them furious.

The four kids walked past the entrance sign. The dinosaurs weren't there anymore since Mrs. Smith had taken them all back to the dogwood grove. Alexis was sure they wouldn't be at the entrance in the morning, but were they running all over the park by themselves? And what about the baby Triceratops? How had it stuck its tongue out without being plugged in?

What was really going on around here?

The four of them walked the entire park, looking for the best places to put the cameras. Kate stuck one near the Triceratops meadow. She crept along the edge of the grass, placed the camera on a rock, and ran all the way back to the trail. She kept glancing over her shoulder, as if she expected the Triceratops to charge any second. Alexis couldn't blame her.

Next they put cameras where the dinosaurs had been found out of place—near the fountain and the entrance sign.

"These things are tiny!" said Megan, leaning on the wall of the fountain and looking at one of the cameras. "Where's the film?"

"Film?" said Kate. "*Please.* These babies are digital."

"Where on earth did you get this many digital cameras?" said Jerry.

"My dad uses them at his work. These are the models from a couple years ago. They have bigger and better ones now. Actually, *smaller* and better." Kate snickered at her joke and led the group through the bushes and toward the Raptors.

"You're such a nerd!" Alexis teased. "What would I do without you?"

Kate smiled and bent down to place the last camera on the ground. She hid it in a clump of fuzzy mule ears. The bright yellow flowers dusted pollen all over her arm. She adjusted the camera so the lens was watching the path to the visitors' center.

"There! It's done!" Alexis said triumphantly.

"So," said Jerry to Kate, "do those cameras just take a picture every five minutes or something?"

"No way," said Kate. "We could miss tons of stuff if we did it that way! I turned on the motion sensor. Anytime these little red lights sense something move, they'll snap a picture." Jerry pushed Megan playfully in front of the camera.

SNAP!

"It works!" he said.

"Of course it works!" said Kate. "And now I have a picture of your sister's ankle clogging my memory card!" Kate leaned down and hit the DELETE button.

"You're amazing, Kate," said Alexis. "I am so glad you came to visit! If it weren't for you, I'd be doing an all-night stakeout."

Megan giggled. "That's not my idea of a slumber party—spending the night in a park of dinosaurs that may or may not eat you!" she said.

"We'd better get back to the front. Mom will be here any time," Alexis said.

On their way back to the parking lot, Alexis stopped to check the donations box. Mrs. Smith liked the idea and had helped her hang it up. It was a simple wooden box with a lock on the lid and a hole in the top so people could drop in additional donations. The small sign on it read, DONATIONS APPRECIATED! ALL FUNDS KEEP THE PARK BEAUTIFUL FOR YOUR ENJOYMENT! THANK YOU!

The box contained seventy-nine cents, three gum wrappers, and a check for fifteen dollars from Mr. Bell, the science teacher.

"Visitors weren't very generous today, were they?" asked Jerry.

"Mr. Bell was," said Alexis. "Did you expect a miracle?"

"Why not?" asked Megan.

"Huh?"

"Why not expect a miracle?" said Megan a little louder. "I've been praying for one a lot lately. I mean, if God could do all those cool things in the Bible, surely He can take some time to help Miss Maria."

"I think He is," said Kate. "She has us to help her while she's hurt. And it's probably only a matter of time before the money comes in."

"How can you be so sure?" asked Jerry.

Alexis wanted to answer him. She wanted to be like Elizabeth and break out a Bible verse that explained exactly why she trusted God to fix this mess, but she couldn't. She couldn't explain why she trusted so completely in something she couldn't see. Jerry believed in God—they went to the same church. But Alexis sensed that he had a hard time trusting anyone but himself.

"I'm not sure *how*," Alexis finally said, "but I know it will happen." She smiled at him, hoping it would make him feel better. He smiled back, but Alexis could tell that he wasn't convinced. Mrs. Howell's old red van pulled up to the curb.

"See you guys tomorrow!" Alexis and Kate called. As Alexis got in the car, she still wished she was better at explaining what was in her heart. Somehow she knew everything would work out.

There was no more investigating to do at the moment. The cameras would do their job, and hopefully the Camp Club Girls would have fresh evidence to go on in the morning.

While they waited for dinner, Alexis and Kate thought of a new way to help Miss Maria. They went to work on the computer designing a poster for the park and then sent a copy to the other Camp Club Girls. Bailey emailed back that it looked like a movie poster.

Alexis smiled. Alexis loved to look at the posters at the movie theaters. In the middle of the poster was a huge Tyrannosaurus Rex. He was standing in the middle of a ring of redwoods, lifting his head in what looked like an ear-splitting roar. In front of him, walking paths wove in and out of the trees. Beautiful flowers and plants were scattered in the shade. At the top of the poster, huge letters read: Aspen Heights Conservation Park: Experience nature, past and present!

"This looks great!" said Kate. "You're really creative, Alexis."

"Thanks, but I couldn't have done it without your help! I'm not good at all of these computer programs." They printed off one copy of the poster and held it up.

"If we put these around town, they should draw more people to the park!" said Alexis.

"Between those and the donations box, something *has* to happen," said Kate.

Mr. Howell brought home pizza, so the girls sat down with pepperoni and pineapple to watch the evening news. Alexis's mom had agreed they could watch TV from the table as long as Thad Swotter was reporting on Aspen Heights.

"It's on, Mom!" cried Alexis. "Come here!"

Nikki, the Channel 13 anchor, was talking to the camera. The picture in the upper right-hand corner of the television screen showed the giant head of Miss Maria's Tyrannosaurus Rex.

"And here's Thad Swotter with the report," she said.

"Thanks, Nikki. Today was a scary day out here at Aspen Heights."

Alexis thought she recognized the scenery behind him. Soon the shape of the Tyrannosaurus loomed just behind the reporter, and she knew she was right.

"He's in the park!" Alexis said. "How did he get in after we closed?"

"Shh! Listen!" said Kate. Thad Swotter's voice barely cut through Alexis's swirling thoughts.

"Any doubts about strange happenings in this park were dissolved today when one of the mechanical dinosaurs actually *attacked* a young girl. As seen in this footage from a cell phone, the girl barely escaped with her life."

Thad Swotter's face was replaced by a video of Alexis diving for the ground as the Tyrannosaurus Rex's head fell toward her. Someone screamed, and at first Alexis thought it had come from the TV. It hadn't. It was her mother.

"Alexis Grace Howell!" she yelled. "What on earth is going on at that place? I said you could help at the park while Miss Maria is hurt, but *this*? It looks like things are getting dangerous."

Mrs. Howell stood with her hands on her hips, waiting for an explanation. Alexis's dad got up and walked toward the kitchen.

"More pizza, anyone?" he asked uneasily.

No one answered.

"It's not as bad as it looks, Mom," said Alexis. "You're always saying the news blows things out of proportion, remember? We were giving a tour, and. . .I'm not really sure what happened, but I'm fine!"

"Well, I don't like the idea of you being so close to those things. If they are prone to sudden movements, or if they break down—"

"We'll be more careful, Mom," said Alexis. "I promise! Please don't keep us away from the park. Miss Maria still needs us!"

"Fine, but I expect you two to be careful while you investigate. And from now on, I want daily updates. If I'm related to the detective, I shouldn't have to hear about everything on the news." Mrs. Howell called over her shoulder to the kitchen, "Now's a good time for that pizza, Rich!"

The next day, Alexis and Kate got to the park before anyone else did. They picked up all of the cameras, and as they walked through the park, they noticed that only one dinosaur had moved. As usual, it was one of the Raptors. The girls put him back where he belonged and settled down in a back room of the visitors' center where they could use the computer.

Only three of the four cameras had taken pictures. Most of them were of nighttime creatures. The tail of a raccoon or a flapping bat. There was a series of pictures of an owl picking up a mouse, no doubt planning to make a meal out of it.

"Wow! Those could be on the Discovery Channel!" said Alexis.

Thad Swotter and his cameraman made appearances in the pictures too. Alexis got excited at first, thinking she'd catch them in action. But then she remembered the newscast. They weren't moving the dinosaurs. The camera had taken pictures of them while they were shooting their story. Alexis sighed.

"Is that all we have?" She was beginning to get frustrated. Usually when she was on a case she didn't have gadgets like Kate's cameras to help her. She thought for sure that they would make things easier. So far they hadn't.

Jerry entered the visitors' center and put two Cokes on the table.

"Thanks, Jerry!" said Alexis.

"No problem, Alex. Are those the pictures from last night?"

"Yeah," said Kate, "but we haven't seen anything so far."

Jerry opened his mouth to say something, but Alexis interrupted.

"Hey!" she said. "I want to know how that guy from Channel 13 got into the park after closing last night!"

"Easy," said Jerry. "I let him in."

"You *what*?" said Alexis.

"I. . .let. . .him. . .in." Jerry pushed Alexis's Coke toward her. "Drink up and don't worry! The news stories have been great for the park. It's like free advertising! Do you know how much it would cost to do a real TV commercial? It's a lot; I've checked. And the park was on the news for ten minutes last night!" He gave the can one last nudge. "Come on, Alex. It's Cherry Coke. . .your favorite."

Alexis took the can and shook her head. She couldn't believe that Jerry had let someone into the park after hours. Why was he suddenly friends with Thad Swotter anyway?

"Wait!" said Kate. "Look at this!"

There, in the corner of a picture, was a Raptor's nose.

"Remember the moved Raptor this morning?" said Kate. "I think we're going to find out how he got there, frame by frame!"

Both of the girls were on the edge of their seats. Kate hit the button to look at the next picture.

Nothing.

But the third picture showed the Raptor's lizard head close up. He was looking directly into the camera lens.

"It's like he knows it's there!" said Alexis. The following pictures reminded Alexis of a comic book: still pictures that told a story.

The Raptor's head again, looking away.

The Raptor's tail, like he was leaving.

The lens covered up by a bunch of leaves.

Leaves pulled away to reveal tons of Raptor footprints.

More dark leaves.

And finally, though the picture was a little fuzzy, a full-frame shot of the Raptor standing in the flowers on the other side of the path—just where they had found him this morning.

"Alexis?" said Kate.

"Yeah?"

"Are you thinking what I'm thinking?"

"That there wasn't even *one* picture of a human?" said Alexis.

"Exactly," Kate whispered. "Not even a finger. I don't understand, Alex."

"Me neither, Kate. I think the evidence is pointing to living, breathing dinosaurs."

"But that's impossible!" said Kate.

Alexis shrugged. Two days ago she would have laughed at the idea of dinosaurs coming to life in a Sacramento suburb.

Now she wasn't so sure.

CHAPTER 5

Crucial Clue

Later that day, Kate sent copies of the digital pictures to the Camp Club Girls. Alex followed it with an email.

TO: Camp Club Girls
SUBJECT: Notes
New Investigation: Could the dinosaurs really be alive?

Yes:
1. We still have not found any evidence of humans being involved. No prints and no people in the pictures from the hidden cameras.
2. The baby Triceratops moved without being plugged in—creepy.
3. The Tyrannosaurus Rex. . .enough said.

No:
1. As far as I know, electronic animals do not come to life. Otherwise, Disneyland would be in a whole lot of trouble.
2. Also, I don't think the dinosaurs eat. None of the plants near them are damaged. . .and Miss Maria's cat hasn't gone missing yet.

Plan: Examine the footprints. Figure out if they are real or if someone is faking them.

The two Camp Club Girls waited until the park was almost empty to make their move. They were tired after another long day of giving tours, but at least nothing crazy had happened today. Mrs. Smith had been afraid that people would stay away because of the Tyrannosaurus Rex, but no one seemed to care. In fact, even more people had been on the trails today.

Alexis filled her pink backpack with giant zipper bags bulging with plaster of Paris. The white goop squelched and squished as she and Kate headed through the park to the most recent set of footprints.

One of the little green Raptors was separated from the rest of the herd. It was the one that kept moving around the park.

"I think he needs a name," said Kate.

"You're right," said Alexis. "How about Jogger?"

"It's perfect! Because he never stays in one place!"

Alexis opened a bag and poured a little of the plaster onto the ground. Then she grabbed Jogger and placed his feet gently in the white mush. After a minute or so, she lifted the dinosaur and wiped his feet. Then she put him back with his herd.

Kate was already comparing the prints in the plaster to the prints that were in the mud.

"They're a perfect match," she said. Alexis bent to examine them and found that Kate was right.

"Almost too perfect," Alexis said. Her thoughts were churning.

When a person walked, did they take the exact same step every time they moved? She thought about the many times she had sped up to catch someone, slowed down to wait, or tripped over something and stumbled.

No, she decided. *People's steps change all the time depending on where they are and how fast they're moving and what they're doing. If a girl is dialing a number on a cell phone, chances are her steps will slow down a bit and the footprints will be a bit deeper. . . .*

She walked around the Raptor area and noticed the same uniform prints everywhere. If these prints had been made by a living, breathing dinosaur, the creature had walked slowly and placed each step perfectly.

Alexis had never known any animal to move like that.

"Let's see what the bigger tracks tell us," she said.

At the site of the mother and baby Triceratops, the girls were disappointed. No fresh prints. Only those from the day Miss Maria got hurt. And emergency workers who helped Miss Maria into the ambulance had flattened all those prints.

While they searched, the girls got an unexpected visitor. Mrs. Smith trudged down the path carrying a heavy backpack.

"Hi, girls!" she said. "How's the investigation going?"

"Okay," said Alexis. "What are you doing?"

"I've got to switch out the battery for the baby Triceratops."

"The battery?" said Kate. "I thought all of the dinosaurs ran on generators."

"Well, most of them do," said Mrs. Smith. "Some of the smaller ones have battery packs. It makes them more versatile. You can put them in places that you couldn't fit a generator, and they'll still move around. The batteries don't last long, though."

Mrs. Smith reached beneath the baby Triceratops and removed a large block. One side of it had greenish skin so it matched the dinosaur.

"I'll take this one back to the center and charge it. Then I'll swap it again in a few days."

She dug the fresh battery out of her bag and snapped it into place. The baby dinosaur sprang to life. Its tail and head moved back and forth, and its eyes sparkled and blinked.

And it stuck out its tongue.

Alexis and Kate were stunned.

"It had a battery!" whispered Alexis.

"What's that?" said Mrs. Smith.

"Nothing," said Kate. The girls didn't want to admit that they had entertained thoughts about the baby dinosaur coming to life.

"Okay," said Mrs. Smith. "You girls take care! Miss Maria is supposed to come home today." Mrs. Smith took off back toward the visitors' center, leaving Kate smiling and Alexis writing furiously in her pink notebook.

"I can't believe it!" said Kate. "Its battery was just going dead! And it actually scared me!"

"Yeah," said Alexis. "You must have seen it using up the last little bit of power."

They were about to move on to the Tyrannosaurus tracks when Kate saw something in the mud that made her stop. She bent down and lifted a branch to reveal a track from the baby Triceratops.

"It's damaged!" said Kate. The back of the track was squashed.

"Perfect," she said dully. "The evidence has been contaminated by a squirrel or something."

"Wait!" Alexis bent down and examined the print.

"Kate," she said. "Can you go back and count how many toes the baby Triceratops has?"

"Sure," said Kate. In seconds she was kneeling near the dinosaur, dodging its moving horns. "Four!" she hollered back over her shoulder.

"I knew it!" said Alexis. "This print only has three toes! It's a fake, Kate!"

"Wow!" said Kate. "Whoever did this didn't do their homework, did they?"

"They didn't think anyone would look this close. But they don't know us, do they?" A triumphant smile stretched across Alexis's face. "Let's check out the Tyrannosaurus Rex."

There was no way Alexis and Kate could lift the Tyrannosaurus Rex leg, so they couldn't make a footprint in the plaster as they had with Jogger. They could only look as closely as possible to see if the foot seemed to match the tracks around it.

"Well," said Kate, "they sure look the same to me. The bottom of the tracks have some weird stripes on them, but I can't tell what they are."

"They do look the same," said Alexis. She handed Kate a bag of plaster to pour into one of the prints. If they could take the print home, they could examine it more closely. Maybe they would see something they weren't noticing at the moment. Alexis walked around the dinosaur's huge legs again. She tried not to think about the head falling toward her.

"Kate?" Alexis asked. "How deep are those footprints?"

"How deep are they? About an inch. Why?"

"Don't you think an animal that weighed this much would make a deeper print in the mud?"

"Come to think of it, yes, probably," said Kate. "At home I have special equipment that could tell us the weight of a print this size and depth. Should I have my parents send it?"

"I don't think we need it," Alex said. "I think we can safely say something that weighs over a ton would have deeper prints."

Alexis followed the tracks away from the Tyrannosaurus Rex and into the forest.

"Everything looks normal—except, of course, dinosaur footprints in the dirt between the plants," Alexis called to Kate.

"*Between* the plants?" Kate asked.

Alexis gasped. "Wouldn't a dinosaur—especially a Tyrannosaurus Rex—do a lot of damage as he walked through a forest?"

"That's what I'm thinking," Kate said.

"I remember seeing a movie with a Tyrannosaurus Rex chasing something. Trees were flying everywhere, torn up by the roots. And whole bushes were stomped down," Alexis said. "I know it was just a movie, but. . ."

"Yeah, not even one of Miss Maria's tiniest flowers is bruised," Kate said. "How could a thirty-foot dinosaur navigate his way through a forest of tightly packed aspens? Especially without damaging one?"

"And look how close the prints are together," Kate added.

Alexis surveyed the prints and then looked back to the Tyrannosaurus Rex. "His legs are at least ten feet apart just standing there," she noted.

"And these are only four or five feet apart at the most," Kate said. "Unless the Tyrannosaurus Rex had tiptoed to the fence, these prints are fake!"

"And whoever made them cares enough about the plants not to damage them," Alexis pointed out.

"Look at this, Alex." Kate was kneeling down in the dirt, about three feet from the footprints. "When was the last time it rained?"

"A couple days ago," said Alexis. "Right before you got here."

"Okay," said Kate. "So how can there be mud for the footprints? Look—the ground where the footprints are was apparently wet to make the tracks. But the path is dusty only a few feet away."

"You're right!" said Alexis. Someone was *making mud* so they could make the tracks.

Alexis got out her notebook to record all of her thoughts. The evidence was beginning to add up.

Evidence for fake tracks:

1. The Raptor tracks are too perfect—like someone picked up Jogger and sat him in the mud over and over, like a kid playing with a doll.

2. The Triceratops tracks are missing a toe.

3. The Tyrannosaurus Rex tracks are too close together, and did not damage plants.

4. There is no mud except where there are tracks.

Now Alexis was sure that someone must be planting the tracks. But who? And why would they do it? She and Kate still hadn't found any clues to help them answer that question.

"The plaster is almost dry," said Kate. "After we make the footprint, let's go see if Miss Maria's home."

"Good idea," said Alexis.

●—●—●

Alexis and Kate didn't make it to Miss Maria's house until after the park had closed for the day. They saw Miss Maria sitting in her favorite chair on her front porch. She hugged an afghan tight around her shoulders, despite the summer heat. Her head was covered with a bright scarf.

As the girls climbed the porch steps, Alexis thought of how small she looked.

"Hello, girls! Come keep me company!"

Jerry came out of the front door. He was about to sit down, but Miss Maria stopped him.

"Jerry dear," she said, "could you get me a glass of lemonade, please?"

"Oh, sure!" said Jerry, and he disappeared back into the house.

Miss Maria beckoned Alexis and Kate with a crooked finger.

"Hurry!" she said in a whisper. "He won't be gone long!" She smiled like a little girl who thought she was keeping an important secret. "How is the investigation going?"

"Good and bad," said Alexis, looking over her shoulder at the screen door. She wondered why Miss Maria didn't want to talk about the investigation in front of Jerry. "We've just found out that the footprints are fake, so we're pretty sure the dinosaurs aren't coming to life."

Alexis thought Miss Maria might say something like, "Well, of course they're not coming to life!" But she didn't. She simply nodded and waited for Alexis to continue.

"The bad part is that we still don't have any evidence linking the incidents to any particular *person*."

"We think Thad Swotter could be doing it just to get a story," said Kate. "But that's just an idea. There's no evidence!"

Their frustration did not go unnoticed. Miss Maria smiled and leaned forward slightly.

"Of course there's evidence!" she said. "You just haven't found it yet! You think you've looked everywhere, but if that were the case, you would have found something."

Noise from inside told them that Jerry was approaching. Miss Maria lowered her voice even more.

"Stop looking where you *expect* to find something. Instead, look where nothing should be."

Miss Maria nodded, as if she had just said the most obvious thing in the world. Alexis was confused, but before she could ask Maria to clarify, Jerry returned.

The girls accepted glasses of tart lemonade and stayed long enough to drink them before going back to the park. They returned to the Tyrannosaurus Rex to retrieve the dried footprint and to make sure they hadn't missed anything.

"I wish we could find something around here *besides* a dinosaur track!" said Kate. She picked up the bag of wet plaster they hadn't used and glared at it as if it were the reason they hadn't found what they needed.

"It will happen," said Alexis. "We just have to look where we wouldn't expect to find anything, like Miss Maria said."

Alexis wasn't sure this would work, but she had to try. She didn't know what else to do. So where was the last place they would expect to find a clue? Alexis pulled her brown curls into a tight ponytail and began to look.

At that moment, they heard a loud bark. They turned to see

Biscuit flying down the trail toward them, his tongue and leash wagging in the wind.

"Where did he come from?" yelled Kate.

"Mom must have brought him!" said Alexis.

"Biscuit! *No!*"

But it was too late. The dog couldn't stop in time. He ran right into Kate, knocking the bag of plaster from her arms and dumping it all over. The gooey white stuff splattered Kate and doused Alexis's foot before flowing beneath a nearby bush.

"Oh no!" said Kate. "I'm sorry, Alexis!"

"Don't worry about it," said Alexis. "After the plaster dries, we can pick it right up." She knelt down to see how far under the bush the mess went, and she froze.

"Biscuit! You're a genius!" Alexis yelled. The dog jumped and wagged his tail, as if he had meant to help her all along.

"What is it, Alex?" asked Kate.

"Look for yourself!" Alexis lifted the lower branches of the bush so Kate could see. The plaster was barely trickling now. It ran over a few sticks before resting in a footprint.

Not a dinosaur print, but the obvious crisscross pattern of a Converse All-Star.

Converse Connection

The next morning Mrs. Howell took the girls to a copy shop. Alexis wanted to print off a bunch of the posters they had made for the park. She would have done it at home, but her printer was out of colored ink. The twins had decided to print fifty copies of their latest creation: a full-color map of the neighborhood.

Mrs. Howell had been aggravated, but Alexis had to admit that the map was pretty good. The boys had marked all of the great hideouts, including a lump of honeysuckle and ivy near one corner that Alexis thought no one knew about. She was impressed. Maybe her little brothers had some detective skills hidden beneath their annoying natures.

Since their copier was out, Alexis decided on a more professional sign than she could do on her computer. She'd have the copy center make the signs full poster-sized and laminated so they'd last for a while.

Alexis dug her savings out of her pocket and put it on the copy counter.

"Honey," said her mother, "you don't have to spend all of that."

"I know," Alexis said. She had thought a lot about it, and she knew that this was what she wanted to do. Miss Maria had spent thousands of dollars trying to save her park. Alexis figured she could spend a few weeks of allowance. She could earn it back before Christmas, anyway, and if it would help the park, it was worth it.

"That will get you twenty full-color, laminated posters," said the freckled teenager behind the counter.

"Okay," said Alexis. "That's what we want then!"

Half an hour later, Alexis and Kate walked out of the shop with the fresh posters draped over their arms. They were still warm from the printer. Mrs. Howell handed Alexis a paper bag full of tape and thumbtacks.

"Stick to the main road," she said. "I'm going to run something to the courthouse, and I'll meet you at the coffee shop on the corner in an hour, okay?" She hugged Alexis and climbed into the red van, pointing it toward the white and silver dome of the capitol in the distance.

"So where do we start?" said Kate. The street was full of small hangouts. Internet cafés and coffee shops were everywhere.

They walked up and down the street leaving posters on community boards inside the shops. They even stuck a few to light posts and bus stops. The twenty posters were gone quickly, and Alexis wished she had saved more of her allowance.

"I guess that will have to do," she said to Kate. They were outside the corner coffee shop drinking iced lemonade the store manager had given them. She was a nice woman who hung one of their posters on the front of her pastry case. From their seat outside, the girls heard her tell each customer to visit the park and support Miss Maria.

Alexis was watching for her mother when something else caught her eye. A familiar-looking man entered the hardware store directly across the street.

"Kate! That's Thad Swotter's cameraman!" Alexis ran to the light post and slammed her hand against the button to activate the crosswalk. "Come on!" she said.

"Why are we following a cameraman?" asked Kate. The walk sign flashed green, and the girls crossed the street.

"Maybe we'll hear something that will link Swotter to the dinosaurs," said Alexis.

"Do people usually let secrets slip to their neighborhood hardware store workers?" Kate asked with a laugh.

Alexis laughed too.

"Probably not, but we have twenty minutes before Mom picks us up, and sleuthing is more interesting than sitting on a corner."

The girls approached the hardware store windows but couldn't see through them. The windows were crowded with signs, shovels, and old newspaper articles with important headlines. Alexis poked her head around the open door. She couldn't see the cameraman.

She motioned to Kate, and the two of them quietly walked inside. From behind a display of leather work gloves, they could see the cameraman. He was at the counter talking to the shop owner.

"If we get closer, we may be able to hear what they're saying," Alexis said.

The girls inched their way around the outside aisle and stood behind a huge stack of red plastic buckets. Alexis glanced at the wall and pretended to be interested in the power tools hanging there.

"Need to replace my fence cutters," said the cameraman. "I'm helping a neighbor build a dog kennel, and I can't find mine."

"What size?" asked the hardware man.

"Pretty small. I only use them for chain-link fencing."

Alexis grabbed Kate's arm, causing her to jump. She tripped backward and fell against the tower of buckets.

Bam! The buckets flew around the girls.

Both the camera operator and the store owner turned toward the commotion. Alex and Kate scrambled to pick up all the buckets.

"Can I help you, ladies?" asked the hardware man.

"Uh, no, thank you, sir," stuttered Alexis. Kate was chasing down a bucket that had rolled down the next aisle. "We were just looking at these, uh, tools."

The camera operator chuckled, and the store owner raised his eyebrows. Alexis turned and looked at the wall. She and Kate were standing in front of the biggest saw she had ever seen. Its round blade must have been three feet wide.

"Now why on earth would you need one of those?" asked the shop owner.

Alexis thought. She didn't want to lie, but she and Kate needed to get out of there in a hurry.

"You're right," she said with a nervous smile. "I probably don't need one this big. We'd better go down the road to the small saw store."

It was Kate's turn to grab Alexis by the arm. She dragged her out onto the sidewalk. The men's laughter echoed onto the busy street.

"Small saw store?" said Kate. "Good one."

"I'm sorry!" said Alexis. "I couldn't think of anything else!"

The girls hit the crosswalk button again and walked back across the street.

"Why did you freak out and grab my arm anyway?" asked Kate. "I wouldn't have knocked over those buckets if you hadn't scared me like that!"

They sat down at a small table outside the coffee shop again. The metal chairs were hot and burned their legs at first.

"The cameraman said he needed to replace his fence cutters," said Alexis. "He can't find his, and he said he only uses them on chain-link fencing!"

"Why did that make you grab me?" asked Kate.

"Remember? When I investigated the Tyrannosaurus Rex tracks, I followed them all the way to the fence. It had a huge hole. And it was a chain-link fence."

"Okay, so whoever is moving the dinosaurs cut a hole in the fence. Maybe that's how the person got into the park in the first place."

"I think they wanted people to think the Tyrannosaurus Rex did it," said Alexis. "To scare people, you know? What if the camera guy was helping Thad Swotter, and he lost his fence cutters that way? Or what if Swotter stole his fence cutters so he could cut the hole in the fence?"

"Maybe," said Kate. "It is a funny coincidence, but we don't have any evidence."

She was right. Maybe they could go back to the fence this afternoon and look for the fence cutters. If they found them, they could connect Swotter—or at least his camera operator—to the mystery.

●—●—●

By the time the girls got to the park, the tours had already started. Since Jerry and Megan were leading people through the park, the area around the visitors' center was vacant—except for Jogger. He was looking at the entrance sign.

"Not again!" said Alexis.

Her emotions were torn. On one hand, she had a new crime scene to investigate. That was always exciting. On the other hand, she was angry at whoever was doing this to Miss Maria's park. She wondered if all detectives had the same struggle. The hunt was thrilling, but wasn't it sad that people were bad enough to make you hunt them in the first place?

"Kate, look!" Alexis had picked up Jogger to take him back to his fellow Raptors. There wasn't any mud, but in the loose dust was another human footprint. It was hardly visible. Kate whipped out her camera and snapped a few pictures.

"It's a Converse, like the other one," said Kate. She bent to get a closer look. "Our suspect is getting sloppy."

"I know," said Alexis. "He didn't leave us a clue for days, and now we find two footprints in a row."

Just then, the girls heard a shout from the visitors' center. Two voices escalated. Someone wasn't happy.

"I think that's Mrs. Smith," said Alexis.

"Yeah. Let's see who else," said Kate. Alexis pushed on the front door, and it swung wide, creaking slightly. The two arguing adults never even noticed.

Mrs. Smith's cheeks were bright red. Strands of dark hair swirled around her face. On the other side of the front desk, with his back to Alexis and Kate, was none other than Thad Swotter.

Only today he didn't have his little notebook and crazy tie. Instead, he wore faded jeans and a fitted polo. An Oakland Athletics ball cap hid his wild blond hair.

"Come on, Mrs. Smith!" Swotter said, trying not to yell. "You can't be serious!"

"I'm just as serious as I was the last time, Thad," said Mrs. Smith. "I said no."

Swotter took off his hat and ran a hand through his gel-matted mop.

"At least think about it," he pleaded.

"Thad, no. I'm not interested." Mrs. Smith wasn't yelling anymore. She just looked tired. "You're welcome to look around the park, Thad, or shoot another crazy story, but this conversation is over." Mrs. Smith gestured toward the two girls. Swotter noticed them for the first time.

"Fine," he said, jamming his hat back on. "I'll go. Enjoy your day here at Bible Land!"

"What's that supposed to mean?" fired Mrs. Smith. Her anger was back.

"I'm talking about the Old Bat's crazy greenhouse! It's not like you guys are giving tours through Jerusalem! A visitor can't bend to smell a rose without getting a cross stabbed in his eye!"

"Come on, Thad," said Mrs. Smith. "I know you're angry, but you're exaggerating just a little—"

"Am I?" Thad Swotter was far from composed. His face was a mixture of red and white blotches, and sweat was running down his neck.

"I've told you before that you should get rid of all that stuff!" he said. "People don't want to see Jesus Thorns or the Lily of the Valley. They come here to see the redwoods and California plants—and they *don't* want to hear that any *God* planted them! People would be lining up to give this place money if it weren't for that stuff!"

He turned and stomped past Alexis and Kate, slamming the door behind him. The girls cautiously approached the desk.

"Was he asking for another interview?" asked Alexis.

"Yeah, something like that," said Mrs. Smith with a weak smile. She pushed a small bouquet of flowers off the desk and into the trash can.

"Those were pretty!" said Kate.

"They smelled funny," said Mrs. Smith. "What are you girls up to today?"

"Just looking for a break," said Alexis.

"Well, you're welcome to grab a Coke out of the fridge and sit in here for a while," said Mrs. Smith.

"Not that kind of break, Mrs. Smith," said Alexis. She grabbed two sodas anyway and handed one to Kate. "I meant we need a lucky break in this case. We found some good clues yesterday. We're going to see where they lead us."

Alexis told Mrs. Smith all about the footprints being fake and the posters they hung up.

"Those posters should help," said Mrs. Smith. "Thanks for doing that. Maybe when the donation box fills up a little more, we should use the money to print more of them. Then we can hang some in other areas of town."

Alexis could see Mrs. Smith's bad mood evaporating. This was good, because Alexis had a favor to ask. She knew from an experience with her grandma that angry adults were not much help when it came to investigating. It was really hard to get good information out of someone who had just turned her hair purple by accident.

"Mrs. Smith, can I ask you something?" Alexis said.

Mrs. Smith was sipping her Diet Coke, but she nodded.

"We were thinking about camping out in the park," Alexis said. "You know, like a stakeout? Do you think that would be okay?"

"That should be okay," said Mrs. Smith. "But we should double-check with Maria first. I'll talk to her this afternoon."

Kate and Alexis left the visitors' center. They were going to inspect the new footprint some more and compare it to the one they had found the day before. Alexis was in the lead, and as she turned the corner, she ran right into Thad Swotter.

Bam! The force of the impact threw her backward. She landed hard on her backside a few feet away. Swotter juggled his cell phone, trying not to drop it. He grumbled an "excuse me" and began walking quickly toward the parking lot, still talking on the phone.

"Oh my goodness!" exclaimed Alexis.

"I know," said Kate. "He didn't even offer to help you up! Are you okay?"

"No! Not that!" said Alexis. She rolled onto her knees and pointed after the reporter. "Look at his shoes!"

There went Thad Swotter—newly famous Sacramento reporter—tromping to his car in a very muddy pair of Converse All-Stars.

CHAPTER 7

Dinosaurs in the Dark

"I still can't believe you guys are doing this!" said Jerry. He was bent over, trying to put Alexis's tent together. He obviously had no idea what he was doing.

"That's the door, Jerry!" said Alexis, stooping to help. "You can't put it against the ground! How will we get in?"

Alexis shook out the tent and laid it right-side up. She grabbed a handful of slender plastic rods and went to work. In minutes, she had the tent standing.

"Here," Alexis teased, passing Jerry a hammer. "You can handle putting the stakes in the ground, right? Just stick them through those loops at the corners and pound them in."

Alexis and Kate had chosen the clearing near the Raptors for their overnight stakeout. They would set up a night-vision digital camcorder and be ready to catch Thad Swotter in the act if he struck again tonight. Even if he showed up and left after seeing the girls' tent, maybe the camera would get a good shot of him first.

"So why *are* you doing this?" asked Megan. She was helping Kate set up the video camera on a hidden stump.

"I told you, Meg," said Alexis. "Nothing else is working. We need to get to the bottom of this before someone gets hurt."

"What makes you so sure someone is going to get hurt?" asked Jerry. "Nothing bad has happened so far. The park is packed every day!"

"Um, Miss Maria was hurt," said Kate. Her voice was almost a whisper—her head hanging down as if she were speaking to her shoes. "She wouldn't have been climbing on the Triceratops if it weren't for those footprints, remember? And what about the day the Tyrannosaurus Rex's head nearly fell on Alex? That could have been because someone was messing around it while making the footprints."

Jerry didn't answer, but he raised his eyebrows. Alexis knew what he was thinking: Miss Maria shouldn't have climbed on top of the dinosaur without anyone around to help. But Alexis also knew that whether Miss Maria was right or wrong, it all came down to the footprints. They had started this whole mess.

"Look at the big picture, guys," said Alexis. "Even if no one ever gets hurt, damage has been done to the park. A whole section of the fence has to be replaced because there's a huge hole in it."

"And besides," Kate added, "whoever's messing around with the dinosaurs might hurt them. I was looking at animated dinosaurs on a website that sells special effects. Some of these dinosaurs cost up to twenty thousand dollars to replace!"

"If something happened to one, Miss Maria might have to use all her savings to pay for it and have to close the park."

Jerry didn't say anything else. He went to Alexis's backpack, pulled out some chips, and chomped moodily while the girls finished setting up camp.

Alexis was aggravated. She loved investigating, but she knew this was taking up valuable time. The sooner she found out who was doing this, the sooner she could focus on Miss Maria's real problem—bringing in visitors and money even after the dinosaurs were gone. All of this craziness was keeping them from finding a solution to the real problem.

Alexis tried to get Jerry and Megan to stay with them, but they were too freaked out about sleeping in the park. Jerry didn't camp. Alexis had learned that much by watching him try to put the tent together. Megan just kept making excuses.

"What if the Tyrannosaurus Rex steps on me in my sleep?" she joked as the group headed in to dinner. Their camp was not far from Jerry and Megan's house, which was just on the edge of the park near the visitors' center. Mrs. Smith had invited the girls to eat dinner there before they began their campout.

Dinner was great, except for Jerry's jokes. He kept telling Alexis and Kate to watch out for dinosaur manure or to keep their snacks locked up so they wouldn't attract the bears. . .or the Tyrannosaurus Rex.

"I heard they found a new species of squirrel in the Sierras," Jerry said with a mouth full of enchilada.

"Really?" said Kate, drawn in by her love of animals.

"Yeah, vampire squirrels. Watch your necks!"

Alexis shivered. For some reason, she couldn't swallow the bite she had just taken.

"Jerry, stop it!" said Mrs. Smith.

Alexis would normally have laughed all night at Jerry's jokes, but she was about to sleep in a dark forest. For that reason, none of the jokes seemed very funny. It wasn't like Jerry to be mean. Maybe he didn't realize he was scaring them.

Kate spoke up as the two of them returned to camp. "If I didn't know better, I would say he didn't want us out here."

"I don't know," said Alexis. "He's probably just trying to scare us because he's embarrassed. Think about it! He was too chicken to stay out here, and two *girls* are going to show him up. Either that or he's just being a boy. By definition they're obnoxious!"

Biscuit tromped along beside Kate on his leash. His presence calmed their nerves, and by the time they reached the Raptor clearing, their laughter echoed through the trees.

The two Camp Club Girls snuggled down into their sleeping bags. They pulled out Kate's computer and filled in the Camp Club Girls until the battery died. Then they fell asleep.

It was still pitch black outside when Kate woke up to find Biscuit's wet nose in her face. He nudged her and then walked over Alexis to the door of the tent.

"What is it?" asked Alexis. She sat up and rubbed her sleepy eyes.

"It's just Biscuit," said Kate. "I think he has to go to the bathroom."

Kate unzipped the tent and led her whining puppy outside. After a second, her head popped back in the tent.

"Forgot the flashlight!" she said. She grabbed Alexis's lantern and went to supervise the excited puppy. Alexis was just about to drift back to sleep when she heard Kate call in a frantic whisper.

"Alexis! Get out here!"

"What is it?" asked Alexis. She fought her way out of her sleeping bag and shoved on her shoes. Biscuit was pulling frantically on his leash, choking himself in his excitement to explore. Kate was standing in the middle of the camp, shining her light on the ground.

"Look!" she said.

"No way!" said Alexis. The camp was absolutely crowded with Raptor footprints. When the girls had gone to bed, the little green dinosaurs had been in their place on the other side of the clearing. Kate shined the light around the edge of camp. Little pairs of eyes glinted in the beam.

They were surrounded.

Alexis didn't know what was creepier, being stared at by a ring of dinosaurs or the thought that someone had been here to move them *while the girls were sleeping.*

"My camera's gone!" cried Kate. Sure enough, the camera she and Megan had hidden on the stump was gone. Jogger was sitting in his place. In the dancing moonlight, he looked as if he was laughing.

"Great!" said Alexis. "We slept through everything!"

Alexis had never been angrier. She thought for sure this campout would lead them to the identity of the dinosaur mover. Instead, they were standing in the dark, looking at a bunch of new footprints that had been put there right under their noses. And now Kate's newest video camera was gone. Alexis reminded herself to add theft to the list of crimes in her notebook.

"Someone is making fun of us!" Alexis huffed. "Every time we get a little closer to figuring things out, we get stumped!"

"I know," said Kate. "It's *extremely* frust–"

Slam!

A loud noise ricocheted through the forest. The girls stood still as statues. Biscuit's ears were standing up, listening for any sign of movement.

"That sounded like a car door," whispered Alexis. She looked at her watch. "Who would be out here at two thirty in the morning?"

"Someone up to no good!" said Kate.

"Come on!" said Alexis. "Maybe it's Thad. Let's sneak up on him. We can't let him see us, but maybe we'll be able to see *him*."

Kate nodded, and the girls started picking their way through the forest. They kept off the paths. The last thing they wanted was to run right into a criminal.

Alexis breathed deeply. Her heart slammed against her rib cage in a frantic rhythm, and she was sure it could be heard a mile away. The girls picked a path through the aspens and dodged the Tyrannosaurus. In the moonlight, the giant reptile looked more than alive. They crossed the Triceratops meadow, and Alexis took in a sharp breath.

The baby Triceratops was missing.

"Look," whispered Kate. "Footprints." Alexis noticed they had only three toes.

The girls followed the fake Triceratops footprints through the meadow. They stopped abruptly at a clump of large bushes. The girls veered to the left to walk around when they heard a loud *click*. A flash of light temporarily blinded them.

Alexis ducked down behind the bush. She pulled Kate down beside her and waited for her eyes to adjust. Spots danced in front of her face like stars.

They heard footsteps. The rustle of dry pine needles. *Click. Flash!*

Alexis edged toward the sound. She peeked around the bush and had to cover her mouth to keep from crying out.

Thad Swotter was standing on the other side of their hiding place. His green and yellow A's hat was on backward, and he was snapping pictures of the newly moved baby Triceratops.

Kate signaled Alexis to keep quiet and crawled deeper into the bush. She positioned her spy watch to point toward Swotter. The small watch, Alexis knew, was able to take pictures. The next time Swotter took a picture, Kate did too, so he didn't notice the flash of her watch.

After a few more minutes, the reporter turned and walked

back through the trees.

"Come on!" whispered Alexis. The girls took off after him, keeping back so they wouldn't be seen.

They were heading northeast through the park, toward the highway. Thad Swotter went faster, and the girls struggled to keep up. Alexis caught her foot on a tree root and stumbled.

"Whoa!" she said. She regained her balance, glad that she hadn't fallen, but Kate grabbed her and pulled her behind a tree.

Swotter had stopped and was shining a flashlight in their direction. The light panned back and forth, igniting the forest around them and casting thick shadows.

"Who's there?" Swotter called. He sounded nervous. Alexis wanted to make some dinosaur noises, just to scare him, but she kept quiet.

"Stupid forest," Swotter said to himself. He turned away again. Alexis noticed that the steps were quicker and his breathing labored. He was running.

The girls followed the spooked reporter to the edge of the park. He climbed over the fence and jogged to the Channel 13 news van parked on the shoulder of Highway 80. Kate was about to take another picture, but a big, masculine hand reached over her shoulder and grabbed her arm.

"I wouldn't do that if I were you."

CHAPTER 8

From Theater to Threat

"Really, I wouldn't do that," said Jerry. "He'll see your flash."

Alexis and Kate spun around.

"Jerry, you scared us to death!" whispered Alexis. "What are you doing here anyway?"

"Couldn't sleep, so I thought I'd check on you," he said. "You weren't in camp, so I got worried."

"We're *fine!*" said Alexis. Swotter's van was gone. She turned and tromped through the forest toward their tent. She didn't care how loud she was anymore, now that the danger of being seen had passed.

The girls couldn't bring themselves to climb back into their sleeping bags and sleep after their discovery. So they sat up in their tent instead, telling Jerry all about it until the sun came up. Then they packed up camp and walked to Jerry's house for breakfast.

Alexis was sure she had solved the mystery. First, there were Thad Swotter's muddy Converse shoes, which matched the only human footprint they had found so far. Now they had caught him in the park in the middle of the night. He *hadn't* been filming a story for the news. Why would he sneak around the park so late at night if he wasn't moving the dinosaurs?

She and Kate had every detective's dream: undeniable evidence. They hadn't just seen Swotter at the scene of the crime. They had a *picture* of him there! There was no way he could deny it—Alexis just had to figure out how to confront him.

Mrs. Howell picked the girls up around ten and took them

home. They went up to Alexis's room and finally fell asleep. Alexis slept until lunchtime, when the twins ran in screaming.

"Lexi! Get up! Get up! Get up!"

They leapt onto the bed, pinning Alexis beneath four bony knees.

"Get up! It's family movie day, remember? Come on!"

And just like that they were gone, pounding down the stairs leaving Alexis and Kate to wipe the sleep from their eyes.

"Family movie day?" asked Kate through a cavernous yawn.

"Yeah," said Alexis. "Once a month my parents take a day off, and we all go see a movie together. It's tradition!" She ran into the bathroom, ran a brush through her hair, and burst back into her room to change her T-shirt. "Today it's the new Glenda McGee movie!"

"Yes!" Kate exclaimed. She rushed to take Biscuit outside before they left.

Alexis and Kate were just as excited as the twins. They had been waiting six months for *Glenda McGee: Hacking Hero* to come out in theaters. Glenda McGee was a teen computer genius who solved mysteries. Kate enjoyed all of the gadgets she used, even though most of them were fictional. The twins liked the fight scenes, where Glenda's cheerleading jumps became killer roundhouse kicks. Alexis just loved the way the heroine balanced saving the world with getting her nails done and studying for exams.

The movie was amazing, and not just because the Howells bought popcorn, drinks, and a ton of candy. The girls talked about the twists and turns of the plot as they walked to the car.

"I can't believe that ending!" said Alexis.

"I know!" said Kate. "The butler was the bad guy! But he was so nice!"

"Yeah! He actually *helped* Glenda solve pieces of the mystery. It was just enough to keep her thinking he was good."

The family piled into the car, and Alexis's mind strayed back to the case the Camp Club Girls were still trying to solve. The movie had gotten her excited. She may not be able to do a double-back flip over a burning car to save the world, but she *could* take down Thad Swotter and save Miss Maria's park.

"Mom," she said, "would it be too far out of the way to take us back to Aspen Heights?"

"No, that's fine," said Mrs. Howell. "I have to run a few errands anyway, and it will be easier if six of us aren't running around the grocery store. I'll drop you girls off and then pick you up on my way home."

Alexis had printed the picture of Thad Swotter with the baby Triceratops before she had left the house that morning. She pulled it out of her pink notebook and examined it as they drove. This picture truly looked suspicious. Should they show it to Maria or Mrs. Smith and let the adults handle things?

No. She was sure he was guilty, but what if he weaseled his way out of it? The other adults were sure to believe him over her. Alexis needed to be completely sure about Thad Swotter before she tattled on him.

What would Swotter say when she and Kate showed him the picture?

●—●—●

The girls didn't see any signs of the news van when they pulled onto the Aspen Heights parking lot. Disappointed, Alexis and Kate entered the visitors' center. Mrs. Smith, Jerry, and Megan were inside, taking a break from leading tours.

"Jerry tells me you girls have things figured out," said Mrs. Smith. She passed Alexis and Kate ice pops from the freezer.

"We think so," said Alexis, opening her banana treat. She wanted to tell Mrs. Smith what they had found but decided to wait. "What are you working on?"

Mrs. Smith had a huge pile of paper in front of her. She was reading through it, highlighting paragraphs and making notes on the edges.

"It's a proposal for the school board," said Mrs. Smith. "I've talked to a couple of local principals, and they might make Aspen Heights a regular field trip location."

"That sounds great," said Kate.

"Yeah. If this works out, it would prove that the park is valuable to the community. We may be able to get some funding."

"Then Miss Maria could keep the park open!" said Alexis.

"Dinosaurs or no dinosaurs!"

"That's the plan," said Mrs. Smith. "Say a prayer. The school board meeting is in two days, and I have to get past them before I can advertise to all of the teachers."

"I'm sure it'll be fine!" said Alexis.

"Oh no," said Mrs. Smith.

"Of course it will be!" said Kate.

"No, it's not that," said Mrs. Smith. "Channel 13 just showed up. I'm going in the back room. . .and I'm *not* doing any interviews." She got up and closed the door to her office.

"Well, *we* want an interview, don't we, Kate?" Alexis threw away her sticky ice pop stick and ran outside. Thad Swotter was coming straight to the visitors' center, so Alexis and Kate just waited near the door. Alexis took out her pink notebook and flipped to the page where she had written down a list of questions for their suspect.

Swotter started to walk past them, but Alexis stepped in front of the door at the last second, and he almost ran into her.

"Whoa! Don't want to knock you over again!" he joked. "Excuse me, girls. I'm looking for Mrs. Smith. Is she in there?"

"Yes," said Alexis. "But she's busy."

"I'm not asking for an interview," he said. "I don't even have the camera today. Can you just tell her I'm here?"

"Actually, Mr. Swotter, we were hoping we could ask you a couple of questions."

Swotter raised his eyebrows.

"A little reporter in the making, huh?" he said, looking pleased. "Ask away."

"Where were you last night?"

"I gave the nightly six o'clock report, as usual," he said. "Which takes a lot of preparation and—"

"And after that?" asked Kate.

"I, uh. . .ate dinner and went home." Swotter shifted his weight and crossed his arms. Alexis's dad had told her that this was a defensive move—people stood like that when they felt threatened or uncomfortable. He saw people do it in court a lot. Alexis was glad she was making Swotter uncomfortable. It meant they were headed in the right direction.

Alexis scribbled answers in her notebook. She had a bunch of questions she could have asked, but why ask tons of questions when one direct shot would get the answers she needed? Besides, if he wasn't expecting it, he might accidentally confess. She took a deep breath.

"And why were you wandering around Aspen Heights at two thirty this morning moving our dinosaurs?" she asked.

"Well, I—*what*? Now wait just one minute." Swotter was definitely caught off guard. He swept his hat off his head and crossed his arms again. "I never touched any of your dinosaurs."

"But you admit you were here?" asked Alexis casually. Swotter's eyes narrowed. He flattened out his mouth, as if to keep it from talking. His nostrils flared. Alexis thought about her father. His nostrils never flared, but when his mouth went flat like that, she knew better than to push him. It meant he was getting angry. Alexis remembered Thad's argument with Mrs. Smith the other day and took a step backward. Would he start yelling and screaming at *them*?

"You *were* here, right?" said Kate softly.

Alexis took the picture out of her notebook and handed it to him.

"It was you!" Swotter said. "I knew there was someone out there! You scared me to death!" Alexis expected him to try to make excuses. She expected him to defend himself, or to confess, or get mad. But Swotter did something far less predictable. He laughed.

"Wow," he said. "You girls are sneaky." He ruffled his hair and crammed his hat back on.

"Sure, I was here last night," he continued. "I come every night, at about midnight, to see which dinosaurs have moved, then I take pictures of them. That's how I get my stories in time for the morning news. We're the only channel that has pictures that early! My boss loves me for it. I fell asleep on my couch last night—didn't make it out here until two."

Alexis put her hands on her hips and raised her eyebrows.

"I know what you're thinking," said Swotter. "It's no secret that I don't love this place. You think I'm moving the dinosaurs to scare people away? Or maybe just to get a good story?" The girls' silence told him he was right.

"Look around," he said. "This place is packed! If I wanted Aspen Heights to go under, I wouldn't do something that brings in *more* business."

"So you admit that you want the park to go under?" asked Alexis.

"No, I said *if*. Look, I may not agree with all of Miss Maria's beliefs, but there's no reason to take the park down because of it! Maybe you and your friends should take a closer look at things. I'm not the bad guy everyone around here seems to think I am."

Swotter moved toward the door of the visitors' center but seemed to think better of it. He sighed and walked wearily back to his news van.

"Come on. Let's take a walk so we can think," Kate said, walking through the door into the park.

Alexis was confused. "I was so sure we had figured it out!" she said.

"Me too," said Kate.

"Who else could it have been, Kate? All of the evidence points to him!"

"You mean his shoes?" asked Kate. "Besides seeing Swotter taking pictures, that's the only real evidence we have. Look around! Those shoes are in style. Half the people in this park are wearing them."

Kate was right. Alexis counted five pairs of black Converse, two pairs of pink, and a group of teens wearing them in crazy plaids. She even saw a two-year-old toddling around in a pair. . .and this was just one section of the park.

"You're right, Kate," said Alexis. "And last night we didn't see him move any dinosaurs. We only saw him taking pictures, and he admitted to that."

How could she have been so blind? Looking back, Alexis could see that the evidence pointing toward Thad Swotter had always been a little shaky. She had made a huge mistake.

When she first met Swotter, he had been rude. She had *wanted* him to be guilty, so she had seen every piece of evidence through her prejudice. She had made a judgment based on emotions not on evidence.

"I guess we need a new suspect," said Alexis.

"Nonsense!" said Kate. "I mean, we can keep investigating and following evidence, but we shouldn't drop Thad Swotter as a suspect too easily."

"But Kate, he said—"

"Alexis." Kate stopped walking. She stood in the middle of the trail facing Alexis. "Get a grip. Since when did the police stop investigating someone just because they *said* they didn't do it? Everyone *says* they're innocent."

"You're right," said Alexis. "We'll stick with the evidence this time, though. If it points to Swotter, we'll question him again. If not, then maybe it will point to someone else."

They passed the entrance sign just as Mrs. Howell pulled into the parking lot. Alexis was climbing in when Jerry ran out of the visitors' center.

"Hey, Alexis! Wait! Someone left this for you on the front desk." He handed a small white envelope through the car window.

"Who was it?" asked Alexis. Jerry shrugged.

"No one saw. It was just there on the desk."

"Then how did you know it was for—oh." Alexis saw her name on the outside of the envelope. Jerry smiled and waved as Mrs. Howell pulled away. The car was crowded, so Alexis didn't open the envelope just yet. What could it be?

Maybe it was an anonymous check. If the amount was huge—big enough to save the park—then whoever left it might have felt better putting it on the desk instead of the donations box. But why would they give it to her and not Mrs. Smith or Miss Maria?

The car pulled in the driveway, and Alexis and Kate tore up the stairs. Finally, they were in her room, at a safe distance from the prying eyes of the twins.

Alexis opened the envelope. To her dismay, there was no check. It was just a folded piece of white paper. Maybe a note from Miss Maria or Mr. Bell. . .

She noticed that her name on the envelope was not handwritten—it looked like the work of an old typewriter. Who would take the time to type on an envelope? Alexis dropped the envelope on her bed and unfolded the note. The words typed there stole her breath away.

STOP SNOOPING, OR ELSE. . .

CHAPTER 9

Litter and Lip Gloss

TO: Camp Club Girls
SUBJECT: New Stuff

1. Creepy note—who could it be from? Is someone just messing with us, or could it be a real threat?

2. Thad Swotter—says he isn't our guy. . .we're not so sure.

Updates:

1. Donations box total to date: $24.37 (obviously not enough to save the park. . .)

2. Posters—most of them covered up by other announcements. Mrs. Smith's school board idea might be our last chance.

"It's ready!" said Kate.

She was kneeling on Alexis's bed in front of the open laptop. On the screen was a live picture of Aspen Heights. Kate had spent most of the day rigging up a web camera in the park. She used Mrs. Smith's internet connection at the visitors' center, so now they could watch the park all night from the safety of Alexis's room. "I'll send a link to the other Camp Club Girls so they can take shifts and help us watch."

"Six sets of eyes are better than two," Alex agreed.

The girls wanted to watch the park by night again, and this was the best way to do it. Spending another night out in the forest was out of the question, since Mrs. Howell had found out about

Thad Swotter wandering around after hours. They didn't admit it, but Alexis and Kate were freaked out too. Not really because of Swotter, but because of the note. They definitely didn't want to be alone in the dark woods if someone was angry enough to hurt them.

Kate placed the web camera near the Raptor clearing. Since Jogger moved every night, they figured some action would probably occur there. It was also pretty close to the visitors' center. That made it easier for Kate to run the tiny wire all the way from the computer in the visitors' center to the tree with the camera in it.

"Everything's set," said Kate, falling back onto the pillows. "Now all we have to do is wait."

"Shouldn't be too long," said Alexis. "Swotter said he usually sneaks into the park to take pictures around midnight. That means whoever moves the dinosaurs and leaves the footprints—if it isn't him—must do it before midnight."

The digital clock on Alexis's bed stand flashed 9:40.

At first they just stared at the screen. Their eyes stung, and they were afraid to blink. After all, the dinosaurs had moved right under their noses the other night. Someone *had* tromped around leaving foot-prints only feet away from their pillows, and they hadn't heard a thing. Alexis was determined not to miss out *this* time.

Finally, after twenty minutes with no movement on the camera, they started playing games to pass the time.

The clock read 10:30.

They ate chips and managed to drink an entire two-liter bottle of Mountain Dew. They couldn't have fallen asleep if they wanted to, and Mrs. Howell had been in twice to ask them to be quiet.

It was 11:15.

They had tossed the deck of cards off the bed and were playing Clue for the third time when Kate got a text from Bailey, asking if she was watching the screen.

"It's happening!" Kate yelled. She clapped her hand over her mouth, hoping she hadn't awakened Alexis's family.

"I know it's happening!" said Alexis. "I'm about to beat you again! I think it was Colonel Mustard, with the wrench, in the conserva—"

"No, Alexis! Look at the computer!"

Alexis dropped her game piece. The bushes across the path from the camera were rustling. To the left of the screen, closer this time, something flashed—the white tip of a Converse shoe.

"If our Converse guy is near the camera, what just moved in the bushes?" asked Kate.

"There must be two of them," said Alexis.

They watched the screen for five minutes. Nothing moved. All of a sudden, the screen went dark. No more dinosaurs, no more bushes. Just blackness.

Or was it green?

Alexis lay down on the bed and got as close to the screen as she could. She pushed a button with a little sun on it, and the picture got brighter. The blotch of black lightened, turning into a bunch of three-pointed shapes that were gleaming in the moonlight.

"They're leaves," said Alexis. "The camera has been blocked by a bunch of leaves."

"I thought Jerry and I rigged the camera far enough away from the plants," mused Kate.

Just then, the leaves moved. Jogger was missing, and his footprints were everywhere.

"No!" cried Alexis. "We missed it again!"

"AAAHH!" both girls screamed and fell off the bed. Game pieces and chips flew everywhere. Somewhere in the house a door banged. Angry footsteps stomped down the hall, but that's not what had frightened them. Something had suddenly jumped into the camera's line of sight. Alexis crept back to the foot of the bed and peeked over the footboard at the computer.

Jogger was looking directly into the camera. His head bent to the side, curious maybe—and then he was gone.

● — ● — ●

The next morning the sun glowed brilliantly, as if it didn't know—or didn't care—that Alexis's case was falling apart. The girls were running out of time. The truth was that the Camp Club Girls *still* didn't have much to go on. Last night's watch hadn't accomplished much.

The girls walked slowly through the park. Alexis wanted to

examine the new crime scene, and they needed to get the web cam out of the tree.

"I still can't believe it!" said Alexis. "Jogger looked right into our camera!"

"Yeah," said Kate. "That means that the people moving him must have found it. They know we're watching them now."

"It's like they are making fun of us. I thought you said you hid the camera!" said Alexis.

"I did!" said Kate.

"Okay," said Alexis. "I'm sorry. Let's focus on what we *did* find out last night." She flipped to a clean page in her notebook and began to scribble.

"We know that there are probably *two* people involved," she said. "Maybe one to move the dinosaurs and one to place the prints? The first person is Converse Guy. He left his print at some other scenes, and we caught a glimpse of his shoe last night. The other person was hiding in the bushes. Man! If it weren't for those stupid leaves, we might have seen their faces!"

When they reached the Raptor area, they headed to the bush on the far side of the trail. Alexis hoped Criminal Number 2 had left some kind of clue. The search didn't take long, but it wasn't because Alexis was fast. There simply wasn't anything to find except an empty water bottle with a bright pink lip gloss around the rim.

"Maybe this means one of the suspects is a girl," said Alexis.

"Maybe," said Kate. "Or maybe some visitor was just too lazy to walk across the clearing to the trash can."

Kate walked over to look at the camera. A lump of oily leaves wilted on the ground beneath it. It looked like someone had pulled them up by the roots. Kate reached down to pick them up.

Alexis glanced over her shoulder. She dropped the water bottle she had been examining and yelled, "Kate, stop! That's poison oak!"

Kate's fingers stopped an inch from the plant. Alexis joined her and poked the leaves with a stick.

"It looks like someone yanked these out of the ground," she said.

"Don't they look like the leaves we saw covering the camera

last night?" asked Kate. "I knew there weren't any leaves where I hung it. What if someone covered the lens on purpose?"

"You're right," said Alexis. "I bet they hid until the leaves were in place. Then one came out of the bushes to do the prints and the other one grabbed Jogger. After they were done, they moved the leaves and gave us a show!"

Alexis felt sure she was right. It made sense that the criminals wouldn't want to be seen on tape. But why cover the camera instead of simply unplugging it? And why dance Jogger in front of the lens?

Alexis could handle a lot without getting angry. The heat of a California summer was bearable. Long lines at her favorite amusement park were no problem. She could even deal with her little brothers when they hid all over the house, waiting to scare her as she walked by. But when her suspects started to tease her, her patience wore thin.

"These people are playing games with us, Kate. It's getting on my nerves." She kicked the poison oak back into the forest, away from the trail. Miss Maria didn't need park visitors going home with rashes.

Rashes.

Suddenly Alexis remembered Sydney telling her about poison oak when they were at camp. "If you get into it, it can give you a bad rash," Sydney explained. She had told Alexis about the rash she'd gotten while in the woods with her park ranger aunt.

Alexis couldn't believe she hadn't thought of it sooner. This was huge. If the Converse Guy touched the poison oak, he would have an awful rash by now. He could taunt her all he wanted—Alexis finally felt like she was ahead. She scribbled in her notebook:

Keep an eye out for someone with a rash. . .and someone wearing bright pink lip gloss.

Alexis picked up the plastic bottle and stuffed it into her backpack. She was excited to continue her investigation now that she had a break in the case, but they had to get the camera down first. They headed back through the park to a storage area behind the visitors' center, where they could get a ladder.

The girls approached the cleared area that held a small greenhouse, piles of terra-cotta pots, and a small storage shed where Miss Maria kept her tools and equipment. A rope hanging between two trees sported a sign that read EMPLOYEES AND VOLUNTEERS ONLY! Alexis stepped over the sign and almost fell on Jerry. He was covered up to his knees in manure.

Alexis and Kate almost collapsed in a fit of giggles.

"It's time to fertilize," said Jerry, leaning on his shovel. "There's no need to laugh so hard!"

"I'm sorry," wheezed Alexis. "It's just, I really needed a laugh!"

"Glad I could help. What brings you back here, anyway?"

"We need to get the web cam down," said Alexis. "I was coming to get a ladder out of the shed."

Jerry was out of the manure in seconds. He reached the shed before Alexis had taken two steps.

"You don't want to go in there! Really, it's unorganized and crazy—there's stuff everywhere. You might get hurt."

"You've been in there," said Alexis, pointing to the shovel. "And you're just fine."

Jerry crossed his arms and shook his head.

"Well, since you're being so chivalrous, can *you* get us the ladder?" said Alexis. "We need to take care of that camera before something happens to it. We already lost one of Kate's cameras the night we camped out."

"Don't worry," said Jerry, glancing over his shoulder at the wooden door. It was cracked open an inch. He backed up and kicked it closed. "I'll get the camera down for you in a bit, when I'm done here."

"Okay," said Alexis. "Thanks." The girls walked away, perplexed. Why was Jerry acting so weird? Maybe he was embarrassed about how messy he had let the shed get while Miss Maria was away.

"Boy, it's hot out here," Kate exclaimed, fanning her face.

"Yeah. But even winter in California can regularly be really warm," Alexis said.

"Jerry must be dying," Kate mentioned. "He's wearing long sleeves."

Alex stood still. Suddenly she remembered a mystery she'd seen on TV, one where the bad guy had worn long sleeves in the middle of summer because the person he'd attacked had scratched his arms, and he was trying to hide the wounds.

She told Kate about it.

"Sounds kind of scary," Kate said.

"It was, kind of. But they caught the bad guy in the end," Alexis said. "I don't think Jerry was bitten by an animatron he moved or anything."

"Probably just protecting his arms from that smelly manure," Kate said. "Who wants that on your skin."

"Yeah," Alexis said. "But it's odd. I don't think I've ever seen him wear long sleeves—even in winter."

Alexis took out the water bottle again. The pink around the rim looked familiar, but she couldn't remember where she had seen it before. She glanced at Kate. Nope. Her Camp Club friend only wore lip balm. Maybe her mom? No. Mrs. Howell favored a mauve-colored lipstick. Oh well. It probably had nothing to do with the case, anyway. More than likely, it was just misplaced garbage, like Kate had said.

Alexis's good mood deflated like a punctured beach ball. They really didn't have anything to go on after all. *Maybe* they would see someone sneaking around the park with a rash creeping up his or her arm. *Maybe* the second suspect was a girl who liked pink lip gloss. Too many "maybes." Nothing was for sure.

Alexis couldn't help but think that maybe Miss Maria would be better off if the Camp Club Girls had stuck to investigating missing Spider Man socks.

An Unexpected Visitor

The girls were bummed out, to say the least. They walked back to the visitors' center and found Mrs. Smith bustling around like a caffeinated squirrel.

"She's been doing this all morning," said Megan as Alexis and Kate walked in. Megan was folding maps on the floor because Mrs. Smith's notes for the school board meeting were clogging up the desk.

"I hope you guys have been praying!" Mrs. Smith said as she searched for her paper clips. "This could be huge! If the school board approves my program, we won't have to worry about money. People will line up to donate!"

"That would be awesome, Mrs. Smith," said Alexis. "Are students allowed at this meeting?"

"Of course! Would you like to come? I can take you home when it's over."

"Yes!" said Alexis. She had never been to something as important as a meeting with the school board.

"Actually, since you go to one of the schools that would be involved in the program, you could really help. If we can show that students are interested in the park, the board can't ignore us."

Alexis had just sat on the floor next to Megan, but she jumped up like she had sat on a cactus. She had an idea.

"Mrs. Smith?" she asked. "Would it help to have a lot of students at the meeting?"

"Sure," said Mrs. Smith. "But they would have to behave

themselves. And they need to know why we're there. There will be a time where you guys will be allowed to speak if you want. If you invite anyone else, make sure they know what we're fighting for and why."

Alexis smiled. She grabbed Megan and Kate by the sleeves of their shirts.

"Come on!" she said, and pulled them out of the visitors' center without an explanation.

"What are we doing?" asked Megan. She was half running, half stumbling down the path after Alexis.

"We're going to your house!" said Alexis. "It's a lot closer than mine. You have last year's yearbook, right?" Megan nodded, out of breath. "Great!"

Minutes later they were at Megan's kitchen table with three Cokes, the yearbook, and a phone book. Kate was matching names in the yearbook to corresponding phone numbers. She was good at guessing. The names in the phone book were usually parents' names, but she had only given Alexis a few wrong numbers. The hardest one to find so far had been Kelli Jones. There were five pages of Joneses in the Sacramento area phone book.

As Kate gave Megan and Alexis phone numbers, the girls took turns calling. They left messages where they could, and when they talked to someone, they told them to call all of their friends too. Alexis hoped that this would help Mrs. Smith at the meeting tonight. If she could get twenty-five or thirty students to show up, they could really make an impact.

●—●—●

That night, when Mrs. Smith pulled up to the Department of Education, a huge group of teenagers was gathered on one side of the doors. Most of the students wore khakis and polo shirts, which made them look like miniature versions of their working parents. The rest of the students stood out in various blue and crimson uniforms, showing their school spirit.

The entire girls' volleyball team had left practice early to be there. So had most of the football team. Alexis got out of the car and straightened out her cheerleading skirt before going over to greet the crowd.

"Wow," said Mrs. Smith. "I never expected. . ."

"Don't worry, Mrs. Smith," said Kate. "You do your thing. We have this totally under control."

The meeting room was short on seats, so many of the students sat in the aisles or stood against the walls. Alexis heard an adult mumble something about the fire marshal. He looked around the packed room, amazed.

The first half hour of the meeting was spent talking about budgets, bus routes, and banning tuna and pea casserole from the cafeteria. The students cheered when the board agreed to rework the cafeteria menus, but they settled down as the board director called Mrs. Smith's name. He was a tall, balding man with a kind face.

"Mrs. Smith, would you like to present your idea to the board? We have all read your detailed proposal, but an overview would be nice. There seem to be many people here to support you!" He smiled.

"Yes, Director Burgess. Thank you." Mrs. Smith stood up and took a deep breath. "I am here tonight as a representative from Aspen Heights Conservation Park. If you have seen the news at all lately, you will recognize our name."

As if on cue, Thad Swotter chose that exact moment to push his way into the room, followed by his cameraman. His ball cap was nowhere to be seen. Instead his bright hair was plastered in place, and his tie was as crazy as ever, though Alexis thought it looked a little loose. Mrs. Smith ignored the interruption. She cleared her throat and continued.

"Our park," she said, "consists of hundreds of acres of native Californian wildlife. There are many species of plants and trees that are common, like the mule ear or Jeffrey Pine, but we take pride in our wide selection of endangered plants as well. In some cases, Aspen Heights is the only place for hundreds of miles these plants can be found.

"This, along with how close the park is to Sacramento, makes it the perfect destination for field trips. It takes less than thirty minutes to get there from any school in the county, and the park appeals to many subjects. Biology and botany are two obvious choices, but the park has a great history as well. There are large stones with grooves where Native Americans used to grind their grains, as well as a stream that was panned for gold during the California Gold Rush in the 1800s.

"I propose a direct connection between our schools and Aspen Heights. We will give regular guided tours and educational walks for students of all ages."

Mrs. Smith finished and looked expectantly at the board.

"And how much would this 'partnership' cost us, Mrs. Smith?" asked Mimsy Button, the oldest woman on the board of education, and quite possibly the oldest woman in the Golden State altogether.

"One of my associates, Alexis Howell, has prepared to talk about that," said Mrs. Smith. "Alexis, would you like to step in?"

Alexis had been prepared to give part of Mrs. Smith's speech. Mrs. Smith told her the board would love hearing from a student, so even though she was nervous, she stood up and faced the board. She repeated a verse, Deuteronomy 31:6, to herself that Elizabeth had texted to her earlier, "Be strong and courageous. Do not be afraid or terrified because of them, for the LORD your God goes with you; he will never leave you nor forsake you."

"It won't cost the schools a dime, Mrs. Button," Alexis said with a shaky smile. "Just gas for the buses, of course."

"Well," said Mrs. Button, "that sounds too good to be true." She turned to Mrs. Smith. "If you don't mind my asking—what's in it for you?"

Mrs. Smith smiled and nodded. She wanted Alexis to keep going. Every eye in the room was pinned on her.

"First of all," she said, "Miss Maria built this park to teach our community. People come and go, but she wants to find a more permanent way to share her knowledge. This program would do that. Also, it would help the park get donations, so we could keep it looking good and keep giving free tours."

"Well," said Mr. Burgess, the board director, "this sounds wonderful. I would love to see this program take off."

The room was filled with the cheers of students. Mrs. Smith smiled and hugged Alexis hard.

"One more question," said Mrs. Button, who had all but

shouted into her microphone. She silenced the cheering crowd with one raised, wrinkled hand. "I have *heard* that there might be controversial elements to your park."

"Controversial elements?" asked Mrs. Smith. Alexis didn't know what Mrs. Button meant, but it didn't sound good.

"Yes," said Mrs. Button. "Christian elements?"

Mrs. Smith threw a scathing look at Thad Swotter, whose face had drained of all color except for a blotchy red area on his neck. He reached blindly behind him and covered the lens of the news camera.

"What do you mean?" asked Mrs. Smith, turning her attention back to the board at the front of the room.

"Miss Maria has scattered her Christian beliefs among the scientific facts of the park, has she not?" said Mrs. Button. "The place is littered with Bible verses."

"Is this true, Miss Ellena?" asked Mr. Burgess.

"No, there aren't any verses. We do have some plants from the biblical regions, and we post some of their history."

"Why haven't you mentioned it before now?"

"To be honest, sir, I didn't think it mattered," Mrs. Smith said firmly. Alexis could see that she was trying to hide her anger.

"Sadly, it does matter. We can't be seen to promote one religion over the other. Surely you understand."

Now Alexis was getting upset.

"But sir," she said, "a historical fact about a plant doesn't promote—"

"I'm sorry, ladies. Please notify us if Miss Maria decides to remove these, um, Christian elements."

"Sir, she never will," said Mrs. Smith sadly. Alexis felt horrible. All of Mrs. Smith's hard work was slipping away.

"Then that is a loss for the community and our students," said the director. He banged his wooden hammer on the desk, and the board filed out of the room. Mrs. Smith and Alexis were standing in the middle of the horde of students, mouths hanging open.

Thad Swotter waded his way over to them, pulling at his collar as if it were suddenly too hot.

"Mrs. Smith," he said. "I never meant to—"

"Leave me alone, Thad," Mrs. Smith said, yanking her arm out of his grasp. "I can't believe you would tell her those things!" Mrs. Smith stormed from the building.

Alexis thought Thad looked stunned and a little sad. Maybe he hadn't done this on purpose, but did it matter? His big mouth had shut down the last chance they had to save the park! Thad turned to go, and Alexis saw him loosen his tie and undo the collar of his shirt. She stopped dead in her tracks.

An angry red rash stood out on the white skin of his neck like spilled tomato sauce on a ski slope. Thad Swotter had poison oak.

Alexis, Kate, Jerry, and Megan filed into the car. All of the other students were speeding off with their parents. No one said a word. They hung their heads, defeated.

Alexis was having a hard time holding back her tears. She kept blotting her stinging eyes on her skirt.

The park was back to square one. The poison oak told her that Thad Swotter probably *was* the one planting prints, but she didn't even care at the moment. In a few weeks, Miss Maria would have to return the dinosaurs, and then it wouldn't matter who was moving them around.

● — ● — ●

Twenty minutes later they pulled into Alexis's driveway. There weren't any words that would make everyone feel better, so she and Kate just waved goodbye. They mumbled a glum "hello" to Mr. Howell, who was watching a baseball game, and tromped up the stairs.

Alexis couldn't believe how things were turning out. How could stuff get so messed up when you were trying your hardest to make it right?

She had been working all week to solve the dinosaur mystery. She had walked miles around the park, spent her entire allowance, and lost a ton of sleep. And besides all of that, she had been praying all week. Praying that God would help her solve the mystery. Praying that God would provide for Miss Maria.

She was on her bed, eyes open, as if she could gaze through the ceiling and past the universe, right into God's office.

"Why won't You just fix things already?" she whispered.

Bling! Alexis looked over at her laptop. She had a new email from Elizabeth, the oldest of the Camp Club Girls. After the meeting, she and Kate posted what had happened on the Camp Club Girls web page. All of the girls had sent back prayers and encouragement, but this was the message Alexis had been waiting for. Elizabeth always encouraged her, but for some reason she calmed Alexis more than anyone else. Maybe it was the Bible verses she always added to her advice.

> *Alex,*
>
> *Don't worry, but be strong and courageous because God is always with you (Joshua 1:9). Don't give up now—because we have God, we will always have hope (Jeremiah 29:11). And God works all things to the good of those who love him (Romans 8:28). The deal with the school might not have worked out, but I believe that He has something bigger and better in mind for Miss Maria. Keep investigating. When I am at my lowest is when the case usually breaks wide open! Love you! Tell Kate hi!*
>
> *Elizabeth*

Kate came into the bedroom. She had just taken a shower and was combing the tangles out of her sopping bob.

"Didn't you use a towel?" teased Alexis. "You're drenching my carpet!"

"You're in a better mood," said Kate. She smiled and tossed Alexis a Coke she had brought upstairs.

"Yeah," said Alexis, stretching out on the bed. "Elizabeth just wrote."

DING!

A clear, high-pitched note rang through the house.

"Was that the doorbell?" asked Kate.

"Yeah," said Alexis. She looked at the clock by her bed. It was nine o'clock. "Who would come to our house at this time of night?"

The Visitor

Alexis and Kate were supposed to be getting ready for bed, but their curiosity got the better of them. The girls slipped out of the bedroom and tiptoed down the stairs. At the bottom, they stood behind a stack of paper and listened. The person outside gave up on the doorbell and began pounding instead. Whoever it was, they were in a hurry.

"Coming," called Mr. Howell. He was out of his chair, but he wasn't moving toward the door. His eyes were still glued to the ninth inning playing out on the television.

"Come *on*, Dad!" whispered Alexis. She didn't know why, but she felt sure that this late-night visitor was the answer to her prayers.

Mr. Howell opened the door, but it was in the way. Alexis couldn't see who was standing on the other side.

"Mr. Howell?" said a man's voice. Alexis couldn't place it, but it sounded familiar.

"Um, yes," said Mr. Howell. Alexis saw her dad stand up on his tiptoes and peer past the visitor into the night.

"I'm alone, sir," said the man on the porch.

"Okay. If you're alone, then why are you here?"

Mr. Howell relaxed a little but crossed his arms. Alexis realized that this was a defensive stance, but her father wasn't scared. Without using words, her dad was saying, "Just try to get by me and see what happens."

Who was on the porch?

"Sir, your daughter has been investigating some strange things at Aspen Heights."

"Yes," said Mr. Howell. "I know. What does that have to do with you?"

"Well, I have some new information. After tonight, I am willing to do whatever it takes to help her."

"All right," said Mr. Howell. "I have to admit that this is more than a little strange. Come on in. I'll call Alexis down."

Mr. Howell moved back to let the visitor come inside, and Alexis gasped.

The porch light shone bright in the night, illuminating the yellow hair and crazy tie of Thad Swotter.

"I know you think I'm the bad guy, but just hear me out."

Thad Swotter was sitting on the edge of a squishy armchair. Alexis and Kate stared at him from the couch, and Alexis wished she hadn't left her notebook upstairs. Mr. Howell sat in his favorite chair, but he wasn't watching the TV anymore, even though the game had gone into extra innings. His eyes were locked on the nervous reporter.

"You know I've been sneaking into the park at night," said Swotter. "I told you that the other day. Like I said then, I've been taking pictures of the dinosaurs before anyone else could."

Alexis tapped the tips of her fingers on her knee. Biscuit trotted into the room and began to chew on the leg of her polka dot pajama pants.

"And?" she said. She had already heard all of this. Did he really have any new information to give her? And what if he wasn't telling the truth? Would he lie to make them think he was innocent?

Swotter smiled.

"Didn't you ever wonder how I knew the dinosaurs had been moved?" he asked.

"Well, yeah," said Alexis. "We thought you just checked the park every night."

"*Or*, of course, that you moved them yourself," said Kate. Her eyebrows arched above the bright green rims of her glasses. "And took your pictures afterward."

Alexis smiled. Like Kate had said the other day, you didn't just believe people were innocent because they said so. The Camp Club Girls had to follow the facts to get to the truth, and most of the facts still pointed to Thad Swotter.

"Is that poison oak, Mr. Swotter?" asked Mr. Howell. "It looks uncomfortable. Would you like something to put on it?"

"This?" said Thad, pointing to his neck. "It's not that bad." But he undid his tie, letting it hang loose around his neck.

"Oh! I forgot," squealed Alexis. "Whoever has been moving the dinosaurs covered up our camera the other night with a pile of leaves!"

Kate almost fell off the couch.

"That's right!" she said, straightening her glasses. "And the leaves we found today by the camera were poison oak!"

Thad opened his mouth, but Mr. Howell interrupted him.

"Can you explain all of this, Thad? There's a lot of evidence against you right now. I've seen my girl's notebook. Your shoes are the same as the criminal's. You've been sneaking around the park at night, and now this? Sounds like too many coincidences. . ."

"But they aren't coincidences!" said Swotter, smiling. "Don't you see? I've been tromping around the woods in the dark. I was bound to get poison oak sooner or later! I think I got this the night you two followed me—had to pull some plants out of the way of my shot. Anyway, I'll stop talking. I have something else I want you to hear."

The reporter plunged his arm into his bag and pulled out—

"Your cell phone?" said Alexis. "How's that going to help?"

"You aren't going to believe me until you hear it," said Swotter. He punched in a number and turned on the speaker phone. The mechanical voice of a woman echoed through the living room.

"Please enter your password," she said. Thad Swotter punched in four digits. "You have. . .two. . .saved messages. First. . .message."

The tinny voice of the woman was replaced by the scratchy sound of silence. After a few seconds, another voice spoke.

"Hello, Thad Swotter."

It sounded low and muffled, as if someone were speaking through a blanket or something.

"They're disguising their voice?" said Mr. Howell.

"Shh!" said Alexis, swatting a hand toward her father. The message continued.

"If you want the story of a lifetime, be at Aspen Heights at midnight. I'll leave directions for you on the entrance sign." The line went dead, and the mechanical phone voice was back.

"Next saved message—" but Swotter turned it off.

"You see?" he said. "I'm not moving the dinosaurs. I've gotten a message every night this week. They tell me where to go to take my pictures. This was the first one."

Alexis and Kate were stunned. Mr. Howell leaned forward, curious.

"What kind of directions did they leave you, Mr. Swotter?" asked Alexis.

"Oh, I saved them. They're right here." He pulled a wrinkled note out of his bag. Alexis grabbed it. Her heart was pounding. The typing on the paper looked eerily familiar.

Mr. Swotter: The story you seek is on the move. Check out the park . . .see anything different?

"That was the first night, after Miss Maria got hurt," said Swotter. "After that, I didn't get any more notes—just the phone calls. I answered the phone a few times and tried to get more information, but the person always hangs up after they tell me where the dinosaurs are."

Alexis couldn't believe this. Her number-one suspect had walked into her living room with amazing evidence! Somehow she knew that Thad Swotter was telling the truth. He usually looked like he was hiding something, but tonight there was something different about his eyes. They weren't smiling, mocking Alexis and her investigation. They really looked concerned. Thad Swotter wanted to help.

"Okay," said Alexis slowly. "So it isn't you, but how will this tell us who it *is*?" Swotter opened his mouth, but Kate was faster.

"The phone numbers!" she said. "Cell phones keep track of who has called! It lists their phone numbers until you decide to delete them." She looked at the reporter, her eyes huge behind her glasses. "Please tell me you didn't delete them!"

"Of course not!" he said. "That's the best part." He pushed a few buttons, scrolling down a list of phone numbers. Alexis couldn't believe her luck. If they got the phone number of whoever was doing this, they might be able to figure out who it was. They could call the number and see who answered, and if that didn't work they could get online. She saw her mom find the name of a prank caller one time by putting in the phone number—like a backward phone book.

"Here it is," said Swotter. "This is the number that came up all week." He turned the phone around so everyone could see. Mr. Howell had been sucked in and was now squished next to the girls on the couch.

"Unavailable?" he said. "How does that help?"

"It doesn't," said Kate. But the reporter informer was scrolling through more numbers.

"I said that was the number that came up all week," he said. "All week, that is, except last night. Last night, the caller got messy and used a landline—a regular phone—instead of a blocked cell phone. Look." He spun the phone around again, and ten digits lit up the screen.

"Do you know whose number that is?" asked Kate in a whisper.

"Nope," said Swotter. "I thought I'd save that for you guys." He handed the phone to Alexis, who looked at her dad. He nodded, and she pressed SEND.

Somewhere, miles away, a phone was ringing. The echo of it came through the tiny speaker of Thad Swotter's cell phone. After the fourth ring, an answering machine picked up.

"Hello, you have reached Aspen Heights Conservation Park. We are not available to—"

The phone slid out of Alexis's hand and hit the floor.

●—●—●

Thad Swotter picked up his phone and glanced at the time flashing on the front of it.

"I hate to run, but I have some work to do," he said. "I'll be at the park this weekend. Will you girls keep me updated?"

Alexis nodded. She was still a little shocked. The phone call came from Aspen Heights. Had someone broken into the visitors' center to use the phone? That had to be it. Nothing else made sense.

Another thought struck her as they walked Mr. Swotter to the door.

"Mr. Swotter, why do you want to help us all of a sudden?"

"Well, really I wanted to help Mrs. Smith. This park means the world to her." Alexis looked confused, so Thad Swotter continued. "We were friends when we were kids, Mrs. Smith and I. Then we grew up and I—well—I forgot what it meant to be a friend. I put everything I had into becoming the best, and I hurt a few people along the way."

Thad Swotter apologized to Mr. Howell for intruding so late at night and then walked back to his car with his hands in his pockets.

"Bedtime, ladies," said Mr. Howell. He laid his large hands on Alexis's shoulders and squeezed. "A lot of new stuff to think about, huh?"

"Yeah," said Alexis. She knew sleep would not come easy tonight. The girls went back upstairs and brushed their teeth. Five minutes later they were sitting cross-legged on the bed talking about who could have made the mysterious phone call.

"Someone must have broken into the center, Alex," said Kate. "That's the only thing that makes sense."

"I know," said Alexis. "Maria was in the hospital most of the week, so she couldn't have been moving the dinosaurs."

"She would never do that anyway, would she?"

"No," said Alexis. "No one at the park would do anything to put it in danger. We all love it too much." Alexis's excitement was deflating by the second. What good would this new evidence be if they couldn't find out *who* had made those calls?

"Hey, do you mind if I read Elizabeth's email?" asked Kate.

"Go ahead," said Alexis. "Just open my mailbox."

Kate walked over to the computer. It had gone into sleep mode, so she wiggled a finger over the touchpad to clear the black screen.

"Oh no!" she said. "Jerry forgot to take the camera down!" Alexis looked over at her computer. Sure enough, the camera was still in the tree. She hoped that nothing happened to it before they could take it down in the morning.

"It's still on," said Kate. "See the Raptors?"

"It must have gotten bumped," said Alexis. "It's sideways now."

"Yeah, it's kind of—" but Kate never finished her sentence.

"Kind of what?" Kate didn't answer, so Alexis sat up to get a better look at the video. "No way! Did you see who that was?"

Kate nodded, her mouth hanging open and her eyes glued to the screen.

The dinosaur movers were back, and they had forgotten all about the hidden camera.

CHAPTER

12

Good Intentions

Alexis's mind was racing. They had hardly slept because of their discovery. As soon as Mrs. Howell was up and about, the girls were begging her to take them to the park.

"I knew I had seen that lip gloss before!"

How could she not have seen this coming? First the shoes—she had never really looked at his shoes, but now she remembered that he always wore Converse when he worked. And the lip gloss? It had been a gift *from Alexis*! How could she have forgotten that?

"It was you!"

Alexis stood over Jerry with her arms crossed. He was knee-deep in a hole he had dug for a new sapling.

"What do you mean?" Jerry said. He blushed, and a crooked smile bloomed on his face. *Does he think this is a game?* Alexis wondered.

"I mean it was you moving the dinosaurs and placing the prints. You and Megan!"

Jerry laughed. "Prove it."

"First of all, your shoes." Alexis pointed at Jerry's feet, which were indeed soled with Converse All-Stars. "You got sloppy and started leaving your footprints everywhere. I don't know *how* I forgot that you wear those old things when you're going to get muddy."

"Lots of people wear these shoes, Alex," said Jerry. She could tell he was enjoying this.

"Sure. But you're wearing long sleeves again today, Jerry. Why?"

Jerry squirmed a little. "Raise up your sleeve, if you don't mind."

Jerry pulled his shirt sleeve up to his elbow, revealing a nasty case of poison oak rash.

"You didn't realize what plant you used to cover the camera the other night, did you? Kate and I found wilted poison oak at the scene. And speaking of that scene. . ."

Alexis stomped past him to the tool shed. Yesterday he had kept her out of it. He said it was a mess. Jerry climbed out of the hole he was digging and followed her.

"No, you can't—" said Jerry, but he was too late. Alexis ripped the door open, flooding the small building with light.

"Ha!" she said. There, in the middle of the floor, was a pile of strange-looking tools. On closer inspection, the girls realized that they were long handles, like broomsticks, with wooden dinosaur feet screwed onto the bottoms. There were two pairs of them. Kate picked one up and noticed thin lines running up and down the foot.

"Those little lines we kept seeing in the tracks—it was the grain of the wood!" she said.

"Cool, huh?" asked Jerry.

Alexis was surprised. She had expected a confession, followed by an apology full of guilt. Instead, Jerry stepped past her into the shed with a huge smile on his face.

"I figured you would catch on sooner or later," Jerry said. "Watch this!" He pulled out the largest pair of wooden feet—Alexis assumed they belonged to the Tyrannosaurus Rex—and stood on them, holding onto the wooden handles at the top. Then he began walking around on them like a pair of stilts.

"See?" he said. "Cool, huh? I thought all this up!" He grinned. Did he expect her to be proud of him? So Bailey had been right after all!

"This isn't a game, Jerry!" Alexis said. "People could have been hurt!"

"Well, no one was," he said. He jumped off the wooden feet and tossed them back into the shed. "Miss Maria needed people to show up. I was saving the park."

"What's wrong?" Megan asked as she walked up behind Alexis and Kate.

"Look, Kate," said Alexis, pointing to Megan. "It's our Lip Gloss Lady." She turned to Megan to explain. "We found a water bottle with your lip gloss all over it in a bush near the Raptors."

Megan looked confused.

"Alexis and Kate finally caught us," Jerry explained. He still sounded as if the whole thing was hilarious. Megan, on the other hand, looked guilty. She stared at her feet and said, "Oh."

Alexis and Kate were staring at Jerry, waiting for an explanation.

"Come on, Alexis!" he said. "You know this place needs help! Thad Swotter gave me the idea, although he doesn't know it. He said in his newscast that this place needed a lot more than toy dinosaurs, and I agreed. You've seen how many people have been coming!"

"Yeah, but that doesn't fix the problem, Jerry!" said Alexis. "When the dinosaurs have to go back, what are you going to do then? They won't bring in any visitors once they're gone, no matter how 'alive' they were while they were here!"

Jerry wasn't smiling anymore. He strode into the shed and pulled a small object off a shelf. He handed it to Kate.

"My camera!" she squealed, delighted to have it back.

"Yeah," said Jerry. "We took it from your camp the other night so you wouldn't see that it was us."

"That's stealing, Jerry!" said Alexis.

"Not really! We were going to give it back!" Jerry stood looking moodily at Alexis until they were interrupted by a familiar figure limping with a crutch under one arm.

"Miss Maria!" they all yelled at once. The group rushed forward to hug her but stopped short so they wouldn't hurt her.

"I trust my park is in one piece?" Miss Maria asked playfully. Then she noticed the tension in the group. "Now what's happened to make everyone so glum?"

"We found out who's been moving the dinosaurs and leaving the prints," said Alexis.

"Oh, that's wonderful!" said Miss Maria. "I knew I could count on you girls!"

"It was Jerry," Alexis said, and Miss Maria's smile disappeared.

"And me," said Megan. "I helped him."

"Well, that *is* a surprise," said Miss Maria. She looked severely disappointed.

"I don't see what the big deal is!" cried Jerry. "It got more people into the park! I was careful! None of the dinosaurs—or *people*," he looked pointedly at Alexis, "have been hurt!"

"You're right, Jerry," said Maria. "But that's not the main point. You were being deceitful. You pretended to help us when in fact you were the problem. If you came up with this idea, you should have just asked me if you could carry it out."

"I was afraid you would say no," Jerry said.

"And you were probably right," said Maria. "I don't want to trick people into loving my park. I want them to enjoy it for the same reasons I do."

"But they don't," said Jerry. "That's the problem! We're going to have to close the park!"

There were tears in his eyes now, and Alexis wondered if all of his joking had just been a cover-up for his real feelings. He was scared of losing the park—of losing his home. She reached out and grasped his hand, which was dirty and hot.

"God will take care of us," said Maria. "You'll see. He's got a way of showing up just when we need Him."

"That's the thing," said Jerry. "We've needed Him for a long time, and you've been praying nonstop. *I've* been praying nonstop!" Jerry pulled away from Alexis's hand and gestured around them. "In case you haven't noticed, He hasn't shown up yet."

Through the open window of the visitors' center, they heard the phone ring.

●—●—●

TO: Camp Club Girls
SUBJECT: Another one solved!

To my Camp Club Sisters,
Thanks for your prayers! The park is going to be okay! Miss Maria got a phone call yesterday from a company who wants to help us. They can't give her the money she needs outright, but they want to sponsor and promote a yearly 5K race through the park! They are going to provide prize

bags for participants and help us with volunteers. Their spokesperson says that the race should raise enough money to help Miss Maria maintain the park and maybe even expand it! We're planning to do the first race in October, when the aspens are golden for the fall! The park will be beautiful!

Some of the local teachers have called too. They want to come to the park for field trips, even though Mrs. Smith's program isn't in place. They say that at first they'll avoid the greenhouse, which has the "Christian elements" the board of directors didn't like. All except for Mr. Chase, the religion teacher at our local community college. He got all excited when he heard about the thorns. He said something about persecution and Roman torture. . .eew.

But the best part is that all of the teachers told Miss Maria that they want to pay her a small fee for guided tours!

Thanks bunches to all of you for putting your heads together on this one! The "criminals" (my friend Jerry and his sister, Megan) realize the mistake they made. I think Jerry also learned a little something about God's faithfulness. Thanks, Elizabeth, for sending those Bible verses. I showed them to Jerry, and he agrees that God always provides, even if it's not in the way or the timing we expect!

Love you all, and keep your eyes open! You never know who will need us next!

Alexis

Kate had flown home at the end of the week. Alexis was back at the park, kneeling in the dirt and planting flowers around a new sign at the head of the park trail. Next to her stood Jogger, who Miss Maria had decided to buy instead of returning him with the other dinosaurs. She said she could afford one of the smaller ones. Since they had all grown so close to the little Raptor, he was the obvious choice. His picture was all over the new brochures, and he was even going to be on some T-shirts they were going to sell in the visitors' center. He had become the perfect mascot.

Alexis had even come up with a great idea for the kids who

visited the park. She drew a map and put a cartoon drawing of Jogger in the corner. The top read "Where's Jogger?" Each time kids came, they would get a map. The goal was to roam all over the park until they found Jogger and marked him on their map. When they had visited the park and found him four times, they would get a prize.

Alexis couldn't help but think about the movie she and Kate had seen. The person they thought was so good ended up being the bad guy. It wasn't too far from what had happened here. She thought Thad Swotter was making trouble because he *seemed* like the kind of person who would. At the same time, she hadn't even thought of Jerry or Megan.

She had learned a lot about judging people before she really got to know them. Thad Swotter had ended up helping her, and she found out he could be a pretty nice guy.

At that moment, as Alexis pressed pink impatiens into the dirt, Thad Swotter walked up behind her.

"Is Mrs. Smith here?" he asked. "She's giving me a tour of the greenhouse."

"The greenhouse?" said Alexis. "But that's where—"

"I know, I know," he said, holding up a hand so he could explain.

"I've never really been interested in where things came from," Swotter said. "You know, creation versus monkeys and all that. But I think the reporter in me is taking over. For some reason, I can't stand not *knowing*. Besides, you guys weren't going to change things around here, no matter what the school board told you. I figure that if you're not willing to compromise, even with everything to lose, this God of yours must be pretty special."

Alexis was awestruck. Was this reporter—the man who would do anything for a story—actually saying he was interested in *God*?

"Mrs. Smith's in the visitors' center," she said. He thanked her and turned away.

"Oh, Mr. Swotter?" said Alexis. He stopped and looked back. "Yes?"

"I'm sorry we blamed you for moving the dinosaurs and stuff," Alexis said.

"That's okay. You were just following your leads, and I shouldn't have been sneaking around the park in the dark anyway. That wasn't very honest of me." He stuck out his hand. "Call us even?"

Alexis shook it. "Even," she said. Swotter left and entered the visitors' center.

God was amazing, Alexis knew. He had helped her solve her mystery, provided for the park, and drawn Thad Swotter to Him all at once!

Alexis finished planting her flowers and stood to admire the effect. The new wooden sign glinted in the sun. The message on it had been her idea, and it made her laugh each time she read it:

PLEASE NO WALKING, JOGGING, RUNNING, LEAPING, TRAIPSING, MEANDERING, WANDERING, JUMPING, DRIFTING, HOPPING, STROLLING, SAUNTERING, AMBLING, MARCHING, STRIDING, PACING, HIKING, TODDLING, SPRINTING, LOPING, SCUTTLING, SCAMPERING, DARTING, DASHING, SCURRYING, BOUNDING, OR SKIPPING BEYOND THE PATH! THANK YOU!

Jogger the Raptor wagged his tail and smiled right along with her.

Camp Club Girls:
Alexis and the Arizona Escapade

The Bridge in the Desert

The noon sun shone bright in a sapphire sky. But twelve-year-old Alexis Howell wasn't paying attention. She stood on the bridge and watched the Arizona heat warping the hills of sand and sagebrush in the distance.

She had never been so afraid in all her life.

Alexis made herself look at the clouds to try to keep her mind off her fear. She liked their shapes, but mostly she was keeping her mind off the water. A crowd of tourists clamored past, and a tall man bumped her into the rail. Her eyes were ripped from the sky as she caught her balance. . .and looked down.

It seemed like forever to the water below. The wind blew, lifting her brown ponytail. The bridge swayed. It rocked beneath her feet.

Maybe it will flip over and throw me off, Alexis thought in sudden panic.

Why had she promised to meet Elizabeth *here* of all places? Why?

Like most children, Alexis had grown up singing the song "London Bridge is falling down. . . ." She'd certainly been surprised to learn that the London Bridge wasn't in London at all. It was here in Arizona.

Another group of tourists nudged past. A large purse landed with a *thud* against Alexis's back, and before she knew it, she had flipped forward. She screamed. She was falling. . .falling. . .falling. . . .

"Alexis?"

The vision evaporated. Alexis turned toward the voice that had said her name.

"Elizabeth! I'm so glad you're here!" She hugged her friend but then couldn't seem to let go. She clung to her friend like a life preserver.

"I'm glad too," said Elizabeth in her soft Texas twang, not seeming to notice the tightness of the hug. "This place is beautiful! The water is so calm and peaceful, and the bridge is magnificent! I *did* think it would be bigger, though."

"Sure," said Alexis, who thought the bridge was quite big enough. She released Elizabeth but then held her arm until they reached the sidewalk at the end of the bridge.

The sounds of vacation echoed off the lake. Laughing children, scolding parents, and the sputter of motorboats. Vendors called out, advertising their wares.

"Cotton candy!"

"Funnel cakes here!"

"Hot dogs! Fresh, cold lemonade!"

Alexis had stopped shaking. Now she was simply trying to keep up with Elizabeth. This was not always easy because her friend's legs seemed twice as long as hers. Elizabeth kept pulling on the bottom edges of her shorts, like they were too short.

"How was the trip?" said Alexis.

"Long," said Elizabeth. "We drove. We just got here, but I needed a break from my brother. Mom said I could meet you and hang out until dinner."

"Great! I'll take you to my hotel. You won't believe it. . . . It looks like a *castle*! It has an amazing pool too. And Grandma got our room for free!"

"Wow!" said Elizabeth. "How'd she do that?"

"She's teaching some classes about British history," said Alexis. "It's a new addition to the London Bridge Days Festival." She gestured to all of the tourists.

They had entered the area of Lake Havasu City that looked like an old English village. People everywhere were dressed up. They all wore a lot of clothes for such a hot day. The women dressed in bright, heavy, velvet clothes. Some wore tattered dark clothes to look like beggars and paupers, poor people. Others were dressed regally to look like princes and queens. They reminded Alexis of the scenes and actors from movies like *Robin Hood* or *The Princess Bride* or even a few of the scenes in *The Chronicles of Narnia.*

Elizabeth turned and looked again at the bridge. She pulled her cell phone out of her pocket and took a picture. "That's really the London Bridge, huh?" asked Elizabeth.

Alexis glanced over her shoulder and shivered.

"Yep. The city of London had to replace it because it was so old, but they didn't want to throw it away, so they sold it to Lake Havasu City."

"I thought the London Bridge was tall, you know? With towers at the ends," said Elizabeth.

"You're thinking of the Tower Bridge," said Alexis. "My grandma told me that people always get them mixed up."

This bridge definitely didn't have towers. It was wide and low to the water, with five long arches supporting its weight. The top of the bridge had a stone rail that held a few old lampposts and a flagpole.

"It's so weird to see something called the London Bridge in the middle of the Arizona desert!" said Elizabeth.

Alexis laughed as she led her friend toward the London Bridge Resort, where she was staying. She was so excited to be on fall break. She had a whole week off from school, so her grandmother had invited Alexis to join her at the resort. Alexis was happy already, but she became super-excited when she found out that Elizabeth was coming too. Elizabeth's dad came to Lake Havasu every year for the bass-fishing tournament. This year he brought the whole family.

Alexis couldn't wait to spend an entire five days with the oldest of the Camp Club Girls! Who knew? Maybe they would get a chance to solve a mystery. Something was bound to happen when crowds this large got together.

"Wow! You're staying *here*?" Elizabeth cried. They had turned into the entrance of the London Bridge Resort. Two huge towers guarded the doors. Every time Alexis looked at them, she expected to see a princess waving from the top or a dragon at the bottom, clawing to get in.

"Hey, stand by the entrance and let me get a picture," Elizabeth directed. "Then I'll send it to the rest of the Camp Club Girls."

Alexis posed until Elizabeth said, "Okay. That'll make them wish they were here."

Then Alexis led the way through the front doors, and a huge scarlet lobby glittered before them. To the left was an expanse of marble floor, which led over to the check-in desk, and to the right was—

Elizabeth gasped.

"I know," said Alexis. "Isn't it awesome?"

An expanse of soft red carpet was surrounded by gold stands and scarlet ropes. Inside the ropes was a gigantic carriage. It looked like it was made of gold. The roof of the carriage was held up by eight golden palm trees, and at the very top sat three cherubs. They were holding up the royal crown.

The girls were leaning in to get a closer look when a boyish voice snapped behind them.

"Can't you see the ropes? No touching!"

Alexis spun around. An officer in a brown sheriff's uniform stood at the edge of the carpet, crossing his arms.

"We weren't going to touch it, sir," said Elizabeth. "I promise—"

"I know troublemakers when I see 'em," said the young man. He couldn't have been much older than twenty.

"Hi," muttered Alexis. She glanced at his badge. "Um, Mr. Dewayne."

He pointed to his badge and said, "*Deputy* Dewayne to you."

"Nice to meet you," said Elizabeth, but it came out more like a question.

"Don't get smart with me, little girl!" said Deputy Dewayne. Alexis smiled. Elizabeth was easily as tall as the officer. "This is my town! I won't have tourists making a mess of things!"

Alexis and Elizabeth simply nodded.

"If I see you even put one finger over those ropes"—he pointed toward the carriage—"I'll clap you in irons!"

Alexis couldn't help it. She sniggered. *Clap us in irons? Whatever that means.*

"You think this is funny?" asked the deputy. Alexis was about to say no, but they were interrupted by a waitress carrying a paper bag.

"Here's your lunch, *Deputy*," she said with a smile. "Grilled cheese with no crust—just the way you like it." She winked at the girls and handed the officer his bag. . .which had cartoon animals all over it.

Deputy Dewayne saw the girls hide a laugh as they looked from him to the bag.

"The kiddie menu is cheaper!" he exclaimed. "And I *like* it! You just remember what I said. This is my town. Don't get on my bad side!" With that, he turned and marched out of the lobby.

"No way!" said Elizabeth.

"I know!" said Alexis. "Kiddie menu?"

"Clap us in irons?"

Elizabeth shot some pictures of the carriage, and then the girls laughed all the way up the stairs to the room where Alexis's grandmother was giving a speech on British literature. When they reached the door of the room where Mrs. Windsor was teaching, Alexis put a finger to her lips to tell Elizabeth to be quiet.

"And *that*," said Alexis's grandmother's voice, "is how the famous Gunpowder Plot was discovered."

The people applauded lightly and then stood to leave. Alexis had to wait for the group of people around her grandmother to clear before introducing Elizabeth.

"This is my grandma, Molly Windsor."

"It's nice to finally meet you," said the short lady, shaking Elizabeth's hand. Her hair was a powerful shade of red, and her face was covered with a smattering of freckles, just like Alexis's. "I hope you two have been enjoying the scenery!"

"We've only just begun," said Elizabeth. "But we *have* been to the bridge."

Alexis shuddered again.

"Really, Alexis!" said her grandmother. "That bridge is hardly twenty feet tall and made out of solid concrete and steel! It's perfectly safe. You need to work on that fear of yours!"

"You're afraid of bridges?" cried Elizabeth.

"It's nothing," said Alexis, changing the subject. "Want to go sightseeing with us, Grandma?"

"Sorry, girls. I have two more lectures today. Why don't you explore together? You're bound to find some fascinating things."

She bustled around her podium, taking out another set of notes. Just then, an older man approached the front. Had he been sitting in the back all that time? Or had it just taken him that long to walk up the aisle?

"Interesting topic, Dr. Windsor," he said. His voice sounded like sandpaper under water—scratchy and wet at the same time.

"Thank you," said Alexis's grandmother. "Girls, this is Dr. Edwards. He is speaking this week as well."

The skinny, slouched man reached out to shake hands but pulled back quickly. He yanked a square white piece of fabric out of his front pocket. He held the handkerchief up to his nose and sneezed into it. The violence of the sneeze had not messed up his perfect mustache, which was a glimmering white, like his short hair.

"Forgive me," he said. "The air here is dusty."

"This is my granddaughter, Alexis," said Grandma Windsor. "And her friend Elizabeth. Alexis is staying with me for the week."

The man eyed the girls and frowned.

"Well, hopefully you two will find something better to do than bother the people attending our conference," he said. "The bed race, for example, usually interests the *loud* youth of the city."

"Bed race?" said Alexis. "What's a bed race?" It sounded so interesting that she forgot Dr. Edwards had just insulted them.

"Ask the crazy lady at the front desk," said Dr. Edwards. With that, he bowed to Grandma Windsor and left.

"Don't mind him, girls," said Grandma Windsor when he was out of hearing range. "He's old and grouchy. Gets along better with books than with people."

Another audience began flooding into the room, so Alexis and Elizabeth fought against the tide and left, waving goodbye over their shoulders. They walked back down to the lobby and saw the woman Dr. Edwards had called *the crazy lady* at the front desk.

Of course she wasn't really crazy. She *did* have a streak of purple hair, though. Alexis was sure that someone like Dr. Edwards would call that *crazy* instead of *creative, interesting,* or *fun.*

They waited at the desk behind a man who had lost his room key and a woman who needed more towels. When it was their turn, Alexis spoke up.

"Hi," she said. "We're visiting here, and we heard something about a bed race. Could you tell us what that is?"

"Of course!" said the lady. She wasn't old, but she wasn't too young either. The color in her hair made it even harder for Alexis to tell her age. "It's exactly what it sounds like—a bed race!" she said brightly.

Alexis and Elizabeth exchanged a confused look. The lady behind the desk explained further.

"The race happens on Saturday, before the parade. Each team decorates an old bed with wheels on it. Then the teams race the beds through town. Someone pushes or pulls the bed, and the others ride on it. You sign up over *there*," she pointed to the wall a few feet away. There was a large poster with a picture of a zooming four-poster and a scribbled list of names.

Alexis looked at Elizabeth and could tell she was thinking the same thing: This could be quite the adventure! A cloud passed over Alexis's smile.

"Where are we supposed to get an old bed?" she asked.

"You'd be surprised," said the woman behind the desk. "I'd start looking around the shopping area. Try the older shops—and don't hesitate to ask around."

The girls turned to leave, but the desk lady called out.

"I'm Jane, by the way."

"I'm Alexis, and this is Elizabeth."

"Well, good luck! The same team has won two years in a row. Maybe you can show them up, huh?" She waved at the girls and gave them a cheerful smile.

The girls waved back and walked across the lobby toward the front door and the sunshine.

Suddenly the lobby door flew open, and a short, round man with messy gray hair stumbled through it. His face was red beneath a bushy mustache, and sweat poured down his cheeks. Everyone in the area stopped moving and talking. The only sound in the room was the slap of the man's polished shoes as he crossed the marble floor.

"Mr. Mayor, what is it?"

The mayor, thought Alexis. *What could be wrong?*

"Mayor Applebee, can I help?" Jane came out from behind the front desk. The mayor stopped. A bead of sweat flipped off the end of his chin. He raised his hands in the air as if he were about to make an important announcement.

His breathing was still labored, but it seemed that he couldn't wait any longer. He gulped at the air and spoke.

"The bridge. . .is. . . It's. . ." He almost fell over, but Jane rushed to support him. After a moment the mayor regained his balance. He drew in a breath—more steady this time—and managed to finish a whole sentence.

"The London Bridge is. . .*falling down*."

Falling Down!

Falling down, falling down.
   London Bridge is falling down. . . .
   Alexis half expected the mayor to finish the old nursery rhyme.

   But there was no "my fair lady." Only a winded man standing in the silence of the lobby and looking distressed. No one spoke because no one knew what to say. Was this some sort of joke? If so, it wasn't a very good one. No one was laughing.

   "The commissioner!" wheezed the mayor. "Where is he?"

   "In the restaurant," said Jane. "Eating lunch."

   Mayor Applebee took off through the lobby.

   "Who is the commissioner?" Alexis asked.

   "The bridge commissioner," answered Jane. "He's in charge of the committee that oversees the bridge. Something must really be wrong."

   Alexis and Elizabeth followed the flow of people out of the hotel lobby and toward the canal. A large group was already gathering on the shore, and it was difficult to see the bridge. They could only see a herd of people being shown off the nearest end of the bridge. The food stands that had been selling treats moments earlier were piling everything into boxes. Over the entrance to the bridge, the sign reading TASTES OF HAVASU had been removed, and a police officer was replacing it with yellow caution tape.

   There must really be something wrong with the bridge, thought Alexis. "Come on, Elizabeth. Let's see if we can get closer."

   The girls edged their way to the front of the crowd and

then carefully walked along the water's edge toward the bridge. Eventually they saw it. A crack—about eight feet long—climbing out of the water and reaching toward the arch in the second bridge support. Even as they watched, a bit of mortar crumbled and plunked into the channel.

The crowd gasped.

Voices chimed together, striking chords of worry and fear.

"It couldn't really fall, could it?"

"The middle will go first, if it does."

"I guess that's what happens when you buy a used bridge!"

"What about the parade?"

What about the parade? thought Alexis. She had been so excited about the festival, but could it go on if the bridge was threatening to collapse? Suddenly a voice from the back of the crowd rose above all the others.

"It's the *curse*." The voice was solid but wavy—like an aged piece of oak. The people on the bank all turned. Their eyes locked onto an old woman. She was wearing a ragged brown dress and a cloak, even though it was hot. Her tin-colored hair hung tangled to her waist, and she was leaning on a warped walking stick.

Alexis couldn't tell if it was a costume or not. The lady definitely looked like some kind of medieval hag. The woman reminded her of the old hag in *The Princess Bride*, who cursed Princess Buttercup in her dreams for giving away her own true love.

"What curse?" someone called from the crowd.

"Don't you people keep up on your history?" asked the old woman. She was speaking from the top of the little green hill near the bridge. Everyone could see her as she lifted her hands to speak over them.

"History!" the woman repeated. "The London Bridge never remains whole for long, no matter how you rebuild it. From the time of the Romans, it has always sunk, burned, or *crumbled*!" She pointed toward the crack with her stick.

The crowd began to murmur. Some were nodding. Alexis made a mental note to ask her grandmother about the bridge's destructive past. The old woman continued.

"When the bridge was brought to Lake Havasu, the curse of

the River Thames followed. Now it will prey on two cities instead of one! London and Lake Havasu City are sisters in destruction!"

The people began talking among themselves again. Some wandered back to whatever they had been doing before the commotion. Some called after the woman, asking her questions, but she was already out of reach. She walked toward town singing softly in a croaking voice, *"London Bridge is falling down, falling down, falling down. . . ."*

When the crowd had thinned out, Alexis and Elizabeth wandered closer to the bridge. From the grassy slope they could easily see the crack. It looked strange—harmless and menacing at the same time. Elizabeth sat on the grass and crossed her lanky legs. Alexis plopped down beside her.

"Do you think a crack that small could really bring a whole bridge down?" Elizabeth asked.

"I have no idea!" answered Alexis. "I'm just glad nothing happened while we were up there this morning." Alexis ran her hand through the short grass.

"I just don't get it," she said, picking a small clover. "This bridge shouldn't just fall down. I read about it before I came. The outside layer of stone is from the real London Bridge, but everything underneath is solid steel and cement. It shouldn't be crumbling, Elizabeth."

Alexis was puzzled. What could possibly bring down such a huge structure? The bridge wasn't old—barely thirty years. And it wasn't like Lake Havasu got a lot of severe weather or anything. That only left one possibility.

"The curse," said Alexis, almost in a whisper.

"Alexis, come on," said Elizabeth. Now her gangly arms were crossed as well as her legs. "You can't really believe what that lady was saying. Curses aren't real!"

"I know," said Alexis. "But it sounds like a mystery, don't you think?" She looked sideways at her friend and raised her eyebrows. Elizabeth's mouth stretched into a wide smile.

"Mmm, I was hoping something like this might happen. . . . I mean, not the crack!" she apologized to the bridge. "You know what I mean. Do you happen to have that little pink notebook of yours?"

"What do you think?" said Alexis. She drew the notebook out of her back pocket and started scribbling as Elizabeth listed people they should try to talk to.

Problem: There's a crack in the London Bridge.

Plan: Track down more information. Start by talking to the old woman—maybe there's more to this curse thing than we realize. Maybe it's a stunt for the tourists.

Alexis thought back to the conversation surrounding the bridge only moments before.

"Elizabeth," she said. "What if they cancel the parade? No parade means no bed race! That would be a total bummer!"

"I know," said Elizabeth. "But it's even worse than that. No London Bridge means no Lake Havasu. They built this town around that bridge, Alexis. How many tourists will come to see a pile of rocks?"

"Who knows," said Alexis. "It works for Stonehenge, doesn't it?"

Elizabeth didn't laugh.

"Stonehenge is a pile of big rocks in England that were propped upright sometime way before Jesus was born," Alexis explained, in case Elizabeth didn't know. "They don't know who put them up or why they're standing in a circle in the middle of a field. . . ."

"Oh, I know about that," Elizabeth said. "I saw a program about it on the History Channel. I was just thinking."

"Look!" Alexis whispered. She pointed across the road to where a short, slouched figure was walking quickly away, leaning on a stick. It was the old woman.

"Come on! Let's go talk to her!" Elizabeth exclaimed.

Both girls jumped to their feet and dusted off their backsides before jogging across the street. They wanted to catch up and ask her a few questions about the bridge and this so-called curse, but it wasn't that easy.

The closer they got to the woman, the faster she seemed to walk. Soon she was almost running. She zigged and zagged through the streets of Lake Havasu City, leading the girls deeper and deeper into the teeming crowds of tourists. The old woman took a sharp left into an alley behind a bakery, and the girls almost lost her.

They stood panting on the sidewalk, being jostled by purses.

Alexis noticed that some of the purses had small dogs in them. She would never understand what made people carry their dogs around everywhere they went.

"It's like she knows we're following her and is trying to lose us!" panted Elizabeth. "She must be up to something devious, or she wouldn't run."

"I know," wheezed Alexis as a Pomeranian nipped at her elbow from inside its rainbow-colored Louis Vuitton. "Can you see anything?"

Elizabeth used her height to peer over the heads of the crowd.

"There!" she cried. The old woman emerged from an alley farther down the street. She bent low, as if she didn't want to be seen.

The girls resumed the chase.

"Maybe she's late for an appointment," said Alexis, fighting against the pressure of bodies as they weaved through yet another crosswalk. At that moment the woman turned around. The girls emerged from a clump of people, and they made eye contact.

The woman ran.

Now Alexis knew that the woman was definitely avoiding them. But why? It didn't make any sense. She was the one who had stood near the bridge yelling about a curse. All they wanted was a little more information, for goodness' sake! And for a rickety, old-looking woman, she sure ran fast!

They ran for half a mile or more, making three left-hand turns and four to the right. Then Elizabeth stopped.

"She's gone," she huffed.

"Are you sure?" asked Alexis.

"Sure." Elizabeth bent over to catch her breath. "I haven't seen her for a few minutes. She got away."

Alexis slumped against the nearest window. It was cold to the touch. The store must have had the air-conditioning going full blast. *Well*, she thought, *there's nothing left to do now but go back.* She looked around. . .and recognized nothing.

"Elizabeth, do you know where we are?"

Her friend only shook her head. Great. They were alone in a strange city, and they had followed the old woman without even thinking about how they would get back. Alexis thought of *Hansel and Gretel*.

"Those two were smart," she said.

"What?" asked Elizabeth.

"Hansel and Gretel were smart. They left a way to get back home."

Elizabeth laughed. "Sure. I'll keep a few bread crumbs in my pocket for our next high-speed chase through a strange town!"

"I guess we can go in a shop and ask someone," said Alexis.

Elizabeth was about to answer when they both jumped.

Hundreds of screams ripped through the streets of Lake Havasu City.

Imposters

The air was quiet for a moment or two. Then it happened again. Hundreds of people screamed.

Alexis looked at Elizabeth. By the fear on her friend's face, she could tell that Elizabeth was also worried. They were two young girls alone in a strange place. Frantic screams filled the air. The did the only thing two Camp Club Girls would have done. They ran. . .toward the screaming.

When they rounded the last corner, the screaming finally made sense. Alexis and Elizabeth stood facing a huge building. Glittering letters on the side of it told them it was Lake Havasu High School, home of the Fighting Knights. The noise was coming from inside the gym. A few straggling students made their way through a pair of double doors.

"Look, Alexis." Elizabeth pointed to another sign. It was splashed bright with purple and gold poster paint: PEP RALLY TODAY! GO KNIGHTS!

"Want to take a look?" asked Alexis. She had been to one pep rally at her middle school, but it had been pretty lame. It hadn't been for a sport or anything. Just an assembly meant to encourage the students to do their best in school this year. Who had ever heard of a "Yay for Homework!" rally?

Alexis had never even been inside a high school. How cool would it be to tell her friends she'd seen a high school pep rally, even if it was from the outside?

The girls edged toward the doors, trying to get a peek before they closed. A voice behind them made them jump.

"Hey! Get in there, or you'll miss it!"

The man ordering them into the building was obviously a teacher. Elizabeth tried to explain that they were tourists, but the man held up a thick, pink pad of paper.

"Please," he said. "Don't make me give out two more detentions."

At that point the girls figured it was useless to protest. He lightly nudged them through the doors, followed them in, and closed the doors with a snap.

Immediately the girls' senses were overloaded.

The horns of the marching band wailed what must have been the school song. The rhythm of the drums was constant and violent, like the heartbeat of an enormous beast. The bleachers exploded with a chant, "Go, Knights, go! Fight, Knights, fight! Go! Fight! *WIN!*" Then more of the screaming the girls had heard from the street.

Alexis didn't know whether to be afraid of high school or extremely excited to be a part of it. Just then she saw something that made up her mind. Five of the cheerleaders, dazzling in purple and gold, gathered in a small clump. The girl in the center disappeared for a moment, and someone yelled, "One, two!"

The cheerleaders moved down together, and when they rose, the tiny girl in the middle exploded toward the ceiling. She completed a backflip before slamming her hands out to meet her toes and falling gracefully back into her teammates' waiting arms.

Alexis's mouth hung open in shock. She had never seen a stunt go that high. Sometimes the girls throwing her in practice barely got her above their heads. She was sure this cheerleader had almost hit the rafters of the looming gym. And she knew that she was going to fly like that one day. No matter what it took.

Someone nudged her. It was the teacher again. He pointed over to the bleachers labeled Freshmen, and Alexis and Elizabeth squeezed into the front row.

"Hey, you don't go to school here." The voice came from a blond boy next to Elizabeth. It wasn't accusing, just amused. "I've never seen you before. You're imposters! I would have noticed you," he added, winking at Elizabeth. The girls ignored him.

A tall girl with purple face paint walked to the center of the gym. She was holding a microphone.

"Attention, Fighting Knights! It's time for the class competition! Now we're going to pick one member from each class. Who will win? The freshmen? Sophomores? Juniors? Or seniors?"

The students roared, and before Alexis realized what was going on, the blond boy had shoved her from her spot on the bench.

"Alrighty! I have a freshman volunteer," the tall girl said, grabbing Alexis by the hand.

Alexis looked at Elizabeth frantically, but Elizabeth just shrugged in a hopeless "What can I do?" expression.

The tall girl with the purple face dragged Alexis onto the hardwood. Alexis stood in front of a thousand teenagers, petrified.

Didn't they know she didn't belong here? Surely it was painted on her like one of their posters. The blond boy had known right away.

Whether or not they knew, nobody said anything. Three older students joined her in the middle of the floor: one sophomore, one junior, and one senior. Cheerleaders pulled two red wagons into the middle of the floor.

"Here, you two work together," the tall girl commanded as she placed Alexis next to the sophomore—a short, chunky boy with glasses. The girl holding the microphone gave Alexis a broomstick and then spoke to the crowd.

"Since this week is the London Bridge Festival, our competition today is the wagon joust!" The gym erupted. "Each team will have two chances to collect as many rings on their broomsticks as possible. As always, seniors and juniors first!"

The other team got ready. One got in the wagon with the broomstick, and the other got ready to pull. Small hula hoops hung from fishing string down the middle of the gym. The person with the broom was supposed to grab them by passing the broom through the middle as they raced past.

All at once, the wagon took off. It was more than a little bit wobbly. The person pulling the wagon had a hard time steering, and the team missed the first three hoops because they weren't close enough.

They weaved some and grabbed two hoops before getting tangled in the third and tumbling over. The students in the gym laughed as the competitors got up and tried their second run. They got three more hoops, giving them a total of five. The older students roared their approval and booed as Alexis climbed in her wagon.

"That's probably a good idea that they gave you the broom," her partner said with a laugh. "I don't think I would fit in that wagon! And if I could, I don't think you'd be able to pull me!"

"Just keep us going straight, okay?" said Alexis. She took a deep breath. How on earth had she gotten herself into this?

They were off. The boy was pulling Alexis a lot faster than she had expected to go. How long had it been since she had been in a wagon anyway? No time to think about it. The first hoop tore by before she realized it, but the next three slid easily onto the end of her stick.

Cheers erupted from the younger side of the gym.

When she picked up a fourth hoop, the broomstick got heavy, and it slipped off before she could lift the handle. They reached the end of the gym and turned around. Alexis only needed to get three more hoops to win.

They tore back down the way they had come, and Alexis aimed for the three hoops left behind. Two slid on easily, but the third spun round and round on the handle, threatening to fly into the audience. The wagon stopped suddenly, and Alexis flew out.

The crowd gasped.

Alexis was lying on her back. She lifted her broomstick in the air, and the girl with the microphone counted out loud.

"Six!" she cried. "The freshmen and sophomores win, probably for the first time in ten years!"

The boos of the older students were drowned out by the higher-pitched cheers of the freshmen and sophomores. Alexis scooted back to her seat, blushing like crazy.

"Alexis, you're amazing!" said Elizabeth.

"Thanks," said Alexis. She elbowed her way in next to the blond boy. "Thanks to you too," she said, pushing him playfully.

"It wasn't that bad, was it?" He laughed.

The microphone girl called for silence.

"Now," she said, "it's time for the reason we're all here in the first place! Let's give it up for your Lake Havasu High School swim team!"

Again the crowd went wild.

"The swim team?" said Alexis and Elizabeth together. Elizabeth leaned over Alexis and addressed the blond boy.

"Aren't pep rallies usually for football or something? I've never heard of a pep rally for the swim team."

"I know," replied the blond boy. "This is the first time the school has had a pep rally for the swim team. But this is more for one guy than the whole team. You see those?" He pointed up to the gym ceiling, and Alexis noticed a collection of banners for the first time. They were purple satin lined with gold. Each one had STATE CHAMPION embroidered along the top with a different event underneath. *100 m Butterfly, 100 m Freestyle, 400 m Individual Medley*. All six of them were labeled with the same name: *David Turner*.

"That's him," said the blond boy. He pointed across the gym to where one member of the swim team stood a little behind the others. "He's only a freshman too. He won all of those last year, before he was even in high school. The guy's a machine. So they decided that the swim team is worthy of being honored this year with a pep rally."

"Wow," said Elizabeth. Alexis was speechless. Something about the swim champion bothered her. Everyone in the school was clapping and screaming for *him*, but he didn't seem to like it. He was off to the side, the hood of his sweatshirt pulled in front of his face and his lanky shoulders stooped. Alexis got the feeling that he wished he were invisible.

The coach who was with the team grabbed a microphone and announced that the team would have a swim meet the following afternoon. It would be held at four o'clock at the Aquatic Center in town.

From the noise and excitement of the screaming crowd, Alexis guessed that just about everyone would be there. She thought it was kind of funny. She wondered if the schools in her area even *had* swim teams. She made a mental note to check when she got back to Sacramento.

The gym began to empty, and students filed out of the gym to go back to their classes. Alexis and Elizabeth slipped out the door to the street, making sure to avoid the teacher who had led them inside. They walked back the way they had come.

Soon they were melting in the heat. A sign up ahead rocked in the breeze. It had a triple-scoop ice cream cone on it.

"What do you think?" asked Alexis. "We can ask for directions to the hotel and get a snack at the same time."

"Perfect!" said Elizabeth.

The girls walked into the shop and sighed with delight as the cool of the air-conditioning mingled with the warm smell of fresh waffle cones. Alexis ordered a scoop of chocolate and a scoop of rainbow sherbet.

"Those don't go together!" said Elizabeth.

"Of course they do!" said Alexis. "What am I supposed to do when I can't decide between chocolate or fruity?"

The girls sat in a squishy booth near the front window and watched the tourists amble by. Their conversation shifted back to the Lake Havasu swim champion.

"I can't believe that!" said Alexis. "He must be really good to have won all of those championships."

"I know!" said Elizabeth. "And he beat a bunch of older swimmers to get them!"

The bell on the ice cream shop door jingled.

The mayor walked through the door and up to the counter, followed by the bridge commissioner and a crumpled old man sniffling into a hankie. Alexis choked on a bite of her rainbow sherbet.

"Elizabeth, look! What is Dr. Edwards doing with Mayor Applebee and the bridge commissioner?"

"Shh!" said Elizabeth. She motioned to Alexis, and the girls slumped down in their booth. The three men sat in the next booth over.

"You sure you don't want anything, Dr. Edwards?" asked the mayor. The only answer was another sneeze. "I suggested the ice cream shop just to get out of the office," continued the mayor.

"All I've heard about all day is that silly curse. My phone has been ringing off the hook!"

"I can assure you, Mayor," said Dr. Edwards, "there is no such thing as the curse of the Thames. History never mentions it. It's just a story someone has made up to scare the tourists."

A deeper, calmer voice broke into the conversation. Alexis knew it had to be the bridge commissioner.

"Curse or not, something's wrong with our bridge. The engineers are flying in tomorrow. If there is any structural damage, the parade can't happen."

"Aren't you being hasty, Commissioner?" said Dr. Edwards.

"Are you trying to tell me how to do my job, Doctor?"

"Gentlemen, gentlemen," said the mayor. "Let's get along, shall we?"

"We can't let years of tradition be stopped by a tiny crack!" Dr. Edwards pounded the table.

"Have you ever seen an avalanche, Doctor?" asked the commissioner. "It all starts with a tiny crack, and then. . .*boom!* Everything goes down, and there's no stopping it.

"To take a chance on the parade would be totally foolhardy. Can you imagine the bridge collapsing with dozens or even hundreds of people on it? Imagine the injuries and even deaths."

"But the chances of that are probably slim," Dr. Edwards said, his voice rising. "If we have to cancel the parade this year, many people probably won't return next year. Our tradition will be lost. *That* would be foolhardy!"

"Yes," said the commissioner. "And imagine how many people will never return and what will happen to the tradition if a tragedy should happen."

"Alright, alright!" said Mayor Applebee. "No more fighting! We all want the parade to go on as planned, but safety must come first. If the bridge is okay, it will happen. If something is wrong. . ." He sighed heavily and stood up, carrying the last of his now dripping ice cream cone. The other two men followed him out of the shop, still arguing.

"Why is Dr. Edwards so concerned about the parade?" asked Elizabeth.

"I have no idea," said Alexis. It didn't make sense. "The mayor might have asked him about the curse, since the doctor is an expert in English history. But why did Dr. Edwards get so angry about the idea of canceling the parade?"

"I wouldn't have thought Dr. Edwards was the type of person who would even enjoy a parade," said Elizabeth. "Actually, I can't imagine him enjoying *anything*."

"That's what I was just thinking," Alexis said.

"Well," said Elizabeth, "do you want to walk back to the hotel? We could hit the pool and go swimming before dinner."

"Sounds good," said Alexis. They got directions and walked the streets silently. Alexis was still trying to figure out why Dr. Edwards cared so much about the problem with the bridge. It sounded like the bridge commissioner was pretty worried. Alexis couldn't stop thinking about one thing he had said. *"It all starts with a tiny crack, and then. . .boom!"*

The more Alexis thought about it, the more she realized the commissioner was right. But not just about the bridge. Sometimes the smallest things could cause the biggest problems. Like this summer, for instance. Her friend Jerry had wanted to help Miss Maria save her nature park in Sacramento. Her business had dropped, and she'd brought in mechanical dinosaurs. But what Jerry had thought was harmless fun ended up as a huge news story and a mystery for the Camp Club Girls to solve. But feelings had gotten hurt, and Miss Maria even got injured because of erry's little idea.

"Elizabeth," said Alexis. "Isn't there something in the Bible about small things causing big problems?"

"Well, there are a few things," said Elizabeth. "A verse or two talk about little foxes spoiling the vineyards, which means small things that we tend to ignore can bring destruction. And in the book of James, we're told that our tongue, even though it's so small, can do big-time damage."

Alexis and Elizabeth walked in silence for a few minutes. Then Alexis suddenly turned to Elizabeth.

"What did you say?" she asked.

"Huh?"

"I thought you said something," said Alexis. She looked around. Not too many people were outside now since it was the hottest time of the day. They were near the alley where they had lost the old woman earlier. Alexis strained her ears and heard it again—a hurried whisper.

She edged toward the alley but didn't look around the corner. The words were muffled, but she heard them loud and clear.

"We have to steal the whole carriage."

A second voice began to argue.

"How are we gonna get it out of the hotel?"

The hotel? Alexis thought. Were these people seriously talking about stealing the golden carriage from the London Bridge Resort?

Elizabeth let out a quiet gasp, and the girls looked at each other.

"Don't worry," said the first voice again. "It'll be easy. And smile—this job is worth millions."

The Golden Coach

Suddenly Alexis heard rustling, as if the people who had been speaking were moving toward them.

Elizabeth grabbed her arm and motioned for them to leave.

Alexis hated to go without at least getting a look at the whisperers. But the rustling seemed to draw closer.

The girls fled. They didn't know what else to do. What would happen if the people in the alley knew Alexis and Elizabeth had heard their plan?

They had run close to two miles when they finally saw the London Bridge Resort. Alexis was grateful to see its towers.

This must have been how retreating armies felt once they had left the danger of the battlefield and found the safety of their castle walls again, she thought.

Alexis and Elizabeth stood in the lobby, panting and trying to catch their breath. Their eyes were drawn toward the carriage. It was absolutely huge. Could anyone really think they would be able to steal this thing?

Alexis walked over to a sign standing near the ropes protecting the golden masterpiece. It gave a brief history of the original carriage and the replica.

The Golden State Coach was built in London in 1762. King George III commissioned it and meant to ride in it on the day of his coronation. The greatness of the coach, however, kept it from being finished until three years later. Nonetheless, King George III and his family used it as the Coach of State. Recent monarchs have used the

coach once a year in their customary parade to open Parliament.
The last time the coach was used was by Elizabeth II in 2002.

This priceless replica is the only full-size model of the original
coach. It was built for the use of the London Bridge Resort and Hotel.

Alexis looked around the hotel lobby. It was filled with people.
Tourists were on their way to dinner. Bellhops ran for the elevators
with teetering piles of suitcases. Jane, with her purple hair, was busily
checking people in and getting fresh towels or extra pillows.

Alexis knew she wouldn't be able to get near the carriage
unnoticed. If she tried, she probably wouldn't make it over the
ropes before someone yanked her out. How did anyone expect
to *remove* the carriage from the room entirely? It just didn't seem
possible.

Alexis felt a bony elbow digging into her side. She looked up
at Elizabeth, who pointed across the carriage to a row of red velvet
chairs. Dr. Edwards sat in one, not seeming to even be aware of
the hustle and bustle all around him. His head was bowed over a
notebook in his lap. His arched hands supported his forehead.

Curious, the girls watched him. Within a few minutes he shook
off his daze, stood up hastily, and dashed out of the lobby more
quickly than the girls thought he was even capable of moving.

A piece of paper fluttered out of his notebook and onto the
floor.

The girls ran over and picked it up.

"Dr. Edwards!" called Alexis. "You dropped something!"

But the man was already in an elevator, and he didn't hear her.
Alexis glanced at the paper in her hand, and her eyes opened wide.
The paper was thick and unlined with frayed holes along one side,
like it had been torn from a sketchbook. On it was a perfect pencil
sketch of the Golden State Coach.

"Man," said Elizabeth. "He's a pretty good artist. Look, he even
drew the swirly detail on the dolphin's tail! What's that writing say?"
She pointed to the bottom corner where a sentence was scrawled.
Alexis pulled the paper closer to her face. She had assumed the
writing was just the artist's name or something, but it wasn't. It was
a question, written in perfect cursive.

Where could it be hiding?

"Where could it be hiding? That doesn't make any sense," Alexis said.

"The carriage isn't hiding at all. It's in plain sight," Elizabeth added. "So what does that mean?"

"I don't know," Alexis said. "I think maybe we'll have to think about it. For right now I'll put this in my notebook. Do you have your computer here?"

"My dad has his MacBook. I can use that," Elizabeth said.

"Good. I don't have a notebook computer, and Grandma's practically in the Dark Ages—she only has a big old desktop back home," Alexis said. "Why don't you go online tonight and set Kate or Sydney busy seeing if they can find anything about the coach being in hiding."

"Will do," Elizabeth said.

"I think we also need more background information than we have," Alexis said. "The sign was helpful, but we need more."

"I can ask the girls to dig up everything they can on the coach," Elizabeth said.

Alexis grinned at her. "You forget that we have an expert right here. I'll ask Grandma about it tonight while you're filling the girls in. There isn't much about English history that she doesn't know. And I know she brushed up on the carriage and everything pertaining to the London Bridge before she came here."

"Perfect," said Elizabeth. "It's about time for me to get back for dinner anyway. See you tomorrow?"

"Definitely. We'll have a lot to look into. Maybe we'll have time to see the swim meet between investigations." Alexis smiled. Why was she so interested in swimming all of a sudden? It must have been the pep rally.

Elizabeth hugged her and left the hotel.

Alexis stood in the crowded lobby waiting for an elevator to take her to the top floor, where her grandmother and she were sharing a suite. Their suite was amazing. It had two bedrooms with king-size beds, a dining room, a living room with a big-screen TV, and its own kitchen. They didn't really use the kitchen, except to store some drinks in the fridge. Most meals they got for free from the hotel—another one of Grandma Windsor's perks.

Alexis entered the room and saw piles of food on the small table in the living room. Grandma Windsor was on the couch, already in her pajamas and fluffy slippers.

"I thought we'd do room service tonight!" she called through a mouth full of pizza. Alexis laughed, imagining what her mom would say if she spoke with her mouth full, like Grandma Windsor had.

"Perfect!" said Alexis. She changed into boxer shorts and a tank top and plopped down next to her grandma in front of the TV. They watched a bit of the news, and Alexis saw that Elizabeth's dad had caught the largest fish in the first day of the bass tournament. She was surprised to see no news of the bridge. She guessed the mayor was keeping everything quiet until they found out what was going on.

After the pizza was gone, Alexis popped open a Mountain Dew and got comfy.

"So, that coach thing downstairs is pretty cool," she said, acting just a little bit interested. For some reason she didn't want to come right out and say, "Someone's trying to steal the coach!" She didn't have any evidence besides a whispered conversation in an alley. And what if the people had only been joking?

"Yes," said Grandma Windsor, "the coach is an amazing replica. The real one was part of a very historical reign in England."

"You mean King George the Third?" asked Alexis, remembering the name from the sign in the lobby.

"Yes, Alexis! I'm proud of you!" Grandma Windsor muted the TV, excited to talk about her favorite subject. "King George the Third was famous for two things, mostly."

"What were they?" asked Alexis.

"Losing the American Revolutionary War and going crazy."

"He went crazy?" Alexis had never enjoyed history class, but for some reason she loved it when her grandmother told her stories like this. The characters seemed so much more real than the ones in her schoolbooks.

"Well, yes," said her grandma. "That's what they say. It may have been the pressure, of course. Being a king isn't easy. Scholars today, however, believe that he was probably genetically predisposed to mental illness and that he had a blood disease."

"What?" asked Alexis.

"It means that his mind might have always been a little fragile. He might have always been mentally unbalanced. If he had been in charge of the country while it was peaceful and wealthy, maybe he wouldn't have snapped. But he didn't live during peace, and he *did* finally snap." Grandma Windsor clicked the TV off.

"How did people know he was crazy?" asked Alexis. She felt sad for this king who had collapsed under the weight of his crown.

"Well, he didn't really lose his mind until his later years. They say it happened after his youngest daughter died. Her name was Princess Amelia, and she was his favorite. In fact, the king was so protective of his daughters that he didn't want them to marry. There were rumors that the young Amelia had fallen in love with someone below her rank. A princess would never be allowed to marry a horse trainer."

"That's awful!" said Alexis. She imagined a beautiful young princess locked in a tower, while her crazy father kept the key on a chain around his neck. The wonderful and extremely handsome boy who wanted to marry the princess stood beneath the tower, day and night, waiting.

Alexis was becoming what her mother called a "romantic type" of person.

Alexis forgot about the mystery surrounding the carriage as Grandma Windsor told story after story about crazy King George III. Alexis learned that Princess Amelia had sent secret letters to the one she loved. Then she had become ill and died without ever getting married.

Alexis asked what happened to the letters, but her grandmother didn't know.

When Alexis and her grandmother stopped talking, she called Elizabeth and passed along what she'd learned.

"The girls all said to tell you hi," Elizabeth said. "McKenzie thought it was a rip-off that you had to ride a wagon instead of a real horse to joust today. Sydney wanted more information on the swimming team since she's so into sports. Kate wishes she would have sent you a prototype her dad has of a new iPad clone so we could keep them posted every minute. Kate is going to look up information. She said any time we have news to text her and she'll circulate it to the rest of the girls.

"Bailey is really proud of you for winning the contest in the school today. She wants to know if either of us are going to try to be the pageant queen. And dear little Biscuit the Wonder Dog even woofed. I think he was saying if he'd been with us today, he would have caught the old hag for us!"

Alexis laughed. The messages sounded so much like the Camp Club Girls! Count on the Camp Club Girls to be there with them in spirit, in thought, and in prayers!

"Can you text Kate and ask her to check into letters Grandma mentioned that were written by Princess Amelia?" Alexis asked.

"Sure," Elizabeth replied. "I think I'll also ask her to check into curses surrounding the London Bridge."

With that, the girls said good night.

When Alexis finally climbed into bed, her mind was swimming with pictures of royalty: beautiful gowns, golden coaches, and lost letters of love. Eventually she fell asleep to the sound of water slapping the bridge outside her window.

And she dreamed.

She was walking along the London Bridge again, only this time she was not afraid. Halfway across she stopped to look over the rail. The reflection of the full moon sparkled brightly in the night, rippling with the small waves. Suddenly she heard a voice. A sweet voice, singing a familiar tune.

"London Bridge is falling down, falling down, falling down. . . ."

It was a girl not much older than Alexis—maybe fifteen or sixteen. Her dress looked old-fashioned but gorgeous. Silver silk sparkling in the starlight. Pearls were strung throughout her long waves of dark hair. They matched the necklace around her delicate throat. The girl's liquid eyes didn't see Alexis, but she stopped to look over the rail too, farther down the bridge.

The young girl took something from the inside of her gown—a folded piece of paper. She hugged it to her chest. Then she kissed it and let it drift down into the lake. She turned away and kept walking toward the other side of the bridge. She kept singing.

"London Bridge is falling down, my fair lady."

The bridge rumbled. The girl disappeared as a thick fog rolled up from the water to engulf everything. Her sweet voice vanished as well and was replaced by an older voice.

"My fair lady!" It shrieked, and then it laughed. The long, dry cackle was all too familiar. It was the voice of the old crone Elizabeth and Alexis had seen earlier in the day. Alexis could see the outline of a bent form through the fog. The figure lifted a walking stick high into the air and brought it down hard onto the stonework of the bridge.

The bridge rumbled again, and this time it rocked. The rail in front of Alexis broke away and fell toward the water. . .and she followed it.

Alexis wanted to scream, but her voice was caught in her throat. Stone and cement surrounded her as she plummeted into the water. It was icy, and the stabbing cold stole her breath. She fought to swim, every moment expecting a piece of the London Bridge to crush her and push her to the bottom.

A few feet away something white was floating on the surface. It was the girl's letter, and it was soaked through. With what? *Alexis wondered.* Tears or water?

One more breath, that's all she could take. Her arms hurt. They couldn't support her anymore. She was sinking.

An arm. A long, thin arm reached out and grabbed her. Alexis was pulled to the safety of the shore by the powerful sidestroke of a swimming prince.

The Message of the Moon

The next morning, Alexis met Elizabeth outside her hotel. There were loud voices coming from the area of the bridge, so naturally they drifted in that direction. When the bridge came into view, Alexis's dream came flooding back. She shuddered.

She almost told Elizabeth about it but decided not to. It had really been weird, and she didn't think she could remember it all anyway.

"Look," said Elizabeth. "The bridge is still closed."

The bridge looked different than it had the day before. It was still decorated with yellow caution tape, but now there were big men in hard hats crawling all over it. They were all using strange instruments that looked like levels. A few of them were even in the water near the closest pillar. It was only up to their waist.

"That's funny," said Alexis. "I thought the water was a lot deeper than that."

"Those must be the engineers," said Elizabeth.

"Good. It shouldn't take them long to figure out what's going on." Alexis led Elizabeth farther down the grassy slope, and they sat on the little beach, about twenty feet from the yellow tape. "Hopefully the festival can pick up where it left off."

The men in the water were pointing toward the second pillar, where the crack had grown overnight. They seemed to be arguing about something.

"That's strange," said Elizabeth.

"What?" asked Alexis.

"The crack. It's reaching *up* the arch of the bridge. See? It's climbing closer to the top every day."

"I know," said Alexis. "That means whatever is causing the crack is under the water."

"I wonder what it could be," said Elizabeth. She shot Alexis a sneaky look. "We could check it out, you know."

"What? You mean under the water?" Alexis's heart began to pound. Not only was she afraid of bridges, but last night she had also dreamed of this particular bridge falling on top of her. "That's crazy! The engineers aren't even getting close to that crack!"

"It's not crazy," said Elizabeth. She leaned forward and shielded her eyes from the sun. She squinted, looking toward the middle of the river where the crack loomed. "The channel under the bridge is only eight feet deep in the middle. A lady at my hotel told me."

"Okay," said Alexis. "Keep in mind that I am barely five feet tall. You, my giant friend, may be able to tiptoe out there, but I. . ." Alexis shivered again. Her dream had been way too realistic.

"Oh come on, Alexis! All we need is a couple pairs of goggles. We brought our swimsuits, right? We can walk out most of the way, swim the last few feet to the pillar, and dunk our heads under to check out the crack."

Alexis was just about to say, "I'll think about it," when a noise behind them made them jump. Chipper whistling. . .to the tune of "London Bridge."

The girls spun around where they sat and saw the old woman dressed as a hag coming toward the bridge. She spotted them, but she didn't run away this time. Instead she turned a little so she was heading right for them. The spring in her step told Alexis the old lady was in a good mood and that maybe she wasn't as old as they had thought. She kept whistling as she reached the bench near the sidewalk. Alexis moved to get up, but a sharp whistle made her freeze.

She looked up, and the old woman raised her eyebrows and shook a finger at her. Then she sat on the bench and looked around, much like a tourist just enjoying the view. *What in the world is going on?* thought Alexis. She watched the woman for almost five minutes before anything else happened.

The lady reached into the pocket of her ragged robe and drew out a small, yellow envelope. She held it in front of her for a moment and looked at the girls to make sure they saw it. Then she placed it beside her on the bench, got up, and left—whistling her tune again.

Alexis and Elizabeth looked at each other. They both asked the same question.

"What was that all about?"

When they could no longer see or hear the old woman, Alexis got up and approached the bench. The little yellow envelope lay facedown on the seat. Alexis picked it up and flipped it over. Three words were scratched on the front:

For the Curious

Alexis looked at Elizabeth and shrugged her shoulders. She tore the envelope open and pulled out a matching note card. The twiglike handwriting said:

442 Lakeview Avenue
7:00 tonight. Don't be late.

That was all. No name. Nothing.

The girls exchanged glances again. What on earth did this mean?

"I guess she wants to talk to us," said Elizabeth.

"Yeah," said Alexis. "But why tonight? At. . .four hundred and forty-two Lakeview Avenue? Why not here and now? Wouldn't that have been more convenient?"

"Maybe," said Elizabeth. "But maybe there's more to it. Maybe she wants to talk where no one can overhear."

They glanced over their shoulders to where the engineers were still investigating the bridge.

"Or," said Alexis, "maybe she wants to lock us in a cage, fatten us up, and throw us into her giant oven."

"Enough with the *Hansel and Gretel* stuff, okay?" said Elizabeth. "Do you want to investigate this stuff or not?"

"Of course I do!" said Alexis. "I think my imagination keeps running away with me." Alexis had no idea why she had been so freaked out lately. Maybe the dream and the bridge had her on edge. Whatever it was, she needed to get over it. She had never thought of herself as a chicken before.

"It's okay, Alex," said Elizabeth. "It's easy to let that happen here.

Half the town thinks it's back in seventeenth-century London. You know what you need?"

"Huh?"

"A little water to wake you up."

Alexis took a fearful step back and pointed to the channel. "I'm not going in there."

"Not the lake, nerd! The swim meet! It will give us something to do until we go meet Miss Creepy."

Alexis lit up. "Yes! Let's go!"

Again she asked herself the question: Why was she so excited about a swim meet? Maybe it was just the allure of something new. She'd never been to one before.

The girls walked across downtown to the Aquatic Center. Alexis thought it looked like a giant concrete ice cube. They were greeted by more purple and gold signs and a gaggle of giggling girls. It looked like the entire female population of Lake Havasu City had shown up.

Other schools were there too. Alexis could tell by the many different colors on the swimming caps of the swimmers. Yellow and black, green and silver, red and blue—just like her school colors back home.

She and Elizabeth found seats halfway up the bleachers. From this place they could see everything. Swimmers were warming up or cooling down in a smaller pool at one end. The huge pool in the middle was divided into eight lanes. Small platforms lined one end.

Within minutes the crowd was on its feet screaming. Alexis and Elizabeth stood too, so they could see. A woman with huge hair was standing right in front of Alexis. Elizabeth looked over and laughed.

"Here," she said. "Trade me spots!" The girls swapped seats, and Alexis saw the reason for the insanity. The Arizona swimming champion was making his way to one of the platforms at the edge of the pool.

"In lane five," said an intercom voice over the crowd, "David Turner!"

The crowd roared. All the other swimmers had waved and smiled up at the crowd when their names were called. Turner kept his eyes on the water in front of him. The swimmers bent forward, ready to enter the water, and the gun went off.

One swimmer on the end had been late jumping off, but everyone else was already gone. In the middle of the pool, Turner hadn't yet broken the surface. He powered through the water, moving his body like a dolphin, until he was almost halfway across. Then his arms came up at the same time, propelling his head and shoulders out of the water as they pushed back under.

It looked as if he were flying.

"So *that's* why they call it the butterfly," said Alexis. She had always heard of the butterfly stroke but had never seen what it looked like.

Turner was at the end of the pool, diving underwater to turn around. When he finished, the person in second place was still in the middle of the pool. The crowd cheered. Turner didn't even look up at the board that showed the swimmers' times in bright lights.

The crowd settled a little as the other swimmers filed out of the pool. The other competitors were greeted by warm hugs of family and the excited smiles of friends. Alexis saw David Turner receive a wet slap on the back from his coach before he slipped away to the locker room. Alone.

His fans, who were still cheering for him, hadn't even noticed he was gone.

"He always looks so sad," said Alexis out loud.

"What?" said Elizabeth, who was watching another race that had already started.

"Nothing," said Alexis. But she couldn't help thinking about the champion. How could someone be so popular—so adored—and still look so alone?

●—●—●

The girls watched the rest of the meet and then went to meet Elizabeth's family for dinner. They ate at a little café near the square, where the jousting tournament was taking place. The sound of clashing metal and pounding hooves made it easy to ignore Elizabeth's little brother, who kept pretending to pick his nose.

"Talk about little things that spoil stuff," Elizabeth said to

Alexis, nodding at her brother. "He's a case in point!"

Alexis's reply was drowned out by the thud of hooves. Every few minutes gigantic horses charged each other. The men on their backs wore real armor and held shields and lances.

Alexis was about to ask why they had to wear the armor when two knights clashed. The lance that the blue knight was holding slammed into the green knight's shield, snapped in half, and then slid up and landed with a crack on the piece of metal protecting the man's throat.

That was why they were wearing real armor.

"Hey, this isn't any game!" she exclaimed to Elizabeth.

"What, jousting?" Elizabeth asked.

"Yes, I guess I thought they were like stuntmen. I didn't realize they were really fighting," she said.

"Jousting is a big hobby all over the United States," Elizabeth said. "A lot of regions have jousting clubs where they're really into it. A lot of cities have Renaissance festivals where jousting is part of the action."

"Do people often get hurt?" Alexis asked.

"I don't know," Elizabeth admitted. "I guess they sometimes have accidents, but I haven't really paid attention or heard much about it."

Alexis had no idea that people still did this kind of thing. Her heart was beating so fast she could hardly eat.

After dinner the girls began wandering through the streets of downtown. Alexis had gotten a map at her hotel that showed them how to get to 442 Lakeview Avenue. They followed the tiny red lines that indicated where streets were block after block. Finally they ended up in a small neighborhood.

The houses were perfect. Each one was small and built of stone or brick. Short fences surrounded each front yard, and wild—but beautiful—English gardens were in full bloom. The fall flowers filled the air with a smell that reminded Alexis of the honeysuckle back home in Sacramento.

When they finally reached number 442, it was getting dark.

"It doesn't look like anyone is home," said Elizabeth.

The girls walked up to the porch, and sure enough, no lights were on inside the house. The flicker of a light with an electrical short licked at the darkness, throwing shadows against the front door.

"Maybe she forgot," said Alexis. "Let's take a look around to be sure she's not home."

Elizabeth knocked, and Alexis left the porch to peek into the first window. The other side was absolute darkness. There was no way to tell what was inside. That didn't matter, really, but Alexis found that she was very interested to see how this woman lived.

"Do you think this woman is really creepy, or is she pretending?" she asked Elizabeth.

"I don't know," Elizabeth said. "Does she dress up and walk around town cackling to entertain the tourists? Or is there more to her?"

"It's awfully dark around here," Alexis said. "Reminds me of a scary movie."

"'People loved darkness instead of light because their deeds were evil,'" Elizabeth quoted. "John 3:19. Sometimes the Bible just has the perfect words!"

"I don't think anyone is home," Elizabeth added.

"Yeah, maybe we'd better leave," Alexis said. "It's too much like a scary movie."

"Yep. It's after dark. Two young girls out alone. Supposed to meet someone at a house, but the house is empty," Elizabeth said.

"And the light is flickering," Alexis added.

"Now all we need is—" She abruptly stopped talking as the girls heard footsteps.

They heard the footsteps turn off the sidewalk and enter the gate of 442 Lakeview Avenue. The girls spun around, expecting to see the old woman. Instead, a tall man raised something over his head. It looked like a short baseball bat.

He was coming toward them!

Alexis tried to scream. Elizabeth covered her head.

Then the object in the man's hand blinded them.

It was a flashlight.

"What are you doing poking around people's houses?"

"Oh no," groaned Alexis. It was Deputy Dewayne, the officer the girls had met on their first day in Lake Havasu City.

"I got a call about some trespassers, so I came to *investigate*."

"We're not poking, really, sir," said Alexis. "We had an appointment. We were supposed to come see this woman at seven."

"*This woman?*" asked the deputy. "And what is *this woman's* name? Huh?" The girls looked at each other. He would never believe them. "That's what I thought," Deputy Dewayne said. He put his hands on his hips.

"I have half a mind to take you in," he said.

"But sir, we weren't doing anything," said Elizabeth. "I promise!"

"Well, get out of here then. If I find you out here again, I won't be so forgiving." He shined his flashlight in their faces, and Alexis turned around to get out of the glare. That's when she saw it. A sentence, scribbled in pencil on the white paint of the front door.

Watch beneath the moon when the bridge calls out.

●—●—●

Deputy Dewayne gave the girls a ride back to their hotels. Alexis didn't dare bring up the writing in the police car. The deputy hadn't noticed it, and she wanted to keep it that way. She didn't want him blaming them for graffiti too. When the officer dropped off Elizabeth, Alexis waved goodbye. She would have to call Elizabeth later.

There was a note from her grandmother when she got to her room. Some old friends from Europe had come to the conference, and Grandma Windsor was going to be out with them until late. Alexis watched some old detective shows on TV Land for a while. But her mind kept going back to the things that had happened that day. Since she had so much to think about, she got in her pajamas and climbed into her bed.

Watch beneath the moon when the bridge calls out.

What on earth did that mean? *Watch beneath the moon* was easy enough. Alexis suspected it meant to watch when the moon was shining, which would mean at night. But what about the last part? What did the woman mean, *When the bridge calls out?* Stone and cement didn't talk, as far as Alexis knew. Bridges definitely didn't *call out*.

Whatever. The lady was obviously a little crazy. And who

knew? Maybe the message wasn't for the girls anyway.

Alexis looked at her clock. Too late to call Elizabeth. She would run the clue by Elizabeth tomorrow and see what she thought. She wondered if Elizabeth had gotten any emails from the Camp Club Girls.

Alexis rolled over onto her side. She had left the curtains and the window open to let in the fresh, cool evening air. The desert smelled wonderful at night—like cooling sage. She drifted in and out of sleep as she watched the moonbeams dance on the wall. And then she heard it: the distinct ringing of metal hitting stone, followed by a splash.

Alexis sat up, looked toward the window, and heard it again. *Ring, thump, splash.*

Was the bridge calling out?

CHAPTER 6

Moonlight Sonata

Alexis pushed the covers away and scooted to the edge of her bed.

Ring, thump, splash!

What could that sound be? It was strange and muffled, as if it were coming from under a pillow. . .or water. Could this be what the writing on the old woman's door was talking about? Did she know something was happening to the bridge during the night? Alexis inched her feet down into the soft hotel carpet and tiptoed toward the window. Her grandma hadn't come back to the room yet. This and the darkness made Alexis feel very alone.

When she reached the window, the breeze stiffened and blew her unruly, bed-head hair out of her face. It was dark outside. The moon was hiding behind a large cloud. The noise had also stopped. Maybe it hadn't been the bridge. Maybe some tourists had been out late playing around the water.

Ring, thump, splash!

Alexis leaned out the window to get a better look. The strange noise was definitely coming from the bridge. The streets were empty. All the tourists and engineers were at home in their beds. She couldn't see anyone. So who—or what—was making the noise?

Alexis heard another splash, so she focused on the water. She couldn't see anything along either shore. No one was skipping rocks or taking strolls along the water's edge. Eventually she looked at the bridge again. If it was dark outside, the areas beneath the bridge were pitch-black. There was no way to see anything without some light. Alexis jumped from the window and grabbed her backpack. She rummaged through it and found what she was looking for: a flashlight.

Alexis carried the flashlight to the window and turned it on. She aimed it across the water toward the bridge. It didn't help much. The beam of light was small, and it didn't penetrate very far into the darkness under the bridge.

Splash.

Alexis turned the light toward the sound. In the second arch, near the crack, the water rippled. Had someone thrown something into the water? She looked to the top of the bridge, but still she saw no one. So what had dropped into the water? Alexis moved the light back toward the water, but it went dark.

Alexis hit the flashlight with the palm of her hand. The batteries were dead.

"Oh come on!" she whispered furiously. "You have to be kidding me!" The light flashed back on but only long enough to blind her before it went dark again.

"Kate would tell me I should have a solar-powered or hand-crank flashlight for emergencies," she muttered, almost hearing the voice of the most techno-savvy of the Camp Club Girls in her mind. "But a lot of good that does me now!"

She dropped the light and leaned out the window again, trying as hard as she could to see without it. She couldn't.

Alexis sighed and was about to go back to bed when the wind blew again. The clouds drifted out of the way, and the brilliant rays of the moon lit up Lake Havasu like it was day. Alexis couldn't believe what she saw under the bridge. Bobbing up and down on the water was a small, wooden rowboat.

That shouldn't have been surprising, because it was a lake. People rowed small boats around Lake Havasu all the time. Even at night. What confused Alexis was the fact that the small boat was empty. Had it come untied from the dock and drifted to the bridge on its own? And she still had no way to explain the noises.

Then. . .

Splash. A head emerged from the water.

Thump. Something heavy fell into the boat.

Ring. Something else fell in on top of it.

Alexis gasped. A long, dark shadow pulled itself out of the

water and slid into the boat. Then it began to paddle in the opposite direction and out of sight. Alexis left the window and grabbed her notebook and a small camera she had brought for the trip. She left the room and sprinted down the hallway to the elevator.

When it opened on the first floor, Alexis ran toward the front doors. The coolness of the marble under her feet made her realize she had forgotten to put on her shoes. *Oh well*, she thought. *I've had dirty feet before.*

But when she saw the automatic doors swing open, she stopped in her tracks. Deputy Dewayne was sitting just outside in his patrol car, as if he was just waiting for her to do something like this. Alexis didn't want to cross his path for the second time in one night, so she turned around and trudged back to the elevator.

On the ride up to her floor, her mind raced. How did all of this fit together? Was it a coincidence that someone was diving in the dark beneath the bridge right where it happened to be cracked? Or could something more sinister be going on?

Alexis was sure the old woman had been trying to tell her something. Maybe she knew it wasn't really a curse. The curse could be a story made up to scare the tourists, like Dr. Edwards had said. In that case Lake Havasu City was in real trouble. Someone was trying to bring down the London Bridge. But *why?*

●—●—●

The next morning Alexis told Elizabeth everything she had seen. First about the scribbled note on the door. Then about the incident with the bridge.

"Do you really think that note was meant for us?" asked Elizabeth as they walked toward the bench near the bridge.

"I guess there's no way to know for sure," said Alexis. "We can ask the old lady the next time we see her. I really think she meant us to get it, though. I mean, she knew we were coming to see her, right?"

"Yeah," said Elizabeth, folding one long leg beneath her as she sat down. "But why on the door? Why didn't she leave another envelope or note like yesterday?"

"Well, she is a little dramatic," said Alexis. "She dresses like a medieval peasant, for goodness' sake! She's secretive too. Maybe she was worried that an envelope taped to the door would be too obvious and that someone else would read it."

"Maybe," said Elizabeth. "We won't know until we talk to her again. So you really saw someone under the bridge last night?"

"Yep. And I just know they were banging on the bridge with some tools. Maybe a hammer or something."

"Did you see the tools?" asked Elizabeth.

"No, but I heard the banging. I saw the person drop them back into the boat when he came up too."

"When he came up?"

"Yeah," said Alexis. "From under the water." Elizabeth looked back at the channel where dozens of engineers were busy at work again. A shifty smile spread across her face.

"You know what that means, don't you?" she said.

"What?" asked Alexis.

"It means that there really *is* a reason for us to check out the bridge! You know, like I said yesterday. We'll get some cheap goggles, and—"

"No way!" Alexis jumped off the bench. "You're crazy! The public isn't supposed to be anywhere near the bridge! And if you haven't noticed, Elizabeth: *We're the public.* Besides, it's just plain stupid to go swimming around under a bridge that's about to collapse!"

"It's not about to collapse," said Elizabeth. "It just has a tiny crack."

"You sound like Dr. Edwards," said Alexis. "Don't you remember what the bridge commissioner said about tiny cracks? They start avalanches, Elizabeth!"

"Okay, okay! Don't freak out. You're right." Elizabeth took a deep breath and looked around. "It really isn't a good idea. So what do we do today?"

Alexis caught sight of a purple flyer taped on a lamppost.

"We haven't thought anymore about the bed race," she said. "Are you still interested?"

"Of course!" said Elizabeth. "We need a little something to distract us."

"We'd better get working on it then. The first thing we'll need is a bed."

"Good job, Einstein!" Elizabeth elbowed Alexis playfully, and the pair of girls walked toward the shopping area of downtown Lake Havasu City.

They passed a mattress shop, and Elizabeth stopped.

"This place sells beds," she said. Alexis pointed to the price tag of the small bed that was sitting in the window.

"Six hundred dollars," she said. "I think we'll need a used one."

They kept walking and turned into an older part of town. The street was narrow, more like an alley than a road. It was lined with antique shops on both sides, with a couple of coffee and pastry shops snuggled in between.

The first store they walked into was called Betsy's Boutique. It was crowded with crystal vases and candleholders and lace doilies. The girls had taken two steps into the shop when a thin woman with a birdlike nose and her hair pulled back into a tight bun stepped out from behind an ancient polished dresser.

"Where are your parents?" she asked.

"Um, back at the hotel," answered Elizabeth. The woman pointed toward a sign in the window that read NO UNATTENDED CHILDREN ALLOWED. Then she coughed and nudged them toward the door.

Back outside on the sidewalk, the girls laughed.

"Well, I guess we'd better find a shop that doesn't have a problem with *unattended children*," laughed Alexis. "What about that one?" She pointed across the narrow street to a whimsical sign that said BILL'S TARNISHED TREASURES. Its windows were crowded with all kinds of things, from worn-out lamps to old bicycle seats.

"Looks good to me," said Elizabeth. They looked both ways and crossed over to the opposite sidewalk. A large jingly bell on the door announced their arrival, but nobody greeted them. In fact the store looked empty.

"Maybe they're in the back?" said Elizabeth.

"Let's look around," said Alexis. The girls didn't see a bed anywhere, but they saw plenty of other amazing things in the piles of junk. Alexis was sifting through a huge crystal bowl full of ancient brass buttons when a voice from behind her made her jump.

"That one is from a World War II naval jacket."

Alexis spun around and faced a large man in glasses. His voice was low and gentle, and his smile was warm and genuine.

"Oh," said Alexis, looking at the button she was holding. It had an anchor etched into it. "That's really neat," she said. "That makes it about. . .sixty years old."

"Just a little older, actually," said the man. "But good job! My name's Bill. This is my shop." Bill stuck out his hand, and Alexis grasped it. This was awkward, since he had a crutch under his arm.

"Nice to meet you, Bill. I'm Alexis, and this is my friend Elizabeth." Elizabeth emerged from a pile of tattered books and waved.

"It's good to meet the two of you," said Bill. "What brings you in here today? Anything in particular?"

"Well," said Alexis, "actually we're looking for a bed. We want to enter the race this weekend, but we're from out of town, and we don't, um. . .have a bed." Alexis looked around the shop. "And it doesn't look like you have one either."

Bill's face lit up, his smile stretching so wide that his glasses bounced on his large cheeks. "We're both in luck!" he said. "Follow me." He turned and hobbled past the cash register, and Alexis saw that he was wearing a full cast on one of his legs. She wondered how such a large man managed to move on crutches through such a crowded store without breaking everything in sight. Bill led them to a curtain at the back of the shop and started through it. Alexis and Elizabeth hesitated, and Bill turned around.

"Don't worry," he said. "Mary!"

"Yes, Bill?" A lovely voice floated into the room from beyond the curtain, and a pretty face followed it.

"Mary," said Bill, "this is Alexis and Elizabeth. Girls, this is Mary, my wife. They're interested in the race, so I'm going to show them the castle!" Bill sounded like a little kid at Christmastime. Mary nodded and pointed through the curtain. The mention of a castle made the girls even more curious. They followed Bill behind the curtain, leaving it open so they could still see the door. Some of her friends called Alexis paranoid, but she got uncomfortable when she couldn't see an exit.

"Whoa," said Elizabeth.

Alexis turned around to see a huge contraption filling the tiny back room. It really was a castle! Bill had built a tower at the head of the bed, where the pillow usually went, and a low wall surrounded the rest of the mattress. At the foot, a real wooden drawbridge was closed, and a blue bed skirt fell to the floor like a rippling moat.

"This is amazing!" cried Alexis.

"Do you think so?" asked Bill. "It's taken me almost a year to build. Go ahead. Climb up and take a look!" He gestured to the back of the tower where a trapdoor revealed an entry onto the bed itself and a couple of stairs leading to the top of the tower. Alexis climbed right up.

"It feels so stable," said Alexis. "But the tower is so tall. Why doesn't it tip over?"

"Well, that's why I used real wood for the drawbridge. The tower makes the back of the bed really heavy. I needed something just as heavy to even out the weight in the front. Otherwise it would topple over the first time it went around a corner. That's also why I put *these* on it." Bill raised a corner of the bed skirt, revealing knobby tires.

"Those things look big enough to go on a tractor!" said Elizabeth.

"Close," said Bill. "They came from a riding lawn mower. The old wobbly bed wheels weren't going to work for something this huge. I also put brakes in it—something most beds in the race won't have. Once this baby gets going, it would be impossible to stop otherwise."

"I see the pedals," said Alexis. "And there's even a steering wheel!"

"Wow," said Elizabeth. "You sure put a lot into this bed. It's amazing, but I don't think we could afford to buy it from you."

Alexis sighed. She knew Elizabeth was right. There was no way they could afford a bed this cool for the race.

"It's not for sale," said Bill. "I'm giving it to you. Just for the race, I mean."

The girls were stunned.

"But why?" asked Alexis. Bill pointed to his broken leg.

"Racing is against the doctor's orders. But I'd hate to see this thing sit back here unused. And I always like to have a bed in the race representing the shop. Instead of my charging you rent, how about if you just finish the work on it and represent us? It still needs to be painted. I've got the paint. It probably wouldn't take you two very long. What do you say?"

Alexis was speechless. They hadn't even been looking for an hour, and they had found the most amazing racing bed *ever*. And they weren't going to have to pay a dime.

"Wow, Mr. Bill. I don't know what to say," said Alexis.

"Just say you'll race her hard. I'd love to be part of a winning team, even if it's just to cheer you across the finish line."

Alexis laughed and shook Bill's hand. "It's a deal!" she said. "Where are the paintbrushes?"

Alexis called her grandmother, and Elizabeth called her parents to tell them what was going on and where they were. Then they painted until late afternoon. Mary brought them turkey sandwiches for lunch and filled plastic cups with iced lemonade every twenty minutes or so.

By the time the girls began to rinse their brushes and close the cans of paint, the bed had been transformed. The walls of the castle were gray stone. White and gray paint had been sponged over it in spots to make it look real. The drawbridge was dark brown. Bill had come in with a hammer and beaten it up a little. The effect made it look weatherworn and very old. He also brought two lengths of chain and attached them to either side of the wooden bridge and then to the castle walls. They hung limp, like real chains that would allow the bridge to fall open.

A few finishing touches still needed to be done, so the girls would have to come back later in the week.

"In the meantime," said Mary as the girls prepared to leave, "Madame Brussau's is a wonderful costume shop. Your costumes should match your bed, Your Highnesses." She curtsied as if the girls were royalty.

"We will visit the shop, Madame Mary," answered Alexis. She and Elizabeth curtsied in return. "Thank you for all of your help."

All the way back to the hotel, the girls talked about their bed.

Hardly any other bed would have brakes or a steering wheel, so they really felt they had a good chance of winning. That was if they could get the hang of driving the bed when they had never done it before.

Elizabeth's parents told her she could stay the night with Alexis at the London Bridge Resort. They were going to watch the bridge. Alexis hoped the person in the boat would show up again. Maybe this time they could sneak down to the water and take some pictures.

When they entered the shining lobby of the hotel, an unusual crowd surrounded the front desk. Dr. Edwards was standing across the counter from Jane. He seemed to be introducing her to two strange men in canvas work suits. They looked like painters.

Alexis motioned to Elizabeth, and the two of them slowed down. Alexis wanted to hear what they were saying as they walked past. Dr. Edwards spoke first.

"These men are Jerold and Jim," he said to Jane. "They have been hired to create a float that will represent the conference and hotel in Saturday's parade. Please allow them unlimited access to the hotel's premises, even though they are not guests. I believe your manager has left you a note to that effect."

Jane dug around on the desk in front of her. She picked up a piece of paper and studied it.

"Yep," she said. "You're good to go! This says he's set up a workroom for you near the ballroom," she said to the workmen.

"Thank you very much," said the larger of the two. The hairs on the back of Alexis's neck stood on end. That voice. It was so familiar. Alexis waited for the man to say something else so she could place his voice, but he didn't. He only nodded and then turned and followed Dr. Edwards around the corner toward the ballroom.

Oh well. It probably just reminded her of someone back home. The two girls went upstairs, ate room service with Grandma Windsor, and went into Alexis's room to get ready for bed.

As Elizabeth opened her backpack and reached inside, Alexis saw a flash of white.

"Is that what I think it is?" she asked.

"Yep. Dad's MacBook," Elizabeth said, pulling the computer out of the canvas bag. "He said I could bring it with me tonight."

The girls put on their pajamas and then sat side by side at the computer desk in the room. Elizabeth turned on the screen, and a glowing apple appeared while the machine booted up.

When she entered the Camp Club Girls chat room, she and Alexis saw that the other girls were already there.

Bailey: *Hi Betty Boo and Lexy.*

Elizabeth: *You know I hate that name. And Lexy? That's a new one. LOL*

McKenzie: *We were just talking about you. Kate was telling us the stuff you texted her all day.*

Elizabeth: *Did Kate send you the photos of the bed too?*

Sydney: *Yeah, that thing's amazing. I wish I was there to push it for you!*

McKenzie: *I don't see why they just don't race horses. Beds don't make sense. If you guys go back there next year, maybe I could come down with my horse. There's a jousting club not too far from here. Maybe I could learn to joust.*

Elizabeth: *That would be cool. Did you guys find anything out?*

Kate: *I looked up Princess Amelia. I found out that she was in love with a stable hand.*

Bailey: *Maybe he's the one who taught her to ride horses.*

Kate: *Maybe. Tradition is that she wrote him letters. After she died, the stories say he couldn't find her last letter. He spent the rest of his life looking for it.*

McKenzie: *What happened to him?*

Kate: *Well, actually he died not too long after Amelia. Of some sort of plague.*

Sydney: *That happened a lot in those times. People died suddenly. He might even have died in the saddle!*

Bailey: *What are you going to do next?*

Elizabeth: *As I texted you earlier today, Alexis saw weird stuff at the bridge last night. We're going to try to keep an eye on the bridge tonight.*

Kate: *Do you have your automatic recording camera with you that you used at Miss Maria's nature park? You know—when you were trying to catch the dinosaurs in action? If so, you can set it up to try to catch any action.*

Elizabeth: *No, we don't have one of those.*

Kate: *Do you want me to overnight a spycam to you?*

Elizabeth: *I think we'll be okay.*

When the girls got off the computer, they weren't tired at all. On the contrary, they were quite excited. They sat at the window for hours waiting for the mysterious person in the rowboat.

He didn't come.

It was one o'clock in the morning, and both girls were asleep on the windowsill. Suddenly Alexis jumped.

"What?" said Elizabeth, immediately awake. "Did you see something?"

"No," said Alexis. "That man in the lobby! I just remembered where I've heard his voice before!"

"Oh. Where?" asked Elizabeth. She relaxed back into her chair.

"Elizabeth, I heard it in the alley! Remember? The two voices were talking about—"

"No way!" Elizabeth sat straight up again.

"Yes way! I have no idea how they are going to do it, but those two men are going to steal the golden coach!"

CHAPTER 7

Priceless or Useless

The girls had breakfast in the hotel restaurant with Alexis's grandma. Alexis still didn't feel the girls had enough information to tell her grandmother what was happening. Still, she was nervous about the speculations she and Elizabeth had. The fact that the con men had gotten jobs at the hotel would make it easier for them to steal the carriage. She had *no* idea how they could do it, but it still worried her.

Alexis knew her grandma would know what to do, but she still didn't feel confident enough to tell her everything. She wondered what she would say about the *idea* of the carriage being stolen.

"Grandma," said Alexis, as the waitress filled her glass of orange juice. "Why is there so little security around the carriage? What would happen if someone tried to steal it?"

Grandma Windsor chuckled.

"Darling, that carriage is huge! No one would be able to get it out of the hotel unnoticed. But even if they could, what would they do with it?"

"Well, it's valuable, isn't it?" asked Elizabeth.

"In its own way, yes," said Grandma Windsor. "But I don't see why anyone would want it. It's the only replica of its kind, so you couldn't sell it to anyone. It would be too easy for the police to track it down again."

"Well, what about a collector or something? Someone like you, who really likes history and stuff?" asked Alexis. She was remembering the many old trinkets her grandmother brought back from her travels. Her house was full of them. Again Grandma Windsor laughed.

"A *real* collector or historian wouldn't want a replica. Deep down, it's only a fake. Would a literature professor be content with a new version of Shakespeare, if there was a possibility she could hold the original? No. Anyone can walk into a bookstore and get a copy of *Romeo and Juliet* for less than five dollars. But the original? Priceless."

"So replicas are worthless?" asked Alexis.

"Now, I didn't say that," said Grandma Windsor. "Take Michelangelo's statue of *David*, for instance. If you walk up to the statue in the plaza, you will enjoy its beauty. You may take pictures and go on your merry way, but if that's as far as you went, then you missed the truth. You have only seen a replica—a smaller shadow of the true art of Michelangelo. The real statue is inside, hidden away from the damaging elements. But the replica is not worthless, Alexis. It is still beautiful; it's just not *as* beautiful. It does not have the same history."

The waitress was back, refilling Grandma Windsor's glass of tea this time.

"So, besides the fact that it is almost impossible to get the coach out of this building unnoticed, I simply don't see why someone would want to steal it in the first place. That is why there isn't much security around it. The hotel has never felt that it was threatened."

But it is *threatened!* Alexis wanted to scream. But after all Grandma Windsor had just said, she thought it would sound silly to voice her thoughts.

After they finished eating, the girls left Grandma Windsor and walked toward Bill and Mary's shop. The bridge was still crawling with engineers, and they would have to wait until night before looking for the rowboat again. So no matter how tempting the mystery surrounding the bridge was, Alexis was going to focus on the carriage for a while.

Alexis knew Jerold and Jim were the same people she had overheard in the alley earlier in the week. But she was starting to have doubts about other things. Would it really be possible for Jerold and Jim, those silly-looking "float builders," to steal the golden coach? There was *no way* they could remove it without someone noticing. As soon as it was missing, someone would sound the alarm. They wouldn't make it very far.

And *why* were they planning to steal it in the first place? They had said it was worth millions, but Grandma Windsor claimed the carriage wasn't worth much at all. Sure, it was probably expensive to make, but you could always build another one. It wasn't like the original coach back in London, which was covered with real gold.

"There's only one way to know for sure if they are going to steal the carriage," said Alexis as they turned down the narrow street to Bill's. "We have to *investigate* these two guys."

"You mean spy on them?" asked Elizabeth, smiling.

"Well, yes," laughed Alexis. "*Investigating* just sounds a lot better! We'll work on the bed for a bit and then go back to the hotel. They're making the float near the ballroom. It shouldn't be too hard to find them."

In the back room of the antique shop, the girls admired their castle. It only needed a couple of touch-ups. Alexis was attaching fake fish to the bed-skirt moat when the bell on the front door jingled. She heard a girl's voice say, "Hello, Uncle Bill."

The voice didn't sound friendly.

Alexis and Elizabeth poked their heads through the curtain and saw a slim brunette standing with her hands on her hips.

"Hello, Emily," said Bill. "Shouldn't you be in school?"

"I heard you have someone driving your bed," the girl said, ignoring his question. Her face was scrunched up, like she smelled something gross.

"Yep, sure do," said Bill. He sounded friendly, but his stiff shoulders told Alexis he had put his guard up. "What brings you down here? Need something for a costume?"

"Eew, gross! Like I would use any of this junk for my costume!" Emily picked up a silver teaspoon with her forefinger and thumb, like it was covered in grime.

"I don't understand what makes you love other people's old stuff so much. Like this spoon." She held it up to the light and then looked around the table where it had been sitting. "It's all dingy, and there's only *one*. What on earth would anyone do with only one spoon?"

"Actually, if you look at the handle—"

But Emily didn't. She rolled her eyes and tossed the spoon toward Bill. He fumbled, and it fell to the ground. Alexis stepped through the curtain to pick it up and hand it to him.

"Who are *you*?" asked Bill's demanding niece.

"This is Alexis," said Bill. "She's the one racing my bed this Saturday."

Alexis smiled and waved. Emily's eyes narrowed to tiny slits.

"Well, she'd better be careful," she said, stepping closer. "The driver who tried to beat me last year ended up in the hospital with a broken arm. And I *don't lose.*"

Emily turned and stormed out of the shop. Alexis was sure she would have slammed the door if it hadn't been for the automatic spring that caught it and made it close gently.

"What was that all about?" asked Elizabeth.

"Oh, don't mind Emily," said Bill. "She's just mad because I wouldn't let her use my bed in the race. She thought I would for sure, because she's family. My brother's kid. Ever heard the term 'spoiled rotten'? Well, that's Emily for sure."

"Why wouldn't you let her race it?" asked Alexis.

"You heard her, didn't you?" said Bill. "She put a guy in the hospital last year—slammed into his bed on the last turn and sent him flying into the crowd. You're not supposed to touch anyone else's bed. Emily told the judges it was an accident, and they believed her and gave her the prize."

"But you didn't believe it was an accident?" asked Alexis.

"Do you, Alexis? I can't have anyone representing my shop doing risky things that might bring bad publicity."

Bill was right. Alexis had just met Emily, and she was pretty sure Emily would have broken someone's arm to get what she wanted.

"Well, she can have the prize for all I care," said Alexis. "I just want to race!"

"That's right," said Elizabeth. "It's like Psalm 37:1 says, 'Do not fret because of those who are evil or be envious of those who do wrong.' No matter what happens, we'll have a blast."

"*And* you'll have the best bed out there!" said Bill. "That thing should be in the parade! It'll be better than any other float!"

Bill still held the small spoon that Emily had tossed at him. He placed it on the table, but Alexis picked it up.

"What were you about to say about the spoon, Bill—before Emily interrupted you?" asked Alexis. Bill smiled. It reminded Alexis of her grandmother's smile when she asked her about history.

"Look at the handle," he said. Alexis held the spoon up in the light, and Elizabeth came close to look as well. A small pink stone shaped like an oval was mounted on the end of the handle. Upon the oval stone, a face had been carved. It was the silhouette of a beautiful young woman.

"Who is it?" asked Elizabeth.

"Princess Amelia, the youngest daughter of—"

"King George the Third!" gasped Alexis.

"You've heard her story then?" asked Bill.

"Pieces of it," answered Alexis. "My grandmother told me some of the stories surrounding her. Something about Princess Amelia and a young man she was forbidden to marry."

"That's what she is most known for," said Bill. "They say the law would have allowed her to marry him after she turned twenty-six, but that was pretty old to be married back then. Her letters may have told him that she would wait. If she hid a letter to give him, no one knows if he ever found it. This spoon is a rare piece. Since Princess Amelia was never a queen, it is quite strange for silverware to have her picture on it. Maybe she really was her father's favorite."

"Wow!" said Alexis. "That means this spoon is more than two hundred years old!"

"Why do you keep that out on a table?" asked Elizabeth. "Shouldn't it be locked away somewhere?"

Bill laughed.

"Probably. A lot of the stuff in my store is more valuable than people think. Like Emily, many think it's just junk—like an indoor yard sale."

"Well, I think it's brilliant," said Alexis. She looked at the spoon again. Was it just her imagination, or did the picture on the spoon look like the girl from her dream? Her imagination was running wild again.

"Hey, look!" cried Elizabeth. Alexis followed her pointed finger toward the large window. Outside, three familiar figures were walking through the alley.

"It's Dr. Edwards—and those two workmen from the hotel!" Alexis looked at Elizabeth and lowered her voice so Bill couldn't hear. "If we follow them, we might find out more about their plan for the carriage."

"They probably won't talk about it with Dr. Edwards around," said Elizabeth. "Maybe he'll leave."

Alexis nodded. "See ya later," she said to Bill. "It's getting to be lunchtime."

"I'm getting hungry myself," said the shop owner. "See you girls later."

Alexis and Elizabeth waved goodbye and left the shop. They were just in time to see the end of Dr. Edwards's walking stick disappear around a corner. They followed, and after a couple of turns, their prey entered a small deli.

"Well, it *is* lunchtime," said Alexis. "Feel like a sandwich?" Elizabeth smiled. The girls allowed a couple more people to enter before they did. They didn't want to be directly behind Dr. Edwards in line in case he recognized them.

After ordering turkey sandwiches and grabbing a couple bags of chips, Alexis led Elizabeth to a booth that hid them from the three men but was still close enough so they could hear everything that was being said.

"I thought you said this job was going to be easy," said the taller of the two men.

"I thought the job was going to be easy, Jerold," said Dr. Edwards. "But circumstances have changed."

"Well, I hope we're getting paid more," said Jerold.

"Yes, yes," said Dr. Edwards testily. "Don't worry about the money! It will come!"

"I don't know what you want with that thing anyway," said another voice. It must have been Jim. "It's a fake. How can it be worth much money?"

Dr. Edwards sighed. Alexis was sure that if she could see him, his eyes would be bulging in exasperation.

"It's not the carriage itself that is priceless," he said, dropping his voice to a whisper. Alexis had to stop chewing her chips so that she could still hear him. "It's something hidden within it."

Alexis stared across the table at Elizabeth. She too had stopped chewing. They sat still, straining to hear every word.

"I have reason to believe that an original document, hundreds of years old, has been hidden somewhere within the carriage. The *document*, my dear fellows, is what's priceless. The carriage just happens to be the hiding place."

The thieves seemed to be happy with the doctor's explanation, because all Alexis and Elizabeth heard after that was the chomping and slurping of the two men eating.

The girls finished their food and slipped out the front.

"So *that's* why Dr. Edwards wants the carriage! He thinks something is hidden inside of it!" said Elizabeth.

"Yeah," said Alexis. "A priceless document. What if it was Princess Amelia's letter?"

"Why would Princess Amelia's letter be hidden in a *replica*?" asked Elizabeth. "The real carriage, maybe, but there's no reason for it to be in Arizona. Your imagination's running away with you again, Alex."

"You're right," said Alexis. "But wouldn't it be cool? No matter what the document is, it's obviously worth a lot of money. *And* it has a rightful owner. I bet if Dr. Edwards were the rightful owner, he wouldn't have to steal it."

"I know," said Elizabeth. "We have to keep him from stealing it. But how are we supposed to do that when we don't know where it is?"

"Easy," said Alexis, smiling wide. "We just have to find it before he does."

Encounter in the Costume Shop

"How on earth are we supposed to do that?" asked Elizabeth. "You saw how that deputy guy reacted when we were just looking at the carriage. What do you think will happen if we actually try to *touch* the thing? Or search it for an ancient letter?"

"We'll just have to be careful," said Alexis. "It might be difficult, but we don't have a choice. If the document exists, it belongs in a museum—not in Dr. Edwards's personal collection."

They walked toward the hotel, thinking about how best to search for the hidden paper. Alexis was so deep in thought that she ran right into a sidewalk display in front of the costume store. She and Elizabeth struggled to dust off the white, curly wigs and hang them back up before anyone noticed.

"Let's go in here," said Alexis. "We need costumes for the bed race and parade, don't we?"

"Definitely!" squealed Elizabeth. They walked in and were immediately hidden in a maze of silk dresses, old-fashioned shoes, and jesters' hats.

"It looks like it's almost all medieval," said Elizabeth.

"Good," said Alexis. "We have to match our bed. It's a castle. What do you think we should be?"

"We could be knights," said Elizabeth, walking over to a suit of armor. "This looks so real!"

"It also looks like it weighs a hundred pounds!" laughed Alexis. They continued through the store, yelling back and forth whenever they found something interesting. Before long they were trying on everything they could reach, making each other collapse in fits of giggles. Alexis grabbed a garish jester's hat with six floppy tentacles and jingle bells everywhere. She smashed it onto her head and spun around.

"Classy, huh?" she asked Elizabeth. But the person behind her wasn't Elizabeth.

It was David Turner, the Arizona state swim champion.

"Very classy," he said, raising his eyebrows and giving her an amused smile. Alexis blushed. It was the first time she'd ever seen David smile. He was twice as cute when he did. She wondered why he never smiled at swim meets or in front of his school.

Alexis yanked the hat off her head but was instantly aware of how messed up her hair must be.

"Um, sorry," she said. "I thought my friend was standing there." She looked around frantically. Where was Elizabeth anyway?

"Don't apologize," said David. "I wouldn't expect any less of someone visiting a costume shop." He was still smiling, as if whatever bothered him at other times was now forgotten.

"I'm Alexis," she said, holding out her hand. David had to rearrange the things he was holding to shake her hand. He dropped a large sword, and they banged heads as they both reached to pick it up.

"Ow!" said Alexis.

"Sorry!" he said, rubbing his head and wiping his long hair out of his eyes at the same time. "You look familiar. Have I met you before?"

"No," said Alexis. "My friend and I went to the swim meet the other day."

"No, that's not it," he said. "Dude! You're the girl from the pep rally!"

Alexis turned crimson. "That was an accident," she said hastily. "My friend and I don't even go to school here!"

"Oh," said the boy. "You don't?" Was Alexis imagining things, or did he look disappointed?

"It's a long story," she said. "We just ended up in the building by accident."

"Well, you're a legend anyway. The whole school's talking about you."

"Great," said Alexis. They both laughed. Then there was an embarrassing silence. Alexis twisted the jester's hat in her hands, and David placed the sword back in a display.

"Not going to get it?" Alexis asked.

"Nope," he said. "I think I'm going to go with the dragon." He held up the head of a costume that was piled under his right arm.

Just then a horrible screech came from outside, followed by a loud crash. Alexis turned and ran to the sidewalk with David just behind her. Elizabeth wasn't far behind. Right in front of the store, two cars were stopped. Apparently one of the drivers hadn't been paying attention and had slammed into the car ahead. Both bumpers were crushed, and the back car was smoking a bit.

The drivers stumbled out of their vehicles and began yelling at each other. No one was hurt, but neither person wanted to take the blame. Within minutes two police cars showed up, and a sheriff approached the arguing drivers.

Someone tapped Alexis on the shoulder.

"Trespassing wasn't enough?" a voice said. "Now you have to shoplift too?"

Alexis spun around to see Deputy Dewayne inches from her face.

"What? Shoplifting?" she stammered. The deputy pointed to her arms. Alexis was still carrying the jester's hat. She looked side to side. David still had his dragon costume, and Elizabeth was holding a pink dress and had a matching crown on her head. None of the items had been paid for.

"Oh this," said Alexis. "We were just looking inside the store when the crash happened. We ran outside to see what happened and forgot we were holding it all."

Deputy Dewayne didn't move.

"Really, Deputy," said David. "She's telling the truth. We were just about to pay."

The officer's eyes narrowed, and then he spun around as the sheriff called his name. Alexis, Elizabeth, and David took that opportunity to slide back into the store and head for the cash register.

Elizabeth had found a great princess costume. Alexis found a crazy outfit that matched her jester's hat. She had wanted to be a princess too, but she loved the hat too much to part with it. They paid and turned to go.

"Uh, see you later?" said David from behind them. His dragon costume was on the counter.

"Yeah, later," said Alexis. She turned and led Elizabeth out the door.

"Um, Alexis?" said Elizabeth.

"Yeah?"

"I think that was a question."

"What do you mean?" asked Alexis.

"What David said just now—I think it was a question. Like, *Can I see you later?* Not, *See ya later.* Get the difference?"

Alexis stopped in her tracks, blushing from the neck all the way up to her ponytail. Her eyes were dinner plates.

"No way!" she said.

"I could be wrong," said Elizabeth. "But it seemed like he liked you."

"What do I do?" said Alexis, frantic. "I don't want him to think I was rude!"

"Go talk to him. He's coming out of the store right now."

Alexis turned around. "David!" she called. He spun around, yanking a pair of earbuds out of his ears so he could hear her.

"Yeah?"

"Um, do you want to hang out with us? I mean, we're not doing anything really, just walking around."

"I've got swim practice now. Maybe later?"

"Tomorrow, maybe," said Alexis. "If not, we'll be in the bed race. Look for the amazing castle."

"Okay," said David, smiling shyly. "See ya."

This time she was sure it was "see ya later." Alexis waved and turned back to Elizabeth, smiling like she had just won a million dollars.

"Chill out!" said Elizabeth. "Take a deep breath. He's a boy, not Superman!" Alexis laughed.

"So what now?" she asked.

"We could try to find out more about the piece of paper Dr. Edwards is looking for," said Elizabeth.

"That's a good idea," said Alexis. "We should check out the area at the hotel where those guys are building the float. We might overhear something else—or at least get an idea of where to look."

Back at the hotel the girls asked Jane for directions to the ballroom. As they approached it, they heard the *tick, tick, tick* of someone shaking a can of spray paint. It was coming from a door across the hall. Fumes and voices drifted out to where the girls were standing.

The door was open a couple of feet, so the girls walked up and peeked inside. Jerold and Jim were working on what Alexis guessed was the float. It was a perfect model of the carriage in the lobby, except that it was white. Alexis waved a hand at Elizabeth to get her to follow, and then she ducked inside and hid behind a tower of empty buckets.

No one saw them come in.

Jerold put down the spray paint he had been using and turned to call across the room.

"Oy! Jim! Hurry up with that stuff, eh? We ain't got all day!"

"I'm a comin', I'm a comin'! Hold yer horses!"

Alexis and Elizabeth held their breath. Jim's voice was just on the other side of the buckets. They heard him rustle around some more and then tromp off toward where the carriage and Jerold waited in the center of the room.

Relieved, Alexis looked through a gap between two buckets so she could see what was going on. Jim had a large roll of something in his hand. It looked like aluminum foil, except that it was gold instead of silver.

"Be careful, dimwit!" yelled Jerold. "You're making it flake! We can't have pieces of gold missing!"

"Why are we doing this, anyway?" asked Jim. "If the boss wants some old paper, why doesn't he just get it out of the carriage while everyone's asleep? We could do that easy!"

"Because it's not just lying on top of the velvet cushion, stupid.

It's in a hidden compartment, and he doesn't know where it is. He needs more time to search."

"So how is a carriage float going to help?" asked Jim.

"Are you really that dim?" said Jerold, smacking Jim upside the head. But he didn't say anything else. Alexis and Elizabeth hid for almost an hour, but the conversation was over. Both men were intent on covering the carriage float with the golden foil.

Alexis was with Jim. She didn't see how this float was going to help Dr. Edwards find the document he was looking for. They needed more information. Alexis felt like she had a lot of clues, but none of them seemed to fit together.

Were the Camp Club Girls at a dead end?

David's Story

Bailey: *Lex, I really like your court jester hat. Are you and Bets going to be in a costume contest?*

Alexis: *How do you know about my costume?*

Bailey: *K8 forwarded the photos of you trying on the hats.*

Sydney: *Who was that hottie standing behind you?*

Alexis: *Beth? How could she be standing behind me if she was taking pictures? And since when do you call her a hottie?*

Sydney: *Not her, goofy. The dude.*

Bailey: *Was he the Man of La Mancha or whatever?*

Sydney: *What's that?*

Alexis: *Oh, I saw that old movie. It was about Don Quixote.*

Sydney: *Who's that?*

Alexis: *Some knight in search of adventure.*

Kate: *I believe that was during the Spanish Inquisition—in a different country and a different century than King George's time.*

Sydney: *Well, he may not be the Man of La Mancha, but I definitely think he's the man of la macho!*

Alexis: *He is cute. And he was really nice in the costume store. You'd like him, Sydney—he's a champion swimmer. But he's been kind of surly the other times I've seen him.*

Bailey: *Surly? What's that?*

Alexis: *Grouchy.*

Kate: *Beth just texted me that you're blushing bright red when you're talking or writing about Daaaavvviiiddd.*

Bailey: *Wait, where's Betty Boo? And who's David?*

Alexis: *She's right here. But I have control of the keyboard, and I'm not giving it up. . . . Mwah- ha-ha. . . (That's an evil laugh, Bailey. And you better be glad she doesn't have control of anything if you're calling her Betty Boo again. She hates that.) And David's the guy in the photo.*

Bailey: *Oh, Groucho—the guy who's the swimmer.*

McKenzie: *So. . . Don't avoid the subject. Why do you blush when the guy's around? Are you and he going to the festivities dressed as Princess Amelia and her horse trainer?*

Bailey: *Do you think Groucho has anything to do with the mystery?*

Alexis: *Oh no. I'm sure he doesn't.*

Bailey: *But you saw someone in the water a couple of nights ago. If he's a swimmer, could that have been him?*

Alexis: *That late at night? It was a school night. What would a kid not much older than us be doing out at that time of night?*

Bailey: *Well, if he's the swim-meister of the century. . .*

Alexis: *I don't think so. I think it has something to do with Dr. Edwards and with the cursing woman.*

Bailey: *She uses bad language?*

Alexis: *No, she is the one who was saying there's a curse on the bridge. I think adults are running this thing.*

Kate: *Well, I researched Dr. Edwards, and he's legit. I couldn't find anything suspicious about him. I even checked his photo from the past against one Beth snapped and sent to us the other day, and it was definitely the same guy who's listed all over the internet with all kinds of credentials.*

Sydney: *I asked my aunt—you know, who works with the park services—if she knew anything about any funny business in that area. She says the rangers in the region have never mentioned anything.*

Alexis: *We're stuck. I keep trying to think of what Sherlock Holmes or Hercule Poirot or McGyver or Jessica Fletcher would do.*

Bailey: *Who are they?*

Sydney: *They're fictional detectives.*

Bailey: *Oh. Or Scooby Doo, Shaggy, Velma, and Daphne.*

Alexis: *Yeah or even them. I'm sure I've seen something on one of those mystery shows that should ring a bell and remind me of one of their plots, but I'm stumped. Ebeth just reminded me we have to go. Have to do a final check on the bed. Will send more photos later. Keep thinking. . . .*

●—●—●

As Alexis and Elizabeth walked back to Bill's shop, they kept trying to figure out what was going on. No matter how exciting the investigation was getting, they had to admit that they were stuck.

Then they were at the shop. As Alexis looked at the bed, she paced back and forth biting her nails.

"I wish we could test-drive it!" Alexis said. She was more than a little nervous about driving in a race when she had never even sat behind the steering wheel of a go-cart.

"I'll push," said Elizabeth. "You can steer. My legs are longer, so I can push and ride at the same time—almost like a scooter."

Alexis almost protested, but when she stopped pacing, she realized that the back of the bed came up to her waist. There was no way she'd be able to jump on when the bed got going very fast.

She was going to have to steer.

Bill climbed up into the front of the bed and called her up too. Since they had been here last, Bill and Mary had made a driver's seat. It was an old recliner painted gold to look like a throne.

"This is the steering wheel, obviously," said Bill, pointing. Alexis sat on the edge of the throne and grasped the wheel so hard her knuckles turned white.

"Mr. Bill," said Alexis. "I would love to be able to say that I drive on a regular basis, but I'm twelve." Bill laughed.

"Well, have you ever played one of those racing video games?

The huge ones with wheels and pedals?"

"A couple of times," said Alexis.

"You'll be fine then. There's only one pedal on this one, though. That's the brake." He pointed his foot below the chair, and Alexis saw the black pedal. It was as big as her foot. *Good*, she thought. *There's no way I'll miss it.*

Alexis turned the steering wheel and pressed the pedal over and over. If she could just get used to it, maybe she wouldn't be so afraid in the morning. She wished she had more strength in her legs.

Maybe I should take up swimming or something, she thought. That reminded her of David.

"Hey, Mr. Bill, do you know David Turner?"

"Yes, I've met him," Mr. Bill replied. "Good kid."

"It seems like he doesn't smile too often," said Alexis. "And I noticed at the swim meet the other day that other people had family members around to congratulate them, but he didn't. He just stood there looking grouchy."

Mary walked into the room with some glasses and a pitcher full of lemonade for the girls.

"Poor kid," she said. "David lost his parents and sister a year or so ago in a car wreck." She handed each of the girls a glass and started pouring out the cool yellow treat. "David wasn't in the car because he was at a swim meet. He lives with his uncle Jeff. Jeff is a good man, but he isn't married and doesn't know what it's like to be a parent. He works a lot of hours, so David's left alone a lot. Often at night, even," she explained. "I understand money is a problem for them too. I've noticed that David is smiling more lately. It's tough to lose your parents.

"I know David's coach too. He told me meets are really hard for David sometimes. Especially when he wins. His parents were on the way to his meet when they had the wreck. It was hard for him to keep swimming. But he does love it and is so good at it. They've thought about training him for the Olympics even if he is a little old for starting that," she added.

"The swim-meister," Elizabeth murmured.

The front door jingled as someone entered. Seconds later,

Emily's better-than-you voice drifted through the curtain.

"Hey, Uncle Bill," she called. "You ready to lose tomorrow?"

Bill sighed and walked into the shop. Alexis and Elizabeth climbed off the bed and followed.

"We're ready to race, if that's what you mean," said Alexis. She smiled, hoping to get a similar reaction out of Emily.

"'Do not answer a fool according to his folly, or you yourself will be just like him,'" Elizabeth murmured.

Alexis smiled. "Proverbs?"

"Yep, 26:4."

Emily did smile at Alexis's comment all right, but it was not a smile of kindness.

"Mmm," she said. "Where's your third, anyway?"

"Our what?" asked Elizabeth.

"Your third. You know, your other person." Alexis and Elizabeth looked at each other, confused. "Don't tell me you don't know!" squealed Emily. Alexis thought she sounded a little too pleased. Emily dug a folded purple paper out of her back pocket. As she unfolded it, Alexis recognized it as one of the bed race flyers.

"Didn't you read the small print?" asked Emily. She pointed to the very bottom of the flyer. "All teams must be made up of three or four people. No more, no less." She refolded the flyer and looked at them with a smile.

"See you in the morning!" Emily chirped, then she turned and left.

Alexis looked back and forth between Elizabeth and Bill. What were they going to do?

"Mr. Bill, can you ride with us?" asked Elizabeth. "I'm sure we could make it safe enough. We'll go slow!"

"No way, girls," he answered. "That's kind of you, but if you went slow enough to keep my leg from getting hurt, you'd have no chance at winning."

"We'd rather race slowly than not race at all!" said Alexis.

"You'll find someone else," said Bill. "There are tons of people in this town willing to jump on a bed just for the ride."

"What about Miss Mary?" asked Elizabeth.

The woman's voice floated from behind the cash register.

"Someone has to keep the store open for the tourists," she said.

Alexis and Elizabeth couldn't believe their luck. They had worked so hard on finishing this bed and had been so excited to race. Now it looked like they might not even be able to. Alexis took a deep breath. There was no way she was giving up this easily.

"Come on, Elizabeth," she said. "We've got to find a partner."

"Well, you know what Matthew 7:7 says," Elizabeth pointed out. "'Seek and you will find!'"

The girls waved at Bill and Mary. "We'll see you bright and early," said Bill. "Don't worry. Not only will your bed race, but it will win if I can do anything about it!"

The girls practically ran back to the hotel. But before long they were sitting outside on the curb sulking. They had run out of options. Grandma Windsor was riding on the hotel float with Dr. Edwards. Elizabeth's dad was riding on the bass float because he won third place in the tournament. And Elizabeth's brother had eaten too much cotton candy and was sick. That meant her mom was staying with him at their hotel. Alexis even asked Jane, the lady at the front desk, but she had to work.

Alexis was trying to be upbeat, but she was really disappointed.

"Excuse me, ma'am!" Alexis called to a complete stranger walking past them. "Would you like to ride with us in the bed race tomorrow?" The lady gave her a funny look and shook her head. Then she walked away mumbling something in a foreign language.

Elizabeth laughed.

"Well, at least I tried!" said Alexis. She couldn't help but laugh too. Something would come up; she just knew it would. There was no way they weren't going to race tomorrow.

After twenty minutes or so, the girls decided to take a walk before dinner. They headed toward the bridge and were surprised to find that no one was there. The caution tape was still up, but the engineers were all gone.

"I wonder where they all went," said Elizabeth.

"Me too," said Alexis. "Why aren't the engineers working? Don't they care if the town has to cancel the parade?"

They were walking past the bridge to the harbor when Alexis saw him. David Turner. He turned onto the street a few blocks ahead of them, hands shoved in his pockets and his hood pulled up over his head.

"Elizabeth, look! It's David!"

"Okay, okay! Calm down! Remember, Alex, he's just a boy."

"No, it's not *that*!" said Alexis, blushing. "The race! I bet he'd ride with us. Come on!" Alexis pulled Elizabeth by the elbow and walked even faster.

"David!" Alexis called, but he didn't turn around. "I bet he has his earbuds in." They sped up even more, trying to catch up, but wherever David was off to, it seemed like he was in a hurry.

"That's odd," said Elizabeth. "Is he pulling a wagon?"

"I think he is," said Alexis. Sure enough, David was pulling a red metal wagon behind him. "What could he possibly be doing with that?" asked Alexis.

David came to a stop near the harbor. He turned onto the wooden pier, wheeling his wagon along with him. When the girls caught up, he was on his knees digging around in a rowboat that was bobbing up and down in the water.

"Hey, David," said Alexis. "How are you—"

Alexis almost screamed. She was looking over David's shoulder into the small rowboat. When he moved an old tarp aside, she saw a chisel and a hammer along with some snorkeling gear. Next to the tools was a large pile of stones from the London Bridge.

CHAPTER 10

Rocks in the Boat

"What is all of this?" squealed Alexis. The music from David's earbuds thrummed. He couldn't hear her. Alexis reached out and tapped him firmly on the shoulder. He spun around so fast that he almost lost his balance and fell in the water.

"Alexis!" he yelled, pulling the device from his ears. "I didn't see you there. You scared me."

David looked between the two girls. Elizabeth's mouth hung open in shock. Alexis's face was scrunched up in fury.

"Bailey was right! It's been you the whole time!" she yelled, pointing her finger in his face. David's mouth opened and closed like a fish out of water. It looked like he wanted to say something but couldn't quite find the words. "You've been the one tearing the London Bridge apart! You're responsible for the crack!"

"What are you talking about?" asked David. "I'm not tearing the bridge apart."

"Then where did those stones come from?" asked Elizabeth. David looked over his shoulder to the pile of stones in the rowboat. There was no doubt—they were the same gray, weathered stones that built the bridge.

"These are from the bridge, but they're just samples," said David. "One of the engineers asked me if I could gather some of the stones for testing. He was supposed to come down here and get them this afternoon."

David seemed like he was being completely honest, but Alexis didn't like the sound of his story. Why would an engineer ask a teenager to take apart a bridge? Didn't they have their own people to do that stuff? Well, the story might sound shifty, but Alexis thought David was telling the truth. He believed he was helping not hurting the bridge. There was one way to find out for sure.

"When did this *engineer* ask you to do this?" asked Alexis. Her face softened, and she was no longer glaring at him.

"About two weeks ago. It takes about two days for me to get one stone loose."

"And didn't you notice you were causing a crack to appear in the bridge?" said Elizabeth.

"I do my work at night because I'm so busy during the day. And I wanted to make some extra money to help my uncle pay bills. I wanted to surprise him, so I've been working at night while he's at work. I never saw the crack until earlier this week, when people started making such a fuss. I asked the engineer about it the last time I saw him, but he said not to worry about it." David turned to Elizabeth. "Why are you looking at me like that?" he asked.

Alexis turned around and looked at her friend. Elizabeth was still looking suspicious. Her eyes were narrow, and her arms were crossed. One of her feet at the end of a long leg was tap, tap, tapping on the wood of the dock.

"No offense, David," Elizabeth said, "but your story sounds crazy. You said you were supposed to meet this engineer today? Well, where is he?"

David looked up the street toward town.

"I'm not sure." He glanced at his watch. "He's late."

"Well," said Alexis, "the engineers who are taking care of the bridge are staying at my hotel. We could go see if he's there. Then you could give him the stones, and we can clear all this up."

"Sounds good to me," said David. "You wanna help me put these things in the wagon? I doubt we'd be able to carry them all the way."

One by one they piled the old stones into the wagon. They were as gentle as possible. The last thing they wanted to do was break one of them in half. Twenty minutes later they were pulling the wagon into the lobby of the London Bridge Resort. The tourists and workers alike turned to watch them wheel the wagon toward the front desk.

"Hi, Jane," said Alexis. "Do you know where the head engineer is right now?"

"I believe the engineers are eating a late lunch," she said, pointing toward the restaurant at the front of the lobby. "What's in the wagon?"

Alexis didn't answer. She turned and led Elizabeth and David toward a nearby table where a team of men in jeans and white polo shirts were eating.

"Um, excuse me," she said. The men stopped chewing and looked at her. One of them sat frozen with his sandwich halfway to his open mouth. "We're looking for one of your engineers."

The men looked back and forth at one another, surprised. Then the one with his sandwich halfway to his mouth answered her.

"I'm the chief engineer, name's Cliff. Which one of my men are you looking for?" Alexis looked at David because he was the one who knew whom they were looking for.

"I don't remember his name," he said, "but I think it started with a *J*."

"I'm John," said a thin man at the end of the table with a bowl of pasta in front of him.

David looked at Alexis and shook his head. The man he was looking for was not at the table.

"This is all of us," said Cliff. "Is there something I can help you with?"

"Well," said Alexis, "some engineer told David that he would pay him to take samples from the bridge for testing. They're right here." She gestured toward the wagon, and Cliff's sandwich dropped onto his plate with a *splat*.

"These are from the bridge? The *London Bridge*?"

David nodded.

"Where did you take them from?" asked Cliff, excited. He jumped up and flew to the wagon, picking up the stones one by one.

"The second pillar, under the waterline," said David. "That's where the engineer told me to take them from."

"Let's get one thing straight," said Cliff. "A true engineer would never tell a kid to remove stonework from a bridge—especially a historical bridge like this one. I think you got duped, kid."

"I don't understand," said David. "The guy was so—"

"Wait!" yelled Cliff. "Did you say you took these from the second pillar?"

"Yeah," said David.

"Right under where the crack appeared?" said another engineer with gravy all over his chin. David nodded.

Cliff jumped out of his seat.

"John, Matt—finish eating, then check this out. I believe this explains the crack. If so, then there's no real damage. These stones can be replaced, and the crack can be filled. It's only surface damage!"

Cliff called over to where Jane was standing at the front desk. "Call the mayor! Tell him the parade is on!" Everyone in the restaurant and hotel lobby erupted in applause. After a minute, David's voice broke through the commotion.

"Excuse me, sir," he said. Cliff turned back toward the three young people. Alexis and Elizabeth were glad that the parade would go on, but David looked troubled.

"I feel stupid," he said. "I should have known that pulling chunks off the bridge wasn't right, but the guy was so convincing. Why would he want these rocks anyway?"

"Don't worry, son," said Cliff. "I believe that you didn't mean to cause any harm. You're no danger to anyone. The person who is a danger is that man who talked you into this. If you see him around, don't let him know we're on to him. You come find me, and we'll get the sheriff. As for why he wanted them, well, maybe he was trying to tear down the bridge for some reason. He might be one of these kooks who wants to get on the news. If he wasn't a kook, he was probably a crook bribed to do it—or he was doing it for money for some reason. You'd be surprised at how much people will pay for pieces of history."

Alexis elbowed Elizabeth. She was thinking of Dr. Edwards. All of this came down to history.

Cliff ran off to help his crew get the bridge ready for the parade and left the three of them standing staring at the floor.

"Well, I guess I'd better get home," said David.

"Yeah, it's almost dinnertime," said Elizabeth. They all walked toward the front doors. All at once, Alexis stopped and yelled.

"Wait!" cried Alexis. David and Elizabeth spun around in surprise. "David! What are you doing tomorrow?"

"Uh, watching the parade, I guess."

Alexis and Elizabeth exchanged excited glances.

"Do you want to ride with us in the bed race tomorrow?" Alexis asked.

"Please! You have to!" said Elizabeth. "I'm going to push, and Alexis is going to steer, but we don't have a third person!"

"You need a shifter," said David.

"A what?" said the girls together.

"A shifter—someone to sit in the middle of the bed and shift from side to side as you go around corners. It keeps the bed from flipping over. You're in luck. I happen to be the best shifter in Lake Havasu. Been on the winning float two years in a row."

"But that means you raced with Emily!" said Alexis.

"Yeah, I did. Until she broke that guy's arm anyway. She's a good racer, but she's too brutal. She'll do anything to win."

"So you'll ride with us?" asked Elizabeth.

"Of course!" said David. "Where should I meet you?"

"Outside of Bill's Tarnished Treasures first thing in the morning," said Alexis. "Don't forget to wear your costume!"

Alexis walked David and Elizabeth to the sidewalk, where the two of them peeled off in opposite directions—David to his home and Elizabeth to her hotel. Alexis turned to go inside and was almost bowled over by a round man in a flapping suit.

It was the mayor.

"Sorry, girl! Sorry! Didn't see you in all the excitement!"

Then he turned and continued running toward the bridge, yelling at anyone who crossed his path. "Did you hear? Did you hear? The parade is on! There's no curse after all!"

Alexis watched him disappear around the corner, half expecting him to do a hitch kick on his way.

CHAPTER 11

The Great Race

The sun was barely up, but the people of Lake Havasu City were already gathering. A variety of beds were ready at the starting line. Racing teams were making final adjustments and getting into position.

Alexis was reattaching a sequined fish that had fallen off when David leaned out over her head from his seat on the bed.

"You almost done?" he asked. Alexis looked up. David's dragon costume was hilarious. It was a glittery blue, and the hood was shaped like a horned dragon's head, complete with three-inch fangs on the front of the snout.

"Yeah, almost," said Alexis. "This fish won't stay put!"

"Well, maybe if your decorations weren't so cheap, they wouldn't fall apart," said a nasty voice from behind them. Alexis spun around and found Emily's knees in her face. They were covered in sparkly tights. Alexis looked up and saw that Emily was dressed like a fairy. Even her makeup was gorgeous, and she had pointed ears and wings.

"Don't you have your own bed to attend to?" asked David.

"Oh," said Emily to Alexis. "I see you had to pick up last year's leftovers to get a third. Well, good luck, *girls.*"

She curtsied to David with her last word and traipsed back to her own bed.

"Don't worry about her," said David as he helped Alexis climb over the wall and onto the bed. "She wouldn't even be talking to us unless she was afraid we might beat her."

"And I think you just might!" It was Bill. He came out of the crowd and hobbled one last time around the castle-bed. "This thing really has a chance with a crew like you three!"

Bill pointed at David and spoke to the girls. "You know this guy's the best shifter in Lake Havasu, right?" he said. "Mary takes the credit. She used to go with his mom to ride go-carts, and she taught him how to take the corners!"

David bowed, his dragon's tail flying up in the air and knocking off Elizabeth's tiara.

"Be careful where you swing that thing!" she said. "Everybody ready? They're about to start!"

Alexis scrambled to the front and sat in the throne. She twisted her jester's hat so she was looking between two of the floppy arms. There was no way she was going to let a couple of jingle bells keep her from seeing where she was going.

Elizabeth climbed out of the bed and took up her station behind the tower, on the ground. She would be the one to start pushing when the gun went off. David plunked down in between the tower and Alexis's throne. There he would squat, ready to shift to one side or the other each time they took a corner. Hopefully he could keep the bed from tipping up or—even worse—from falling over.

"Alexis! Hey, Alexis!"

Alexis looked over and saw her grandmother's shocking red hair bobbing up and down in the crowd. She was waving frantically, elbowing Dr. Edwards in the side as she did so. He did not seem the least bit interested.

"Hi, Grandma!" called Alexis.

"Drive that thing well, baby!" called Grandma Windsor.

"I will!" cried Alexis. "And I'll meet you at the end of the parade!"

Their conversation was interrupted by the mayor's amplified voice. It roared over the noise of the crowd, causing a hush that was unnatural for so many people. The air hummed, as if the noise was just waiting for the right moment to explode again.

"*Ready! Set!*" called the mayor, the cap gun raised high over his head. *Snap!*

And they were off.

Along the starting line, beds began to roll forward. All of them were slow at first, but after a few seconds they picked up some speed.

"Come on, Elizabeth!" yelled Alexis. Just then David's head appeared over her shoulder.

"Alexis!" he said. "Just around the first corner is a hill! When I tell you to, lean forward as far as you can without falling out!"

"What?" Alexis cried. "What for?"

"You'll see," he said. Alexis didn't like the grin on his face.

The corner came faster than Alexis had expected. They were in the middle of the road with beds on either side. The street curved a little to the right, and David crouched down along the right wall of their castle.

"I'm on!" cried Elizabeth. She had stopped pushing and was now standing on the back of the bed.

"*Now!*" cried David. Alexis leaned forward, keeping her hands on the steering wheel. To her surprise, David was beside her, adding his weight to hers at the front of the bed. Soon she saw why they were doing it.

At first it was only five inches, but soon their castle-bed was a good twenty feet in front of everyone else! Their weight was forcing the bed down the hill faster than all the others!

The wind in her face made Alexis whoop in excitement. *This is how it must feel to fly*, she thought. The road continued straight at the bottom of the hill, so Alexis just sat back in her seat and held tight to the vibrating steering wheel. David returned to the middle of the bed, and Elizabeth got ready to jump off and push—but they were going too fast. She didn't need to.

"Whoo-hoo!" cried Elizabeth. Her head peeked up over the top of the tower. "You guys are doing great!"

"Here comes another corner!" said David. "Alexis! Tap the brakes once, then lean into the turn!" Alexis did as she was told. She tapped the pedal with her foot—but she did it twice. The bed lurched and took the turn at a crawl. They had lost most of their momentum, and two beds flew past them.

"Push, Elizabeth!" called David. Alexis felt the pressure from behind as Elizabeth struggled with the weight of the bed. She could see that the road up ahead dropped off in another hill, and she hoped they could catch up on the way down.

"All right!" shouted David. "Let's do it all over again! Elizabeth— get on! Alexis, lean forward and, no matter what you do, *don't touch the brakes!*"

Once again they were flying. In no time at all they had overtaken two teams. Now only one bed was ahead of them. Alexis looked up and recognized the sparkly wings of Emily's costume.

"We're going to pass her on the curve at the bottom!" said David. "Put our bed on the inside of the turn! Between her bed and the curb! If we lean left, you won't need the brakes! Plus," he said with a smile, "even if we tip, all we'll do is bump her a little. Ready? *Lean!*"

And she did. Alexis leaned to her left with everything she had. The force pulling the bed to the right was crazy. Alexis thought for sure they were going to topple over. Once, their left wheels lifted into the air, but David's weight put them back on the ground.

They came out of the turn just ahead of Emily's bed. An angry screech came from behind them. Then there was a jolt, and their castle-bed almost flew off the road and into the watching audience.

Cheers turned to boos, and after she got control of her bed, Alexis looked over to see Emily passing her.

"Oops!" said Emily. "Guess I got a little close. Sorry!" And she kept rolling.

"No way!" cried Alexis. "She cheated!"

"She always does," said David. "One more curve, then it's a slight hill to the finish. Don't pass her yet. Stay behind her on the turn, and we'll lean down the hill again, okay?"

Alexis nodded. Elizabeth joined them up front. They were going so fast there was no way she could push anymore. The last turn behind them, Alexis gripped the wheel and leaned. David and Elizabeth leaned forward too, one on either side of her.

They were even with the back of Emily's bed—they were at the middle—they were nose and nose—

The finish line was feet away. Without warning, David put his feet on the castle wall and leaped forward, grasping the finishing ribbon in his hands before falling and rolling beneath the bed with a crash.

Cheers erupted from the crowd. Alexis slammed on the brakes

as the medical staff ran out to pull David from under the bed. He was fine, except for some minor scrapes, and one of his dragon's teeth had been knocked out.

"Dragons have tough hides!" he said with a laugh as Alexis and Elizabeth ran up to him.

"That was *crazy*!" said Elizabeth.

"Why did you do that?" asked Alexis.

"I couldn't let her win," he said. "Not like that."

Alexis noticed there was quite a commotion near the side of the finish line. Most of the beds had finished, but the judges seemed to be fighting over something. Alexis led the way over to the judges, her jester's hat flopping in her hands.

"Where's the picture? We have to have the picture!" called one of the judges. He was a short man with a huge mustache.

"It's coming, Wilbur," said another judge. She was tall and was looking around the crowd. "Where's the photographer?" she shouted.

"I'm right here!" called a man in a tweed coat. He was running as fast as he could, huffing from the exertion. A digital camera was around his neck. He stopped near the judges and played with the buttons for a few seconds. Then he passed it to the judges. After a few moments of silence, the tall judge spoke.

"I just don't believe it!" she said.

"Me neither," said the little man with the mustache. "But the rules say—"

"The rules say what, exactly?" said Emily. She had abandoned her bed and was stalking toward the judges. "They had better say that I won!"

"Well, actually, young lady," said the man, "you didn't."

He showed her the camera. Emily's mouth dropped open, and she shoved the camera at Alexis. Alexis grabbed the camera. There was the proof, clear as day. David's long arms outstretched, grasping the finish line and beating the front of Emily's bed by a good six inches.

"But their bed didn't cross before mine!" argued Emily. "He jumped off!"

"The rules state that each team member is considered a part of the bed as long as they are touching it," said the lady judge. "And as you can see, his feet were still on the wall when he crossed the finish line."

Emily looked ready to argue, but the mayor burst past her, shoving her to the side.

"Congratulations!" he said, shaking hands with Alexis, Elizabeth, and David. "Great job! New winners!"

He squeezed them all in close, and the photographer took a picture. Then, without a moment to spare, the mayor was gone again.

"The parade!" he called. "Ten minutes until the parade!"

Alexis couldn't believe it. Not only had they been able to race, but they had also won!

"I can't believe we beat Emily!" Alexis exclaimed. "She's so mean that I was sure she'd win!"

"Well, I guess when we do the right thing and try hard, well, maybe the good guys don't always finish last," Elizabeth said. "It's kind of like 2 Samuel 22:25 says, 'The LORD has rewarded me according to my righteousness, according to my cleanness in his sight.'"

The three winners walked through the crowd and found a grassy spot on a hill to watch the parade pass. People kept stopping to congratulate them, and many shop owners told them to come by later for something or other "on the house." They made a plan to get free ice cream and chocolates but *not* to visit the taxidermist who had promised a special surprise.

The parade was all they had hoped it would be. The school marching band opened up, and not far behind them was the golden float from the hotel. Dr. Edwards sat in the driver's seat, accompanied by Grandma Windsor. They were both dressed in authentic costumes from the era of King George III, and Alexis thought it looked like her grandmother was having the time of her life.

You know, she told herself, *Dr. Edwards even looks happy. He looks like a gentleman driving his lady.*

Alexis gasped and stood up.

"What?" asked Elizabeth and David at the same time.

"A gentleman driving his lady," she murmured. "A gentleman. . . driving his *lady*!"

Without explaining, Alexis tore off through the crowd. Elizabeth and David followed, catching up outside the London Bridge Resort.

"What's going on?" Elizabeth panted.

"I think I know where the letter is hidden!" said Alexis. She ran through the automatic doors and stopped. The lobby was empty. Even Jane was nowhere to be seen. Alexis turned toward the golden coach.

"I think I know where it is!" she said again. As she went to cross the red ropes, she tripped, putting out a hand to stabilize herself on the coach. When she touched it, a huge sheet of golden foil came off in her hand.

"Wow," said David. "I thought the replica was sturdier than that!"

Alexis and Elizabeth looked at each other in horror.

"It is," they both said. Then they took off running back out the doors.

"Wait!" called David. "What's going on?"

"It's Dr. Edwards!" said Alexis. "He's stealing the replica from the hotel!"

"How?" asked David. "What are you talking about?"

"You saw the foil slip off," said Elizabeth. "He must have replaced the real carriage with his phony 'float' while everyone was watching the bed race."

"Right now, he's driving the actual replica of the golden carriage through Lake Havasu City!" said Alexis. "And everyone just thinks it's a float!"

The three teens ran across the street and down a couple of blocks. They stopped outside the Lake Havasu City Sheriff's Department. Inside, they met a bored-looking woman sitting at the front desk.

"Excuse me, ma'am," said Alexis. "We have an emergency."

"What is it?" said the woman, sitting up a little straighter and looking alert.

"Someone has stolen the golden carriage from the London Bridge Resort!" said Elizabeth.

The woman behind the desk burst out laughing. She laughed so hard that she began crying. Alexis tried to explain, but the lady just kept laughing and showed them out the door.

Alexis was stupefied. If the police didn't believe them, who would? They walked back slowly to the parade. Grandma Windsor hollered to them, and Alexis pushed her way through the crowd to get to her.

"You're already done, Mrs. Windsor?" asked Elizabeth.

"Yes," Grandma Windsor said. "Dr. Edwards and I were leading the parade, so we were done first. Hey! Why's everybody so glum?"

Alexis didn't think her grandmother would believe her, but there was no reason to hold back anymore. She told her the whole story, from hearing Jerold and Jim in the alley to finding the fake carriage in the lobby only minutes earlier.

"The police don't believe us," Alexis finished. "There's nothing we can do."

"What do you mean, nothing?" cried Grandma Windsor. She disappeared into the crowd, and within minutes honking filled the air. People parted as it came closer. Grandma Windsor was behind the wheel of her cherry red convertible, motioning for Alexis to jump in.

"I don't want to leave you two behind," she said to David and Elizabeth, "but we haven't asked your parents, and we don't have time. I just saw Dr. Edwards loading the carriage into a semitruck. He's already on the interstate, heading west!"

With that they were gone. Alexis buckled her seat belt as Grandma Windsor hit the gas pedal.

"I called the sheriff," said Grandma Windsor. "Told him he'd better listen to me since he ignored my granddaughter. They should be on their way."

When they got on the freeway, Alexis could barely make out the shape of a truck in the distance.

"It's time to see what this baby can do!"

The engine thrummed as the car went faster. . .and faster.

A siren wailed behind them, and Alexis saw the red and blue of flashing lights in the rearview mirror. *Thank goodness!* she thought. *The sheriff will catch Dr. Edwards in no time!* The car pulled up next to them but didn't drive past. Alexis looked over and gasped.

It was Deputy Dewayne, and he was motioning for Grandma Windsor to pull her car over.

Busted!

"What is he doing here?" hollered Alexis over the noise of the car's engine.

"Well, I did call the sheriff," said Grandma Windsor. "Maybe he wants to question me." She coasted to the side of the road. When the car stopped, Deputy Dewayne pulled in right behind them, lights still flashing and siren blaring.

Grandma Windsor rolled down her window, and Alexis spun around in her seat to watch the deputy approach. He swaggered up to the car and stood with his hands on his hips. The look on his face reminded Alexis of a starving lion that had just found something to eat.

"Ma'am," said Deputy Dewayne to Grandma Windsor, "do you have any idea how fast you were going back there?"

"I'm sorry, Officer," said Alexis's grandma. She put on her best smile. "I must have gotten carried away. I didn't want the fugitives to get away." Alexis leaned over so she could see Deputy Dewayne's face.

"She's telling the truth, sir," she said. "We were trying to catch up to Dr. Edwards before he gets away with the golden coach."

Deputy Dewayne's eyes narrowed.

"So it's you!" he said. "I should have known!"

"Now Deputy," said Grandma Windsor. "There's no reason to talk to my granddaughter that way." The deputy took off his sunglasses and leaned through the window.

"Now ma'am, you need to understand something," he said.

Alexis wondered why he was suddenly talking to her grandmother like she was a five-year-old. "Every time there's been a disturbance this week, I've found this girl in the middle of things."

Grandma Windsor was still smiling, but Alexis could tell that it was getting harder for her to keep it up.

"I'm sure there have been a few misunderstandings," she said, "but that is not the issue right now. Right now we are trying to keep a thief from—"

"I don't think you are qualified to tell me what is or is not the issue, ma'am," said the deputy.

"Maybe not, but if you would just radio the sheriff, he'll tell you—"

Deputy Dewayne stepped back and yanked the car door open.

"Step out of the car, ma'am," he said. Grandma Windsor's mouth dropped open. Alexis dropped her head into her hands with a sigh.

"Don't fight it, Grandma," she said. "This is a losing battle."

Grandma Windsor huffed in anger and got out of her car. Deputy Dewayne spun her around and pulled out his handcuffs.

"Molly Windsor, you're under arrest for obstruction of justice and failure to comply."

Alexis was about to complain when more sirens filled the air. She turned to see four sheriff's cars blow past them on their way to catch Dr. Edwards. Deputy Dewayne stared after them, stunned. He fumbled with Grandma Windsor's handcuffs and ran toward his car. Alexis had a sudden thought. She had to be with the police when they caught Dr. Edwards. She was the only one here who really knew what was going on. But how was she going to get there? Grandma Windsor couldn't drive with her hands cuffed behind her back, and it would be too far to walk. She glanced at Deputy Dewayne and got an idea.

"Um, you'd better take me with you," she said.

"Why would I do that?" he asked suspiciously.

"Well, you said it yourself—I've been involved in every crazy thing that's happened this week. Don't you think I have something to do with this too?" The deputy opened the passenger door to his car.

"Get in," he said. Alexis smiled at her grandmother as she

jumped in the front seat of the police car. She was about to say something when Deputy Dewayne jumped in the other side and took off, siren blazing—and left Grandma Windsor standing in handcuffs on the side of the road.

Neither of them said a word during the drive. Within five minutes they were pulling up behind a gaggle of red and blue lights that had surrounded a huge semitruck. They were just opening the back end when Alexis and Deputy Dewayne walked up.

Alexis saw that Jerold and Jim were already in handcuffs. Alexis watched two officers lead them into one of the patrol cars in front of the truck. The sheriff was near the golden coach, talking to Dr. Edwards. Alexis edged nearer so she could hear what they were saying.

"I just don't understand it, Doc," said the sheriff. "Why would you steal this thing? What on earth could you do with a replica of a golden coach?"

"Well," said Dr. Edwards, "it's very pretty. Thought it would look good in my garage." He pulled out a handkerchief and blew his nose.

"You expect me to believe that?" said the sheriff. He kept ranting, adding question after question. Dr. Edwards kept answering with one or two words. It was as if he wanted to keep the sheriff talking as long as possible. Alexis got the impression that he was biding time.

"Good, they got him!"

Alexis turned around to see David and Elizabeth standing near her. She looked back and saw Elizabeth's parents wave at her from their car fifty yards behind everyone else.

"How did you know where we were?" Alexis asked.

"When we saw the deputy taking off after your grandma onto the highway, we knew the direction you were going. I called my parents, and they agreed to bring us out."

"So we could be in on the catch!" David said with a big smile.

"Well, *catch* is the right word." Alexis turned to Elizabeth. "Jim and Jerold are up in the front patrol car," she said. Then she explained to David, "Those were the two men who were building the float for Dr. Edwards, the ones we heard talking about the robbery in the alley."

"So what's going on here?" Elizabeth asked, motioning at Dr.

Edwards and the sheriff.

"The sheriff's asking questions, like why the doctor stole the carriage, but Dr. Edwards isn't answering them very quickly. I was just thinking that it's almost like he's stalling," she said. And then she realized why he was stalling.

Every few seconds Dr. Edwards scooted a little bit closer to the carriage. He must have known this was his last chance if he wanted to find the document.

"Wait!" cried Alexis. The sheriff spun around, surprised to see her. Dr. Edwards noticed her and gasped. She had never seen his ancient face look so angry.

"Little miss," said the sheriff, "what are you doing here?"

"My grandma was the one who called and told you about the theft," Alexis said. "But it's not really about the carriage at all, is it, Dr. Edwards?" The old professor wiped his nose again.

"Of course it is," he sniveled. "I have no idea what you're talking about, little girl."

Alexis turned toward the sheriff.

"Sir," she said, "Dr. Edwards believes that there is a priceless letter hidden somewhere in the carriage. He came to Lake Havasu City so he could look for it, but when he couldn't find it, he decided to steal the whole carriage instead."

"Is this true?" asked the sheriff, turning toward Dr. Edwards.

Dr. Edwards's lips tightened into a flat line. He was obviously trying not to say anything. When there was no answer, the sheriff turned to Alexis again.

"This is an interesting story," he said. "But there's no evidence that it's true. We've still got him on the theft charge, though."

He turned back to Dr. Edwards, as Elizabeth nudged Alexis and showed her something on the cell phone.

Alexis read the words that were texted there and looked up at Elizabeth in amazement. Elizabeth grinned and nodded.

"Sir," said Alexis, touching the sheriff on the elbow. "I know where the letter is hidden—at least I think I do."

Dr. Edwards smirked. "Little girl, I have been searching this carriage for years—visited London Bridge Resort every vacation. There's no way *you* would have been able to find the document after four days in town!"

Alexis ignored him. "May I?" she asked the sheriff.

"Be my guest," he said. Alexis climbed up into the back of the trailer and made her way toward the front of the carriage. A golden wave of water hid the driver's seat from view. When she was level with the seat—where Dr. Edwards had been only this morning—she turned and spoke to the crowd of curious police.

"There's a story that the princess Amelia, King George the Third's youngest daughter, hid a letter for the man she loved in her father's coach. Dr. Edwards was probably looking throughout the inside of the coach, since that's where the princess would have sat, but one of our other mystery-solving friends who loves horses, McKenzie, thought of somewhere else to look. The man the princess loved worked with the horses. In that case she probably would have hidden the note where he would have found it while harnessing them to the carriage."

Alexis grabbed the golden post that was meant to hold the horses and slid her hand into the hollow end. She pulled out a thin box and opened it. The hinges creaked in the silence.

And there it was—a small, folded package, yellowed with age.

"'For the Son of Man came to seek and to save the lost,'" Elizabeth murmured. "Luke 19:10 doesn't quite fit the situation, but I think God must have nudged McKenzie's brain!"

"No!" hollered Dr. Edwards. "That's mine! Mine by right!"

"How do you figure that, Doc?" asked the sheriff. "And what on earth is a priceless letter doing here, in Lake Havasu City? Shouldn't it be in the real coach in Britain?"

"I did all the research decades ago, while I was in college," said Dr. Edwards. He spoke to the sheriff, but he was glaring at Alexis.

"I finally figured that the letter was probably in the carriage," he continued, "so I wrote to the royal family and got permission to search it from the queen herself. But before I could save the money to go back to Britain, my professor stole my permission letters and went himself. He found the letter, but he told me he had hidden it from the royal family so he could keep it for himself. He died in a train accident on his way to Southern California, and it took me fifty years to figure out that he'd hidden it in the carriage. So you see? I did all the work! It's rightfully mine!"

The sheriff smiled sadly.

"It's a sad story, Doc," he said. "And I wish I could take your side, but the truth is that you committed a crime when you stole the replica. Why didn't you just ask permission to search the carriage? We could have helped you take it apart if need be."

Dr. Edwards looked crestfallen. Alexis felt bad for him, but the sheriff was right. Dr. Edwards had committed a crime, and they couldn't reward him by giving him the letter now. Another deputy handcuffed the doctor and led him toward another car with flashing lights.

"I guess we'd better figure out what to do with this," said the sheriff. He stepped forward and reached into the box that Alexis was still holding.

"Stop! Don't touch anything!"

Everyone spun around to see Grandma Windsor leap out of yet another police car. Her wrists had been freed from the cuffs, and she strode toward the back of the truck trailer with purpose, her costume dress flapping behind her.

"You can't just go and grab a two-hundred-and-fifty-year-old document like it was a letter from your mother!" she yelled at the sheriff. The man smiled and stepped back.

"Of course, Professor Windsor. I'm glad you're here. Would you mind helping us out with this?"

"Not at all," Grandma Windsor said with a smile. She slipped a white glove onto her hand and reached into the compartment. She lifted the letter out with a flat hand and slipped it into a large plastic Ziploc bag. "It's not perfect, but it will do," she said.

●—●—●

The next morning Alexis was sad because it would be her last day in Lake Havasu City. At least for now. David and Elizabeth met her in the hotel lobby after breakfast. David was carrying three neon-colored rubber duckies.

"What are those for, David?" asked Alexis as he handed her a pink one. He gave the purple one to Elizabeth and kept the green one for himself.

"You'll see," he said. "Follow me!"

They left the hotel and made their way toward the bridge. Alexis noticed quite a crowd gathering along the railings.

For a moment she was afraid that something was wrong, but then she realized the people were smiling.

"What's all the commotion?" she asked. "I thought the festival was over."

"Not quite!" said David. "We close it out with the duck race!"

Alexis looked at the bridge again and saw that everyone at the railings had a rubber ducky in their hands. They were passing the sheriff's department when Elizabeth grabbed Alexis's arm.

"Look! Wonder where they're taking Jim and Jerold?" she said.

Alexis looked across the street. Two police officers were putting Jim and Jerold into the back of a police car.

"Hey!" said David. "That's the engineer I told you about! The one who wanted the stones from the bridge!" He was pointing to Jim.

"It doesn't surprise me," said Alexis. "Those two were helping Dr. Edwards, but I don't imagine that's the only shady deal they were involved in. I wonder what they wanted them for, if not to destroy the bridge or ruin the race."

"Bet I know what they wanted the stones for," Elizabeth said. "I updated the girls last night on what was going on. Awhile ago Kate texted me that she'd done a search on London Bridge artifacts and found someone selling stones from the London Bridge on several internet auction sites."

"You mean like eBay?" David asked.

"Well, I'm not sure if it was eBay, but there are a lot of sites out there like that now," Elizabeth said. "One of the sites she saw them on that requires a selling location listed Lake Havasu City. And the sellers' names were words like Jerold, and J and J Auctions."

"We'll have to tell Grandma so she can let the sheriff know. Then he can look into it," Alexis said.

"Has your grandma found out what's going to happen to the letter from Princess Amelia?" Elizabeth asked.

"Yes, she called the British Museum, and they are super-excited about finally having the letter. They even offered to let Lake Havasu City borrow it each year during the festival," Alexis explained.

Elizabeth looked at David and frowned. "You know there's one other thing I don't get. If it was you making the crack in the bridge, then what was the thing with the old hag cursing the bridge?"

"I know which woman you mean," David said. "That one dressed up to be really ugly? I heard her saying something about the bridge."

"Do you mean Meghan?" Suddenly the young teens realized that Grandma Windsor had joined them. "Are you talking about my friend Meghan?" she asked, linking arms with Alexis.

"I don't know. She was some old lady who looked like she stepped out of the movie *The Princess Bride*," Alexis explained.

"Oh yes, that's Meghan!" Grandma exclaimed. "She's actually not old. She's quite young. She's a drama student who likes to come to the festival dressed up as an old woman. She seems to have a talent for that kind of voice and for living in character. She's great at curses."

"Grandma!" Alexis exclaimed.

"Well, not real curses, silly. They're all make-believe," Grandma said. "She is convincing, isn't she? If she can't make it as an actress, I'm sure she has a future as a makeup artist."

"But she left a message for us," Elizabeth said. "And why would she run away from us if she was your friend?"

"Well, that's just it, dears," Grandma Windsor explained. "I had told her about this fabulous Camp Club Girls you have and all the mysteries you solve. I'm quite proud, you know. She was so afraid you'd be bored that she said she was going to try to stir up a bit of a mystery for you. Secret messages, anyway. She thought it would just be a spot of fun for you."

"You mean you knew all along?" Alexis asked.

"Oh yes, dear. I meant to tell you about it before you thought there was a real mystery there, but it seems like you found your own mysteries to solve without Meghan's help. I think she had a few more messages planned, but she had to leave town and go back to where she normally lives—Tucson, I think. Her mother got ill and needed her," Grandma Windsor said. "Now Alexis, I need to scoot for a few minutes. I'm on my way to the sheriff's office. Have to see him about that silly ticket his silly deputy gave me. I'll see you at the hotel in a bit."

Grandma Windsor trotted off.

"Well, at least that answers that!" said Elizabeth. "Oh, you know, I decided I'm going to talk to Mr. Bill about buying that spoon with Princess Amelia on it. Mom gave me some money this morning. Alexis, I guess I'm as much of a romantic at heart as you are. I'm going to run and get it and will meet you at the bridge in about ten minutes. Here, hold my ducky for me, will you?" she said as she thrust the purple duck in Alexis's hand.

"So you're a romantic at heart, hmm?" David asked, with a tender smile on his face.

Alexis blushed and shrugged.

"So any chance your grandma will be back in Lake Havasu?" asked David. "Maybe this winter?"

"I don't think so," she said.

"Oh," said David. "I just know some old people like to come to Arizona in the winter. I mean, not like she's old!"

Alexis laughed.

"No, she's not really old," she said. "And I think she's coming to visit us for the holidays. Dad mentioned a trip up to Tahoe, but I don't think I'll be back down here anytime soon."

"Do you have an email address then?" asked David.

"Better than that," said Alexis. "The Camp Club Girls have a website!"

"The *what*?"

"It's a long story," said Alexis. She and David walked to the bridge while she explained to him about the Camp Club Girls and their mysteries. Then Elizabeth joined them, and all three leaned over the railing of the bridge and dropped their ducks into the water.

Alexis didn't know if it was because she had solved two cases, because she was with such good friends, or because God had just erased her fears. But for some reason, she wasn't scared of the bridge anymore.

Camp Club Girls:
Alexis and the Lake Tahoe Tumult

CHAPTER 1

Cat's Out of the Bag

"Only about twenty more minutes to the hotel!" said Mr. Howell. Alexis's dad hummed as he guided their rented car up the winding road that would take them to Lake Tahoe.

The flat, icy landscape scattered with sagebrush had turned into snowy peaks. As Alexis gazed at them, her imagination started to go wild. She decided the snowy peaks reached into the bright blue sky like the jagged teeth of a crocodile—like the crocodiles she'd seen in a documentary on the Discovery Channel earlier in the month.

And, of course, her thoughts of documentaries and the Discovery Channel made her think of the real purpose she and her friend Bailey, a fellow Camp Club Girl, had for going to Lake Tahoe with Alexis's mom and dad and twin brothers.

"Hey, Dad?" Alexis called. "Can we go straight to the animal reserve?"

"I don't see why not," Mr. Howell said. "It's too late to ski today, anyway. I'll drop your mom and brothers off at the hotel. They can check in and hang out while I drive you out there. We'll be back by dinner."

Alexis yawned and closed her eyes. She thought again about those big teeth on the crocodiles.

Suddenly the car began to swerve and shake as if those crocodile teeth had gotten hold of the Howells' car.

"What's going on?" asked Mrs. Howell.

"Not sure!" said Mr. Howell. He was struggling to keep his

hands on the steering wheel. Alexis looked out the window and realized that the car wasn't all that was shaking.

"Dad, is this an earthquake?" she asked.

Mr. Howell didn't answer. He was focused on dodging the rocks that had begun rolling down the hill above them.

But almost as suddenly as the bouncing of the earth had begun, it stopped. Within a matter of minutes, the car was driving smoothly again.

"What a way to start a vacation, huh?" Mr. Howell laughed nervously. "I think that *was* a small earthquake."

Alexis turned to Bailey, but her fellow Camp Club Girl was fast asleep, face pressed against the window. The breath from her gaping mouth was fogging the glass. Alexis peeked into the back of the van where her little brothers were also sleeping.

There was no way Alexis could have slept, even before the earthquake. She was too excited about her documentary.

The owners at the Tahoe Animal Reserve and Rescue at Lake Tahoe had agreed to let her tour and film their facilities. Her video would be about remembering nature in the middle of our world full of cement and SUVs.

She was planning to enter the video in a contest for young amateur filmmakers. The winner of the contest would not only see the film shown on the Discovery Channel but would also receive scholarship money. And knowing how much her mother's youngest sister was still paying on loans she'd taken out for college, Alexis knew it was never too early to start saving money for college!

So even though she was only twelve, Alex, as most of her friends called her, was going to get started. She loved movies. She knew when she grew up, she wanted to work with films in some way, perhaps as a director. She'd lived in Sacramento all her life and knew of several good colleges that offered classes to prepare students for the film industry.

Since she loved to operate a camera, Alexis was very excited to enter the contest.

And what better place to record nature than in Lake Tahoe? From the time pioneers had discovered the lake in 1844, it had been a tourist attraction. People from all around the world visited the area to enjoy its beauty.

The lake sat in a bowl of earth surrounded by mountains and pine trees on every side. Tahoe was the world's third clearest lake. Alexis had been waterskiing here before, and she remembered how she could see the bottom in places that were over one hundred feet deep. The lake was on the border of Nevada and California, with half of the lake in each state and the border running from north to south.

No matter which side of the lake you were on—the California side or the Nevada side—the lake was lined with plenty of resorts, vacation homes, and convention centers. In the winter, the area was also a popular place to ski and snowboard. Olympic medal winners had even been known to practice there.

Alexis had even seen these award winners practicing the last time she'd been at Lake Tahoe. Her dad attended conventions once or twice a year at the lake. And whenever they could, the whole Howell family accompanied him. They enjoyed the activities while Mr. Howell went to his business meetings.

Alexis recognized the landscape and held her breath for her favorite part of the drive. One last corner, and there it was. The view before them was a wonderful panorama. The brilliant lake shone in the sunlight like a perfectly smooth sapphire. The sight made Alexis gasp, even though she'd expected it. Suddenly the view was gone, replaced by walls and darkness.

Beep! Beep! Beep-Beep! Alexis's dad honked the horn.

"What's wrong?" Bailey jerked out of her slumber. "Are we falling off the cliff, Lexi?"

"Lexi? I'm Lexi now?" Alex asked with a smile. Bailey was well known for the nicknames she gave others.

Bailey didn't answer. She just grabbed Alexis's coat in fear. She frantically looked around. "It's dark!"

"No, Bailey! We're not falling off the cliff. We're passing through Cave Rock. It's a tunnel that has been around forever."

"Well, why was your dad honking the car horn?" asked Bailey, still a little dazed. "Scared me to death!"

"Sorry about that," said Alexis. "My dad honks every time we go through a tunnel. This wasn't bad because the tunnel was short.

You should have seen this one time! We were on the East Coast, and we went through this tunnel that was about a mile long. Dad honked *all the way through!* Doesn't your dad honk the car horn when you go through tunnels?"

"You really need to come to the center of the nation," Bailey answered. "Where I live, we're in the middle of the United States. The land is pretty flat there."

"Flat? You mean like the desert?"

"Well, we have hills and stuff. But we don't have mountains—especially not with tunnels," Bailey explained. "You have to go up to Wisconsin to see the bigger hills and huge rocks. They might have tunnels up there. I don't know."

Bailey lived near the middle of the state of Illinois, outside a city named Peoria. She was also still a preteen and the youngest of the group who called themselves the Camp Club Girls. The girls had all met when they shared a cabin at Lake Discovery Camp. They had become the best of friends as they solved a mystery together. And since then, the Camp Club Girls had continued to solve mysteries—mysteries that had baffled many adults!

As they drove into the resort area of Lake Tahoe, Alexis pointed out the hotel and convention center where they'd be staying. "It's called a hotel, but it's really a resort," she said.

"What's the difference?" Bailey asked.

"I'm not sure," said Alex. "I think resorts have more activities going on, and this place has a ski run and all sorts of fun stuff.

"And we can also enjoy any of the activities in town. They have a great transportation system—it's a cute little shuttle bus that has places to get on and off it. So we can explore the whole city if we want," Alex explained.

In no time they had dropped off Mrs. Howell and the twins at the hotel. The girls waited in the car while Alexis's dad checked in Mrs. Howell and the boys and helped them get their luggage to the room. Then he returned to the van.

"Chauffeur's back," Mr. Howell announced cheerfully as he climbed into the driver's seat. "Next stop: Tahoe Animal Reserve."

Bailey and Alexis had their eyes wide open, trying to take in all the sights as Mr. Howell drove through town and out into land that was still on the brim of the lake, but not as filled with resorts.

In only moments they were pulling up a long, snowy driveway to the animal reserve. A large wooden sign topped with snow read TAHOE ANIMAL RESERVE AND RESCUE. Mr. Howell parked in front of a small cabin that was painted a light shade of moss green. There was more than a foot of snow piled on the roof.

"I guess this is it!" said Mr. Howell. He got out of the car and immediately slid, nearly falling to the ground.

"Ouch!" he called. "Watch out for the ice!"

Just then the front door to the cabin opened, and a lady in a parka came running out.

"I'm so sorry!" she said. "I must have forgotten to put the salt out this morning!"

"Salt?" Bailey asked Alexis. She shut her door gently, trying to keep her footing. "Did I miss something?"

"Salt melts ice," said Alexis. "Something to do with lowering the freezing point of water."

"Very good!" said the woman. She reached down to help Alexis and Bailey up the steps. "You're a smart one! You must be the documentary girls."

"That's us!" said Bailey. "Are you ready to be famous? If we win, our video will be on the Discovery Channel!"

"That would be fabulous! I'm Karen Ingles. My husband and I own the reserve." Karen Ingles reached out to shake Mr. Howell's hand and then the girls' hands. "Come on in, you three! I'll show you around, and you can tell me more about your video."

The inside of the cabin was very cozy. Alexis noticed that it looked to be half house and half office. A roaring fire filled a beautiful stone fireplace. A few old couches were near the fire, and Alexis felt it would not just be a comfortable place to sit but would be a great location to film an interview or two. Looking toward the side of the cabin, Alexis could see a small kitchen and a large desk with papers strewn all over it. A door behind the desk led deeper into the cabin. Karen hung her parka on a coatrack and told the rest of them to do the same.

"Thank you so much for allowing us to do this, Mrs. Ingles," said Alexis.

"Please, Karen is fine. And don't mention it. We don't usually give tours, let alone allow people to film our animals, but your email was so wonderful that I couldn't refuse. I could tell you two girls really cared about the animals, and it's a chance for college scholarships too! Besides, you made me laugh."

Alexis smiled and was about to say something when her father yelped.

The girls spun around to see Mr. Howell jump up on the couch. He was shaking and pointing to something on the floor.

There, curled up on a rug in front of the fire, was a full-grown bobcat!

"Don't worry, sir," said Karen. "That's only Bubbles. He's kind of a pet."

Bubbles opened his eyes and lifted his nose in the air, sniffing.

"Dad, get off the couch!" said Alexis, embarrassed. "I don't think he's going to hurt you. Besides, you do know that bobcats can jump, right? The couch won't do you much good."

Everyone laughed. Mr. Howell even chuckled nervously as he stepped down off the striped cushion.

"Why do Bubbles's eyes look strange?" asked Bailey. She had crept closer and was sitting on the stone of the fireplace, only feet from the large cat.

"He's blind," said Karen. "That's the only reason he's kept as a pet. The vet couldn't fix his sight, so he'll never be released into the wild again. He'd die out there, so we let him stay here."

"That's so cool!" said Bailey. "I want a bobcat!"

"Well, some people do keep them as pets, but it's dangerous. They are wild, no matter how sweet and fluffy they look. See Bubbles's poufy paws? The claws in them are three inches long and could cut your throat in seconds."

Bailey backed slowly away and coughed.

"Oh, don't worry," said Karen. "He won't hurt you. We've had him for years. But that is something you need to remember while you're around the other animals in our sanctuary. No matter how cute they are, they're wild. They will react according to their instincts, no matter what your intentions are. Things like bats and raccoons can give you rabies not to mention nasty scars. The owls' talons aren't very friendly either. If you're going to do this documentary, you have to remember to follow our rules, and never—*never*—approach any animal without us. Got it?"

"Yes, ma'am!" said Alexis. Bailey nodded her head so fast Alexis thought it might pop off. Alexis dug her little pink notebook out of her backpack. She wanted to write down the rules Karen gave her as well as any information that might be great for the documentary.

Bang! Suddenly the door behind the desk burst open. A tall man in a flannel shirt stumbled into the room, his eyes bulging.

"Karen! The deal's off! Call those kids, and tell them that they can't film here! The mountain lions are out of their cages!"

Mischief and Mystery

It was obvious from the look on the man's face that he hadn't known the girls were there. He glanced around frantically.

"It's okay, Jake," said Karen. "Let's go get those cats back in their cages!" The two owners turned and ran out a back door.

"Wait!" said Alexis. "We can help!"

"What?" shouted Bailey, glancing at Bubbles nervously. "Didn't you hear? They said *mountain lions*!"

"I know! Come on!"

Before her father could stop her, Alexis followed Karen and Jake out the back door. Bailey was just behind. They followed a trail in the snow to a small barn structure not far away. Alexis reached out to open the door, but her father's large hand pushed it shut again.

"Dad!"

"Listen first, then open," said Mr. Howell. "The last thing we want to do is let a sick mountain lion out of this barn."

Alexis was shocked. She thought for sure he was going to keep her from going in.

She and Bailey crept closer and put their ears against a small crack in the wood. They only heard the tramping of heavy boots and Jake's and Karen's panicked voices.

"Get that one! He's by your elbow!"

"No! Ow! The other one! She's too high up. You're going to have to get the ladder!"

But Alexis couldn't figure something out. She couldn't hear the mountain lions at all. Bailey seemed to be thinking the same thing.

"What? No ripping of claws? No earth-shattering roars?" she asked. Alexis shrugged and pushed the door open enough for the three of them to slide through. Just as she entered, something landed on her head and leaped ten feet to the top of one of the cages. It looked like a ball of fur with a tail.

There were six of them, and they were everywhere.

"They're kittens!" cried Bailey. "How cute! Come here, kitty, kitty. Come here."

Another ball of fluff tore by them, snagging Bailey's shoelace with a tiny, sharp claw.

"Oops. I forgot they had those things," said Bailey.

Alexis watched as Karen and Jake chased the litter of mountain lion cubs around and around the barn. They managed to get one back in the cage, but when they opened it again to put in another one, the first one escaped.

"It's useless!" cried Karen. "We'll be doing this all day!"

Another cub leaped from a rafter onto Alexis's head. This time it tried to stay put, but it was too heavy and slid to the floor instead.

"Ouch!" Alexis cried. "What's the deal?"

Bailey, who was reaching behind a barrel for one of the cubs, looked around.

"Lexi!" she cried. "It's your hat! The kittens like your hat!"

She was right! Alexis had forgotten about her hat. She had picked it out especially for this trip. It was a cozy striped winter hat with a huge fluff-ball pom-pom attached to a string at the top. Of course the lions would like it! The way the pom-pom bobbed, it looked like a huge cat toy!

Alexis studied the cage. She thought she could get the kittens in with her big pom-pom hat. If she walked in the cage, they would probably bound after her to get the fuzzy cap. But she couldn't figure out how she'd get out again without releasing them.

The cages in this barn were for larger animals. They were made of simple chain-link fencing—something Alexis could easily reach her arm through. Before anyone noticed, Alexis was climbing up the side of the mountain lion cage.

"What are you doing, Alexis?" asked her dad. He was following

Jake around the barn trying to help. Instead, he ran into Jake every time he stopped, causing him to miss a kitten more than once.

"Don't worry, Dad! I think I have an idea!" Alexis reached the top of the cage and crawled carefully to one of the back corners. Then she took her hat off and shoved it through the chain link into the cage. She held it by the rim, allowing the huge fluff ball to dangle and swing.

"Here, kitty, kitty!" she called. It didn't work. The mountain lion cubs were way too interested in terrorizing the rest of the barn. "Bailey, help me! Get their attention!"

"Okay!" Bailey picked up a broom and ran over to the lion cage. She began running the handle along the metal, making a huge ruckus.

"Come on, kitties! Over here! Come on, kitties!"

The cats started noticing the noise and looked toward the dangling hat. Then, as if by some secret command, all six of them charged toward Bailey as fast as they could.

"*Ahhh!* Yikes!" Bailey screeched and lurched out of the way. "Lexi, it's working! Here they come!"

"Wait, Bailey!" said Alexis. "You have to open the door. They can't get in."

"Oh, right," said Bailey. She ran back over to the cage and struggled to open it against the tide of fluff and claws. Once it was cracked wide enough, the kittens pushed their way in. They dashed to the dangling hat and leaped, one after another, into the air. Their tiny paws reached over and over for Alexis's hat, but she pulled it out of reach every time.

"Are they all in?" Alexis called to Karen. Karen counted out loud.

"Yes! They are. Close the door!"

Bailey slammed the door, and Jake rushed to lock it before the kittens could run out again.

Alexis yanked her hat back through the cage and climbed carefully down. The ordeal was over with only one minor casualty: Alexis had lost one long piece of red yarn from her hat, and all six of the mountain lion cubs fought for it.

"Wow, that was great!" said Karen. "Thanks for your help, girls!"

Mr. Howell was still trying to detangle himself from a stack of buckets he had knocked over.

"Yeah," said Jake, pointing to Alexis's hat. "I guess I need to get one of those."

"Does this happen often?" asked Bailey.

"Well, it's not supposed to," said Karen.

"And it never used to," said Jake.

Alexis pushed her hat back onto her head and straightened it. "What do you mean, it never *used to*?" she asked.

"Come back to the office, and we'll tell you all about it," said Karen. She led the guests back through the snow and toward the cozy office.

"What's this?" Bailey asked. She stooped and dug something out of the snow. It was a small key ring with a few tiny golden keys on it.

"That's funny," Karen said. "I could have sworn those were in the office. Thanks!"

She took the keys and opened the office door.

"Looks like we need more firewood," said Jake, looking at the dying fire.

"I can help you get it," said Mr. Howell. Jake stepped right back out the door, looking scared.

"No, no, that's all right. Why don't you pour yourself some coffee over there?"

Mr. Howell fixed himself a cup of coffee. He brought the girls some hot cocoa too as well as a plate of doughnuts. Soon they were all circled around the living room fire. They could hear Jake splitting a few larger logs just outside.

"This has happened a lot lately," said Karen. She stirred some more sugar into her coffee and tasted it.

"What has?" Alexis asked. "The mountain lions getting out?"

"Well, yes and no. They *do* keep getting out, but other things are happening too. Animals are getting loose when they shouldn't. But others have gotten sick or started acting strangely. One or two have escaped altogether, and that's a nightmare. In weather like this, there are very few animals that can survive. If they're not healthy or fully grown, they really don't stand a chance."

"So this is new?" Bailey asked, with her mouth full of doughnut. She swallowed, wiped frosting from her lips, and tried again. "I mean, it's never happened before?"

"No, not until recently," said Karen. "Jake's mom and dad owned this place long before we came along. It's been in the family forever, and nothing like this has ever happened. Jake feels like he's failing and is afraid we'll lose the family business. He just can't figure out what's going wrong."

Jake came back through the door and dropped a pile of wood in a box near the fireplace. Bubbles the bobcat jumped up and glared at Jake through his misty eyes before moving to the other side of the rug.

"So you see," Jake said, "it's like I said before we ran to the barn. You girls can't do your documentary here. It's just too dangerous. We never know when this stuff is going to happen. This time it was the cute little guys, but what if it's something bigger and more dangerous next time?"

Karen sighed. "That's why we don't give tours. If a visitor got hurt by a sick animal, that would be awful. We could get into a lot of trouble, not to mention the fact that we would feel horrible."

Alexis was heartbroken. They couldn't be serious, could they? She loved snowboarding, but she had really come here to do this documentary. Where else could she find a place like this reserve? This was the only one of its kind in all of California. And this was the only spring break she would get. She wouldn't have time to shoot the video after school started again next week.

"But we're not just anyone!" said Bailey. Alexis looked at her friend and smiled. She could tell that Bailey would not take no for an answer. "I mean, we helped you catch the baby mountain lions, right? And no one got hurt. We're really smart, and we're always careful! We've done all kinds of things that other kids haven't, right, Lexi? Our club has solved all kinds of real mysteries, and if this isn't a mystery, then I don't know what is."

"What club is that?" Karen asked, sipping her coffee.

"The Camp Club Girls," Bailey explained. "We all met at Discovery Camp and solved a mystery there. Since then we've solved several mysteries together."

"Oh, so you all live in the Sacramento area?" Karen asked.

"No," Alexis said. "Only I live in California. The other girls live in different places in the United States—Montana; Washington, DC; Texas; Philadelphia—and Bailey here is from Peoria, Illinois."

Jake ran his thick hands through his hair and sighed.

"Sorry, kids. First of all, this isn't a mystery. It's just a case of too many mistakes made by *me*."

"That's not fair, Jake," said Karen. "We've been running things as usual. Name one mistake you have actually made."

Jake just stood, frowning.

"That's because you're not making mistakes," said Karen. "Ever since this started, we've been even more careful!"

"But if it's not a mistake, Karen, what is it?"

"It's a mystery," said Mr. Howell. "It sounds like you *do* have a mystery on your hands."

Jake crossed his arms. "Prove it," he said jokingly.

"Okay," said Alexis, jumping to the challenge. "First of all, how did those cubs get out this morning? Who opened the cage last?"

"I did," said Karen. "This morning when I fed them, I opened it to check on Tiny Tim. He's the runt of the litter, and I had to make sure the others didn't take his share."

"Okay, so can you remember everything you did, step-by-step?" asked Bailey.

"Of course. I waited for Tiny Tim to finish eating, and then I left, locking the door behind me. Then I brought the keys inside and hung them on the rack. I remember I locked it because I had to try three keys before I found the right one. They all look the same."

"Little and gold?" asked Bailey. "Were they the keys I found outside in the snow?"

"As a matter of fact, they were," said Jake, puzzled. "I saw you put the keys on the rack this morning, Karen. How'd they get outside again?"

"You see?" said Alexis. "It's a mystery. You both know the keys got put away this morning, and you're sure the door was locked. The door was *open* when we went into the barn, which means *someone* must have taken the keys out of the office and opened the cage."

"But that's impossible!" said Jake. "We've been in here all morning!"

"No," said Karen.

"What?" Jake asked, puzzled.

"No, we haven't. We both left to pick up Lisa from the bus stop this morning. We were gone for about fifteen minutes." She turned to the girls. "Lisa is our daughter. She's out right now, but you'll love her, I'm sure."

Jake and Karen stared at each other wide-eyed. Could someone have broken into their beloved reserve and let these animals out on purpose?

"So you see, this *is* a mystery," said Bailey.

"And we can help you solve it while we do our documentary," said Alexis. "Maybe we'll catch something on tape that will help us figure out what's going on."

The girls looked sweetly up at the two reserve owners. Their big eyes pleaded for the chance to do their video and solve a mystery at the same time.

"Okay," said Jake. "But you won't be allowed to go anywhere on the reserve alone. One of us, or Lisa, will be with you at all times for your safety. If at any time things get too dangerous, we will pull the plug on the project. Sound fair to you?"

"Yes!" chimed both girls at once.

"And you're okay with this, Mr. Howell?" Karen asked.

"Yep," he said. "As long as they're supervised. Alexis almost got eaten by a T. rex last summer, so I'm sure she can handle some sick animals." Jake and Karen looked puzzled. Mr. Howell winked. "It's a good story. You should ask her about it sometime."

Threatening News

"I hope we can do all of this, Lexi," said Bailey.

She followed Alexis through the breakfast-buffet line, stopping every few feet to make sure she wasn't about to drop their camera bag. It was just a little too heavy for her. But Alexis didn't notice. She just kept piling cream cheese on her bagel.

"All of what?" she asked.

"I mean, I hope we can shoot this documentary *and* solve a mystery," Bailey said, the camera bag slipping off her shoulder. "We're only here for a few days, you know."

"It's almost a whole week," Alexis said, putting the top back onto her bagel. "Besides, we're the Camp Club Girls! Or have you forgotten? We can solve things like this in our sleep."

Bailey smiled and pushed the camera bag back on her shoulder. Then she dumped milk onto her bowl of fruity cereal.

"I guess you're right," she said. "Hey, there's a table open by the fireplace!"

The girls gingerly stepped around the other tables and chairs in the room to a knobby wooden table in front of a huge stone hearth. The hotel they were staying in was amazing. It was massive, but it still felt warm and inviting.

Bailey set down her food tray and gasped.

"Oh no! Where's the camera?" She spun around to see if she had dropped it.

"Ouch!" someone behind her cried out.

Bailey turned and realized that she had hit the boy at the next

211

table with the camera bag. It had been on her shoulder the whole time.

"I'm so sorry!" she said, turning to the boy. He looked a little bit younger than Alexis.

"Everyone's always sorry!" exclaimed the boy. "Why don't people try watching what they're doing and where they're going? Then they wouldn't have to be sorry all the time!"

"Um, well, we are really sorry," said Alexis. She was now standing beside Bailey looking down at the boy, who was still rubbing a spot on his head. "My friend was just worried. She thought she might have lost—"

"I really don't care what she thought she lost," the boy said, facing Alexis. "She just needs to watch where she's swinging her stuff."

He got up and stormed off, taking his tray to the other side of the dining room.

Alexis turned around and saw tears in Bailey's eyes.

"It's okay, small fry," Alexis said. "Some people can't help but spread their bad moods."

"I really didn't mean to hit him, Lexi," said Bailey. "I was thinking about the camera, and I didn't realize he was sitting so close to our table."

"Don't worry about it," said Alexis. "Let's eat. We have a bus to catch, remember?"

After breakfast Alexis and Bailey waited outside the hotel for the bus that would take them across town. They were supposed to get off at a little convenience store and ice cream parlor that was near the reserve. Then Lisa, Karen and Jake's daughter, would meet them and drive them the rest of the way. She was home for spring break too—only she was taking a break from college.

On the bus ride over, Alexis and Bailey went through their recording equipment. They had a digital video camera and enough disks to record hours upon hours of footage. Alexis had also borrowed an external microphone from her drama teacher at school. It would help them pick up voices and sounds from farther away. This could really come in handy when they recorded animals from a distance.

When the girls got to their stop, Lisa was already waiting for them on the porch of the store.

"You must be the documentary girls," she said. She shook their hands. She was wearing thick skiing mittens. A hat that matched her mittens covered most of her long, brown French braid.

"That's us!" said Alexis. "This is Bailey, and I'm Alexis."

"It's good to meet you," said Lisa. She led them to a red Jeep that was still running in the nearby parking lot. It was toasty when the girls climbed in. "So my parents told me about the kitties escaping yesterday and your help in getting them back in the cage. I hear you two think these things aren't just accidents, that something fishy is going on up at the reserve?"

Alexis was nervous. Would Lisa laugh at them? Did she think it was silly that two girls wanted to investigate what was going on at her parents' place? She was in college, after all. She was probably really smart.

"Yep!" Bailey answered before Alexis could get the right words together in her mind. "Something *very* fishy is going on up there. I mean, animals just don't unlock their cages by themselves, do they?"

"No," Lisa said, pulling away from the store parking lot onto the main road. "I guess they don't."

"And your parents have run this reserve for years without problems, right?" Alexis asked. "So if they haven't changed the way they do things, then there is no logical reason for things to be falling apart."

Alexis couldn't quite bring herself to look at Lisa. She was sure the girl was about to laugh at them.

"I couldn't agree with you more," said Lisa.

"Really?" cried Alexis.

"Of course. I've been telling my mom for a while that something's not quite right. I hope you two can help. I would love to, but I've been away at school. And even if I were here, I wouldn't know where to start an investigation!"

"Well you're in luck!" said Bailey. "That's what we do!"

"My mom and dad told me about your success with solving mysteries," Lisa said as she turned the car around a corner. "I went on the internet last night and read about how you solved the problems at that dinosaur park. I hear you've helped with other adventures too."

"Yes, a bunch of them!" Bailey exclaimed. "We helped find a missing millionaire. Lexi helped rescue some sea lions. Our Camp Club Girls group of sleuths also solved a problem with sabotage in Wisconsin, a plot to harm the president in Maryland, a mystery with horses, and bad stuff going on at the London Bridge in Arizona. We even found lost jewels in Amarillo, at the Cadillac Ranch!"

"Hey, I've been there," Lisa said.

"All six of us Camp Club Girls always work together to figure out the mysteries," Bailey said.

Lisa drove up the driveway to the reserve, but she passed the small cabin where the girls had met Jake and Karen the day before. Instead, she kept driving around a few barns until she stopped at one of the smaller ones in the back.

"What's this building?" asked Alexis.

"This is the building where we start your documentary!" said Lisa. She jumped out of the Jeep and trotted off through the snow. "C'mon! Follow me!"

Bailey grabbed the video equipment off the seat next to her and followed Alexis out of the car. The snow was knee deep, and Bailey had a hard time keeping up with the two taller and older girls.

"You want me to carry something else?" called Alexis.

"No thanks!" said Bailey. "I'm almost there!"

Lisa was waiting for them at the door to the barn. When they got close, she put her finger to her lips to signal them to be quiet. She opened the door and ushered Alexis and Bailey inside.

The room was dark, and the only noises were a small series of squeaks coming from the farthest corner of the barn. Lisa flipped a light switch, and a few lightbulbs flickered to life above their heads. The barn was warmer than Alexis had expected it to be.

There must be heaters in here, she thought.

Lisa peeled off her coat, and Alexis and Bailey did the same. After hanging them on pegs near the door, Alexis and Bailey walked quietly over to the corner where Lisa was. It was the same corner the squeaks were coming from.

"What are those things?" asked Bailey. "Baby mice?"

Tiny brown bodies huddled together in the bottom of the cage. The only body parts Alexis could really see in the pile of fluff were a bunch of round, pink ears. Maybe Bailey was right. They sure did look like mice.

"No, they're not mice." Lisa laughed. "They're baby bats."

"What?" whispered Alexis.

"That's so cool!" Bailey said.

"Yeah," said Lisa. "We've been taking care of these for a while now. Eventually, when it gets warmer and they get bigger, we'll be able to let them go. But right now they don't have any parents, so they don't have a way to get food."

Lisa opened the cage and took out one of the little creatures.

"Wait!" said Alexis. "Let me get out the camera!" She took the bag from Bailey's shoulder and pulled out the camera. It was fully charged and had a new disk in it already. "Ready, Bailey?"

"Ready!" Bailey said. They had decided that Alexis would run the camera and that Bailey would do most of the on-camera work. Alexis loved movies and usually did her own commentaries when filming. But she knew how much Bailey longed to be a star. She knew that giving the younger girl the turn in front of the camera would be a gift that would make Bailey happy. And since Bailey was younger, Alexis figured it would make her feel more confident and sure of herself around the other Camp Club Girls.

"This is a baby California Myotis bat," said Lisa. She brought the small animal closer to the camera and stretched out one of its wings. With the wings expanded, the bat was much bigger than Alexis had expected it to be.

"At first we fed them on milk," said Lisa. "We twisted the corners of small rags, dipped them in warm milk, and let the baby bats suck the milk out of the rags. Now they're big enough to eat bugs."

She placed the bat back in its cage and pulled a jar from a nearby shelf. Using a spoon, she scooped what looked like maggots out of the jar and sprinkled them into the bottom of the cage, which looked like it was covered with a fine mesh.

"The mesh allows their little claws to grab hold," said Lisa.

"So they can crawl to get the food, right?" Bailey asked.

"Yup! Look!"

Sure enough, the baby bats had detached themselves from their pile and were crawling toward the wiggling food. Alexis had never seen anything so gross and so cool at the same time. She taped the feeding. Then she put the camera on a tripod so it would tape while she and Bailey helped Lisa clean out the owl cages.

Baby great horned owls sat above them on branches, watching curiously. They were big, even for babies. Each one was about eighteen inches tall, and their fluffy baby feathers made them look even bigger.

"I don't know why on TV owls are always shown as spooky or around scary places," Alexis said. "They don't seem creepy at all."

"Probably because they're nocturnal animals. They mainly hang out at night and sleep during the day. Night animals seem spooky to most people. Can you see where they got their name?" Lisa asked as she shoveled dirty straw into a bucket.

"The feathers on their heads, above their eyes," said Bailey. "They look like horns!"

The day flew by, and before they knew it, the girls were walking to the office for some lunch.

"Uh-oh," said Lisa as they approached the small building.

"What is it?" asked Alexis. Lisa pointed to a shiny black Mercedes-Benz.

"That always means trouble," she said. "Or at least it means that Dad's going to be in a bad mood."

Alexis tromped up the steps with the others and entered the office.

"I'll be right back. You wait here," Lisa said as she disappeared into the other room.

Like the day before, a fire was burning in the fireplace. But Bubbles was nowhere to be seen. Instead, someone strange was at the counter talking with Jake. It was an older man in an expensive coat. His gray hair was slicked back away from his round face, and he hadn't taken off his sunglasses, even though he was no longer outside.

"Come on, Jake," the man was saying. "This is the last time I'm coming out here."

"Good," Jake said with a smile. "Then this is the last time I'll have to tell you no."

The other man slapped his hand down on the desk.

"Jake, you can't be serious!"

"You know exactly how serious I am, Bruce. I don't want your money."

"You'll wish you'd taken my money when they shut you down," said Bruce. He had spoken in a quiet voice. Alexis was glad she had good ears.

Jake's smile vanished, and he leaned across the desk toward Bruce. "Is that a threat?" he growled.

"No, Jake, no! Of course not!" Bruce laughed, but Alexis thought it sounded fake—like he was trying too hard to make the right sound come out. "I just mean that you're in trouble. It seems like you've been having a few. . .*problems* here at the reserve."

"How would you know about that?" asked Jake.

"Oh please, Jake! This is Tahoe! Tourists or no tourists, it's a small town. People talk." Bruce took his car keys out of his pocket.

"You know where to find me if you change your mind, Jake," he said. He placed a card on the desk, and then he was gone. As Alexis moved closer, she saw that the card said *Bruce Benton, Land Developer.*

Jake picked up the card. "We can just throw that in the trash," he said as he tossed it into the wastepaper basket.

Karen and Lisa came through the door, each carrying a stack of mail.

"I saw that Benton guy's car and heard you talking to him. What was that all about?" Karen asked Jake as the ladies handed their piles of mail to him.

"Oh, same old stuff," he answered. He took some of the mail from her and started opening it. "Bill, bill, bill," he said. Then he stopped. "Another threat letter," he said. He tossed it onto the desk.

Alexis and Bailey had wandered over to look out the window, but now they hurried back to the desk.

"Really?" Alexis said. "You got a threat letter?"

On the desk was a sheet of white paper with different sizes of lettering on it. Someone had cut words out of a magazine and pasted them together.

You think you're helping, but you're interfering with nature. Leave the forest alone! It will heal itself! If you don't, more than letters will come your way!

No one had signed it.

"What in the world?" Alexis said. "This is awful!"

"It's not as bad as you think," said Lisa. "We actually get them a lot. A lot of people are unhappy with places like this reserve."

Bailey and Alexis looked at Jake. They were puzzled. How could anyone be angry with a place that helped animals?

"It's the same old thing, Alexis," said Jake. "You can't please everyone. Some people think we do too much." He pointed to the letter Alexis held in her hand. "Others think we don't do enough. Nothing ever comes of the letter, though. We don't worry about them. We keep them all, just in case something worse happens, but that's it."

Alexis was still alarmed. She had received a threatening note once before, and she remembered how scared she had been. It had made her feel like someone could jump out at her at any moment. She opened her mouth to mention it.

"Ahhh!" Karen suddenly cried out.

"Oh no, Jake! Look!" She was holding another open letter.

"Is it another threat?" asked Bailey.

Jake took the letter and looked it over.

"No," he said. "It's worse. It's a letter from the government. They say they've had complaints about our facility, and that if they continue, then we'll lose our license to operate."

"What does that mean?" asked Alexis. Lisa walked up and put her arm around her dad's waist.

"What it means, Alexis, is that we'll have to close down the reserve."

Moneybags Bruce

I think there's a lot more going on in this mystery than I ever imagined.

Alexis typed the last line onto the screen for the Camp Club Girls to read. She was using her mom's laptop and had just typed a long email to all the girls to let them know what was going on.

Bailey read over Alexis's shoulder.

"It's scary to think that not only is someone letting animals out of their cages but that the government has even heard about it," Bailey said thoughtfully.

"Well, as you read in my email, I told the Camp Club Girls that if we can't solve this mystery, the reserve might not exist anymore. And that would be terrible!" Alexis exclaimed. "Then what would happen to those precious baby bats?"

"And animals that can't take care of themselves, like Bubbles," Bailey added.

"Good thing Mom and Dad picked this time to bring us here," Alex said.

"Or as Beth would say, 'There's no such thing as coincidence. God has you there now for a reason!'" Bailey laughed as she thought of their friend from Amarillo, Texas. Elizabeth was a walking Bible—and not because she was showing off, but because she believed that God directed people through His words in the Bible. Elizabeth believed God could do anything and often reminded the girls of that truth.

"I'm just concerned," Alexis said.

"About the mystery?" Bailey asked.

"Yes, but I'm also kind of worried that we won't be able to solve the mystery and do the documentary too," she said slowly. "I really, *really* wanted to win this documentary contest, but what good will that be if the reserve we film gets shut down?"

Alexis bent over to lace up her heavy snowboarding boots.

Bailey had a mouthful of ski mittens as she used her hands to lace up her boots, but she nodded to show that she was listening.

"Karen and Jake are really doing us a favor by letting us film our video here," continued Alexis. "It would be sad if we couldn't pay them back by solving this case. I mean, it's what we *do*."

"So we'll just have to keep doing what we're doing," said Bailey, taking her gloves out of her mouth and tossing them onto the bed. "I mean, we'll solve the case *while* we work on the documentary."

"That's what I thought too," said Alexis, "but that's a lot to do in a few days."

"No, Lexi!" said Bailey. "I mean *really* work on them at the same time. We were going to shoot a documentary about the reserve, right? Like, about what they do for the animals and stuff? But now something better has come up! They do amazing things for the wildlife here, and someone is paying them back by sabotaging them! So, we can still make our film about the reserve. . ."

A lightbulb flashed to life in Alexis's head.

"But we can make it about the *mystery*! Then filming our documentary really *is* solving the case! Bailey, you're a genius!"

Alexis hugged Bailey so hard that the two of them practically fell off the bed. The worry lifted like it had never been there.

Why didn't I think of that in the first place? Alexis wondered. *We can document the trouble at the reserve!*

If they solved the case, their documentary would be different from any other—like a real-life *CSI* show! And even if they didn't solve the case completely, they would draw attention to what was happening. They could send a copy to the government and maybe get more help for Karen and Jake. *And I bet the Tahoe Tourism Bureau would help too,* Alexis thought.

The girls spent the morning on the ski slopes. Alexis had

promised her dad that she and Bailey would take at least one day to enjoy the snow with the family. It was a vacation, after all.

Alexis loved snowboarding. She had learned to ski in fifth grade but had always felt awkward. In the back of her mind, she was always afraid her legs would tangle up at any moment and send her flying down the mountain on her face.

The next year, her dad had signed her up for snowboarding lessons. It was so much easier! Or at least she thought so. There was no chance that her feet could tangle, because they were anchored securely side by side.

There had been one time that a face-plant had brought the snowboard up from behind to whack her in the back of the head. . . not fun. But overall it was always a great time.

Bailey hadn't skied much, so the girls spent the first hour on the bunny hill. Alexis taught her how to wedge the tips of her skis together (in the shape of a triangle), and they cruised along slowly until Bailey got the hang of it. It didn't take long. Soon she was tearing down the mountain so fast that Alexis could hardly catch up.

"You should have your camera along!" Bailey called to Alexis. "Then you could do a documentary on a midwestern girl learning to ski! I could be a star!"

On their fifth run down the mountain, Alexis took her time. She always got more confident after a few hours on the slopes, so she wanted to try some smaller jumps. By the time she got to the bottom, Bailey had been waiting for almost ten minutes.

"Come on, Lexi! You take forever!"

"Sorry! I wanted to try some tricks!"

"Well, I'm starving," said Bailey. "Let's get lunch!"

The girls left their boards outside the lodge and went in to find the cafeteria. They ordered a pizza to share and then giant cups of hot chocolate. Alexis had to admit that it felt good to take her gloves off and wrap her fingers around something warm.

"The sun's out," said Alexis. "Want to sit outside?"

"Sure," said Bailey. They wiggled their way through tons of tourists. Alexis thought she heard at least four different languages being spoken in the crowd. People came to Tahoe from all over the world it seemed. Alexis was trying to understand a woman speaking French when Bailey elbowed her in the ribs.

"Hey, look!" Bailey said. "Isn't that the boy I hit in the head with our camera at breakfast yesterday?"

Alexis looked in the direction Bailey was pointing. Sure enough, the same boy was sitting on a bench looking up at the mountain. Alexis wondered why he wasn't wearing any snow gear. Who came to the ski lodge and didn't ski? As the girls got closer, Alexis noticed something else. The boy was holding a walking stick. But it wasn't like the walking sticks people used when they hiked in the mountains. It was thinner and white.

"Bailey," Alexis whispered. "I think he's blind!"

"No way!" said Bailey. "Yesterday he walked all the way across the dining room without help. And he was carrying a tray of food!"

"I know, but that's normal. Blind people don't need help all the time—only when they're in unfamiliar or crowded surroundings. Come on."

And before Bailey knew what she was doing, Alexis was sitting down beside the boy on the bench. Bailey sat next to her, more than a little nervous. Was the boy still angry with her?

"Hi," said Alexis. "I'm Alexis, and this is my friend Bailey."

"Hi," squeaked Bailey. The boy didn't even turn to look at them when he spoke.

"Oh, it's you," he said. "Going to knock me in the head with a ski pole this time?"

"Of course not," said Alexis. She was trying to be friendly. The last thing she wanted to do was argue. "So what are you doing up here?" she asked.

"Observing," said the boy.

"Observing?" said Bailey. "But you're—"

"Blind? Yeah, thanks for reminding me. I almost forgot."

"We're sorry," said Alexis. "My friend was just curious. What kinds of things do you observe up here?"

The boy turned to Alexis but didn't say anything. Alexis got the feeling that he wanted them to leave.

"Are you on vacation?" asked Bailey.

"Yep. My family and I come every year."

"Do you ski or snowboard?" asked Alexis. Bailey was about to ask how he could do either, but Alexis shushed her.

"I would like to ski, but it's not going to happen this year. My dad is here in meetings on business so it's just my mom and me having free time. She forgot to reserve me a guide, and I'm not good enough to go down the mountain without one."

"Where is she?" asked Bailey. "Couldn't she guide you?"

"Nope. She never bothered to learn how." The bitterness in the boy's voice made Alexis sad. "Dad usually does it."

"So you're just going to sit around your whole vacation?" asked Bailey.

"Bailey!" said Alexis.

"No, she's right," said the boy. "That's about all I can do."

He leaned back on the bench and crossed his arms. Just then, Alexis had an idea.

"Hey!" she said. "We're filming a documentary at an animal reserve outside of town. We're taking today off, but we're going back tomorrow if you'd like to come!"

The boy's eyes looked less grumpy for a split second. Alexis could tell he was interested, even if he was pretending not to be.

"Come on," she said. "It will be fun."

"Okay," he said. "Sure. I mean, it's not like I have anything else to do. My name's Angelo."

"All right, Angelo," said Alexis. "Meet us in the hotel lobby at seven thirty tomorrow morning. We take the bus across town. Your mom can call my mom if she has any questions." Alexis jotted her phone number on her receipt from lunch and thrust it into his hand.

Angelo nodded and then got up and walked away. Alexis noticed that he used his walking stick to find his way through the crowd.

"I think I made him mad again!" said Bailey.

"I'm sure you didn't," said Alexis. "You were just curious. I'm sure he knows you're not rude. People probably get their words all mixed up around him all the time. Plus, he's coming with us tomorrow. You can show him how awesome and sweet you really are!"

"Okay," said Bailey. "But Lexi, I think we have a new mission now."

"What?" said Alexis. "Another one?"

"Yep. Whatever it takes, we're going to make Angelo smile."

The girls walked back through the lodge. There were still a few hours of daylight left, and they could get at least five runs in if they hurried. Near the front door, Alexis stopped. Bailey ran into her from behind.

"Ouch! What'd you stop for?"

"Look over there," said Alexis. "That man by the fireplace—isn't he the man who was at the reserve yesterday? Jake called him Bruce."

Sure enough, there he was, warming his hands by the fire and talking to the owner of the ski resort. Alexis didn't know why, but she just *had* to hear what they were saying.

"Let's sit by the fire for a minute," she said. "There are two chairs open."

So Alexis and Bailey sat next to the fire in a pair of squishy armchairs and strained to hear every word they could.

"How's the new resort coming, Bruce?" asked the second man.

"Too slow for my taste," answered Bruce. "I'm having some trouble getting the land I want."

"The city isn't giving you trouble, is it?"

"No, no," said Bruce. "It's the owners. They're not interested in selling, no matter how much I offer! I don't get it. The money I could give them would buy five animal reserves somewhere else! What's so special about this one?"

"You're trying to buy from Jake and Karen?" asked the other man. "I don't think you'll win that battle. That reserve is Jake's whole life."

"That's what he said too. But I wouldn't be so sure. Money always gets people in the end, and I always get what I want."

The two men walked off toward the cafeteria. Alexis turned to look at Bailey, whose mouth was hanging open.

"That's why he was at the reserve yesterday!" said Bailey. "Moneybags Bruce wants to buy it!"

"Yeah," said Alexis. "And it sounds like he'd do anything to get it too."

"I'm going to write down the clues we're looking at right now," Alexis added.

She unzipped a pocket in her snowboarding pants and took out her small pink notebook. It was time to start taking notes on this case. Alexis had gotten in the habit of carrying a small notebook with her everywhere she went. She'd seen it done on one detective show on TV and thought it was a good idea. And her notebook had come in handy before as she'd worked on other Camp Club Girl mysteries.

"We already know someone probably unlocked the mountain lion cage," said Alexis as she scribbled. "You found the keys in the snow, and Karen swore they had been hanging up inside that morning. Then we have that threat letter too. Maybe we can take a closer look at it tomorrow."

Last but not least, Alexis wrote the most recent piece of information: *"Moneybags" Bruce Benton wants to buy the reserve to put up another ski resort. Would he sabotage the reserve to get what he wants? He did say he would do anything. . . .*

"Come on," Bailey said. "Let's go to our room. We need to send an email to the Camp Club Girls to fill them in! They need to know about the mountain lions and Moneybags Benton saying he'd do anything to get the reserve."

CHAPTER 5

Bellyaches and Bears

The bus ride the next morning was pretty quiet. Alexis and Bailey tried over and over to get Angelo to talk to them, but he only nodded his head or shrugged his shoulders. By the time they got to the reserve, Alexis was sure that since Angelo was with them, it would be a very long day.

"Things have been a little crazy here," said Lisa as she led them into the office.

"What do you mean?" asked Bailey. But as soon as they saw Karen, they knew something was up. She was sitting at the desk, staring blankly at a cup of coffee that looked as if it had gone cold. Large dark circles were under her eyes.

"Been up all night?" asked Alexis. Karen jerked out of her stupor and nodded.

"The coyotes are sick. I was up late taking care of them. Then, when I finally went to bed, the phone rang. It was three in the morning."

"Who in the world would call you at three in the morning?" asked Bailey.

"That's what we're trying to figure out," said Karen. "I answered, thinking it might be an emergency, but I only heard breathing. Then a voice said, 'You're lucky they're only sick this time.' And the phone went dead."

"It was a threat?" asked Angelo. It was the first time he'd spoken.

"Yes," said Karen. "I guess it was. Alexis, who's your friend?"

"This is Angelo. We met him at our hotel, and he was interested in our documentary. I hope it's okay that we brought him along."

"That's fine," said Karen. She walked over to where Angelo was standing and grabbed his hand to shake it. "It's nice to meet you, Angelo. You all want some hot chocolate?"

Alexis took out her pink notebook while the group sat down on the squishy couches near the fireplace. She hadn't expected to have new information so quickly, but now seemed like the perfect time to ask some questions. Karen set five cups of cocoa on the coffee table and sat down.

"Karen, you said the call came at three in the morning, right?" asked Alexis. "Do you remember what the voice sounded like?"

"Well, it was definitely a man's voice. I didn't recognize it, so it wasn't anyone I know. It was kind of high-pitched."

Alexis scribbled down every word. Bailey took a gulp of her cocoa then put it down.

"What if the caller was just disguising his voice?" she asked. "Like this?"

Bailey said the last two words in a silly high-pitched voice that reminded Alexis of Elmo. She laughed.

"That's possible," said Karen. "I was also exhausted. I mean, it *was* three in the morning. Jake probably could have called, and I wouldn't have recognized him."

That made everyone laugh, including Angelo. Bailey elbowed Alexis and pointed. It really was nice to see him smile.

"Someone's at the back door," said Angelo suddenly. Everyone turned, and sure enough Jake opened the door, stomping snow off his boots. Bailey leaned over to Alexis and whispered in her ear.

"How did he know there was a back door?" she asked. Alexis had been wondering the same thing, but Lisa answered.

"I imagine he has amazing ears," she said. Angelo grinned.

"That's what my dad says," he said. "It's fun to freak people out sometimes, though."

"Often, when people don't have their sight or hearing, their other senses become keener to help their bodies and minds compensate," Lisa explained. "Often, blind people can hear better than the rest of us. Or they may be able to distinguish odors that the rest of us can't even smell."

"Looks like you guys are having a party," said Jake. He leaned over the back of the couch and spoke to Karen. "The coyotes are getting worse, and the vet can't come till tomorrow."

"Okay, I'll be right out," Karen said.

"Can we come?" asked Alexis. "We don't have to film the sick animals, but we could look for clues. I mean, I really think whoever called you did this on purpose. Didn't they say something about the sick animals?"

"They sure did," said Jake. "We just don't know *how* they made them sick. Did they poison them, or what? We can't help the coyotes until we know what's making them sick. But I don't know if you should go near them. . . ."

He looked around at the concerned group and sighed.

"Okay," he said after a minute of silence. "Come on out. And grab the cameras. There might be some stuff worth filming."

Lisa left to do some other chores, but everyone else followed Jake to the coyote barn. Angelo didn't have his walking stick, but apparently he didn't need it. He followed close beside Bailey with his hand on her elbow and never stumbled.

"Just let me know if we have to go up or down stairs," he said, tapping Bailey gently on the head.

"You got it!" she said. She was glad he didn't seem to be angry with her anymore.

The coyotes were a very sad sight. They were all curled up in their cages, whimpering, and one or two of them were barely breathing. Alexis felt a surge of anger. Who could do this to poor defenseless animals in cages? And *why?*

She noticed that most of the coyotes had bandages or casts on. So they had already been hurt before someone came in and made them very ill.

"Someone is definitely not playing fair," said Alexis. She took out her camera and began shooting footage of the poor creatures.

"Bailey," she whispered, "get on camera and explain what's happening."

Bailey smoothed out her short hair and jumped in front of the camera next to the first coyote cage.

"Today, we came to the reserve excited to help, but the day

has turned sad. Someone broke in during the night and gave the coyotes something to make them ill. Since we have no way to know what they have eaten, it's hard for Karen to treat them. Everything will have to go on hold until Karen, Jake, and Lisa can figure out how to help these poor creatures."

"And cut!" said Alexis. "Good job, Bailey. That was great."

Alexis was stuffing the camera back in the bag when Angelo grabbed Bailey by the arm.

"Don't move," he said. "What did you just step on?"

Bailey looked down at her boots.

"Nothing, unless you count the straw on the floor," she said.

"No," said Angelo. "It was definitely *not* straw."

Angelo knelt down and tapped Bailey's left boot. "Lift this one up, please. If you could."

Bailey looked puzzled, but she did what Angelo asked. She lifted her boot, and he placed his hand on the floor. He moved the straw around for a minute and shook his head.

"Nope. Can you lift the other one?" Bailey did what he said, and Angelo searched the straw again. After a few seconds, he lifted his arm up in triumph.

"Here it is!" he said. "What is it? It feels like foil."

"It *is* foil," said Alexis. "It's a chocolate wrapper!"

"A what?" asked Jake. He came across the barn and looked at the crumpled piece of brown foil.

"A chocolate wrapper," said Alexis again. "You guys don't eat in here, do you?"

"Of course not," said Jake. "Karen! Good news! It's just chocolate!"

Karen came over to look at the wrapper as well.

"This is good news?" asked Bailey. "Maybe they just ate too much! I get sick every Easter because I eat too many chocolate eggs. I guess it wouldn't be so bad if I didn't combine them with jelly beans."

"Well, chocolate isn't *good* for them, but at least now we know what to do for them," said Jake.

"So is it like the time my cousin's dog ate my giant candy bar?" Alexis asked. "We thought the puppy was going to die."

"Yes, something like that," Jake said. "Chocolate can kill dogs in the worst cases, and coyotes are of the dog family, so chocolate can make them very sick too."

"Wow, Angelo," said Alexis. "We wouldn't have found that wrapper if you hadn't been with us. I'm really glad you came!" Angelo smiled. Again. Alexis was really glad he had decided to come with them. Not just because he found the wrapper, but because she was sure this was taking his mind off the fact that he couldn't ski. She tucked the wrapper into her notebook to keep as evidence.

This keeps getting weirder and weirder, she thought. Someone had wanted to make the coyotes ill but hadn't gone far enough to kill them. Maybe the person had a soft spot after all. Or maybe he or she was too afraid to poison the coyotes with something more toxic, like antifreeze.

Not only did someone feed the coyotes chocolate, but then they had called Karen in the middle of the night. What was it the caller had said? *You're lucky they're only sick this time.*

Does that mean that next time they will *kill an animal?* Alexis was suddenly afraid for all the animals on the reserve. Why would someone do something like this? What could they have to gain?

God, Alexis prayed, *please help us get to the bottom of this before one of your creatures gets hurt.*

Her thoughts were interrupted by Lisa, who came into the barn carrying an armload of helmets.

"You three want to take a ride?" she asked. "I thought I could show you the bear caves today!"

Alexis looked at Bailey and smiled.

"Awesome!" said Bailey. "Do the bears go away in the winter?"

"Of course not!" said Lisa. "But they do hibernate. They're all sleeping right now."

Bailey's smile wavered, but she was the first one to run outside and climb onto the monstrous snowmobile that Lisa indicated. It was big enough for all four of them. Lisa climbed onto the front so she could drive, and Bailey held on to her coat. Alexis and Angelo climbed up behind Bailey.

"Hold on tight!" Alexis said to Angelo over her shoulder.

"You too!" he said. "It won't do me any good to hold on to you if you fall off!"

The ride up the mountain was fun. Alexis had never ridden on a snowmobile before. Most of the wind was blocked by Bailey's hat, but her nose was still starting to tingle in the cold. It felt strange—almost like they were sledding uphill.

When Lisa stopped the vehicle, Alexis was confused. She couldn't see a cave anywhere.

"We have to walk the rest of the way," Lisa explained. "We can't take the snowmobile any closer because it's too loud. The last thing we want to do is wake a hibernating bear!"

Lisa went to the back of the snowmobile and untied a big bundle. She pulled out four pairs of snowshoes. Alexis strapped on the purple ones. She was really excited. She had heard of snowshoes but had never worn them herself. They really did allow her to walk on *top* of the deep snow!

Alexis took the camera out of its bag and began taping. She felt like she was in a scene from *The Call of the Wild*. It was one of her favorite books.

The group hiked for about five minutes before Lisa stopped them.

"There, up ahead," she said. "Can you see it?"

Alexis had to strain her eyes, but she could just see the cave. It was a small, black opening in the snow beneath a huge pile of granite. The pine trees were heavy with snow. They bent in toward the cave, as if they were protecting it from outsiders.

"We won't get too much closer," said Lisa. "Just to be safe. But I thought you might like to get it on tape."

Alexis moved a few feet to the left to get a better angle. Angelo was still barely holding on to her back.

"Can you smell them?" he asked.

"Who? The bears?" asked Bailey.

"Of course. I wouldn't want to get too close. Never mind the teeth and claws. They stink!"

Alexis couldn't smell a thing. She zoomed in with the camera lens, and Bailey said a few words into the camera. Alexis was about to turn around when Angelo's grip on her coat tightened.

"What is it?" she asked him.

"A sound," he said. "I heard a strange sound. . .one that doesn't belong in this forest."

"What kind of sound?" asked Alexis, but then she heard it—a small popping noise—right before something hard stung her cheek.

"Ow!"

Alexis stumbled and almost pulled Angelo onto the ground. There were a few more popping noises, and then a completely different sound tore through the forest.

It was the roar of a cranky bear.

"Run!" called Lisa. She grabbed Bailey and took off toward the snowmobile. Alexis and Angelo followed, but the snowshoes were hard to run in. Alexis looked back just in time to see a huge brown bear emerge from the mouth of the cave. It took one sleepy look around and started running right for them!

Fortunately, the snowmobile was a bit downhill from the bear cave. That downhill slope helped the young humans run faster, while it slowed down the bear. Alexis briefly remembered a Discovery Channel special on bears, which revealed that bears run uphill much faster than they run downhill.

Of course, it's not good to have bears running after you, fast or slow! she thought.

Lisa and Bailey reached the snowmobile and clambered on. Lisa fired up the engine and turned to pull Alexis and Angelo aboard. Soon they were on their way back down the mountain. Alexis turned to see if the bear was still following them, but she wasn't holding on to Bailey. She slipped sideways and fell into the snow. She hit hard and rolled down the mountain about ten feet before stopping near a half-buried tree stump.

Lisa circled back around, and Angelo helped pull Alexis back onto the snowmobile.

"Good thing I wasn't holding on to you!" he laughed.

"Wait!" said Alexis. "My camera! I dropped it when I fell!"

Luckily, the bear had taken off in another direction, and the camera was easy to find. It was right where Alexis had fallen, tangled up in a pile of dead branches. The branches kept it from falling into the wet snow, which might have damaged it.

"It's still on," said Bailey. "You might not want to waste the battery!"

The group headed back to the office. All of them were quiet. They knew that they had barely escaped being attacked by an angry bear. What were those strange noises? And what could have awakened the bear? Alexis asked Jake her questions back at the office, but he wasn't worried about answering them at the moment.

"The most important thing, Alexis, is that we find that bear! We need the tranquilizer gun, Karen. Call the ranger too. Maybe if we put it back in its den, it will sleep out the rest of the winter."

"What if you can't find it?" asked Bailey.

"That's what we're worried about," said Karen. "Bears that wake up early run into lots of problems. Right now, most of the smaller animals are hibernating too, and the rivers are frozen over. There isn't much food out there for a bear. If he's awake long, he'll burn up all of the fat he stored for the winter, and then he'll have to be put in captivity or. . ."

"Or what?" asked Alexis.

"Or he'll die," said Jake.

Kate's Helping Hand

Back at the hotel, the girls left Angelo to go meet Alexis's family for dinner. First they went to the room to change clothes. When Alexis looked in the mirror, she saw a huge red bruise with a purple center on her right cheek.

"Eew!" she said. "That looks awful! Bailey, why didn't you say anything?"

"Well, we were too worried about the bear, weren't we?" said Bailey. "Besides, it didn't look that bad at the reserve. It's definitely pretty."

Alexis pressed her fingers gently to her cheek.

"Ouch! What could have done this?" she asked. "I remember getting hit with something before the bear woke up, but I never saw what it was."

"Could it have been a rock?" asked Bailey.

"Maybe. Oh well. We'd better get down to the restaurant."

Alexis threw on fresh jeans and a sweater before slipping on her sneakers. They were so much easier to walk in than her heavy snow boots. After tromping in boots all day, she felt as light as a feather. Bailey tied her hair up in a tiny ponytail, and they took the elevator to the second floor to find the steak house.

"There they are!" said Bailey, pointing into the crowded restaurant. Alexis looked up and saw her two brothers waving their arms to get her attention. Her mother was frantically grabbing water glasses to keep them from being knocked over.

Alexis sat down next to her father, and he poked gently at her cheek.

"I thought you two were shooting a documentary out there, not BB guns!" he said.

"BB guns?" said Alexis.

"Yeah," said Mr. Howell. "I'd recognize a BB bruise anywhere! My brother and I used to play with those things all the time. It's a miracle we never shot an eye out."

Alexis's eyes opened wide, and she kicked Bailey under the table. So she had been shot by a BB gun? That meant someone else had been out at the bear cave at the same time as their group. What if a BB had awakened the bear? What if that's what the person was trying to do?

It reminded Alexis of Cruella DeVille, the villain in *One Hundred and One Dalmatians.* Her first name started with the word *cruel,* and in the movie she would have done anything to get the puppies for a fur coat. If turning cute puppies into a coat wasn't cruel, Alexis didn't know what was.

She thought about how it felt to see the bear charge out of the cave. It had been really scary. One of them could have gotten hurt, or even worse. At that moment, Alexis knew she and Bailey and the Camp Club Girls had to solve this case as soon as possible. The person doing these things was becoming dangerous. Like Cruella's character, they didn't care who they hurt. As long as they got what they wanted, they might do anything. . .but what *did* they want?

After dinner Alexis and Bailey took their camera to their hotel room and borrowed Mrs. Howell's computer again. Alexis plugged her camera into the USB port on the computer so the girls could look at what they'd filmed near the bear cave. The camera had been rolling the entire time. Maybe it saw something—or *someone*— that they hadn't.

They started by watching the spot on the sick coyotes.

"You do such a great job in front of the camera, Bailey!" said Alexis.

"Thank you, dah-ling," said Bailey. She tossed her hair and did her best movie-star impression.

"We have to remember to add the stuff about the chocolate," said Alexis. "I don't think we filmed—"

"Shhh!" said Bailey. "Here's the bear cave!"

They sat and watched as the camera rolled over the snowy landscape. Surrounding pine trees were drooping from the weight of the snow. Shafts of sunlight peeked through the branches and made the white sparkle. Soon the cave came into view—a small opening beneath the rock.

"Is it just me, or does that cave look too small for a bear to get in and out of?" asked Bailey.

"Well, a bear sure did come out of it," said Alexis. "We're about to see it happen."

The camera rocked a little.

"That must have been when you got hit by the BB," said Bailey.

Alexis nodded. She was watching the screen as closely as possible. Soon the bear came charging out of the cave, throwing snow everywhere. But Alexis wasn't watching the bear. She was looking everywhere else for any sign of a fifth person in that forest.

Soon the film got hard to watch. The picture jumped all over the place as Alexis tried to run in her snowshoes. Most of the shots showed either her clumsy feet or a piece of the sky.

"Well, that's it," said Bailey. "That's where you dropped the camera when you fell off the snowmobile, right?"

"Yup," said Alexis. "Now all we can see is snow and a couple trees." Alexis reached for the EJECT button, but Bailey grabbed her hand.

"Wait! I see something," she said. "Rewind it!"

Alexis skipped back a few frames and leaned in closer. Sure enough, something was moving in the background. Near a group of trees in the distance, a shadowy figure climbed onto something and sped away in the opposite direction.

"Was that another snowmobile?" asked Bailey.

"I believe it was," said Alexis. "What else could it have been? Bailey! We have this person on tape! Whoever was out there waking up the bears—"

"*And* shooting people with BB guns," said Bailey.

"Right. That too. They're on our video, Bailey! This is great! All we have to do is blow up this frame, and we'll have a picture. What if this solves the case?"

"That would be great," said Bailey. "Can we blow up the picture on this computer?"

Alexis messed around with the keyboard for a few minutes and then sighed. There were hardly any programs loaded onto it.

"No, we can't," said Alexis. "I mean, there might be a way, but I have no clue how to do it without the program I'm used to using at school. I wish Kate were here. She would know how to do it."

Bailey laughed so loud that someone talking outside their hotel room abruptly stopped.

"Come on, Lexi! Do you or do you not know how to email?"

Alexis couldn't help it. She began laughing too. Why had she forgotten all about the internet? It was her main link to the rest of the Camp Club Girls.

"Right," Alexis said, going to work at the keyboard again. "All I need to do is cut out this piece of video and send it to Kate. I hope the file won't be too big."

After a few minutes of tweaking the video file, Alexis typed an email to send to their friend, the technogeek, and copied in the rest of the Camp Club Girls so they'd know what was going on. If anyone could help them, Kate could.

Dear Kate,

Bailey and I were going to see sleeping bears today when someone woke them up! Apparently the person shot a BB gun into their den (and hit me with one too!). I have a video with a person in the background. The person is too far away to see now, but I was hoping you would know how to zoom in and maybe get a few still pictures. I hope this isn't asking too much. As Princess Leia said in the old Star Wars *movie: "You're our only hope!"*

This could be the big break we need. Bailey says, "Hi, Katie Cat!" We love you and miss you!

Alex and Bailey

"Hopefully, she'll get to it soon," said Bailey.

"Are you kidding? Kate checks her email every five minutes. If she's not already asleep, she'll probably get it tonight."

Just then there was a gentle knock at the connecting door, and Mrs. Howell popped her head in.

"Hi, Mom. We're done with the computer now," Alex announced.

"Oh, that's okay. I didn't come in for that," Mrs. Howell explained. "I got a call from the restaurant. They said I left my purse there, and they've taken it to the front desk. I'm trying to get your brothers to bed, so I wondered if you girls would run down and get it for me."

"Sure, Mom," Alex said with a smile.

"Great. I'll call them and let them know you're on the way," Mrs. Howell said.

The girls quickly entered the elevator and rode to the lobby.

"I wonder how Angelo's doing," Bailey said.

"Hmm. Maybe we should call him and invite him to join us tomorrow," Bailey said.

As the girls picked up Mrs. Howell's purse, Alex noticed a "house" phone near the front desk—a phone for guests to use to call the hotel rooms. She punched in the operator's number and asked for Angelo's room.

No one picked up in Angelo's room. She left him a message and told him to meet them at the bus stop if he was interested. Then they headed up to the room.

The girls got back in the elevator talking about their plans for the next day. When they got off the elevator, they could already hear the commotion coming from their room at the end of the hallway. To Alexis's surprise, a hotel manager was standing at their door, knocking. She and Bailey stood slightly behind him to see what was going on as Mrs. Howell opened the door.

"Yes? Can I help you?" she said.

"Yes, ma'am," said the manager. "I wonder if you could have your little ones calm down a bit? It's just that we've had a number of complaints from your floor—"

"Oh, I'm so sorry—"

"And the floor below you—"

"Sir, I promise they won't—"

"*And* the floor above you as well," the man finished.

Alexis's mother looked sorry, but Alexis could tell that underneath she was furious. Not at the manager, but at her twin sons.

"Thank you, sir," she said through clenched teeth. "It won't happen again." The man smiled and walked back toward the elevator. Alexis barely caught the door before it closed, and she and Bailey made it into the room just in time to hear the melee that ensued.

"I told you two to settle down!" Mrs. Howell was yelling. "If I have to tell you again, you're not skiing tomorrow! I'll sign you up for the hotel day care instead, and you can play with the two-year-olds! I'm not kidding!"

Alexis and Bailey sat down with Mr. Howell on the couch. He was watching the Discovery Channel and checking email, completely unaware of the chaos in the bedroom.

"It's hard to believe you two could make it onto real-life TV!" he said to Alexis and Bailey. "How's the filming coming anyway?"

"Really well," said Alexis. She told him all about the baby bats and the sick coyotes. She even told him about the bear cave and the one that woke up, though she failed to mention how close she and Bailey had been when it happened.

Ding!

A small screen popped up on Mr. Howell's laptop.

"Here, Alex. Looks like you've got an email," he said, handing her the computer. From the next room over, they heard a lamp crash to the floor.

"I'd better go help your mother," laughed Mr. Howell, and he left them alone on the couch.

Bailey got so excited that she almost knocked the computer to the floor. "It couldn't be Kate, could it? It's too soon!"

"Let's see," said Alexis, and she opened up the email.

Alex and Bailey,

It's so great to hear from you, and it's SUPER great to know that I can help you! Pulling a pic out of that vid was easy. You'll find the pics attached to this email. I gave you what you asked for—close-ups of the guy on the snowmobile, but I zoomed in a little more for a few pics I thought might help you more. You'll see what I mean. Love you lots! Happy investigating, and don't hesitate to call if you need me again!

Kate

Alexis hurried to open the files. There were four of them. The first was a picture of the whole scene: a man bundled up from head to toe climbing onto a snowmobile. They couldn't see his face, but they could see what he was carrying over his shoulder.

"Is that a gun?" asked Bailey.

"Probably a BB gun," said Alexis. She opened the next picture.

It was a close-up of the man's face, but it was fully covered with a ski mask. That didn't help much. The third picture was just of the snowmobile, and the fourth was a super close-up of the side of the vehicle.

"Why would she send us that?" asked Bailey. The computer bounced on Alexis's lap as Mr. Howell sat back down on the couch.

"Oh!" he said. "A Yamaha Phazer! Those are great snowmobiles. Super expensive, though. You two interested in riding?"

"You could say that," said Alexis. She was staring at the make and model of the snowmobile, trying to figure out why Kate had zoomed in far enough to see it. All of a sudden, it hit her.

"Bailey, this is huge! We may not have his face, but we know what kind of snowmobile he was driving! Maybe that will lead us to who he is!"

"Maybe," said Bailey. "But it's not like this is *CSI*. We don't have access to all of the registered snowmobile owners in California. And even if we did, how would we know which one was this guy?"

"You're right, Bailey. This isn't *CSI*, but we can still use the info. Didn't you hear Dad? These things are expensive. I bet whoever was riding it rented it. Tomorrow we can call around to the rental places in town and see if anyone took out a Yamaha Phazer today. That's a start anyway. Then we'll go investigate the area near the cave again. Maybe this guy left something behind."

When the girls climbed into bed, Alexis couldn't fall asleep. Bailey's light snoring wasn't keeping her up. Her mind was. It seemed to be going about a million miles per hour. She hoped this snowmobile would lead them to whoever was sabotaging the reserve. She knew it could be a dead end, but she refused to think about that right now.

Please, God, she prayed. *Help us tomorrow. We need a break. The reserve needs You. We need You. This is where the real investigating begins.*

CHAPTER 7

Starstruck

The next morning, the girls awoke to a wall of white. Snowflakes as big as silver dollars drifted toward the ground—so many that they melded together to form a frozen fog. There had always been snow on the ground since they arrived, but at least four more feet had fallen while they slept.

Alexis looked out the window and felt like she had landed on another planet.

"I hope we're not stuck in the hotel today!" squealed Bailey from behind her.

"Me too," said Alexis.

"One thing's for sure," she continued, layering on her thick socks and snow boots. "Even if we can get to the reserve, there's no way we'll be able to examine the site near the bear cave. Any evidence will be covered up."

Alexis and Bailey weren't too hopeful as they rode the elevator down to the lobby. They were surprised to see that it was business as usual outside. Cars and buses chugged by the hotel. Bundled-up tourists trudged into the corner coffee shop. The only things out of place were the huge piles of snow on the sides of the street. Every few minutes a huge snowplow roared its way through. It pushed the newly fallen snow out of the street, adding to the piles.

As the girls waited to see if the bus would come, they didn't see any sign of Angelo. The bus picked them up as usual, though now there were metal chains clacking on all of its four wheels. Lisa picked them up in the Jeep. A small plow was sticking out of its front bumper. It took much longer than usual to traverse the road to the reserve office. Every once in a while, Lisa had to let the plow down to push through the snowdrifts.

"You're really good at that," said Bailey from the backseat.

"Thanks," said Lisa. "Thankfully, this only happens a few times a year. I don't know what we'd do if we had to deal with it all the time!"

"I even saw a school bus on our way here," said Alexis. "My cousin in Tennessee gets out of school if they *think* it's going to snow! Wait until I tell her that kids in Tahoe go in a blizzard!"

"Yeah," laughed Lisa. "It takes a lot to get a snow day here."

By the time they were inside the office, warming themselves by the fire, Jake and Karen were already doing their rounds with the animals.

"Hey, Lisa?" Alexis said. "We have a lot of video of the animals. Do you think we could interview you about the reserve and your parents?"

"Sure!" said Lisa. "I finished a lot of my work early this morning. Besides, if you two win, I'll be on TV! And I'm *sure* you'll win. You just have to! People will love this."

Alexis spent the next hour behind the camera filming as Bailey asked Lisa question after question. They learned everything they could about the reserve. Lisa's grandparents had started it with their life savings, and the Ingles had worked continually to expand it since then. It was the only reserve of its kind in California or Nevada—the only option for the animals that animal control and the humane society couldn't deal with.

The Ingleses felt their setup was still too small. Just last month they had had to turn away a wolf that someone had tried to keep as a pet. They just didn't have the space. The wolf had gone to a sanctuary near Olympia in Washington State, but he had been lucky—most animals Karen and Jake couldn't keep had nowhere else to go. If a zoo couldn't take them, they had to be released or put to sleep.

After the interview, Lisa had to leave. The local high school was having a college fair, and she was going to help answer questions about her university. Before she left, Alexis caught her at the door.

"Lisa?" she called into the snow. "Do you think we could use the phone for a bunch of local calls? We were going to follow up on a lead."

"Sure! Mom and Dad will be busy until lunch anyway."

Alexis got out her pink notebook and placed it next to the phone while Bailey scrounged around the office looking for the phone book. There was a whole page full of numbers for snow-mobile rentals, so the girls decided to go in alphabetical order.

By the time Alexis had called half the rental places, she still hadn't written anything down. Bailey was getting bored. She started making origami out of a pile of yellow sticky notes lying on the desk.

Finally, on about the twentieth call, they got a break. Alexis learned that the snowmobile they were looking for was rare because it was expensive. Only two places in South Tahoe even rented them—and one of those places was only minutes away from the reserve! It was called Rainbow Rentals.

"This makes sense, Bailey!" said Alexis. "If the person we're looking for rented the snowmobile just down the road, they wouldn't have had to transport it at all. They could have just taken off up the mountain and circled around onto the reserve's property! Bailey! Are you even listening?"

Bailey's head had drooped onto the desk. She was sleeping comfortably and drooling on a half-made paper bird. Alexis shook her.

"Bailey!"

"Huh? What?" Bailey said. She sat up and Alexis laughed. One of Bailey's sticky-note creations had stuck to her cheek.

"I might have found the right place," said Alexis. "I just need to make one more call to check."

Alexis made the call and scribbled furiously on her notebook the whole time. It turned out that someone *had* rented a Yamaha Phazer the day before. It was a girl who rented the machine all the time. Her name was Chloe. She had long, red hair and was a bit of a snob according to the guy on the phone. Alexis thanked him for the information and hung up.

"So, do you think this Chloe girl is the one who is doing all of this damage?" asked Bailey.

"If she rented the snowmobile, then she might be the one waking the bears," said Alexis. "But we still have to figure out who she is and tie her to the crimes if we're going to get her to stop. That's what has to happen before the reserve will be safe."

Bailey opened her mouth to say something else, but nothing came out. She was staring over Alexis's shoulder at the front door to the office. Her mouth was hanging open, and when Alexis asked her what was wrong, she just pointed toward the door. Alexis turned around, and it was all she could do to keep her mouth from dropping open as well.

Standing in the doorway was none other than Misty Marks, one of Hollywood's most popular actresses. Miss Marks shrugged off her coat and hung it on the rack, just as if she were at home. Then she turned to the girls.

"Hello!" she said, crossing the room. "I don't believe I've met you two. I'm Misty, Karen's sister."

Alexis shook Misty's hand.

"Oh, hello," she said. "I'm Alexis and this is Bailey."

Alexis elbowed her friend, and Bailey finally closed her mouth.

"You still have a bird stuck to your face!" Alexis whispered. Bailey swiped at her cheek and sent the paper pigeon flying across the room. It landed near Bubbles, startling him awake. Misty Marks looked like she was trying not to laugh.

"Are you two new here at the reserve?" she asked.

"Oh no," said Alexis. "I mean, yes! Well, we don't work here or anything. We're shooting a documentary for a contest."

"That's right! My sister told me about that! Is she around?"

Just then, Karen burst through the back door.

"Misty! I thought I heard your car!" The two women hugged, and then they both began talking at the same time. Bailey leaned toward Alexis.

"Karen's sister is *Misty Marks*?" she said. Alexis just nodded. How exciting! Alexis *loved* movies, and here she was meeting one of the hottest stars in Hollywood. It was obvious that Bailey was even more excited. She simply couldn't sit still.

"So, Misty, have you met our detectives?" asked Karen.

"Detectives? I thought they were filming a documentary."

"Yes, they are, but Alexis and Bailey have offered to help us figure out what is behind all of the strange happenings here," said Karen.

"Well, not really what," said Bailey. "It's actually a *who.*"

"Really?" said Misty. "How interesting! Any leads?"

The actress leaned down toward the desk to get closer. Alexis was surprised. She had always thought that movie stars would all be rude in real life. Apparently Misty Marks was really interested in their mystery.

"Well, we did figure out who rented the snowmobile we saw yesterday. We think this girl could be the one who woke up the bear," said Alexis.

"*And* the one who shot Alexis with a BB gun!" said Bailey.

"What?" said Karen. "Someone *shot* you?"

"Well, we didn't know it at the time, but my dad said my bruise was caused by a BB. See?" Alexis pointed at the blotchy bruise on her right cheek.

"And we think that's how the person woke up the bear. She was shooting BBs into the cave."

"This is a lot more serious than you made it sound, Karen," said Misty. "I thought you all had just forgotten to lock the cages a couple of times."

"That's what we thought too," said Jake. He was at the back door stomping snow from his boots and shaking it out of his hair. "Hi, Misty. Good to see you."

"You too, Jake," said Misty. "So what's really going on?"

"Well, we thought everything was falling apart and that it was all our fault," said Karen. "But then these girls showed up, and we realized that someone is sabotaging us. We found chocolate wrappers near the coyote cages the day they got sick, so we think someone fed them chocolate to purposely make them sick. And we think someone has been sneaking our keys and letting out animals. And just yesterday someone woke up a brown bear out of hibernation."

"How is the bear?" asked Alexis. "Did you find him?"

"Oh yeah," said Jake. "We tranquilized him and took him back to the cave. Hopefully, when he wakes up, he'll realize he's comfortable and go back to sleep."

"Speaking of getting comfortable, let's go sit down and talk about this for a few minutes," Karen said. She led the group to the couches, and everyone sat around the fire.

"Alexis," Karen said. "I'm worried. You could have really gotten hurt. What if that BB had hit you in the eye?"

"She got hit by a BB?" asked Jake, and Alexis told her story all over again. She could see Jake was getting angry, so before he could suggest that she and Bailey stop investigating, she told him about the snowmobile and the "Chloe" girl they thought was responsible.

"We're getting close to figuring this out, Jake," said Bailey. "It won't take too long now."

"Okay," said Jake. "So you know that a girl named Chloe rented the snowmobile. How are you going to find her? Do you even know where to start looking?"

Alexis hadn't thought that far ahead yet. Tahoe was a big place, and her dad wasn't just going to let her and Bailey wander around it looking for some girl with red hair.

"We'll just have to pray for another clue that leads us in the right direction," said Alexis. She smiled her most confident smile.

"Well, I guess we already know it's not a tourist or any of our environmentalist groups," said Jake.

"Really?" said Bailey. "How do we know that?"

"Well, the environmentalists usually ride around town on bicycles. They're not really the type to rent a top-of-the-line snowmobile. And a tourist wouldn't have known where to find the bear caves."

Jake was right. Alexis's head was spinning. What did this mean? Whoever was doing this was probably a resident—someone who lived in the Tahoe area. Either that, or they were very familiar with it. What she and Bailey really needed was another clue. A *real* one that would point them in the right direction.

Laughter interrupted Alexis's thoughts. The group's conversation had shifted. Now they were talking about Bruce Benton, the rich guy from the resort.

"Yeah," Misty was saying, "I ran into him at breakfast, and he wanted me to remind you how far all that money could go. He really thinks this mountain would be the perfect place for an upscale resort. It's on the quiet side of town, away from all of the noise and gambling over in Stateline. He's right, you know—"

"*What?*" said Jake. "You really think I should sell my family's heritage to that no-good, slimy—"

"No, no! Jake, let me finish," said Misty. Alexis was amazed. Jake had all but yelled at the actress, and Misty Marks was still smiling her Oscar-winning smile. It was like there was a joke that no one knew about but her.

"What I was *going* to say, Jake, is that he's right about the location. It would make a great resort, but there are plenty of resorts around this lake. I reminded him that this was the only reserve of its kind in the area. And it's in a great central location to serve both California *and* Nevada. Even if you did want to sell, it would be almost impossible to find another tract of land this perfectly suited to what you do."

"Oh. Well, thank you, Misty," said Jake. "Sorry about before. I've been a little on edge lately."

Alexis was lost in thought again. So Bruce Benton wanted the reserve, huh? Hadn't she and Bailey heard him discussing his new resort the other day? He had said there were some complications... but he had also said that they wouldn't last long.

Was it possible? Could this Bruce guy be involved in sabotaging the reserve just so he could have the land? It *was* a very "Cruella" thing to do. Alexis scribbled a reminder in her notebook. She would talk to Bailey about her idea as soon as they were alone again.

"Well," said Misty, bringing Alexis back to the conversation again. "It looks like everyone needs to get back to work. How would you girls like to hear *my* take on all of this?"

"You mean like an interview?" asked Alexis.

"Sure! If you need it, that is. I don't have a lot of time, but I'm willing."

"It would be great to have an outside perspective on the hard work Karen and Jake have put into the reserve. Bailey? Would you like to take the camera and interview Miss Marks?"

Bailey was speechless again, but a huge smile broke her face almost in two.

CHAPTER 8

Out Cold

Bailey chattered away as she dug the tripod out of Alexis's camera bag. The thought of interviewing one of her favorite actresses had finally loosened her tongue, and now she was asking Misty Marks about a million questions a minute. Misty just laughed as she followed Bailey into the back office. It would give them a quiet place to conduct most of the interview.

Alexis decided it would also be a good idea to get scenes of Bailey and Misty walking around the reserve. "I'll set up the camera and let you two get started with the interview. Since Misty's time is limited, while you're doing the interview, I'm going to find some areas where we can have good shots of you two to show. Then we'll edit it all together later."

"Sounds great to me," Misty said, flashing another of her famous smiles.

Before Alexis shut the door, Bailey looked back and waved at her.

"Thank you!" she mouthed. Alexis gave her two thumbs-up and smiled. She wondered if the actress would get a word in.

Alexis sat back on the couch and got out her notebook. As she looked over her notes about the mysterious "Chloe," Bubbles jumped up onto the cushion next to her and put his head in her lap. His misty eyes looked up into hers like he was asking her for something. Alexis looked at Karen nervously.

"He may be three times bigger, Alexis, but sometimes Bubbles thinks he's just a plain ol' house cat. I think he wants you to pet him."

Alexis rubbed Bubbles's head. The little tufts of hair sticking out from the tips of his ears were extremely soft. She realized that long tufts stuck out from between each of his toes as well. Alexis could see how people might think a bobcat would make an awesome pet. It was like holding a giant kitten. . .until Bubbles yawned and reminded her that his teeth were much bigger.

Jake was walking back toward the couch with two steaming mugs of coffee when they heard it—a muffled cough from somewhere outside and a faint rattle.

"Is someone outside?" asked Karen. "I thought I heard a cough."

"Shh!" said Jake. He was frozen in the middle of the room, his head bent toward the sound. "It's not the cough I'm worried about. It's the can of spray paint!"

He dropped both cups of coffee and bolted out the back door. Karen and Alexis stared at each other for a minute before following. They ran to the back steps just in time to see Jake disappear around the corner of the building.

"Be careful, Jake!" Karen called. There wasn't a path through the snow here, so Alexis and Karen waited under the eave.

"He won't catch them," said Karen. "He never does."

They stood in silence for a minute. Then for two. Then almost five had gone by, and they hadn't heard anything. Karen took off through the snow calling after Jake. Alexis followed again, tripping through the feet of loose powder. They rounded the corner, and Alexis saw the paint. The messy, red letters stood out against the snow like spaghetti sauce spilled on a new, white shirt.

GET OUT WHILE YOU CAN.

The last letter trailed off at the end, as if the painter had been caught before finishing.

"Jake?" Karen called again. Still there was no answer. The women left the first barn and circled around so they were near the outside edge of the parking lot. As they rounded another corner, Karen stopped so suddenly that Alexis ran into her.

"Jake! Oh no!"

Karen stumbled through the snow and knelt on the ground. Alexis came up behind Karen and gasped. Jake was lying in the snow, unconscious. At first Alexis thought the dark red all over his face was paint. Had the mysterious painter sprayed Jake in the face so he could get away? Then it hit her.

It wasn't paint. It was blood.

"Jake! Jake!" Karen said. She was wiping blood away from his mouth and nose. Jake opened his eyes. He sat up and looked frantically around.

"Did you see him? Did you see the car?"

"What? No," said Karen. "You were alone when we got here. Out cold. What happened?"

"I saw the guy painting the barn and tried to catch him. He must have waited for me around this corner, because when I rounded it, his fist was there waiting. I never saw a thing—just his black coat."

Alexis left Karen's side and walked toward the parking lot. A series of footprints led her through the parking lot to the other side where tire tracks showed where the person's car must have been parked. Near the parking spot, two things caught her eye—the can of spray paint was on the ground, and something red glinted on the bark of a nearby tree. Alexis took a step closer and saw a large handprint in red paint.

It was too big to be a woman's hand. And a woman had probably not hit Jake hard enough to knock him out and mess up his face like that. So if "Chloe" didn't paint the barn, who did? Were the two connected? Or were there many different people out to mess with Karen and Jake and ruin their reserve?

Alexis made her way back to Karen, who was helping Jake up the front steps and into the office. Inside, Bailey was helping Misty Marks clean up the broken coffee mugs. Alexis noticed that the puddle of liquid was no longer steaming.

"What happened, Karen?" asked Misty. "We heard you yell. Oh Jake! What happened to your face?"

As Karen told her sister the story, Alexis went to the small kitchen and filled a bag with ice from the freezer. When she got back to the couch, she handed it to Jake, who had just hung up the phone.

"Thanks, kid," he said. Jake laid his head on the back of the couch and balanced the bag of ice on his throbbing nose and cheek. "The police said it will take them quite awhile to get here—with the weather, they have a lot of accidents they have to get to first."

"Oh no, Jake! What about the benefit? You can't get on stage with your face looking like that!" Misty exclaimed.

"Misty," Jake laughed, "I think a flashy party is the least of our worries right now, don't you? Maybe we should think about canceling it anyway. What if word gets out that we're having these problems?"

"Jake, we can't afford to cancel the benefit," said Karen. "It's our number-one source for donations all year!"

"What benefit?" asked Alexis.

"Did you say a flashy party?" asked Bailey. Her eyes lit up, and she scooted to the edge of the couch.

"Well, yes," said Karen. "Every year we have a benefit party at one of the resorts. This year it's at the one you're staying in. People come from all over the country to hear what we've been doing and what we plan to do in the next year. Then they donate the money that helps us run this place. We were hoping that this year we would get enough to expand—maybe even enough to build our own animal hospital and to hire a vet."

"Yes, it's a tradition!" chimed Misty. "And Karen's right, Jake. You can't afford to cancel the benefit. It's tomorrow night! People are already in town just for you!"

Alexis saw the light in Misty's eyes and figured she was the reason for most of the donations made to the reserve. If Alexis was right, there would be more than one movie star at that party. By the look of awe on Bailey's face, she had the same idea. Misty noticed too.

"I have an idea!" she said. "How about if we invite our movie makers to the party! They can film some of it for their documentary . . .*and* get to meet some really cool people!"

"That's a great idea!" said Karen.

"I don't know," said Jake. "Haven't we gotten them in enough trouble?"

"It won't be an issue, Jake," said Misty. "The party's at their hotel this year! They won't even have to go anywhere."

The girls sat on the edge of the couch, leaning toward Jake.

Alexis tried not to look too excited, but the idea of being in a room full of stars had her head spinning.

"All right," said Jake with a smile. Bailey and Misty squealed together and then immediately began talking of dresses and high heels. Alexis was excited, but her mind went in another direction. She was thinking about the spray paint and the red handprint again. She and Bailey *had* to solve this case, because it wouldn't matter how much money was donated to the reserve if the government shut it down.

Alexis went over all of the clues in her mind. There had to be something she was missing—somewhere they hadn't looked. And then it hit her.

"The letters!" she said, startling everyone in the room.

"What d'you mean, Lexi?" asked Bailey. "What letters?"

"The threatening letters Karen and Jake have been getting—we haven't looked at them yet. Jake, do you think we could browse through them?"

"Sure, Alexis. They're in the top drawer of the desk."

Alexis and Bailey sat behind the desk again like they had that morning making phone calls. Alexis spread about twelve letters out in front of them. A few were old and wrinkled and looked as though they had been made out of old newspapers. The newest ones, however, were very different. Their words weren't cut from dull gray newspaper. Instead, they were shiny or glossy, like a magazine.

Alexis prodded the edge of one of the glued words and realized that, unlike a magazine, the paper was thick—almost like cardstock, the heavy paper used for index cards, menus, and other things that need heavier paper.

"Look, there's a picture on the other side of that word! That's a picture of our hotel!" shouted Bailey. Sure enough, as Alex pulled the word up, the back side of it showed the stone tower and part of the hotel's title in lights. Bailey was right!

"Bailey," said Alexis, "I think these letters are made out of brochures! Pamphlets advertising hotels around Tahoe!"

By this time, the others had gathered around the desk to look over the girls' shoulders.

"I think you're right," said Karen. "Look—this is Harrah's!"

"And this one's from Caesar's," said Jake. "These are the most recent letters we've gotten. What could this mean?"

"I'm not sure," said Alexis. "But it narrows things down. Whoever is bothering you guys must hang around the resorts, where it's obviously easy for them to get their hands on these brochures."

Alexis pulled out her camera and started taking pictures of the brochures.

A horn honked from outside.

"That's Lisa," said Jake. "Time for you all to get back to the hotel. We'll be in touch about the party."

The girls smiled and said their goodbyes. The bus ride back was quiet. Both Bailey and Alexis were thinking about the new clues they had. What did "Chloe" and the snowmobile have to do with the brochures and the man with the red spray paint? Were they connected? Alexis looked out the window into the wall of white and pleaded with the One she knew could help them piece together the puzzle.

Please, God! We need a break. We have all of these clues but no way to connect them.

When the girls got back to the hotel, they zoomed straight to Mrs. Howell's laptop. Alexis uploaded the photos of the letters and posted them on the CCG website. Then she started writing in the CCG chat wall. She told the girls about the threatening letters and about the message in the red spray paint, as well as the handprint.

Soon the girls were responding to her words.

> Sydney: *Did you find anything out about who was renting the snowmobile?*
> Alexis: *Sounds like some woman named Chloe.*
> McKenzie: *Do you think she's the one who left the message in the snow and knocked out Jake?*
> Alexis: *No, Bailey pointed out that the handprint is too big for most women—unless she's a real amazon. And it would take quite a punch to knock out Jake. Karen thinks from the way the injury looks that the*

person did it with his knuckles, not with any weapon.

Kate: *Unless she's an amazon and a wrestler or something too! Or a policewoman! They learn how to pack punches.*

Sydney: *Well, if the words on the letters look like they're all on Lake Tahoe brochures, you're probably right about it being someone who's hanging around the resort area.*

Kate: *Although any public place sixty miles around Lake Tahoe probably has racks of brochures promoting their attractions.*

Alexis: *Yeah, they do, but I just have a feeling it's someone who hangs around the resorts. It's definitely someone who's familiar with the reserve—enough to even know where the bears sleep.*

Elizabeth: *I think you should go with that gut feeling. I think it's God directing you.*

Alexis: *Well, He'd better direct fast. Bailey and I feel like we've hit a dead end, and we only have a couple of days left here.*

McKenzie: *Don't be discouraged. I think you're way closer to solving this than you were twenty-four hours ago.*

Elizabeth: *Yes, you've learned that the person sending them hangs out around the resorts, probably.*

Sydney: *And the spray painter made a big mistake by leaving a handprint. And since most spray paint is permanent, it will probably be a few days before he—assuming it's a he—can get the paint off his hand.*

Alexis: *So all we have to do is go around asking if we can see every man's hand?*

McKenzie: *Well, let's hope it doesn't come to that. . . .*

Elizabeth: *But whatever it takes! LOL!*

Sydney: *Yeah! If you keep your eyes open, you'll catch him.*

Alexis: *You're right. We'll even catch the criminal red-handed! Literally! ROTFL.*

CHAPTER 9

A Redhead Red-Handed?

Before dinnertime Alexis and Bailey took to the streets. Their goal was to watch people, and they were looking for something very specific. Jake had mentioned that the painter had been wearing a black coat. They were looking for someone who looked like he had money—since he hung around at the resorts all day, and they weren't cheap—and who had an obvious red stain on his hand.

Soon, however, they hit a roadblock. They found that, on the Nevada side of the state line, they couldn't go *inside* any of the hotels. All of them had casinos on the ground floors, and Alexis and Bailey were obviously not old enough to walk around those without parents.

"That's all right," said Bailey after they had been shown politely out of their third casino. "It's nasty in there anyway. . .all smoky, and it's hard to hear myself think over the blinging noises of all those crazy machines!"

Bailey was right. Alexis hadn't enjoyed being inside the casinos, but she also knew that they didn't have much of a chance of finding who they were looking for if they were limited to walking the sidewalks.

The snow started picking up, swirling thick around their heads. Bailey spoke up again.

"What if he's wearing gloves, Lexi? We won't be able to see his hands if he's wearing gloves."

Alexis hated to admit it, but Bailey was right. After more than an hour, Alexis led Bailey back to their hotel. They sat down in the lobby in front of the big fire to thaw out a little and talk about what to do next. The only other person nearby was a young woman using a laptop computer. She was wearing a scarf over her head, so Alexis guessed she had just come in from outside too.

The girls chatted until the woman's phone rang. She picked it up with a huff and answered it stiffly.

"Chloe Stevens, how may I help you?"

Alexis and Bailey froze when they heard the name. They sat very still and eavesdropped, pretending to watch the fire dance in the hearth.

"No, he is unavailable tomorrow night," snapped the woman named Chloe. "In fact, he won't be in the office until next week. Yes. Thank you."

She hung up the phone and went back to her computer. After less than a minute, her phone rang again. The woman tore the scarf off her head in frustration, and Alexis gasped.

The woman's hair was bright red.

Alexis looked at Bailey, and it was obvious that Bailey was thinking the same thing. They had found "Chloe," and they hadn't even been looking for her! Alexis waited patiently for Chloe to finish her phone call, and then she began a conversation.

"So, are you enjoying your stay in Tahoe?" asked Alexis. "Are you on vacation?"

Chloe looked up from her computer, surprised to be addressed by two young strangers.

"No, and no," she said. Then she lowered her head to the computer screen again. Alexis wasn't turned off by Chloe's obvious attempt to ignore her. She pressed on.

"Done anything fun, though? Skiing? Snowmobiling?"

Chloe made a disgusted sound.

"Ugh, no! I hate the snow. I can't wait to get out of this place and get back to the Valley." The phone rang again. Chloe snapped her laptop closed and stood up quickly.

"Thanks for the conversation," she said rudely, "but I'm going to bed. It's the only way to get away from the boss who never stops calling."

With that, she stormed off toward the elevators and was gone.

"I guess that wasn't her," said Bailey. "You heard her. She hates the snow. Some other red-haired Chloe must have rented the snowmobile."

"Hmm, maybe," said Alexis. She wasn't convinced. She didn't believe in coincidences, and it would be a huge one if there were two young redheaded "Chloes" walking around the small town of South Lake Tahoe. The good thing was that it seemed like Chloe must be staying at their hotel. If she were somehow connected to the painter, they would probably find him here as well.

She couldn't help but feel that God had answered her prayer on the bus. He was leading them closer to the answer, she just *knew* it. Before she could say what she was thinking, Bailey nudged her arm.

"Look, Lexi. Several computers are empty. Let's go see if the Camp Club Girls have found out anything."

The girls walked to a huge column that was surrounded by computers and chairs. FOR PATRONS' CONVENIENCE, the sign above each computer read. Alexis knew that this was a hotel where a lot of companies and organizations held conventions, like her dad's company. She'd seen people dash out between meetings to check their messages. She knew from being around her mom and dad that they were making sure nothing important had popped up at work while they were in the meetings.

So Alexis felt rather important sitting down and logging in to the Camp Club Girls' website. She felt almost like an adult dashing to get the latest news from her coworkers in solving mysteries and mayhem.

She and Bailey started to read the messages on the chat wall together.

> Sydney: *You know, girls, I've been thinking about the woman named Chloe who rented the snowmobile. Even if she didn't KO Jake, I have a feeling she might be involved in this.*
> Alexis: *That's amazing. Just wait until you hear WHOM we just sat next to in the hotel lobby.*

Alex took a few minutes to explain what they'd seen and heard from the woman next to them.

Sydney: *Well, even if she doesn't like snow, she still could have rented the snowmobile for her boss. Assistants do that kind of thing, you know.*

McKenzie: *If I were you, I'd try to follow her until you know for sure that it's not the Chloe you're looking for. I think Sydney's right. I have a feeling about her too.*

Elizabeth: *She sounds like she might lead you to bigger fish, as we say here in Texas.*

Alexis: *Bigger fish?*

Elizabeth: *Yes. The person who's really at the helm of the dastardly deeds.*

Sydney: *If she is the right Chloe, she might lead you to the person who's really responsible for sabotaging the reserve.*

McKenzie: *I've also been thinking about your new friend, Angelo.*

Alexis: *You think he did this stuff? But he's* blind, *Kenz. I* don't think he could have ridden a snowmobile.
I guess he could have written with paint in the snow, but I don't think it would be as legible. . . .

McKenzie: *No, silly. Bailey's been up here in Montana, so she can tell you how many mountains we have in parts of our state. Some people from my church have a ministry helping people with disabilities do sports things, like participating in rodeos and even skiing.*

Elizabeth: *How do they do that?*

McKenzie: *People who can see and help skiers get around are called guides. They ski the trail with the blind person and help him or her avoid obstacles and learn the course.*

Elizabeth: *That must be a really hard thing to do.*

McKenzie: *They say it's not as hard as people think. Although blind people don't have their sight and can't follow a guide with their eyes, they can follow the guide with their ears and other senses. And they tend to have good instincts that help them find their way around.*

Alexis: *Really? Do they have friends who help people around here?*

McKenzie: *Well, no, I don't think so. But I went online and looked up the resort where you're staying. They're having a ski meet in a couple of days. I emailed them to see if people with disabilities can compete, and they told me yes. I told them about your friend, Angelo, and they said they had guides available to help at the meet. The guides give the people with disabilities a little bit of help so they can compete. All Angelo has to do is register for the meet and request one ahead of time. He just needs to talk to Mark at extension 378 in the resort.*

Alexis: *Terrific! I'll make sure he knows that!*

McKenzie: *The guy named Mark was really nice. He said if you guys had any questions to just ask him.*

Bailey nudged Alexis's shoulder. "Look, Angelo just walked by. He's sitting over there. Maybe we should go talk to him about it."

"Good idea," Alexis said as she typed their goodbyes to their online friends and logged out of the public computer.

As the girls approached Angelo, they saw that his eyebrows were crumpled into a scowl.

Bailey said, "Hey, Angelo! Over here!"

The boy's face lit up as he turned toward the girls.

"What's up, Angelo? You look bummed," said Alexis.

"Well, it's not a big deal," said Angelo. "I found out about a ski race the resort's sponsoring later this week. I just wish I could be part of it."

"But you can!" Bailey exclaimed.

"We told one of our friends about meeting you the other day and how you wished you could ski," Alexis explained.

Bailey picked up the story. "She contacted the hotel and talked to a guy named Mark at extension 378."

"He said they have guides for skiers who need help!" Alexis said. "All you have to do is call him to register and to request a guide."

"That's awesome, Angelo! You should totally enter!" cried Bailey.

"Hey, you can do it right now!" Alexis exclaimed, noticing the house phone nearby.

"Well, I guess I could," Angelo said hesitantly.

"Here, we'll help!" The girls led Angelo to a bench by the phone. They sat beside him as he punched in the extension number 378.

The girls listened to Angelo sign up.

"Okay," he said. "Do you have anyone who can help me practice? . . . Oh, I see. . . . Well, yes, let's go ahead and leave me signed up for the event. Maybe I can figure something out."

Angelo sighed heavily as he hung up the receiver and leaned back in his chair.

"Is there a problem?" Alexis asked.

"Well, a bit of a challenge." Angelo smiled weakly. "They have guides to help at the race, and I'm signed up for one. But they don't have any practice guides available. I need to practice if I'm going to compete. Oh well."

Alexis could tell he was trying not to kill the mood and depress everyone else. She thought hard for a minute, and then her eyes lit up.

"Angelo! I've got an idea!" she said. "Meet us tomorrow morning at the ski lodge—as soon as the lifts open!"

"But, Alexis—"

"No buts! Just do it! And be ready to practice!" Alexis jumped off the couch and grabbed Bailey by the arm.

"Come on, Bailey! We have a lot to do before tomorrow!" The girls took off toward the elevators, leaving Angelo baffled but smiling in the lobby.

●—●—●

The next morning, Alexis and Bailey waited impatiently for Angelo to show up. They still had half an hour before the slopes opened, but Alexis was excited. She wanted to get started right away. She had spent most of the last evening getting what she needed from the rental shop. Then she had called Mark at extension 378 and talked to him. He had explained what to do and had told her that all she needed besides skis and poles were two vests.

One was for Angelo. It was orange, and it said BLIND SKIER in black. Alexis's vest was orange as well. It said GUIDE. Alexis was already in her vest when Angelo came around the corner with his skis.

"Good morning, ladies!" he chimed. "So what's the plan?"

"First, you have to put this on," said Bailey. She tossed the vest into Angelo's chest, and he caught it easily.

"Sweet!" said Angelo. "If you're giving me a vest for practicing, you must have found me a practice guide? Who is it? I thought they were all busy."

"They are all busy," said Alexis. "I'm the one who's going to lead you through the course. Mark at extension 378 and the guy in the ski shop walked me through what to do and gave me the vests. He said he remembered you from when you were here skiing with your dad before. He said you probably wouldn't need a guide for long, anyway, because you're so good."

Angelo looked more than a little nervous.

"Have you ever done this before, Alexis?" he asked.

"No. But I'm sure we'll do great! Come on!"

Alexis led Bailey and Angelo to the ski lift, which took them to the top of the race course. More than once, she tried to help Angelo when he didn't really need it.

"The chair's almost here. Get ready to sit."

"I know, Alexis. I can hear it," Angelo teased. Alexis had to remind herself that Angelo had skied much more than she had. If he'd known the race course already, he wouldn't even have needed her.

Their first time down the course, Alexis realized just how good Angelo was. She weaved slowly in and out of the blue flags that made up the course, calling back to him only to say "left" or "right." After three times through, Angelo was simply following the sound of Alexis skiing ahead of him. Bailey stayed behind them, taking her time.

"Okay, Alexis!" Angelo called. "You can speed up now! I should practice going fast."

"I'm going almost as fast as I can!" Alexis called back. "I've never done a race course before today, and I'm not a good skier to begin with!" As if to demonstrate her last claim, Alexis took the final turn on the race course, and her skies got tangled. She did a rolling dive down the rest of the hill and came to a stop near the end of the lift lines. Bailey and Angelo caught up, barely holding in their laughter.

"Are you okay, Lexi?" asked Bailey.

"Yeah, I'm fine. I'll be a little sore, but nothing too bad."

"Thanks a lot for your help, Alexis," said Angelo. "I'll be fine tomorrow. My race guide will take me through a couple practice runs in the morning. I know the turns by heart, and that's the main thing."

"Are you sure, Angelo?" asked Alexis. "I don't feel like we did much."

"It was perfect," said Angelo. He kicked off his skis and held out a hand to help Alexis up. "If it weren't for you, I wouldn't be able to enter the race at all. You two will come watch tomorrow, right?"

"We wouldn't miss it for the world!" said Bailey.

"Good. I'll see you both in the morning! Have fun at your fancy party!" Angelo picked up his skis and made his way back up to the lodge.

Bailey was smiling ear to ear, but when she looked at Alexis, she scowled.

"What's wrong, Lexi?"

Alexis looked as if the bogeyman had just jumped out at her from under the bed. Her eyes were wide with fear.

"Lexi, what is it?"

"The party!" said Alexis. Her voice came out in a hoarse whisper. "It's tonight!"

"Yeah, it is," said Bailey. "What's the big deal?"

"We don't have anything to wear!"

Within thirty minutes the girls had changed out of their ski clothes and stuffed down a couple of sandwiches. They left the hotel and walked a couple of blocks away from the state line, passing all kinds of tourist shops.

"The lady at the front desk said there was a great thrift store down here," said Bailey. "It's secondhand, but apparently everything's really nice."

"Good," said Alexis. "I have about thirty dollars for my entire party outfit!"

The thrift store was a gold mine as far as the girls were concerned. The woman at the register led them to a rack packed full of evening gowns and party dresses.

"Girls don't usually come looking for these until prom," she said to Alexis and Bailey. "That's still a couple months away, so you two have tons to choose from! After you find a dress, the purses and shoes are near the register. Fitting rooms are just through those curtains."

"Thanks," said Alexis. She and Bailey had a blast moving through the racks. There were dresses with feathers and sequins in bright colors, as well as simple black gowns. They all looked as if they could have been worn on the red carpet. Alexis and Bailey each took a small pile into the closest dressing rooms and took turns modeling their choices.

Alexis was trying on a long peach-colored dress when Bailey jumped through the curtain into her dressing room.

"Oh, good," said Alexis. "I need help zipping this up."

"Forget the zipper!" said Bailey. "Look who just walked into the store!"

Alexis poked her head through the curtain and stared. Chloe, the redhead from the hotel, was laughing with the cashier. The woman pointed toward the back of the store, and Alexis dove back into the dressing room as Chloe headed for the dress rack.

"I guess she needs a dress too," whispered Alexis. "Let's pick our stuff quickly so we can follow her when she leaves!"

Bailey and Alexis tried on the rest of their dresses in a hurry and made their choices on the dresses they liked best. Then they moved to the front of the store to find shoes and accessories. As soon as they had finished, they paid. Then they lingered, pretending to look at jewelry. Alexis kept an eye on Chloe the whole time.

Chloe seemed to be annoyed again. Her phone kept ringing, but she was ignoring it.

"I'm on my lunch break!" she yelled at it when it rang for the seventh time. "Leave me alone!"

"Boss working you too hard, sweetie?" asked the shop owner.

"Not really," answered Chloe as she hung a teal dress back on the rack. "I think he just has something against free time. That's him again, making sure I'm going to be on time for our meeting in twenty minutes."

Soon Chloe checked out at the register. Alexis and Bailey walked outside to wait for her to come out.

"She's going to meet her boss," said Alexis. "This is our chance to see who he is!"

"He could be our guy with the red hand and black coat!" said Bailey. Alexis had a feeling Bailey was right, but she didn't want to get too excited.

At that moment, Chloe came out of the shop and buzzed past them heading back toward the hotels. She was on the phone.

"Yes, sir," she said. "I'm on my way. . . . Yes, your tuxedo for the benefit should be in your room. . . . Yes. . . . Yes, I have my dress. Yes, I'll see you in a few minutes."

She started to put away her phone when the girls heard it sound again. She answered it. "Hello? . . . Well, I'm sorry! I told you the paint was permanent. Did you try lemon juice and sugar, like I told you to? . . . Okay then. I don't know if you'll be able to get it off for the event tonight or not. . . . No, you'd look silly in gloves. Try the stuff again, and if it doesn't work, keep your hands in your pockets as much as you can."

She hung up again, and the girls followed at a bit of a distance. They wanted to get a glimpse of Chloe's boss without letting her know she was being followed.

"Oh no!" Alexis said. She grabbed Bailey's arm and pulled her along faster. Chloe was losing them. She had passed the hotel and was headed for a restaurant in one of the casinos.

"No!" cried Bailey. "We can't go in there!"

The girls sped up, hoping they could get a glimpse of the man Chloe was meeting before she entered the restaurant. They came to a street crossing, and Alexis sighed. A little red hand was flashing at her from the other side of the crosswalk. They would have to wait for the walk signal, and by then Alexis was sure Chloe would be gone, along with any chance of finding out who her boss was.

Alexis turned to say something to Bailey, but she was gone. Alexis looked up again and yelled.

"Bailey, no!"

Bailey hadn't noticed the flashing red hand. She had plowed right into the crosswalk and into the path of a bus!

Last Chances

A huge arm came out of nowhere and shoved Alexis away from the street. A second later, something heavy landed on top of her. She had no idea what had happened—there was just this incredibly painful worry deep in her chest.

Bailey! What had happened to her friend?

After half a minute, Alexis realized the pain in her chest wasn't just the worry. She couldn't breathe. *Chloe's boss has found out about us and knocked me down!*

Then she realized the man who'd shoved her back on the sidewalk was her father. He was sprawled next to her, clutching Bailey in his arms. He rolled off, and the three of them sat on the slushy sidewalk, staring wide-eyed.

"Are you okay, Bailey?" Mr. Howell asked, out of breath.

"Um, yeah. I think so." Bailey's voice barely squeaked out. Alexis thought she sounded like a very small chipmunk.

"I came looking for you two. I'm glad I was here too. That bus almost had your name on it, Bailey. It's a good thing we're leaving tomorrow. You girls don't need to go looking for any more trouble. Let me guess—you two were following a lead."

"Well, yes," said Alexis. "But Bailey just got excited, that's all! This investigation isn't dangerous, Dad, I promise!"

Mr. Howell scowled and pointed to the bruise on Alexis's cheek. He crossed his arms, waiting for her to explain her way out of that one. Her answer surprised him.

"It's okay, Dad. We've solved the case!"

"You have?"

"We have?" echoed Bailey. She was just as surprised as Mr. Howell.

"Yes! I almost forgot because of the whole bus thing, but didn't you hear what Chloe said to her boss just before we lost her?"

Bailey scrunched up her face, trying to remember. She shook her head. Mr. Howell was scratching his.

"Well, you two better get up to the room if you're going to have enough time to get ready for your party," said Mr. Howell. "Your mom's up there dancing out of her shoes. She's more excited than you are—her makeup's all over the place, and I think she has out five different curling irons, or straighteners, or something like that."

"Thanks, Dad. Come on, Bailey!"

Alexis towed Bailey toward the elevator. Once the doors closed, Bailey spoke up.

"So what did she say?" she asked.

"Shh!" Alexis whispered. She pointed to the three businessmen on the elevator. The doors opened on floors three and five, and eventually Alexis and Bailey were alone.

"So?" pressed Bailey.

"I can't believe you didn't hear her!" said Alexis.

"I was so worried about catching up to her that I wasn't really listening, Lexi. Now come on!"

"Okay, okay!" said Alexis. "There are two things. First of all, she mentioned permanent paint! It sounded like her boss was having a hard time washing it off of something!"

"Wow! So her boss really *is* the one sabotaging the reserve," said Bailey.

"Yes! Unless it's a really big coincidence, and you know how I feel about those."

"There's still a problem, though," said Bailey. "We don't know who her boss *is*."

Alexis didn't stop smiling. The elevator doors opened on their floor, and she pranced down the hall toward their room.

"I know, but do you know what else Chloe said?" Alexis asked. Bailey shook her head, jogging down the hall to catch up.

"She told her boss that his *tuxedo for the benefit* was in his room! Bailey! He's going to be at the party tonight! Even if we don't know who he is now, we'll definitely know by the end of the night! We just have to watch Chloe to find out who she's working for."

Alexis dug around in her bag for the room key.

"Come on! Let's call Jake and tell him the good news!"

Mrs. Howell was buzzing around the room like a queen bee. Alexis thought she might be more excited than the girls were about the party.

"Over here, ladies! Did you get dresses? Here, let me iron them for you." She swept the shopping bags out of Alexis's hand and headed toward the bedroom. Alexis picked up the phone and dialed the number for the reserve. Lisa picked up, but within a minute she had given the phone to Jake.

Alexis told him all about finding Chloe and that they were absolutely sure her boss was the one sabotaging the reserve.

"He'll be there tonight, Jake!" said Alexis. "We can turn him in and get him to confess! Then the disasters will stop, and the government won't be able to take away your license!"

Silence filled the other end of the phone. Alexis was sure that Jake was speechless. He was probably amazed that they had solved the case in under a week.

"Um, Alexis?" Jake said after a minute or two. "I hate to break it to you, but we can't just go around accusing members of Tahoe's elite society of being criminals. If this guy really does have money— and it sounds like he does—he's not just going to confess to all of this. There's a reason he's sabotaging us, anyway. He's not going to just give up because some kids are on to him. No offense!" Jake sighed.

"You girls have done a great job, Alexis," Jake continued. "But we're going to need hard evidence if we're going to stop this guy."

"Okay, Jake," said Alexis. "See you in a few hours."

"Okay," said Jake. "Hey, let me know if you come up with anything else, okay?" It sounded like Jake felt sorry for them.

"Mmm-hmm," said Alexis. Then she hung up the phone.

Ugh! It was so unfair! They had worked so hard. How was it possible to be so close and so far away at the same time?

"He's right, you know," said Bailey. "We have to have evidence.

This guy isn't going to roll over and admit his crimes to a couple of girls."

"I know!" Alexis said. She stomped her foot in frustration. "There *has* to be a way."

"Girls! Dresses are ready!" called Mrs. Howell.

For the next hour and a half, the girls allowed Mrs. Howell to dress them up as if they were Barbie dolls. She ignored them as they talked about the case and searched for ways to pin the sabotage on Chloe's boss.

"There's still the red paint," said Bailey as Mrs. Howell tugged a wrinkle out of her slip. "His hand should be red, right?"

"Yeah," said Alexis. "That's good, but it may not be enough. He could come up with a ton of reasons why his hand might have gotten paint on it."

Mrs. Howell had started working on Alexis's makeup, and it was really hard to think through the case with the makeup brushes tickling her face.

"Careful, Mom," Alexis said. "I don't want to look like a clown."

"Don't worry, hon," said Mrs. Howell. "No one will even be able to tell you're wearing any makeup. It's just a light blush, lip gloss, and a little bit of mascara to make your gorgeous eyes pop on camera. You two are filming the benefit for the documentary, right?"

"Yep!" Truthfully, Alexis had forgotten all about the documentary. She was glad her mother had mentioned it, but it also made her nervous. She would have to do two things at once tonight—finish filming the documentary *and* solidify their case against Chloe's boss. And she wasn't sure how she and Bailey would get both tasks done at the same time.

"Okay, now that you two are ready, I'm going to go finish fixing my own face," Mrs. Howell said with a smile.

"Let's go check our email, Lexi, and see if the girls have worked any of their magic while we've been out today."

"You know if she could hear you, Elizabeth would say it's not magic!" Alexis said as she retrieved her mom's computer from the other room.

"You bet! Betty-boo would remind us that God cares about every detail of our lives and is always at work—even when we least expect it," Bailey said with a grin.

"Speaking of which, looks like everyone is signed on, including Betty-boo. We hit it at the right time."

Alexis: *Hi CCG! We're getting ready to go to a banquet with the celebrities.*

Elizabeth: *I've been praying for you all day. I sense that the Lord is going to break through some confusion tonight.*

Alexis: *Good! It's about time for us to leave, so it's almost like it's tonight or never! And we haven't failed a CCG case yet! I don't want this to be the first one.*

Elizabeth: *Jesus asked His disciples: "You of little faith. . . why did you doubt?" And I think that's the message He has for us today too.*

Sydney: *Speaking of messages for today, I've been doing some pretty intensive work on the internet.*

Alexis: *About what?*

Sydney: *I just have a feeling that developer who has been bugging Jake and Karen is involved in this in some way. The feeling wouldn't go away.*

Elizabeth: *That's exciting because God often works in our lives by giving us ideas that won't go away!*

McKenzie: *I've been thinking about the developer too. If he's rich and he's used to having his way, well, it sounds like he's pretty ruthless. Sounds like he can only think about what he wants, not about what's best for the animals and people around the reserve. Those kinds of people can be pretty impulsive.*

Sydney: *Wait. You haven't heard what I did.*

Alexis: *Well, what did you do?*

Sydney: *I took the name of the company you gave us the other day, and I looked it up on the internet. I thought maybe it would tell us the name of his assistant or secretary. Then we could see if that Chloe girl was his assistant. Assistants often do*

> things like scheduling equipment—like snow-blowers or snowmobiles or whatever that thing was—for their bosses.

McKenzie: *What did you find out?*

Sydney: *Nothing. From the website, that is.*

McKenzie: *Aww. You got our hopes up for nothing. . . not to mention Alexis and Bailey's.*

Sydney: *Wait a minute. You keep interrupting. I couldn't find the names of any of his staff people at his office, but I found the phone number. And I called it.*

Alexis: *Did you ask him if he'd been threatening anyone or committing acts of sabotage?*

Sydney: *No, silly. But I did ask if I could talk to his assistant. And I told the person who answered the phone, "Now what's her name?"*

Alexis: *And? . . .*

Sydney: *And your instincts are completely true! The assistant's name is Chloe Stevens!*

Alexis: *Chloe Stevens! Wow, so Bruce Benton is Chloe Stevens's boss!*

Kate: *I hate to throw a damper on things, but even if Chloe Stevens rented a snowmobile for her boss, how do you know that her boss is the spray-paint person?*

Alexis: *We haven't told you yet, but we heard Chloe talking on the phone earlier today. She told the lady at the store she was talking to her boss. And then she said something about his getting the permanent red paint off of his hands.*

Bailey suddenly spoke up. "Uh, Lexi, I just realized something. That was on another call. She'd hung up from her call with Benton and was talking on the phone again when she said that."

Alexis sat stumped for a moment. *Bailey's right! We don't know for sure that she was talking to Benton again.*

After she got her breath back from the surprise, she typed this new information onto the screen for the girls to read.

McKenzie: *So all we really know is that she was telling someone how to get red paint off his or her hands, right? We don't even know it was a man.*

Alexis: *Yeah, her tone of voice hadn't changed much, so I just assumed she was still talking to her boss. But it might not have been. What are we going to do? Any suggestions?*

Sydney: *Can you shadow Chloe tonight? Watch her and see who she talks to. See if any of the men have a red hand.*

McKenzie: *Will you have time to keep on her trail?*

Alexis: *I don't know. I have to work on filming the event and filming Bailey interviewing people.*

Kate: *Too bad you can't pull a James Bond and plant some sort of monitoring device on her.*

Alexis: *Kate, you're brilliant! I can go James Bond on her. I forgot about the lapel mic! It's actually to put on Bailey while I'm taping her. She talks into the lapel mic, and I can receive it through a device in my ear, even if I'm in another room. If I could plant the mic on Chloe, I could hear everything she says.*

Elizabeth: *But wait, you wouldn't be able to see the men or their hands.*

Kate: *Too bad you don't have a tiny video bug you could plant on her purse or dress and see the hands of the men she talks to.*

Sydney: *I'm still thinking about this Bruce Benton guy. If he's the one trying to destroy the animal reserve, do you think he'll try to ruin the event tonight? Could you plant the mic on him? Then you could hear if he's up to something.*

Alexis: *I don't see how I could. Bailey's sitting here and just said she doesn't see how we could either.*

McKenzie: *And what if he's not the man with the red hand? You could be concentrating on him and wouldn't even realize if anyone is popping Jake with another punch or shooting another BB gun— or worse. . . .*

Elizabeth: *Maybe that's what you should do with the lapel mic. Maybe you should put it on Jake where no one can see it. That way if anyone threatens him or does anything else, you'll hear it.*

Alexis: *Brilliant idea, Elizabeth. I hope no one harms Jake, but he's the one most likely to have someone bother him. And we can only plant the bug well on someone who knows we're doing it. I'm sure he'll let us.*

Sydney: *Well, also keep an eye on Bruce Benton. . . .*

McKenzie: *And Chloe Stevens!*

Alexis: *We need a few more of you here on site with us! We've gotta run if we want to get hold of Jake before the benefit starts.*

Elizabeth: *Okay. Check in tonight, and let us know what happened since you don't have cell phones with you. And we'll all be praying that God gives you wisdom, understanding, and eyes that can see everything!*

Alexis and Bailey were ecstatic. Alexis wasted no time in pounding the number to the reserve into the hotel phone. She hoped that Karen and Jake hadn't left yet.

"Yes?" a voice answered.

It was Jake, and he sounded like he was in a hurry.

"Hey, Jake, it's Alexis. Can you guys drop by our room when you get to the hotel? We'd like to put a microphone on you for the evening, if that's okay. It won't take long."

"A mic?"

"Yes, we'll explain later, but we think it will help us catch whoever is trying to ruin the reserve," Alexis said.

"Yeah, yeah—sure. We'll be there in half an hour. What room?" After Jake jotted down the room number, he quickly hung up.

"He's going to do it?" asked Bailey.

"Yep!" Alexis said. "He sounded a little agitated, though. I wonder if something else happened."

Mrs. Howell came into the front room carrying the girl's miniature purses. Bailey's was silver and went beautifully with her sapphire-blue dress and silver heels. Alexis's purse was the same color as her dress—a light peach that looked good with her pale skin and dark hair.

"I put the lip glosses in there for you," said Mrs. Howell. "You can borrow them for the evening in case you want to refresh."

"Thanks, Mom," said Alexis. She doubted that she would reapply the lip gloss, because she hardly ever wore the stuff. This one matched the color of her dress perfectly, though, and went great with her blue eyes, so maybe she would try it.

Before long, someone knocked on the door. Bailey rushed to open it, and Misty Marks swept into the room trailing her long, white dress behind her. Feathers ran from one of her shoulders down the back of the dress and all the way to the train, which rested on the floor. Her outfit was stunning.

Right away Alexis realized that she had forgotten to mention Misty Marks to her mother. Mrs. Howell stood in the middle of the room touching her hair absentmindedly with her mouth hanging open.

"You girls look absolutely gorgeous!" chimed Misty. She glided over to Mrs. Howell and introduced herself. Alexis was glad Misty was there to keep her mother busy while she and Bailey hooked up Jake, who looked like he'd rather be in one of his flannel shirts than the rented tuxedo he wore.

Alexis could tell that something was bothering him. His face—bruised pretty badly from the punch he'd taken the day before—was covered with worry.

"What's wrong, Jake?" Alexis asked as Bailey untangled the cord on the lapel mic.

"What? Oh, nothing, nothing," said Jake. "Everything's fine. Do you really think this will work?"

"Well, it's a long shot, but if anyone suspicious approaches you or threatens you tonight, we'll get it all on tape, and I'll hear it through the receiver," said Alexis.

"Mmm," was all Jake said. His face darkened even more.

"Is there something you're not telling us, Jake?" asked Alexis. "We can't help if you keep us in the dark, you know."

Alexis and Bailey faced the large man in front of them with their hands on their hips. That made him smile.

"Okay, okay," Jake said. "You mentioned threats? Well, I received one just before we left the reserve to come over here. That's why I was so short with you on the phone. Look, it's right here."

Jake reached into the inside pocket of his tux and pulled out a folded letter. Alexis recognized it at once as another message glued together out of resort brochures. The glue was still fresh. Alexis's fingers stuck to the letter in the damp places. She and Bailey stared at the single sentence with wide eyes.

Tonight's your last chance.

CHAPTER
11

Thank You, James Bond

Bailey and Alexis followed Jake and Misty through the hotel and into the gigantic ballroom. They were early, so the room was empty except for a few waiters here and there, and Karen. She was putting some animals in their cages in places that would be highlighted throughout the evening.

Karen's dress was bright red, matching her lipstick. When the girls reached her near the stage, Alexis saw that Bubbles had come to the party as well. He was wearing a brand-new collar that matched Karen's dress.

"The other animals will stay in their cages," said Karen as she hugged the girls. "Bubbles is used to people, and he's great at getting donations! All I have to do is walk around with him and tell his story every time someone asks about him!"

Alexis looked up onto the stage and saw two large golden cages. In each cage sat a golden eagle—the largest in the eagle family. Their feathers were a golden brown, and their eyes sparkled bronze. One of the creatures spread his wings, and Alexis understood why the cages were so large. The bird's wingspan was six feet across!

"They're so majestic!" squealed Bailey. "They look like gorgeous statues!"

"This is Kelly and that one's Ben," said Karen. "They were shot last year. We're hoping to release them as soon as it warms up."

"They're a surprise!" squeaked Misty. "The curtains will be closed most of the night. We'll open them just before Jake's speech and let people ogle the birds before we ask for their money!"

Misty chuckled. The girls could tell she was having a blast, and the party hadn't even started yet!

Jake took the girls to a prime table right in front of the stage. Their names were scrawled in gold on two beautiful place settings. Alexis had never felt like a princess before, but she was pretty sure that this was what it would feel like.

"You girls are free to mingle all night," said Jake. "Film anything and anyone. Even the movie stars. They know there'll be cameras. Here—these will keep anyone from thinking you're in the wrong place or giving you a hard time."

Jake pulled two badges out of his pocket and handed one each to Alexis and Bailey. They were press passes.

"You don't have to wear them," he said. "I know they won't match the dresses. If you want, you can just keep them with you in case anyone gets nosy about your camera."

"Thanks, Jake!" said Alexis. "Be sure to turn on your microphone before the party starts."

"I will. Look—I don't expect anything to happen, but if you hear or see anything fishy, I want you to notify one of the police officers who will be on duty, all right? No being the hero?"

It was clear that Jake was still thinking about the threat he'd received. He was more than a little edgy.

"Gotcha," said Alexis and Bailey together.

Not long afterward, music began playing. Alexis noticed a DJ near the back of the room. People began streaming into the ballroom, and in no time the party was in full swing. It was hard not to be dazzled by all the stars. A couple of times when they spotted a favorite, they jabbed each other and whispered excitedly. The girls found they really had to focus to keep their mission in mind.

"First let's just do general taping," Alexis suggested. "We'll go around taping the event and people, and decide which stars we want to talk to later."

"What about Chloe?" Bailey asked.

"We'll look for her while we're wandering around and getting an overview. That's why I just want to start filming and wandering— that will give us an excuse to go around looking for her."

"Then we can follow her until we see who her boss is?"

"Yes, that's what I was thinking," Alexis said. "Or even better, I hope she'll arrive with him, so we get that figured out right away."

"I wonder if she knows how he got the red paint," Bailey said. "I wonder if she's in on it too."

"I don't know. I guess we'll just have to wait and see."

"What are we going to do when we see her with her boss?" Bailey asked.

"Well, first of all, let's get close and see if his hand is red with the spray paint. Then we're going to have to come up with some way to see if we can get some evidence to confront him with.

"I hate to say this," said Alexis, "but I actually hope this guy threatens Jake to his face. I mean, I don't want him to hurt him, but if we could get a threat on tape, it would be something to take to the police. . . . Bailey?"

Alexis turned and saw that Bailey had wandered off. She was back at their table chatting away with yet another Oscar winner. Alexis shrugged and kept walking lazily through the crowd. To an outsider, it would look like she was simply listening to the easy party conversations going on all over the room. In reality, though, she was only listening to one person—Jake.

The earpiece in Alexis's ear caught a signal from his microphone and allowed her to hear everything. She figured it looked pretty natural for a camera operator to have an earpiece. At best, she just looked like she was listening to a director in the other room. At worst, she just looked like she had an earpiece for a cell phone in.

She was surprised to find that she could actually hear the other people talking to Jake as well. Alexis had been unsure if the mic would pick them up, but it did. Now all she had to do was wait for the *right person* to talk to Jake.

As if on cue, Alexis saw Chloe—the red-haired assistant— waltz through the door. She was in a beautiful, brown, floor-length gown, but her face looked the same as usual—grumpy. If Alexis was right, Chloe was not in the mood for a party.

And she was alone.

Alexis's high hopes plummeted. She had been so sure that Chloe's boss would arrive with her. Now, though, she realized that had been a silly thing to be sure of. They had never seen Chloe with her boss, so why should this party be any different?

Alexis left her video camera at the table so she wouldn't be conspicuous and followed Chloe around. She watched the woman from a distance and kept track of every man she talked to. As soon as Chloe finished a conversation, Alexis would move in and do what she could to check the man's left hand for red paint.

She had to get pretty creative. Some of the men made it easy by waving to her with their left hands. Other times, she had to introduce herself and offer a hand to shake—the left one. She knew this made her look clumsy and naive, but it worked. Most people simply smiled at her mistake and shook her left hand anyway.

Soon it felt as if she had talked to every person in the room. She wasn't used to high heels, so her feet were beginning to hurt. Alexis returned to the table and found Bailey messing with the video camera.

"I got some great footage of the guests!" Bailey said as Alexis sat down. "Now I have it all set up to tape Jake's speech. Have you met anyone cool?"

Bailey went into detail about all the stars she had met and gotten autographs from, but Alexis didn't hear her. Misty was on the stage in front of the red curtain. She had a microphone and was getting ready to introduce Jake and the eagles.

But that wasn't what caught her eye. She had just seen Jake go backstage—and he hadn't gone alone.

Seconds after he disappeared behind the side of the curtain, another man followed. Alexis didn't see his face, but as the man moved the curtain back into place after himself, she saw the palm of his left hand.

It was red.

"Bailey, I'll be right back!" Alexis said. "Do me a favor and start filming now, will you?"

"But it doesn't look like anything's happening yet."

"I know, but trust me! Just start taping!" Alexis took off across the front of the room to the stairs at the side of the stage. The boy in charge of opening the curtain was bobbing his head to whatever song was playing on his iPod. He didn't even see her pass by.

At the bottom of the stairs, Alexis almost took off her heels, but she decided not to. Instead she tiptoed up the staircase as quietly as possible. She could hear the conversation in her earpiece before she saw Jake. Whoever was talking to him sounded angry, but Jake was furious. Alexis poked her head around a pillar and saw the two men nose to nose between the eagle cages.

"This is it, Bruce! I mean it!" Jake whispered.

"What do you mean, this is it?" said Bruce calmly. "You don't think I'll really just let you walk away from this idea, do you?"

"Are you threatening me?" asked Jake.

"That's up to you, Jake." Bruce was growling now. "Take this deal. I want your land, and I'm going to get it one way or another. This is your last chance to sell it. You can announce it here!"

"And if I don't?"

"Well, as you've learned, accidents happen," Bruce said. "Even accidents with kerosene spilled over from heaters in the barn and fires erupting. I wouldn't want to be you and hear the cries of injured animals. . . ."

Alexis gasped! Sydney had been right! Bruce Benton was the man who'd been trying to make Jake abandon the animal reserve.

And now he was going to burn down the reserve if Alexis didn't act quickly!

Surprise, Surprise

Jake pulled a piece of paper out of his front pocket.

"You sent this, didn't you?" Jake asked, waving the paper in Bruce's face. Alexis recognized it as the latest threat letter. Bruce didn't answer, but a large smile spread across his wide jaw.

"You did all of this! You painted my barn? You poisoned my coyotes and woke up a hibernating bear? You shot a kid with a BB gun? Bruce—you *hit me in the face!*"

Jake was furious now. If it hadn't been for the music outside, Alexis was sure that everyone would be able to hear this.

That was it! Everyone *needed* to hear this! It was all the evidence they needed to stop Bruce Benton. The music stopped, and Misty's voice drifted over the ballroom. Alexis had an idea.

She ran back into the ballroom, finally tossing off her heels as she leaped down the stairs. Alexis made straight for the DJ's booth in the back. The young man running it looked at her bare feet and raised his eyebrows. Alexis ignored him.

"Jake needs another microphone," she said. She was shocked when he simply nodded and handed her a cordless microphone.

"It's on," he said. "You just have to push that button to un-mute it."

"Thanks!" Alexis said.

In a matter of moments, she was sliding through the curtains again.

"You're being stupid, Jake! We're talking about millions of dollars!" Bruce Benton nearly shouted.

Alexis took the earpiece out of her ear and put it up to the microphone. She propped it there with one hand. Then she took a deep breath, pushed the MUTE button, and tucked the microphone a little behind her body, where her skirt would partially hide it.

"So you admit you're the one who's been hurting the animals and trying to ruin the reserve?" Alex called out evenly from several yards away.

Bruce Benton turned on his heels with alarm. . .until he saw it was only a young girl standing there. He didn't even notice the mic she held.

"So what if I did?" Bruce Benton said with a sneer. "It's my word against old Jakey-boy's here. And I have more money. . . . Are the police going to believe an animal nut or a fine, upstanding businessman?

"Yeah," he said, looking at Jake. "That's a great angle. We'll tell 'em this animal nut has gone nuts and is causing his own attempts at sabotage. Going crazy. Trying to get insurance money. . ."

"No one will ever believe that!" Jake exclaimed.

"Sure they will. It's your word against mine. No one will listen to a little girl like this, so it's just your word against. . . Hey, what are you doing?"

While Benton had been talking, Alexis had slowly edged over to the curtains and started to pull the ropes to open them. Sometime during Benton's speech, Misty had stopped talking.

"What's going on here?"

Now with the curtains open, Bruce Benton could hear what he hadn't heard behind the curtains—his voice booming over the room's sound-system speakers, through Alexis's microphone.

News reporters dashed from the back of the room toward the stage, but a police officer who'd been stationed in the back of the room beat them. Quietly, the officer stepped up to the stage, "Mr. Benton, we've heard your whole conversation there, sir. You're under arrest for willfully harming animals and destroying property. You have the right to remain silent, sir. Anything you say can be used against you in a court of law. . . ."

Alexis's eyes met those of Bailey's at the head table, and both girls exchanged smiles of pure glee.

The next morning, Alexis and Bailey barely made it to the slopes in time for Angelo's race. They had stayed out so late that they had slept right through the hotel alarm. As a result, both of them were wearing beanie caps shoved low over their leftover curly hairdos from the party.

With Bruce's arrest, Jake and Karen had told the group about the sabotage attempts on the animal reserve.

And after the grand unveiling of what Bruce Benton had been doing, Karen and Jake had told the whole room about Alexis, Bailey, and the other Camp Club Girls solving the mystery. When they told the room about Alexis and Bailey doing the documentary, stars had literally lined up in the room, eager to help the girls by saying a few words to their camera about the reserve and why they supported it.

With all the excitement, some of the tightest of fists had opened to spur a flood of donations. Everyone attending was so inspired that they all gave something. Even the DJ slipped a twenty-dollar bill sheepishly into the donation bin. Alexis and Bailey had been blown away by the selfless giving. Karen had called that morning to tell them that they had raised enough to build an animal hospital and hire on-site veterinarian help.

Now as they stood outside in the bright sunshine, Alexis took a deep breath. A unique fragrance drifted in on the cold air. It was the smell of snow—something that Alexis had never noticed before—and it made her smile.

"Look! There's Angelo!" Bailey was standing on the top of a picnic table to get a good look at the race course. Alexis jumped up beside her and squinted into the sun. It was a beautiful day, and the snow was as bright as a mirror reflecting the sun.

"Where?" asked Alexis.

"Up at the start!" said Bailey. "He's wearing his green jacket and a bright yellow helmet."

"I see him! Go, Angelo!" Alexis shouted.

Within minutes, the horn sounded, and Angelo took off down the mountain. His guide stayed well ahead of him, and the way Angelo skied made it look like he'd been born to fly over the snow.

He weaved in and out of the red and blue flags, shaving so close to them he made the crowd gasp.

"You would never know he was blind if you didn't know him," said Alexis. She was amazed. When she had first met Angelo, she remembered feeling sorry for him and a bit protective. This week had taught her a lot of things, though, and one of them was that people and things that seem helpless almost never are. In fact, without Angelo they might not have solved this case. . .and she might have been eaten by a cranky bear. It had been Angelo, after all, who pulled her back onto the snowmobile when she fell off.

Within minutes, the race was over. Angelo had beaten his opponent by a wide margin, and Alexis and Bailey ran to meet him.

"Angelo! That was amazing!" said the girls together.

"You totally toasted that guy!" said Bailey.

"Did I? I thought it felt like I was alone up front," Angelo said, but Alexis could tell by his smile that he knew exactly how badly he had beaten his opponent. "That was the semifinals. This afternoon I'll race for first place!"

"That's awesome, Angelo!" said Alexis. "I wish we could stay to see it, but you'll have to email me. We have to leave after lunch. Bailey flies out from Sacramento tomorrow morning, so we have to get home tonight."

"I'll miss you," said Angelo, "but I'll send you pictures. My mom's watching."

Angelo pointed over to the stands, and Alexis and Bailey saw a beautiful woman waving at them. She looked just like Angelo, only prettier.

"I wanted to thank you two," said Angelo. "I wouldn't have been able to race without you. I had a blast yesterday practicing too. You really made this vacation great. It started off awful. . .but most of that was probably my bad attitude."

"Don't mention it," said Alexis. "You taught me a lot too. I'll never assume that a 'disability' makes someone need me. I think I needed you more than you needed me anyway!"

"I *did* save your life, I guess," laughed Angelo.

"Hey," Angelo said, looking serious. "Remember the day we met?"

"When I hit you in the head?" said Bailey.

"No, the next day, just over there on that bench." The girls nodded. "Well, you asked me what I liked to 'observe,' and I was really rude. I never answered you."

Alexis and Bailey looked puzzled.

"You see," continued Angelo, "I observe with all of my other senses. That day I was paying particular attention to the smell of snow."

"The smell of snow?" asked Bailey.

"Yep!" said Angelo. "Try it sometime, and think of me."

Bailey and Alexis each gave Angelo a hug and waved good-bye to his mother. Within an hour they had eaten and were back in the car with Alexis's family driving Highway 89 back down toward the Valley and Sacramento.

In the back of the car, Bailey and Alexis had the laptop open and earphones on. They were editing tape for their documentary, and they were surprised to see how much it looked like a suspense movie. They had tons of information about the animals on the reserve, but they had also documented the reserve's struggle against Bruce. Bailey had taped a lot during the party, and she had caught Bruce's confession too.

The final two minutes of film were a huge surprise.

"Did you tape this?" Alexis asked Bailey.

"No," she answered. "I thought you had."

The girls sat in silence and watched. It was a close-up of Misty Marks, famous actress, speaking directly into the camera.

"The goal of the Tahoe Animal Reserve is simple," she was saying. "Watch over those who cannot watch over themselves. This applies to our animals, but it applies to our everyday interactions as well. Everywhere we go, there are people who *need*. Look around you. Notice the needs and fill them when you can. The smallest good can fill the largest gap."

Misty smiled broadly into the camera.

"Thank you, Camp Club Girls, for filling our gap. We are forever grateful."

Alexis couldn't see the screen anymore. The tears in her eyes were getting in the way. She wiped at them with the back of her hand and turned to Bailey, who was smiling through her own tears.

As Alexis watched the Jeffrey pines race by outside the window, she said a silent prayer: *Thank You so much, God. Thanks for helping us. Thanks for helping these people. Please help me to always see the little gaps that I can help fill in people's lives—even when they look too small to be important.*

Alexis looked back at the screen. She had never been so excited about a project in her life. She knew this documentary would be a winner—whether it made it on the Discovery Channel or not.

Camp Club Girls:
Alexis and the St. Helens Screamer

That's No Bear!

Screeeech!

The driver of the van slammed on his brakes with all of his power.

Alexis glimpsed something huge and furry disappearing into the woods. The impact of the brakes jarred her head forward. Then the seatbelt yanked her firmly back against the seat.

"What is it? What's going on?" Alexis gasped.

But the driver was too busy to answer, frantically trying to keep the vehicle on the road.

Alexis grabbed her seat cushion and held on for dear life as the back of the van swung from one side of the highway to the other. The van almost hit three trees and another car before it finally settled on the side of the road.

The driver looked back at Alexis. His hands were shaking.

"You okay?" he asked.

"Yeah," said Alexis. She glanced into the rearview mirror and realized her eyes were the size of dinner plates. "What was that thing?"

"I don't know," said the driver, "but it was huge. Looked like a bear or something."

The driver pulled back onto the road and took off up the mountain again.

Slowly, Alexis's heartbeat returned to normal.

To keep her mind off of the near-accident, she began to think again about the task ahead.

Alexis Howell couldn't believe she was doing this. She couldn't believe she was hundreds of miles from home riding in a taxi van toward a smoking volcano—without her parents.

Alexis loved to travel, and she had flown a lot, but this time she had come by herself. She had flown into Seattle, Washington, the night before, and now she was on her way to Mount St. Helens.

At first the van had been full of tourists traveling to the volcano. Some came from far away on family vacations, Alex learned from their chatter. Others were native Washingtonians who just wanted to see the mountain one last time before it was expected to change forever. That's what had brought Alexis here. The rumor that St. Helens was about to blow.

The driver had dropped off most of the passengers in the small town below the mountain before driving Alexis up Spirit Lake Road to her destination. Alexis looked out the windshield as they wound their way up the mountain. Her ears popped. She was about to ask how much farther they had to go when she noticed that the driver kept glancing nervously at the sides of the road.

There must be a lot of wildlife up here, thought Alexis. *He must be afraid of something else jumping out of the trees. I'll have to ask McKenzie if that happens a lot around here.*

Alexis was on her way to meet McKenzie, one of the other Camp Club Girls.

The Camp Club Girls were six girls from different parts of the country who'd met and shared a cabin while spending a week at Discovery Camp, a rustic camp in the midwest part of the United States. While there, the girls had solved a mystery involving jewel thieves. They had decided they liked being amateur sleuths.

Since then, by working together, they'd solved twenty mysteries. Each girl had her different strengths she brought to the team. Sydney Lincoln, from Washington D.C., was quite the sportswoman and nature lover. She'd even participated in the junior Olympics.

Kate Oliver, from Philadelphia, was dubbed Inspector Gadget by the girls because she'd introduced them to things like infrared cameras, robotic spies, and other tools to help them solve their mysteries. It helped that Kate's dad was a professor and brought home many prototypes of inventions his students created. Kate was also the caretaker of the girls' dog, Biscuit the Wonder Dog. Sometimes when Biscuit was on the scene or even from Kate's home, he had a knack of helping the girls find the answer to their problems.

Bailey Chang, from Peoria, was the youngest of the girls and dreamed of being a star someday. She had an enthusiasm and a knack for coming up with nicknames that actually led to answers.

Elizabeth Anderson, from Amarillo, loved music and God and the Bible. She was the oldest Camp Club Girl and had a scriptural insight that often helped lead to answers.

McKenzie Phillips was often the heart of the group—she had a knack for figuring out motives and seeing how thoughts led to actions.

And Alexis herself, often known as Alex, was well versed in the cultural aspect of cases. Sometimes they reminded her of things she'd seen on TV or in books and helped her give valuable insight to the mysteries. She wanted to be Nancy Drew when she grew up. Or else a documentary director. Alexis was already well on the way—she frequently did *A Kid's Eye View* documentaries for TV stations around her home in San Francisco, and Discovery Channel had even expressed an interest in her.

That's what led Alexis to Mount St. Helens now.

McKenzie's mom had a friend who lived near St. Helens. Her name was Kellie Sanderson, and she ran a small pottery shop that a lot of tourists visited. She was letting Alexis and McKenzie stay with her for almost a week while they researched the mountain for Alexis's latest documentary.

Alexis *still* couldn't believe her mom had let her come!

The driver sneezed. Alexis jumped and started paying attention to her surroundings. Tall trees called lodgepole pines reached toward a flawless blue sky. They were so tall and thick that Alex didn't get too many glimpses of that beautiful sky. Most of the trees in the area were coniferous, which Alexis had learned meant they had pine needles and cones and stayed green all year-round, giving Washington State its nickname of the "Evergreen State." Most were tall with their needles at the top, like the lodgepoles, but the forests also contained pine trees shaped more like Christmas trees, as well as spruce, birch, oak, and other trees. The last time Mount St. Helens had blown its top, the lava and impact had destroyed 230 square miles of forests. Alexis had seen pictures of the huge, tall trees toppled over like wooden toothpicks.

The driver was still looking back and forth nervously.

"I hope this isn't the only sunny day we have this week," Alexis said, trying to take the driver's mind off of his apparent nervousness. "I hear there aren't too many sunny days in Washington."

The driver looked at her in his rearview mirror.

"No, not this time of year," he said, beginning to put on the tour guide personality that Alexis had seen earlier. "That's why it's so beautiful here. Lots of rain to water all the trees!"

In minutes the driver was unloading Alexis's duffle bag out of the back. She thanked him for the ride and waved goodbye.

As the dust from the taxi's tires faded into the air, Alexis turned around. She was standing in front of Kellie's shop. It was called Sanderson's Ash Works. It looked like a little red cabin with a wooden front porch. Statues of all shapes and sizes looked out at her from shelves along the windows.

"Alexis!" cried a voice from the side of the shop. Alexis looked to see McKenzie running toward her. McKenzie's auburn hair bounced brightly in the sun. The light brought out the red in it and the green in her eyes too. Alexis loved McKenzie for many reasons, but she really loved that they shared their pale skin and freckles.

Rawl! Ruff!

McKenzie was followed by a white and black dog that looked like it was mainly Siberian husky—she later learned with a little German Shepherd blood thrown in. The dog's bark was deep, but he wagged his tail as he jumped around the girls.

"That's Husky," McKenzie explained. "He's Kellie's dog, and we all adore him. Sit, Husky."

Immediately, the dog dropped his haunches to the ground.

"I'm so glad you're here!" said McKenzie. Her bear hug squeezed Alex's breath out of her.

"Me too!" said Alexis. She pointed at the shop. "This place looks so cool!"

"You don't even know! Wait 'til you see the mountain. And we have our very own cabin to stay in! By ourselves! It even has a kitchen!"

McKenzie grabbed Alex's bag and led her around the side of the shop. The building was longer than Alexis had expected it to be. They went around the back corner, and McKenzie led her through a door and into a bright kitchen. The stove and refrigerator looked like they were fifty years old, but they were still shiny white and chrome. In fact, the whole kitchen looked like it had been pulled out of the 1950s or '60s.

One statue on an old shelf caught her eye. It was shaped like a human, but something about it looked shaggy. It looked like it had long hair all over, and it was slouching forward, like some kind of big monkey or werewolf.

Alexis turned around. A young woman was standing at a wooden kitchen table. She was piling sandwiches onto a huge platter.

"You must be Alexis!" she said, flinging the leftover turkey and cheese slices onto the table. "I'm Kellie Sanderson. This is my house."

Alexis shook the woman's hand.

"Your house? But I thought it was a shop," said Alexis. Ms. Sanderson motioned for the girls to sit at the table. She poured them both tall glasses of water and then sat down too, reaching for the tower of sandwiches.

"It's a shop too," said Ms. Sanderson. She pointed toward the front of the building. "The shop is in the front room. This back here and the upstairs are my living quarters. I love it. It definitely makes for a short commute between home and work!"

The girls laughed, and soon they were eating and chatting away.

"So Alexis," said Kellie, "you do documentaries? Is it a hobby?"

"I guess you could call it that," said Alexis. "I did one in Lake Tahoe for a contest. It was about an animal refuge. One of our local TV stations saw it and really liked it. They have a show called *A Kid's Eye View*. They asked me to be their nature correspondent. That means I do special stories that have to do with nature. A story on St. Helens will be perfect! Thanks for letting me come, Ms. Sanderson."

"Please! Call me Kellie," Ms. Sanderson insisted. "I feel like I'm only old enough to be your big sister; not old enough to be called Ms."

"Are you sure?" Alex asked.

"Yes!" said Kellie. "And I'm glad to have you here. It's nice to have visitors."

While the girls ate, Kellie told them all about the mountain. The last time it had erupted was in 1980. The eruption had been so huge that the ash it had blown into the sky had drifted over five states.

"My mom remembers it," said McKenzie. "She said the ash fell in Montana like gray snow for days. They had inches of it."

Alexis's glass of water began vibrating on the table. She stared at it for a moment before Kellie spoke.

"Oh no, not again," she said. She stood up and grabbed a few of the closest breakables just as the rumbling got worse. Alexis could feel her feet vibrating on the floor.

"An earthquake?" asked Alexis.

"Yep," said Kellie. "They've been happening more often. It always happens when a mountain is thinking about erupting. I think it's how God lets us know to get out of the way."

"Aren't we supposed to get under the door jamb or the table or something?" asked Alexis. She had been in earthquakes before, but they always made her nervous.

"Usually," said Kellie. "But these have been happening four or five times a day, and they are really small—just rumbling, really."

"The earthquakes are what first started worrying the scientists," said McKenzie. Alexis was going to ask why they were so worried, when someone else walked into the kitchen through the back door. It was a young man about Kellie's age. He had long, shaggy blond hair and dark brown eyes.

The man stopped in the doorway for a minute until the small earthquake passed. Then he plopped down at the table with them and grabbed three sandwiches off the platter.

"Another new friend?" he asked, pointing to Alexis.

"This is McKenzie's friend, Alexis," said Kellie. "Alexis, this is Chad Smith. He is my right-hand man around here and helps me run the shop. In fact, he's usually the one who really knows what's going on and the man with a plan who makes this whole enterprise work."

"Okay, what are you buttering me up for?" Chad said with a grin, looking at Kellie. "Flattery will get you everywhere, you know."

Then Chad turned back to the girls and saluted Alexis like a lazy soldier. He grinned again.

"Good to meet you," he said. Alexis noticed he was a little out of breath. Sweat was beading on his forehead too.

"Run a race to get here?" Alexis teased. Chad Smith wiped his forehead with a napkin and laughed.

"Nope," he said. "I'm just hot-natured. I've been hiking this morning."

"Ooh, be careful out there, Mr. Smith!" squealed McKenzie. "Didn't you see the paper this morning?"

"I hate to tell you this, girls, but I suspect Chad would rather be called by his first name too. We don't have much formality up here on the mountain—not even between adults and kids."

"Except for teachers," Chad said. "I was twenty-three before I knew teachers even had first names."

"No way!" Alexis said.

"Seriously!" Chad responded. "But Ms. Sanderson's right. Please call me Chad."

He turned to McKenzie. "Okay, what were you saying?" he asked. "What should I be careful about?"

McKenzie pointed to a folded paper that was half-hidden beneath the plate of sandwiches. Alexis saw that the main headline was a story about a missing hiker.

"We have way too many hikers get lost up here. You know that, Chad. . . ."

McKenzie heard Kellie begin to lecture Chad about taking a hiking buddy when he went into the forest, but then a different article in the paper caught her eye. Well, really it was the picture. The black-and-white photo was of what looked to be a furry animal. The headline read ANOTHER SIGHTING NEAR ST. HELENS.

"Have you guys had a problem with bears lately?" Alexis asked when the others had gone back to their lunches. "My taxi almost hit one coming up the mountain."

"Bears?" asked Chad.

"Yeah," said Alexis. She pointed to the paper. "It says here there was another sighting."

"Oh that?" said Kellie. "Look real close, Alexis, honey. That's no bear. That's Bigfoot."

CHAPTER 2

Slipping Up

"Bigfoot?" said Alexis. "Right. Are you going to tell me to watch out for Care Bears and My Little Ponies too?"

Alexis started to chuckle, but then she looked around the table. No one else was laughing.

"What? You can't be serious," she said.

Chad grinned.

"Kellie's dead serious," he said. "We've had a lot of different people reporting Bigfoot sightings this spring. Everyone from family campers to forest rangers have seen something big and human-like walking through the forest."

"But couldn't it be a bear?" asked Alexis.

"Bears don't walk around on their hind legs very often, Alexis," said Kellie. A smile spread across her face. "This is the most we've ever seen of a Sasquatch. That's Bigfoot's native name. It means 'wild men.' For a long time he's been a legend for scary stories around the campfire, but I really think he's a species of animal. And I think we're close to pinpointing and discovering exactly what he is. He must be getting used to people."

The smile on Kellie's face was contagious. Alex's mind began racing. Could this be true? Could there really be a Bigfoot walking around St. Helens? If so, maybe the mountain wasn't the only story for her to cover while she was here.

The first statue caught Alexis's eye again. Now she understood. It wasn't a shaggy human or a werewolf—it was Bigfoot. Alexis turned to look over her shoulder. A short walkway led to the front of the cabin and the shop. Now Alexis could see that the shop's shelves were full of similar statues.

"You want to take a look?" asked Kate, noticing Alex's interest in the shop.

"Sure!" said Alexis. She and McKenzie helped clear the table. Then the group went into the shop. Chad walked to the front door and flipped over a sign so people would know the shop was open.

Alexis was amazed. She had never seen such amazing artwork before. Everywhere she turned, she saw beautiful figures that Kellie had molded from the gray clay. So many of them resembled the Bigfoot in the kitchen. Even though none of them had detailed faces, Alexis could see emotion in every statue.

"Each one is handmade," Kellie explained. "Even though a lot of them may look similar, they're all unique. None are from molds."

"You know what?" Alexis said, turning to Kellie. "They all seem a little sad."

Alexis thought her words might offend Kellie. Instead, Kellie smiled and nodded her head.

"You're very observant, Alexis," she said. "I don't know why, but every time I sculpt Bigfoot, I seem to create him that way. I think it's because that's how I think of him."

"Why do you think he's sad?" asked McKenzie.

"Well, every time he's spotted, he's always alone. Plus, I've heard him calling at night a few times. He sounds like he's looking for something."

"What does he sound like?" McKenzie said to Kellie.

"I don't know how to describe it. Not quite like a dog. Not quite like a wolf. It almost has a bit of a human sound to it. Like it has a soul that's in a bit of anguish."

"You think he might be lonely?" asked Alexis.

"I *know* he is," said Chad. Alexis turned and saw him staring out the front window. He seemed to be talking under his breath and not really to them, so Alexis asked Kellie another question.

"This clay is a strange color," she said. "I've never seen this color of gray in pottery before."

"That's because you've never been to St. Helens before," said Kellie. McKenzie picked up a small statue and showed Alexis the bottom of it. It read MADE BY KELLIE SANDERSON FROM THE ASH

OF MOUNT ST. HELENS.

"It's ash!" said Alexis.

"Yep!" said McKenzie. "Isn't that cool? Everything Kellie makes comes from the mountain."

McKenzie reached out to grab Alexis as another tremor rocked the shop. The statues around them wobbled dangerously.

"I really should put everything in bubble wrap or do something to secure it better," said Kellie. She looked at the girls and said, "If you guys want to see the mountain, you'd better go soon. If these tremors get any worse, they'll probably shut down the visitors' center—maybe the road too. You won't get any video footage of the mountain if they shut you out!"

Chad wandered back to the group.

"She's right," he said. "I'll drive you up if you want. I have a friend up there I want you to meet. He's a scientist from the university, Alexis. I know he'd love to help with your project."

"That's great!" said Alexis.

"You might want to change your shoes first, though."

"What's wrong with my shoes?" Alexis looked down at her old Converse high-tops. She had brought them because she didn't care if they got yucky. She figured they'd be good for tromping around on the mountain.

"They don't look like they have much traction," Chad explained. "Hiking boots are best around here. But if you just stay on the trails, you should be okay," he added. "I'll get the truck."

A short time later, McKenzie and Alexis were climbing out of the truck and crossing a large, circular parking lot. To the right was a building with a sign welcoming visitors. Tourists were streaming in and out, reading information about the mountain and buying souvenirs.

Chad didn't take them inside. Instead he led them to the left. They approached a low rock wall that overlooked a slope, a small valley, and then. . .the mountain.

"Wow!" said Alexis. "It's huge!"

The lookout was pretty high up, so Alexis was looking almost straight across at Mount St. Helens. It was still a large mountain, a beautiful grayish color. It had snow at the very top. But Kellie had warned her that even the summer could be very chilly in the Northwest. Sometimes, Kellie had told them, the roads to the mountain weren't even open this time of the year because of the snow. But this year had been a dry, warm year.

The thing that made Mount St. Helens different from any mountain she'd ever seen was the crater. The 1980 eruption had blown a giant hole in the mountain's top and side. It didn't sit right on top, like the many cartoon volcanoes Alexis had seen. Instead, it was crooked, like someone had taken a bite out of the side of the mountain.

"It looks like a big bowl," said McKenzie.

"A big, snowy bowl," said Alexis. "I didn't know the crater was so big. It looks like half the mountain's gone!"

"The 1980 eruption was huge," said Chad from behind them. "You can see why the scientists are so worried. Speaking of scientists, come with me. I want you to meet my friend."

The girls followed Chad farther away from the visitors' center. A young man with rectangle glasses and messy hair was perched on a rock. He was busy reading a small machine that beeped every few seconds in his hand.

"Rick!" called Chad. "I have visitors!"

The young man looked up and grinned. He jumped off the rock and was with them in two long strides. Alexis noticed a bunch of name tags and badges hanging around his neck. They all said Dr. Rick Porter, University of Washington Department of Geology.

"You're a doctor?" Alexis exclaimed when Rick shook her hand. "But you're so young!"

"This is Alexis, and that's McKenzie," said Chad. "They're researching the mountain for a documentary."

"It's great to meet you two!" said Rick. He picked up one of his badges and laughed. "Yup, I'm a doctor. Not the kind that fixes broken bones, though. I'm the kind that studies rocks and mountains about to blow." Rick gestured toward St. Helens.

"So it really is going to blow up?" asked McKenzie.

"Probably," said Rick. He showed them the beeping machine in his hand. It had a series of numbers running across a small screen. "This is a seismometer. It measures seismic activity," he explained.

Alexis and McKenzie stared back at Rick. Their eyebrows had become high arches of confusion.

"What kind of activity?" asked Alexis.

"*Seismic.* That's the fancy name for the rumbling and small earthquakes you've been feeling," said Rick. "This measures how strong they are. The bigger they get, the more likely the mountain will erupt. What we don't know is how bad it's going to be. Is it going to burp up a little ash and seep a little lava out of a crack, or is it going to blow away its other half? We're trying to figure that out."

Alexis got out her video camera.

"Would you mind repeating that with my camera rolling?" she asked Rick.

"Not a problem," Rick said. After she had recorded Rick's explanation and gotten a good shot of the mountain, she zoomed the lens on Rick's little machine. The number on the screen was 3.3.

"What does that number mean, Dr. Rick?" she asked, lifting the camera to his face again.

"Oh, it means that the last little rumble was a 3.3 on the Richter scale—that's the scale we use to measure movement in the ground, like earthquakes and stuff. It goes from 0 to 10."

"So a 3.3 is really tiny, huh?" asked McKenzie.

"Yeah, just a rumble," said Rick. "You can feel it, but it doesn't do any damage."

"What's a 10 look like?" asked Alexis.

"No one knows," said Rick. He wasn't smiling anymore. "A 10 has never been recorded, but in 1960 there was a 9.5 in Chile. We're talking total devastation over thousands of miles. It was awful. Let's hope we never have to see a 10. I doubt we'll see anything close to that here at St. Helens. The big eruption in 1980 was only a 5.1."

Rick lifted the machine closer to his face and played with a few knobs.

"But the higher the number gets, the closer we get to the mountain erupting."

Alexis turned off her camera and looked around. She wanted to get some footage of the mountain before they left.

"It was nice meeting you, Dr. Rick," she said. "Thanks for the interview."

"Anytime!" Rick said. "I'll see you girls around if you're staying a few days."

Chad stayed to chat with his friend while Alexis and McKenzie explored the lookout. It really was an amazing view. If the tourists in Bigfoot sweatshirts and crazy Hawaiian shirts and hiking boots would get out of the way, she would have some great shots for her film.

Why were they wearing Hawaiian shirts anyway? Alexis had done pretty well in geography at school, and she didn't remember Washington State being anywhere near Hawaii. Thinking of Hawaii reminded her of the volcano. She had always thought of volcanoes as a part of history, but she never would have thought she'd be standing on the edge of one, wondering if it would blow. The thought was creepy.

"Alexis!" called McKenzie. "Come look at this!"

Alexis put her camera away and jogged over to a trail that led down the hill toward the mountain. McKenzie was kneeling in the dirt.

"Look," said McKenzie. "It's a footprint! What kind of animal do you think made it?"

Alexis looked where McKenzie was pointing. The print was bigger than any that Alexis had ever seen. It looked almost like a human foot, but there was something very strange about it. "It looks like a professional basketball player ran around down here without his shoes on!" said Alexis. "Those feet have to be size fourteen, at least!"

"What if it wasn't a human, Alex?" said McKenzie. Alexis stood up and shielded her eyes from the sun. The prints continued down the steep hill and toward a scraggly bunch of trees. They crossed a line of orange tape that the scientists and forest rangers had set up to keep tourists away from the mountain.

Alexis stepped out to follow them.

"Alex, Chad said to stay on the trail," said McKenzie. "That's steep! It's practically a cliff!"

"I'm not going far," said Alexis. "I just want to—"

McKenzie screamed. Alexis slipped on the dusty ground and fell toward the drop-off and the valley below.

A Mountain Mystery

As she fell, Alexis's arm got stuck in something, and her body jerked to a stop. She thought for sure her arm was going to come off, but at least she had stopped falling down the mountain. But what had caught her? She hadn't seen any trees. . . .

"I told you those shoes weren't going to work on the mountain," said Chad. Alexis looked up and saw that he was leaning over the rock wall. He had her arm in a vise-like grip. Alexis got to her feet, and Chad helped her clamber back over the wall. Soon she was standing in the safety of the level parking lot.

"Wow, thanks," Alexis said, dusting herself off. She looked over the edge again and shuddered.

"What were you guys doing down there anyway?" asked Chad.

"I found some tracks," said McKenzie. "We thought they might be Bigfoot's."

"Yeah," said Alexis. "We wanted to see where they went."

"Well, Kellie will be interested in that," said Chad. "I'll have to bring her up here later to take a look. You two about ready to head back?"

But the girls didn't get a chance to answer. A blaring car horn filled the air, and a huge white van burst into the parking lot. It barely missed clumps of scientists and tourists as it made its way to where the girls and Chad were standing. When it parked, a swarm of cameramen jumped out of the sliding back door. Alexis noticed that the top of the van was full of antennae and satellite dishes. The writing on the side said SEATTLE SEVEN NEWS.

"Great," said Chad. "I knew it wouldn't take long for him to get here."

Alexis didn't have time to ask whom Chad was talking about. Before she knew it, a tall guy with spiked black hair jumped out of the front seat and ran to the rock wall. He looked out at the mountain and then turned to yell at the cameramen.

"Right here, guys!" he called. "Set up for the evening shoot!"

"What's all this?" asked McKenzie.

"It's Jeremy Jones," said Chad. "He's a reporter with Channel Seven News. He must be doing a story on the mountain."

Chad sounded really annoyed, and Alexis thought she knew why. She had experience with news reporters, and she knew they weren't always fun to be around.

Alexis and McKenzie watched Jeremy Jones tell his crew where to stand, and in a minute he was right on top of them.

"Excuse me, people," he said. "We're going to need this area."

Chad didn't budge. He waited until the reporter actually looked up and saw them.

"Oh, hey Chad!" said Jeremy. "Who are your little friends?"

"These are some friends of Kellie's," said Chad. "They're here to do a video on the mountain."

"Alright!" said Jeremy. "A couple of little reporters, huh? Well, be sure you get this shot, it's gorgeous!"

He pointed out toward the mountain. Alexis was going to tell him that she already had that shot, but Jeremy Jones wouldn't stop talking. He began giving them all kinds of advice about reporting. This would have been really great, if Alexis had thought he really cared about her report. But she got the feeling that he just liked to hear himself talk.

"And last," Jeremy said, "always remember to get tourists out of your shot, unless you are interviewing them. They really get in the way."

"Uh, okay," said Alexis. "Thanks, Mr. Jones."

Chad nudged Alexis with his elbow.

"He means us, Alexis. He wants us out of his shot," said Chad.

Jeremy shrugged and shot the girls a smile.

"I've got to get this story done, don't I?" he said. "I'm sure we'll bump into each other again soon!"

Jeremy Jones turned his back on them and started ordering the cameramen around again.

"Well, that was interesting," said McKenzie.

"I would say weird," said Alexis. Chad just turned and walked back to the truck.

By the time they pulled in to Kellie's shop, it was starting to get dark. A chill had settled around the mountain now that the sun was no longer shining. Alexis took a deep breath. The air smelled like warm pine needles and cool water. It was so fresh that Alexis thought part of her would like to stay in this forest forever.

"Alexis, are you coming?" McKenzie was waiting at the back door. Light from the kitchen poured out into the night, and Alexis smelled something wonderful. She followed McKenzie inside.

"What's that smell?" she asked.

"Tacos!" said Kellie. "They're my specialty!"

As the four of them settled around the table to eat, the girls filled Kellie in on all the stuff Rick had told them about the mountain.

"It sounds like they know what they're doing," said Kellie. "We should have plenty of warning if the mountain's going to blow. Rick's at the same college my dad teaches at, and they have good people there."

"What does your father teach?" Alex asked.

"He teaches anthropology, which is the study of humanity, or the study of people," she explained.

"Speaking of the study of people, weird people anyway, we met someone else up there too," said Chad. "Your old buddy Jeremy Jones is in town."

Kellie choked on her taco. She coughed until her face was red. Alexis passed her a glass of water.

"Are you okay?" she asked.

"Fine," Kellie said, still choking a bit. She turned to Chad. "So what's *he* doing at St. Helens anyway?"

"He's doing a story, as usual," said Chad.

"What's wrong?" asked Alexis. She knew that the reporter seemed a little stuck up, but she didn't know why Chad and Kellie seemed to be upset about his presence in the area.

"Oh, it's nothing," said Kellie. "Jeremy Jones came out here last summer to do a story on my shop."

"That's awesome!" said McKenzie. "Did it bring in a bunch of tourists?"

Chad snorted. It sounded like a pig's version of his usual laugh.

"We thought it would," he said. "But when the story went on TV, we realized that he didn't really want to help the shop out."

Kellie was angrily chomping on her taco again. When she spoke, her mouth was still half-full.

"His story ended up being on my statues, but he wasn't very nice," Kellie said. "Instead of telling people how unique and pretty they are, he made fun of them."

"He made fun of them?" said Alexis.

"Yeah," said Kellie. "He laughed at them because most of them have something to do with Bigfoot. He doesn't believe Bigfoot exists."

"Oh," said Alexis. She went back to eating her taco, a little disturbed.

"That's awful," McKenzie said indignantly.

"Yeah," Alex added. "Even if Jeremy Jones didn't believe in Bigfoot, how could he make fun of someone as nice as you on the news?"

Alexis didn't even know if she believed in Bigfoot, but she would never make fun of someone just because they did. It wasn't like Kellie was crazy or anything.

"Oh well," Kellie said with a sigh as she finished her food. "At least he'll probably stay away this time."

But just then there was a knock on the back door, and the porch light illuminated the spiked silhouette of Jeremy Jones.

"You've got to be kidding!" said Chad. He stomped into the shop, away from the reporter. "I'd better make myself scarce until he leaves, or I may say something I shouldn't."

Kellie crossed the room and opened the door an inch. Jeremy Jones pushed it open the rest of the way and walked right in. Husky immediately began to growl and show his serious-looking fangs.

Raaaawwwwwwlllll! Rrrrrruuuuuffffff!

"Husky, sit," Kellie commanded. Husky looked at her like he

wanted to obey, but he also wanted to take a piece out of this man.

Rraaaawwww. He growled a bit more softly as he obeyed his owner.

"I see you still have that demented dog," Jeremy Jones said with a sneer. "You need to get yourself a dog that's not so psychotic."

"Can I help you, Mr. Jones?" asked Kellie, ignoring his barbs.

"Come on now, Kellie!" said Jeremy. "Is that any way to greet an old college friend?"

"It's how I greet an old college friend who has turned into a rude reporter," said Kellie. She was still holding the door open. Maybe she hoped Jeremy Jones would turn right back around and leave.

Jeremy ignored her comment and turned toward Alexis and McKenzie.

"Did you two get some good video today?" he asked.

The girls just nodded. Jeremy turned away from all of them and studied the big statue on the shelf. It was the same one Alexis had noticed that morning.

"Are you *still* hooked on this Bigfoot thing, Kell?" he asked.

Kellie flopped down at the table and put her face in her hands.

"Whatever you want to call it, Jeremy," she said. "I'm still making my pottery, if that's what you are asking."

"Mmm," said Jeremy. "And your, um, research? Are you still following your crazy dad's notes all over the mountain?"

"Don't call him crazy!" said a rough voice from the hallway. Chad had wandered back into the kitchen. "Dr. Sanderson is a genius!"

"Spending half of his life chasing around after a mythical creature doesn't sound like genius to me. It sounds deranged," Mr. Jones said.

"Well I should—" Chad said, raring back his fist.

"It's okay, Chad," said Kellie, putting her hands on his chest and keeping him away from Jeremy Jones. "I'm used to this by now."

Kellie turned back to Jeremy. He had started snacking on their bowl of chips and salsa.

"Jeremy, is there a reason you're here?" she asked.

"Just wanted to say hi and let you know I'm in the area," he said. A few chip crumbs sprayed the table. He winked at Alexis and McKenzie and then turned back toward the door. "We should do dinner, Kell."

"Mmm, I'll think about it," Kellie said.

Alexis tried not to laugh. Kellie looked angry. It didn't look like she would have to think very long. She was trying to be nice, but Alexis could tell that she definitely didn't want to go to dinner with Jeremy Jones.

"Well, think about it. I'm staying at the Dewdrop Inn while I'm here. Just call me anytime," he announced as he walked out the door.

"Yeah, she'll go out with you after Bigfoot is found," Alexis heard Chad mutter under his breath. She bit her lip again to keep from laughing.

When the door closed behind the intruder, Kellie started cleaning up. "The nerve!" she exclaimed, looking at the door.

As the girls rinsed their plates and slipped them into the dishwasher, she wiped down the table with a wet cloth.

"You girls should get to bed," she said to Alexis and McKenzie. "You have a long day tomorrow! Alexis, I took your luggage to the cabin while you were gone."

As Alex thanked her host, she noticed that Kellie's smile was back. The girls hugged Ms. Sanderson and waved goodnight to Chad. They went out the back door and crossed the yard to their little cabin with Husky right behind them.

Alexis hadn't seen it yet, but McKenzie had been right. It was like their own little house!

"Kellie told me that this used to be a tourist cabin that was rented to people," McKenzie explained. "But when she bought the shop, she also bought this cabin to offer to guests and when her family comes to visit. Her dad likes to spend time down here when he's not teaching. He likes to look for Bigfoot."

"So it runs in the family, huh?" Alexis asked.

"Yep, apparently," McKenzie said.

As the girls walked in the door, to the left they saw a small living room with a couch, a small TV, and a fireplace. Behind the couch two bunk beds were stacked against the wall. Alexis saw her bag on the top bunk. There was a small door near the beds, and Alexis guessed that was the bathroom.

To the right, on the other side of the cabin, were a small kitchen and a tiny table with two chairs. The kitchen had a sink and a small stove. There was also a mini-fridge. Alexis popped it open and found that it was stocked full of snacks and soda.

"This is so great!" said Alexis. She popped the top off a Coke and tossed one to McKenzie. "I thought we'd be lucky to have a place to put our sleeping bags on the floor!"

"I know!" said McKenzie. She had her camera out and was snapping pictures of Alexis and the room. "I'll put these on the Camp Club Girls website when I get home. The others would love to see this!"

"Speaking of the Camp Club Girls," said Alexis. "I think there might be a bit of a mystery around here."

"What do you mean?" asked McKenzie.

"Well, what was all that about Kellie's dad?"

"Oh," said McKenzie. "Dr. Sanderson used to bring Kellie up here a lot during the summers. I think they might have seen what they thought was Bigfoot sometime while they were camping. Dr. Sanderson became obsessed with finding Bigfoot. So he spends his winters teaching, and when he's not teaching summer school, he spends his time up here. Meanwhile, Kellie takes up where he left off. She uses all of her free time to look for clues."

"Wow," said Alexis. "So that's why she loves to sculpt Bigfoot. And if her dad stays in this cabin doing his research, I guess we're staying in Bigfoot central itself!"

While McKenzie had first turn using the bathroom to get ready for bed, Alexis thought about Jeremy Jones making fun of Kellie and her Bigfoot research. She had never thought about Bigfoot before. She really had no idea if he was real or just some story made up to scare campers. Or if he was just a make-believe creature played up to help draw tourists to the area. But it wasn't like Alexis to make a decision without all of the facts, so she turned to McKenzie.

McKenzie came out of the bathroom with her pajamas on and a toothbrush in her mouth. Alexis started pulling her pajamas out of her bag too.

"You know, McKenzie," said Alexis, "it really would be a shame if two Camp Club Girls got together without solving a mystery."

McKenzie spit in the bathroom sink and put her toothbrush back in its plastic bag.

"I can agree to that. But what mystery?" she asked.

"Well, we are here to report on the mountain, but that won't take all of our time," said Alexis. "What if we spent a little time looking into the whole Bigfoot thing? There have been a lot of sightings. At least that's what the newspaper said. And don't forget the footprints we found today. Maybe we could do some interviews and look around."

McKenzie slid under the covers, and Alexis climbed up to the top bunk. She had to be careful not to hit her head on the rafters of the roof. McKenzie turned off the lamp by the bed. Now it was dark, and talking about Bigfoot became a little spooky.

"That's not a bad idea, Alex. I bet Kellie would tell us anything we wanted to know."

"I bet you're right," said Alexis. "And we can keep our eyes open for more clues."

The girls were drifting off to sleep when a noise from outside made both of them jump. Something was rustling around in the forest not too far from their cabin window. Alexis thought she heard a low growl.

But it sure didn't sound anything like a dog!

CHAPTER 4

Hunting for Trouble

"What was that?" McKenzie whispered nervously.

"I don't know. Something outside. Bears don't growl, do they?" Alexis asked.

"I don't think so," McKenzie said. "Not like that. Did we make sure the door's locked?"

"Yes. I checked it."

"It wasn't Husky, was it?" McKenzie asked.

"No, it was outside," Alexis said, but she still looked down at Husky just to be sure.

With the movement of Alex's bed, Husky raised his head and looked at her calmly. He sniffed the air. Then he put his head back on his paws.

The girls didn't hear the growl again and soon fell into an exhausted sleep.

By the next morning, the girls had forgotten all about the scary noise in the night. They quickly dressed and scurried to the house for breakfast with Husky right behind them.

When the girls walked into the kitchen, an extra person was sitting at the breakfast table. Rick, the geologist, was scooping piles of scrambled eggs onto his plate. Kellie slid a plate full of toast onto the table and sat down.

"Did you girls sleep well?" she asked.

"Yup!" piped Alexis. She was so excited about getting to the bottom of the Bigfoot mystery that it showed in her huge smile. She had her pink notebook in her backpack. She was ready to take notes if she heard anything about Bigfoot while she and McKenzie worked on the volcano film.

McKenzie nodded and poured a glass of orange juice.

"What's new, Dr. Rick?" she said, glancing up at Rick through sleepy eyelashes.

"A lot, actually," he said. "The mountain started emitting gases this morning like it might be getting ready to blow, so they've closed it to tourists."

Alexis's jaw dropped, and her fork clattered to the floor.

"Oh no!" she said. "How am I supposed to get my story if I can't get to the mountain?"

She was frantic. All Alexis could think about was going home and telling the TV station—and her parents—that the whole trip had been a waste. Her brilliant mood shriveled like a helium balloon in the cold.

"Don't worry, Alexis," said McKenzie. "We'll find a way to get your story. We can still interview the people in town. And I bet Dr. Rick will give us any information he can."

"I can do better than that, actually," said Rick.

Alexis tried not to be annoyed. He was still smiling from ear to ear, like he hadn't just crushed her hopes. What could he possibly do for her now?

"What do you mean, Dr. Rick?" McKenzie asked. "If the mountain's closed, there's not much more to do than interviews."

"I said it was closed to tourists," said Dr. Rick. "But I never said it was closed to scientists. We can still go up there all we want."

Alexis raised her eyebrows. She didn't want to be rude, but how was it going to help her if the scientists were still allowed on Mount St. Helens? They might be able to do their jobs, but that would not help her do hers.

Dr. Rick opened a leather messenger bag at his feet and pulled out two badges. They were something like the one he had around his neck. He placed them on the table and slid one to McKenzie and one past a plate of bacon to Alexis.

Alexis read the badge and gasped. There, beneath the university seal and the title "Amateur Geologist" was her name.

"Wow, Rick, what are those?" asked Kellie. She came around

the table to look over Alexis's shoulder.

"They're just name tags," he said. "But as long as you two are with me, you'll be allowed on the mountain. You should be able to keep filming for your story."

Now Alexis knew why Rick had been smiling. She was smiling again too.

"That's amazing!" she said. "Dr. Rick, thank you so much!"

"No problem," Rick said. "I'm a bit busy this morning, but I should be able to take you guys up later this afternoon if you have time."

"That sounds perfect, Rick," said Kellie. "I can keep the girls busy for a while."

After breakfast, Alexis and McKenzie helped Kellie in the shop for a few hours. Kellie showed them the tools she used to shape the clay into figures and the pottery wheel she used to create bowls like those the Native Americans of the area had taught her to use. "Some of them took me under their wing when I first started out," she explained. "They taught me how to make pottery from the natural resources around here, including the unique dyes they used from flowers and plants.

"In fact," she continued, "I spent a lot of my summers around here as a child, camping with my parents. So I was familiar with this place. When I first graduated from the Art Institute, I worked here with an old Native American woman who'd had this store for decades. She taught me how to make her pottery and figurines and how to improve my art skills. And she taught me the practical side of succeeding in a business. Her children weren't interested in living in the woods and trying to make a profit from things like this. So when Mrs. Running Deer was ready to retire, she sold me the business."

Next Kellie showed the girls the kiln, where she fired all the clay pottery and figures to make them hard and strong. The kiln was huge and could fire many pieces at once.

"It's old and heavy, but it does the job," Kellie said. "The temperature in here gets up to more than 2,300 degrees. That's twice as hot as the lava coming out of a volcano. After being in there, a figurine could withstand a throw from Bigfoot himself," she said with a little chuckle. "If Mount St. Helens behaves itself, while you're here I'll let you make a figurine to take home as a souvenir."

After the intricate tour of the shop, the girls dusted figurines most of the morning. Even though they worked hard, the time seemed to fly.

Alexis never had so much fun cleaning before. She noticed that not all of Kellie's sculptures were of Bigfoot. There were tons of small animals native to the Northwest. There were tiny beavers and soaring eagles. Ashy turtles and salmon were displayed near gurgling fountains. Kellie really was good at what she did.

A silver bell jingled, and Alexis turned around to see two women enter the store. They were wearing baseball caps with "I Love Bigfoot" on them. They hardly noticed the girls as they chatted to each other about the guide they'd had on a helicopter tour they'd taken over the volcano a week earlier.

Alexis and McKenzie stopped their dusting and hovered near the cash register to stay out of the ladies' way and let them look around. Kellie greeted them and told them to ask if they had any questions. She didn't have to try to get them to buy anything. Within thirty minutes they were piling all sizes of statues on the counter near Alexis.

One lady took off her cap and leaned on the counter.

"We sure were glad to find your little shop," she told Kellie. "With the mountain closed, there's not a lot to do in the area."

"You're right," said Kellie. "If they've closed the mountain, they probably will close the nearby parks as well. No swimming or boating. I'm glad I could give you somewhere to spend your time!"

"And our money!" said the other lady. She wobbled up to the counter carrying one of Kellie's larger statues. Kellie laughed.

"There are a couple of shops in town too," she said. "The jewelry place has a lot of local art."

"We were going to shop there this morning but decided to wait until everyone calms down a little."

Kellie looked at Alexis and McKenzie. She was as confused as they were.

"What do you mean, *calms down*?" asked Kellie. "What's going on in town? Usually it's a pretty quiet, low-key place to be. Not much drama there."

One of the women put her hand on her hip and rolled her eyes, but she was obviously more than happy to share the gossip.

"Well, honey, we're not locals, but something has people all worked up."

"And it's not just the mountain that's grumbling," said the other lady.

"People are grumbling?" asked Kellie. "But the town is usually so friendly."

The first woman leaned on the counter and lowered her voice, even though no one else was around to hear her secret.

"Dogs and cats have started disappearing," the lady said. "The rangers haven't had any complaints of bears or mountain lions in the area, so some of the local people are starting to blame it on Bigfoot. It's causing quite a stir."

At the mention of Bigfoot, Kellie's eyes got really big. Alexis thought she could guess what Kellie was thinking. She wanted nothing more than to find Bigfoot, but Kellie would be heartbroken if he turned out to be some sort of monster who ate people's pets.

Alexis put her hand on Kellie's shoulder.

"We could go check it out," Alexis suggested. "We could interview the ranger about the volcano, and while we're down there we can see what all the talk is about."

"That's a great idea!" said McKenzie.

The girls looked at Kellie with pleading eyes. The town would be a great place to start digging up clues about Bigfoot, since so many people from town had reported seeing him.

"Well," said Kellie, "I guess Chad could watch the store for a bit. We could go in and get lunch at the diner and then stop in and talk to the rangers."

"Yes!" said both girls together. They ran through the kitchen and grabbed their things. They wanted to get their backpacks if they were going investigating. Alexis made sure her notebook was still in her bag. She grabbed her small video camera too. In less than five minutes the girls were back with Kellie in the store.

"That was fast," Chad said. He was washing the front window. Husky sat beside him as if checking to make sure Chad didn't miss any spots. "If you guys are going to the diner without me, you'd better bring me back a burger!" Chad turned to Husky and rubbed the fur between his ears. "Isn't that right, boy?" Husky thumped his tail. "And bring one back for my friend here. And hey, while you're at it, add some onion rings. And maybe a chocolate malted. And—"

"And we'd better get out of here before he has us buy out the whole diner," said Kellie with a laugh. She waved at Chad.

"Now sell billions of dollars worth of merchandise while we're gone," she called as she walked out the door.

"Is that all? I was going for trillions!" he called in reply, returning their waves.

The ride to town only took twenty minutes. There wasn't any traffic going to or from the mountain, so the only other people on the road were the scientists. The little town was just outside the borders of the St. Helens National Park. It was very small, with only the diner, a couple of shops, a tourist information shack, a few old-fashioned motels, a general store, and the ranger station.

A lot of people were hanging around when Kellie parked near the ice cream parlor. Tourists were there, as usual, but there were a lot of locals too, and the locals looked angry. Alexis, McKenzie, and Kellie followed a group of people toward the diner. Many were stopping to look through the windows at some commotion inside.

Kellie led the girls inside. They sat at a table covered with a checkered tablecloth and ordered lunch, and then Kellie pointed to a table across the room.

"That's what all the commotion is about," she said. Alexis looked over her shoulder and saw a man in a ranger's uniform eating with a man in a thick flannel shirt. A huge dog lay on the floor at the second man's feet. Alexis thought it looked like a wolf.

"What? Are they staring because a dog's in here? Is that even legal?" McKenzie asked. "What kind of dog is that, anyway?"

"It's an Alaskan malamute," Kellie answered. "No, it's not the dog. I don't know if it would be legal in the city, but Sam, who owns this place, is best friends with the dog's owner. The dog's the best-behaved dog in three states, I hear. Next to Husky, of course."

"Then what's everyone staring at?" Alexis asked.

"The man in the uniform is Ranger Davis," said Kellie. "The

other guy is Bill Randall. He's a hunter who lives just outside of town. We usually just call him Randall. He and the ranger have never been friends. I wonder why they're eating together? I bet that's what has everyone so curious."

The girls paid little attention to the two men as they decided to follow Chad's example and order burgers, rings, and malts.

"You're looking a little distraught today, Melody," Kellie said to the waitress as Melody placed their orders on the table a few minutes later.

"Oh, my cat disappeared this week," Melody explained. "I've had him a long time, and he's never wandered away from home."

"That must be really upsetting," McKenzie said.

"Well, it is," Melody said. "But on the other hand, there are so many wild animals around here that once in a while a pet disappears. It's the price we pay for living near bears and mountain lions and wolves and such.

"In fact, that's what those two are discussing. A lot of pets have been disappearing lately. Billy Randall insists it's because Bigfoot's on the prowl," Melody explained.

"Really?" Kellie said a bit sharply. The girls craned their necks to look at Mr. Randall.

"Yeah, he's trying to get a special license to go into the national park land and hunt down Bigfoot," Melody added.

Almost as if on cue, the men's voices rang louder through the shop. Alexis and McKenzie stopped eating to watch.

"We have no evidence of *any* large animal around town," said Ranger Davis. "I've said it a hundred times! There's no reason to go hunting down anything! Especially not a mythological creature!"

"It's no myth!" cried the hunter. "I've seen him myself, just outside my property!"

"Well, if that *is* true, then it's the scientists that need to find Bigfoot *not* the hunters," said the ranger. "Besides, Randall, you can't hunt anything without a license."

Someone growled. Alexis couldn't tell if it was the hunter or his dog.

"No license exists for hunting Bigfoot," said the hunter.

"Exactly!" said the ranger, flinging ketchup from one of his french fries. "So hunting him is out of the question! If the scientists find a new species of animal, and we figure out that there are enough of them to allow hunting, then you'll be the first to know. Although most of the sightings have been near the mountain, and you can't hunt in the national park anyway."

Some of the people in the restaurant laughed at this. The hunter glared around the room.

"What about that missing hiker?" asked the hunter. He wasn't yelling anymore, so people had to lean in to listen.

"What about her?" asked Ranger Davis.

Alexis remembered the woman in the newspaper. The girls had heard on the radio on the way into town that the woman still hadn't been found.

"Well," said the hunter, "if this Bigfoot creature is out there eating our cats and dogs, what's he going to do to a helpless human lost in the woods?"

Ranger Davis stopped chewing his food and stared at the hunter.

I guess he hadn't thought of that, thought Alexis.

The hunter stood up and glared down at the ranger. There was another growl, and Alexis saw the dog get up too.

"Davis, I'm warning you," said the hunter. "There's something worse than starvation waiting for that poor girl if the creature finds her before we do."

The hunter slapped a ten-dollar bill onto the table to pay for his lunch and stomped out of the diner.

The ranger sighed and added some money to the pile. Then he got up and walked out the door, leaving half of his burger untouched.

"Come on, girls," said Kellie. "I want to talk to Ranger Davis. This doesn't sound good."

They stopped at the counter to pay and order Chad's burger to go. They would come back and get it after they talked to the ranger.

Outside, the crowds had disappeared. Locals went about their own business, and tourists crowded into the shops as usual. There wasn't anything else to see for the moment.

The girls found the ranger in the ranger station across the street. He was sitting at his desk with a cup of coffee at his elbow.

It didn't look like he was interested in drinking it. Ranger Davis looked up when the three girls came in.

"Oh, hi, Kellie," he said. He took off his hat and ran a hand through his dark gray hair. "I heard that you have some company staying with you. Young television gals." He turned to the girls. "Welcome to our lovely area," he said.

"Hi, Ranger," said Kellie. "This is Alexis and McKenzie. You're right; they're doing a documentary about Mount St. Helens. Hey, is everything okay?"

"Well, it's been better in St. Helens, that's for sure," he answered. "I knew I could expect to see you down here sooner or later, with all this Bigfoot blabber. I wish your dad were still around. He'd know how to handle these crazy hunters."

"Is it that bad?" asked Kellie. "You told Mr. Randall no, right? He wouldn't hunt anything without permission. He's a little rough, but he's not crazy."

The ranger sighed again.

"I'm not sure of anything anymore, Kellie," he said. "All I know is that if Bigfoot's out there, he'd better be careful. He's got more enemies than the average animal."

The Call of the Creature

Alexis hoped that Bigfoot knew he might be in danger.

If he really is out there, she thought. He was supposed to be big, but could he defend himself against a forest full of hunters—with their high-powered guns?

"McKenzie," said Alexis, "is it silly to worry about an animal that may not even exist?"

"No, Alex. Of course not," said McKenzie. "I'm worried too. Even if this creature isn't Bigfoot, he's being hunted. What if the creature is innocent? What if he's not the one making cats and dogs disappear?"

"I don't know," said Alexis. "I can't believe that hunter just wants to run around the forest with his gun without knowing the facts."

Alexis finished tying her shoes and pulled on her backpack. Rick would be there any moment to take the girls back up the mountain.

"You have a point, Alex," said McKenzie.

"What do you mean?" asked Alexis.

"Well, you're right that the hunter doesn't have the facts, but neither does anyone else," said McKenzie. "No one really knows what's going on here."

"Then we have to find out," said Alexis. "The first thing we need to do is email Sydney."

"Why Sydney?" asked McKenzie.

"Because you know what a nature nut she is. She knows

everything about the weirdest animals. The last time we talked, she was telling me all about a new fish they found somewhere near New Zealand."

"You're right!" said McKenzie. "If this news about Bigfoot is on the internet, I bet she has seen it."

"Yep. She might be able to help us separate the facts from fiction. It will save us a lot of time, since we're only here for a few days."

Alexis grabbed her notebook computer and then put it back on the bed with a frown.

"We should have thought of this earlier," she said. "Now we'll have to find a ride back into town to send the email."

"What do you mean?" asked McKenzie. "This may be the woods, but it's not *Little House on the Prairie*. Every cabin has wireless internet."

"Really? I thought maybe we couldn't pick it up here because of the trees," Alex said. "I just brought my notebook in case I needed to go ahead and start doing some editing while we're here."

Alexis turned on her computer and waited. Sure enough, it detected a signal that would connect her to the internet. Alexis was about to open a new email when a tiny picture popped up in the corner of her screen. It was Sydney.

"Sydney's online!" Alexis said to McKenzie. "I bet we can IM her instead of emailing. We'll get her answer right away!"

Alexis's fingers flew over the keyboard.

Alexis: *Hey there, Sydney!*

Sydney: *Hey, Al! What's up? I'm a little busy. I'm writing a report on ring-tailed lemurs.*

Alexis: *Well, I'm in Washington State with McKenzie, and we've stumbled onto something interesting.*

Sydney: *Well, hi, Mack! Ooo, Washington State? Watch out for Bigfoot!*

Alexis: *LOL, very funny. Seriously, though, that's what we wanted to ask you about.*

Sydney: *I'm being serious too, Alex. Watch out for Bigfoot. It's all over the internet. People have been running into him a lot this spring.*

Alexis: *So you know about it?*

Sydney: *It's hard to pick out the truth from the other crazy things people say, but there have been enough sightings to make it seem real.*

Alexis: *What makes you say that?*

Sydney: *Usually people writing about Bigfoot are all the same. They're weirdoes who spend too much time in the woods. But lately all kinds of people are talking about him. Old ladies visiting the mountain, kids on field trips, people like that.*

Alexis: *School kids?*

Sydney: *Yeah, I'll email you the article.*

Alexis: *Thanks! You know, Syd, if this really is Bigfoot, it would be a new species, right?*

Sydney: *Right. And that doesn't happen very often. When scientists find a new animal, it's usually a weird fish or something that lives at the bottom of the ocean. It's really the only place that hasn't been explored all the way. I'll do a little more searching and see what I find. After my report is done, of course!*

Alexis: *Thanks, Syd!*

Sydney: *No problem, Alex! Talk to you soon! Ta-ta for now, Mack!*

Alexis set the computer on McKenzie's bottom bunk.

"Well, that was interesting," she said.

"Yep," said McKenzie. "So all kinds of people are seeing Bigfoot now? I wonder what that means."

"Maybe he's not as shy as he used to be," said Alexis. "Or maybe he's being forced out of the forest because he's looking for food. That happens with bears and coyotes back home."

The girls shivered as they thought of the missing cats and dogs in town. Alexis hoped that Bigfoot wasn't really eating them.

A horn sounded from outside.

"I bet that's Rick!" said McKenzie. The girls grabbed their backpacks and flew out of the cabin. A university van was waiting in front of Kellie's shop. They jumped in with Rick and a female scientist and headed up the mountain. Before they got to the parking lot of the visitors' center, a park ranger stopped the van. The girls flashed their name tags that Rick had given them, and the ranger waved them through.

"Wow, that was easy!" said McKenzie.

"Yeah," said Rick. "Security isn't too tight right now. They just don't want tourists up here in case they have to evacuate. We scientists know what we're running from and how fast to move out of the way. Tourists tend to linger to take one last picture."

Alexis jumped out of the van and looked around. There weren't very many people in the parking lot. A few scientists were clustered around their gadgets, scribbling frantically in notebooks.

"What are they doing?" asked McKenzie.

"It's called forecasting," said Rick.

"Like weather forecasting?" asked Alexis.

"Very much like that," said Rick. "But instead of telling you when it will rain, we try to tell you when a volcano is going to erupt. First, we look at the earthquakes. Hot lava, called magma, moves into a holding chamber under the mountain. When it moves, it causes earthquakes."

"So keeping track of the earthquakes tells you how much lava there is?" said Alexis.

"Sometimes," said Rick. "But just because there's lava doesn't mean the mountain will blow. Sometimes it just cools and turns into rock inside the mountain."

"What else do you look for?" asked McKenzie.

"We watch the mountain to see if it's bulging."

"Bulging?" said Alexis. "That doesn't sound good!"

"Well, the hot lava lets off gasses. Eventually, there is so much gas that the mountain starts to expand, like a balloon."

"But it's not a balloon!" said McKenzie. "It's a *mountain*! How does it expand?"

Rick sat down on the stone wall and took a deep breath.

"In 1940," he said, "a bridge up in Tacoma collapsed."

"Gallopin' Gertie!" squealed McKenzie. "My mom told me about that last summer when we drove over the new bridge."

"The real name was the Tacoma Narrows Bridge," said Rick. "It collapsed in mild winds because conditions were just right. If you watch the video, it looks like the steel and concrete had turned to liquid. It twisted like a piece of taffy for a while before it finally broke and crashed into the water."

Rick looked out over the mountain.

"To us, a mountain seems so strong. What could possibly move it? But when conditions are right, just like the steel and concrete of that bridge, the mountain will blow. Think of it like the balloon again. If you blow and blow into a balloon, soon it won't be able to hold any more air, and it will pop."

Alexis looked across at the mountain. For the first time since she had arrived at the mountain, Alexis was afraid. The forces of nature could be scary. Earthquakes and volcanoes were powerful things. Alexis took a deep breath and suddenly smiled.

But I know who made the earthquakes and volcanoes, she thought, *and the Creator is always more powerful than the creation!*

Psalm 27:1 popped into her head, and she said it to herself a few times. "The LORD is my light and my salvation—whom shall I fear? The LORD is the stronghold of my life—of whom shall I be afraid?"

In an instant her smile grew even bigger.

"Alexis!"

McKenzie had crossed the parking lot. She was looking at the mountain from another angle. When Alexis looked up, McKenzie started waving at her wildly.

"What is it?" asked Alexis as she jogged over. McKenzie pointed to the dirt on the other side of the rock wall. It was another set of footprints left by huge, bare feet.

"It looks like they follow the wall," said Alexis.

"Good!" said McKenzie. "Maybe this time we can follow them without you falling down a cliff."

"Ha, ha," said Alexis. She pushed McKenzie playfully. "Come on, let's go!"

They followed the tracks along the wall until they almost ran into the visitors' center. The footprints ended there.

"Why don't they go off into the woods?" said Alexis.

"Because whatever left them didn't go into the woods. Look.

The last two prints are facing the wall, like he was getting ready to climb over it."

"Into the parking lot?" said Alexis. "I wonder why Bigfoot would be wandering around in a human parking lot?"

"We don't know this is Bigfoot, Alexis."

"You're right, but I don't think some big basketball player with huge feet is running around the area barefoot either."

Alexis took out her digital camera and snapped a few pictures of the tracks. When she got to the wall of the visitors' center, something tickled her elbow. She looked down and saw a clump of brown fuzz. She picked it up and put it into a plastic baggie she dug out of her backpack.

"What do you think it is?" asked McKenzie.

"I think it's fur," said Alexis. She looked at McKenzie and raised her eyebrows.

"Man, Alexis! I wish we had a science lab like they have on TV. Then we might be able to tell for sure what kind of fur it is. Alexis? What are you staring at?"

Alexis pointed across the parking lot to where Rick was helping another scientist load gadgets into the van. He looked up and waved the girls over. It was time to go back down the mountain.

"Come on," said Alexis. The girls trotted back over to the van, and Alexis held up her plastic baggie. "Um, Rick, do you have any way to tell us what kind of animal this hair came from?"

Rick took the baggie and held it up.

"I study rocks, Alexis. I don't have the right tools to do that," he said.

"Oh," said Alexis.

"Bummer," said McKenzie.

"But I know someone who does," said Rick. The girls looked up. Alexis hadn't been so excited since she found out she was coming to St. Helens.

"Margaret, the girl who rode up here with us today, would have exactly what you need," said Rick. "It might take a day or two to get any results, though."

"Wow, thanks, Rick!" said Alexis.

"No problem. If this really is Bigfoot, it's a big deal!"

The girls got into the van with the other scientists, and Rick dropped them off at Kellie's. Alexis almost didn't recognize the shop. It was crowded with tourists.

McKenzie and Alexis pushed their way through the crowd until they found Kellie. She was behind the cash register filling shopping bags with her statues. The shelves were clearing out fast.

"Hi, girls!" she said when she saw them. "Isn't this great? The Bigfoot sightings are getting people excited. They love my statues, and tonight I'm leading a camping trip."

"You're going camping with a huge unknown animal on the loose?" asked McKenzie.

"That's the point, McKenzie," said Kellie. "People *want* to see Bigfoot. We go and hang out around a campfire. If we're lucky, Bigfoot might come to see us. He may not get too close, but maybe we'll get a glimpse. If you want to come along with us, go get your sleeping bags ready!"

Alexis followed McKenzie out the back of the store and across the yard to their cabin. It was beginning to get dark. They had to hurry. Alexis stuffed an extra pair of clothes into her backpack and grabbed her sleeping bag and pillow. She made sure her video camera was still in her backpack too, just in case. If they saw Bigfoot, she wanted proof.

That night they stayed up past midnight. They sat around a campfire, listening quietly while Kellie told stories of her father and how he had seen Bigfoot.

"Come on out, Bigfoot! We won't hurt you," one lady yelled into the darkness.

Alex and McKenzie looked at each other, rolling their eyes.

Alex wasn't sure if Kellie was trying to spook the people on the trip. She didn't know if that was part of the thrill for the campers. But she caught people apprehensively looking into the darkness as if they thought Bigfoot would suddenly appear and eat them!

No matter how long the girls tried to keep their eyes open, they never got a glimpse of Bigfoot. When they finally rolled out their sleeping bags, Alexis was having a hard time keeping her eyes from closing. As she drifted off to sleep, she heard a noise. It sounded almost like the lonely howl of a wolf, but it was deeper. She was sure it came from a much larger animal.

What the Neighbor Saw

The next morning, Alexis and McKenzie followed the rest of the weary campers through the woods. They hadn't seen Bigfoot, but it had still been a fun night. Most of the tourists were convinced they had *heard* Bigfoot. That would be a great story to tell too.

Alexis was about to ask McKenzie a question when she heard Kellie yell from the front of the group.

"What in the world is going on here?"

The campers stopped in their tracks. Alexis and McKenzie ran to the front and saw what had surprised Kellie. Police cars surrounded her shop with their lights flashing. One man was tying yellow crime scene tape to a nearby tree. Husky was tied around another tree, frantically wresting his body around, trying to get the muzzle off that someone had put on his face.

"My dog!" Kellie cried, running to her pet.

"Sorry, ma'am," one of the police officers answered. "He was going crazy when we got here and seemed like he was going to bite us, so we had to muzzle him and tie him up for a while. Please leave him tied up until we leave."

"What happened?" Alexis asked McKenzie. She tried to see what had happened, but there was too much commotion.

"Over there," said McKenzie. She poked Alexis's arm and then pointed to the back door that led into Kellie's kitchen.

It had been torn completely off its hinges.

"Oh no!" said Alexis.

Kellie turned around and thanked all of the campers for a good trip. Then she asked them kindly to leave so the police could do their job. As the tourists left the scene, Kellie stormed off to find whoever was in charge.

"It looks like someone broke in," said Alexis. "But why?"

"Maybe they wanted to steal the statues. Or maybe they took the money out of the register."

"There's only one way to find out for sure," said Alexis. She dropped her backpack near a tree and dug out her pink notebook and a pen. "We have to ask some questions."

Alexis walked toward one of the officers, but McKenzie grabbed her elbow.

"Those cops aren't going to talk to us, Alexis! This is a real investigation."

"Our investigation is real too, McKenzie!" said Alexis.

"I know it is," said McKenzie. "That's why we should talk to *that* guy over there."

McKenzie pointed across the yard to the young policeman who had been tying up the yellow tape a moment before. He was standing at the corner of the shop looking bored.

"See what I mean?" said McKenzie. "The other cops are too busy to talk. He looks like he would love to answer our questions! We just have to act like we're curious and scared because we're staying here and all."

"I don't have to act," said Alexis. "It's creepy to think about someone breaking into the shop. What if they come back to break in to our cabin?"

The girls shivered, and then McKenzie walked across the yard to where the young police officer was standing. He was drawing pictures in the dirt with his black boot.

"Um, hello," said McKenzie. "I'm McKenzie, and this is my friend Alexis."

The young man nodded.

"I'm Officer Johnson," he said. "Can I help you? I don't think anyone is supposed to be back here."

"We are staying here right now, Officer. Kellie Sanderson is our friend, and we are here visiting," said Alexis.

"Oh," said Officer Johnson. "Well, be glad you weren't here

when the break-in happened. Whoever did this is strong and violent. Just look at what he did to that door!"

Alexis realized that the glass in the top of the door was gone. Broken pieces littered the ground around the back steps. Two chunks of wood were missing where the door had been attached to the house.

"That's crazy!" said McKenzie. "Was the inside destroyed too?"

"No," said the officer. "That's the funny thing. There's a little bit of mud inside, but nothing else was messed up. We don't even think anything was taken."

"So why would someone break in if they weren't going to take anything?" asked Alexis.

"Not sure," said Officer Johnson. "Maybe they just wanted to make a mess. Is there anyone who doesn't like Ms. Sanderson or her work?"

Alexis remembered that Jeremy, the news guy, didn't like Kellie's Bigfoot sculptures. But she didn't think he would break down her back door. She shook her head.

"Well, I would be careful if I were you," said Officer Johnson. "Don't go anywhere without an adult, okay?"

"Yes, sir," said McKenzie and Alexis together. They waved goodbye and walked toward the back of the shop. Kellie had just gone inside, and Alexis wanted to see if the police officers would let McKenzie and her in too. They might find some clue the police had missed. McKenzie walked past her, and Alexis grabbed her arm.

"Not so fast!" Alexis said. "If we walk slowly, we might hear what some of the other police officers are talking about."

"Good idea!" said McKenzie. They strolled through the yard, waiting to hear something interesting. Two officers were arguing over their favorite doughnuts.

"No way!" said one officer. "Chocolate frosting with sprinkles!"

"Nope," said the other officer. "I like it simple. Just a light glaze."

Alexis rolled her eyes as McKenzie tried not to laugh. They obviously weren't going to get any useful information out of those two.

Near the broken door, a policewoman kneeled to snap a few pictures of something in the dirt. Alexis leaned over her shoulder and saw a boot print.

"Is that the only print you guys found?" said Alexis. The woman jumped and almost dropped her camera.

"Yes, it is, but you two need to back away. You're going to contaminate my crime scene." The woman went back to taking pictures. Alexis got out her camera and shot a quick picture over the officer's shoulder. When the policewoman turned around, Alexis and McKenzie were already a few feet away examining the door. Alexis took a few pictures of it too.

"Man," said McKenzie. "Someone had to be incredibly strong to yank this door off its hinges."

"Yeah," said Alexis. "But maybe they used a tool of some sort. Why would they rip it out anyway? The glass was broken. They could have reached through the window and unlocked the door from the inside."

"Hmm," said McKenzie. "Ooo! Here comes Kellie!"

Kellie's voice drifted out the back door seconds before she came tromping out of it.

"What do you mean *nothing is missing*? My favorite statue is gone!"

Kellie was nose to nose with the lead investigator.

"I'm sorry, ma'am," he said. "It was hard to tell. It didn't look like anything had been disturbed."

"Well *I'm* disturbed!" said Kellie. "Please tell me you're going to find this guy."

While Kellie and the officer kept talking, Alexis spotted something on the doorjamb. Stuck on the splinters where the door had been ripped out was a small, brown piece of fluff. She gasped and jabbed McKenzie in the ribs.

"Look at that!" she whispered. "It looks just like what we found at the mountain today!"

"You're right!" said McKenzie.

Alexis took a picture before she interrupted Kellie's conversation.

"Excuse me," she said, tapping the lead investigator on the shoulder. "I think your officers missed something. There's a tuft of hair caught in the doorway."

She pointed up, and the officer stared. He looked around to

the woman officer who had told Alexis and McKenzie to go away.

"Officer Keith!" he said. "Why was this overlooked?"

"Uh, well, I'm not sure, sir," she stuttered.

"Well, take care of it!"

"Yes, sir!" The woman nudged Alexis out of the way so she could begin taking pictures of the hair.

Kellie led the girls under the yellow tape and away from the crime scene.

"I'm going to go around front and look for Chad. I haven't seen him yet," said Kellie.

"Okay," said McKenzie. "We're going to our cabin for a bit. We'll be out in a little while."

Kellie nodded and turned to walk around the shop. Alexis looked sideways at McKenzie.

"What are we going to do in the cabin?" she asked.

"Well, our clues are beginning to pile up. We have the tracks at the mountain, the noises we keep hearing at night, and *two* tufts of dark brown fur. I think we need to get our facts straight and start figuring this thing out."

"I agree," said Alexis. "But why do we have to be in the cabin?"

"Because of the internet connection," said McKenzie. "I think it's time we called in the rest of the Camp Club Girls, don't you?"

Alexis smiled.

"It would be nice to hear what they think," she said. "Let's invite them to a video chat later tonight!"

"That's exactly what I was thinking!" said McKenzie.

The girls entered the cabin, and Alexis headed straight for the laptop. She flipped it open and went to the website that all the Camp Club Girls shared. Once the page was up, she typed her invitation.

Hi, everyone! McKenzie and I are in Washington, and some pretty weird things have been going on. We'd like to see what you guys think! If you can, meet us online at eight o'clock tonight. Sorry, Sydney and Kate. . .I know that's late on the East Coast! Hope you can make it!

Love, Alexis

"There!" said Alexis. "The others will definitely be able to shed some light on this."

Alexis went to close her computer, but McKenzie stopped her.

"Wait! You have an email from Sydney!"

"You're right!" said Alexis. "It's that Bigfoot article she was telling us about yesterday!"

Alexis opened up the article and read it out loud to McKenzie.

"Last Tuesday, a busload of fourth graders from Olympia, Washington, went on a field trip to Mount St. Helens. They hoped to see some wildlife, but they got more than they bargained for. Their teacher, Mrs. Hawkins, says that they saw Bigfoot."

"Wow!" said Alexis. "They were *here*! At St. Helens!"

"I know!" said McKenzie. "Keep reading!"

Alexis continued, "Mrs. Hawkins says the children were getting on the bus to go home when a large, brown animal jumped out from behind the visitors' center. 'They screamed because they thought it was a bear,' said the teacher. She pushed the last children onto the bus and closed the doors to keep them all safe.

"One of the fourth graders says that's when it got strange. 'We were watching out the windows, waiting for the animal to go away. It was bigger than any bear, and its hair was long and shaggy, like my grandma's dog. It came closer to the bus, and then it started dancing!'

"All of the witnesses saw the same thing: a large animal dancing through the parking lot on its two hind legs."

Alexis and McKenzie stared at each other. This was not just a rumor. This was a busload of people who had seen Bigfoot. . .or something like him. At least sixty students, a teacher, and a bus driver had all seen the same thing.

"Well, at least we know there's *something* out there," said Alexis. "It's not just some story someone made up."

"I wonder if Kellie or Chad know about this article," said McKenzie.

"Only one way to find out," said Alexis. "Let's go ask!"

The girls left the laptop on the bed and went back outside. The police officers were beginning to leave, so Alexis and McKenzie walked around the crime scene to the front of the shop. They saw

Kellie standing near the porch talking to Chad, but before they could ask their question, someone else interrupted.

"Nice day for a break-in, huh, Kell?" Jeremy Jones was leaning against his news van with his arms crossed and a huge smile plastered across his face.

Kellie rolled her eyes. Chad ran his hand angrily through his blond hair and stomped off into the shop.

"What are you doing here, Jeremy?" asked Kellie.

"There's a story to cover," Jeremy said. "Why wouldn't I be here?"

"Of course," said Kellie. "Well, if you want an interview, we'd better get to it so you can leave."

Jeremy smiled again, but he didn't look sweet. Alexis thought his expression looked like her brothers' faces when they had put worms in her bed or dirt in her hot cocoa.

"I already got my interview," said Jeremy. "I talked to the little old lady who lives across the road. She said she saw everything. She *said* she saw Bigfoot."

The Secret Cave

Jeremy's news van left the shop, and all three of them stood there with their mouths hanging open. Kellie looked down at Alexis and McKenzie.

"Bigfoot broke in to my shop?" she said.

"According to your neighbor," said McKenzie.

"But that doesn't make any sense!" said Kellie. "Why would he do something like that? If he's been hanging around here, he should know that I care about him. I would never hurt him! Why would he steal one of my statues?"

"Maybe he just liked it," joked Chad, who was coming back out of the shop. Everyone except Alexis started laughing. "That's the ultimate compliment—when the subject of your favorite piece of artwork steals his own statue!"

"What if he's right?" Alexis said. The others stopped laughing and stared at her.

Alexis could see they were confused, so she told them what she was thinking.

"There was only one statue missing, right, Kellie?"

"Yes," said Kellie.

"Which statue was it?" asked Alexis. "You said it was your favorite."

"It was the only statue with *two* Sasquatches. They were standing together holding hands and looking up at the stars. It was my favorite because it was the only one where I thought Bigfoot looked happy."

"Maybe that's why he liked it too," said McKenzie. "You said you thought he was lonely. Maybe you're right."

"But it still doesn't make sense," Kellie insisted. "Husky was loose in the house. The person would have walked all the way through to get the statue. Husky never would have allowed someone he didn't know into the house. The police officers had to tie him up to get near the house. Even if it was some sort of animal, Husky would have gotten ferocious."

"That's an interesting idea, ladies," said Chad. "Let's talk more about it in the truck."

"In the truck?" said Kellie. "Where are we going?"

"To Spirit Lake," said Chad. "They have to replace the door, and the shop's closed for the day. We might as well show the girls something cool."

"Good idea!" said Kellie. "Come on, ladies! You're going to love this!"

All four of them piled into Chad's truck. After a bit they turned off the main road and onto a dirt trail. Alexis didn't think many cars made it back this way.

It was a gorgeous day. There hadn't been any sunshine since the day Alexis arrived, but for some reason even the dreary day was beautiful. Gray sky poked through the pines. The dull color only made the green brighter. The only dirt on the ground was the road itself. On either side bushy ferns filled the forest floor. Every now and then, Alexis saw a fallen tree covered with yellow-green moss.

When Chad stopped the truck, Alexis looked out the front window. There, spreading out in front of her, was a huge lake. It was unlike any lake she had ever seen, because it was covered with floating logs.

"Welcome to Spirit Lake!" said Chad. Everyone got out of the truck and began walking down to the shore.

"Why are there logs in the water?" asked Alexis.

"They're trees," said Kellie. "The last time the mountain blew there was a huge landslide. The force of it swept hundreds of thousands of trees right off of the mountain. Many of them ended up in this lake."

"Wow," said McKenzie. "That's crazy!"

"It's better now," said Chad. "At first the lake was almost completely covered by the dead trees. The lake was dead too. After the eruption, nothing could survive in it because of the gasses and chemicals the mountain released."

"Scientists thought it would take a long time for the lake to recover," said Kellie. "But it only took three years. By 1993, there were even fish."

Alexis was amazed.

God allowed that eruption, she thought, *but He also helped the mountain heal. I shouldn't be scared of what might happen if the mountain erupts. It's all in God's hands.*

Alexis got out her video camera and started filming for her report. She had hardly worked on it since her first day here, and she needed to get it done. She filmed Chad and Kellie as they told the story of Spirit Lake again, and then got some close-ups of the floating trees. When she was about to put the camera away, she heard McKenzie call her name.

Alexis followed the voice around a corner. McKenzie, Kellie, and Chad were kneeling over a spot near the truck.

"What is it?" asked Alexis.

"It's another footprint," said McKenzie. "Just like the ones we found at the visitors' center up on the mountain."

Alexis ran over, and sure enough, there were more of the giant, bare footprints leading toward the lake.

"You two have seen these before?" asked Kellie. "Why didn't you tell me?"

"We're sorry, Kellie," said McKenzie. "It's been a busy couple of days."

"That's true," said Kellie. She was bubbling with excitement. "Tell me all about them!"

The girls told Kellie about the tracks they had found on the first day of their visit. Then they told her of the tracks near the visitors' center that led them to the tuft of brown hair they had found.

"Dr. Rick is checking the hair out," said Alexis. "We think he might be able to tell us if it was left by Bigfoot or not."

"This is amazing, girls!" said Kellie. "You may have discovered evidence that Bigfoot exists! DNA testing could prove that he is a new species, even if no one can catch him or snap a good picture!"

"Well," said Alexis, "if we follow these tracks, we just might get a good picture."

Alexis turned her camera back on, and the group began following the footprints. They went down near the water and then turned to the right. After about fifty feet, they disappeared into some bushes.

"I don't know if we should go in there, girls," said Chad. "I don't know if this is Bigfoot or not, but what I do know is that it's something very large and very wild. We probably don't want to sneak up on it."

"You're right," said McKenzie. She picked up two sticks and started banging them together and yelling into the bushes.

"What on earth are you doing!" said Alexis.

"I'm letting him know that we're coming," said McKenzie. "My dad taught me. It tells bears, mountain lions, and other large animals that you are coming so you don't sneak up on them. They are less likely to attack you that way. If they hear you, they usually leave and go somewhere else."

"But I thought we were trying to get a picture," said Kellie, disappointed. "Why are we scaring him away?"

"It's either scare him away or take a chance that he might not like us," said Chad. "Come on."

He pushed his way through the bushes and gasped.

"Come on, girls! You're not going to believe this!"

Alexis, McKenzie, and Kellie followed Chad's voice through the bushes and found themselves in a cave. Dull light from outside trickled in between the leaves of the bushes, but it was still pretty dark.

"Here," said McKenzie, and she dug out her cell phone. When she pressed its flashlight button, it filled the cave with a bluish light.

"I think this is his home," said Alexis. "I think Bigfoot *lives* here!"

She ran to the back of the cave.

"Look at this!" She started snapping pictures of a pile of pine needles. It looked like a giant nest, and there were tufts of brown hair all over it. McKenzie brought her phone closer so they could get a better look.

"This must be where he sleeps," said McKenzie. "There's some different hair over on this side. Look." Alexis looked closely. It was blond hair, and it looked to be about shoulder length.

"Maybe Bigfoot has a girlfriend," joked Kellie. Alexis dug another plastic bag out of her backpack and dropped the blond hair into it. She didn't know what she was going to do with it yet, but it was another clue.

"The other Camp Club Girls might have some ideas," said McKenzie. Alexis nodded. She was glad they were going to talk to the others tonight. They needed some fresh eyes to tell them if they were missing something. One thing she didn't want to do was jump to conclusions.

"Is there any chance this could be a bear cave?" Alexis asked. She shivered, remembering too well what it was like to be chased by an angry bear. That had happened when she and Bailey were on site at Lake Tahoe, doing a documentary on an animal refuge. With the Camp Club Girls' help, Alex and Bailey had figured out who was trying to sabotage the refuge.

At Lake Tahoe the girls had gone to see hibernating bear caves, when someone had awakened the bears. Only by God's help and grace had the girls gotten on their snow sleds and away from the angry bears.

Alexis looked nervously at the entrance to the cave. Maybe they should get out before whatever lived there came back.

"There's no way it's a bear cave," said Chad.

"What do you mean?" said Kellie.

"Look over here," said Chad.

McKenzie moved her phone so the light was shining on where Chad was standing. There by his feet were the remains of a small campfire.

"As far as I know, bears don't build campfires," said Chad. Alexis bent down to snap a few shots of the fire. She could tell it was old because there was no warmth coming from the charred logs. There were fish bones scattered among the ashes.

●─●─●

On the way back to the shop, Alexis couldn't stop thinking about the cave.

"Do you really think that's Bigfoot's home?" Alexis asked McKenzie quietly, hoping Chad couldn't hear them over his iPod.

"I don't know. I've never heard of any animal being able to make a fire," McKenzie answered. "Not even gorillas can do that, I don't think. And they're supposed to be the closest to humans, aren't they?"

"Well, one of those primates," Alexis answered.

"And aren't animals generally scared of fire?" McKenzie said.

"Well, they always were on the old Tarzan movies I used to watch," Alexis said, laughing.

"I don't know. This seems nuts," McKenzie said. "If Bigfoot did live in this cave, it means he's much more than just another animal. He would be nearly human."

"Did you ever see *Harry and the Hendersons*?" Alex asked.

"I think my mom used to have the VHS," McKenzie replied. "Wasn't it some movie about Bigfoot living with some people?"

"Yeah. They accidentally hit him with their car in the woods," Alexis recalled. "They thought they killed him, so they took him home to stuff as a trophy. But he was only knocked out and regained consciousness. The family became really good friends with him."

"And this came to your mind because. . . ," McKenzie asked.

"I don't know. I would just think that to be able to make a meal, Bigfoot would have to be nearly human, not an animal. I think it's more likely that a person was in that cave. But what was he or she doing with hair from the Bigfoot?"

Back at Kellie's place, they found that Kellie's repairman had already been out and put a brand-new door on her home. He was just packing up to leave. The girls went to their cabin for a few minutes while Kellie talked to the repairman.

A little later, Kellie, Chad, and the girls were about to eat lunch back at the shop when there was a knock on the back door. Kellie opened it, and Rick walked in.

"Congratulations!" said Kellie. "You're the first one to walk through my new door!"

"Thanks," said Rick. "Ooo, hot dogs!"

The scientist sat down with them at the table and began piling his plate with hot dogs and chips.

"Well, girls," he said through a mouth full of sour cream and onion chips, "I got the info back on that hair you found."

"You did?" said both girls at once.

"Yep," said Rick. He took a drink of water, and Alexis rolled her eyes. Did he *have* to take a drink *now*? She was waiting for vital information! This might break their case wide open! Rick wiped some ketchup from his cheek and continued.

"It looks like the hair is both human *and* animal," he said.

"What?" said Alexis.

"How is that possible?" asked McKenzie.

"I don't know," said Rick. "It's blended together. Some hairs were human, and some were not. We don't know what animal they came from, though. We'd need more equipment to figure that out. I can send the sample back to the college, but it will take a few days."

"We'll probably be gone by then," said McKenzie.

"Yeah, but thanks for the help," said Alexis. "It's still good information."

Alexis opened her mouth to take another bite and then dropped her hot dog back onto her plate.

"I almost forgot!" she said. She bent over and dug through her backpack. "We found this with some of the brown hair near Spirit Lake."

Alexis handed the baggie with the blond hair in it to Rick. He looked at it through the plastic for a minute and then handed it back.

"This is definitely human," he said. "And I think you should take it to the police."

Rick's face was very serious.

"Why?" said Alexis. "What would they want with it?"

"Well, you remember that hiker who disappeared earlier this week?" Rick said. "She—"

His words were interrupted by the sound of someone running through the shop in the front of the cabin. The front door slammed.

"What was that?" said Chad. "Someone was in the shop!" He ran into the shop and the others followed him. They got to the front porch just in time to see a green truck screech out of the gravel parking lot and head toward town.

"That was Randall," said Chad. "The hunter you girls saw in town the other day. He comes up here sometimes to look at Kellie's new statues. But why didn't he let us know he was here? He usually likes a friendly chat. And I don't know why he left so fast."

Kellie gasped.

"I do," she said. "He heard us talking, and he might have peeked in and seen the hair we found in the cave."

"What do you mean?" said Alexis.

"The missing hiker—she had blond hair."

CHAPTER 8

Man-Eating Monster?

"That hunter is sure going to cause a stir now," said Kellie. "If he thinks Bigfoot is responsible for the missing hiker, he's going to want to find him. He'll use this as an excuse to go on the warpath against Bigfoot even more. And Randall isn't known for his patience. I think he'll shoot first and ask questions later," she said.

"Maybe he'll miss," Alexis offered hopefully.

"I wish, but I doubt it," Kellie said unhappily. "He's the best shot for miles around."

She didn't say anything else, but Alexis knew what she was thinking. If the hunter found Bigfoot, the animal would be in trouble. And what if that hair really *did* belong to the missing girl? Could Bigfoot really have taken her? If so, why? And would he have harmed her?

Rrrrrmmmmbbbmmm.

The group had turned to go back into the shop when a deep rumble made them look toward the mountain. The gray sky turned almost black, and the ground rocked beneath their feet.

"Oh, no," said Rick. His cell phone started ringing like crazy. "Get in the truck!" he yelled as he answered his phone. "Hello?"

Alexis followed Chad and Kellie to the truck after she grabbed her video camera. She jumped in the backseat and pulled McKenzie in with her. Rick jumped in just before Kellie closed her door.

"Oh no, I left my keys in your kitchen," he said.

"No time to go back now!" Kellie exclaimed as Chad roared out of the parking lot and drove as fast as he dared down the winding road toward town. No one said a word, but Kellie looked worried. When Rick finished his call, she turned toward him.

"How bad?" she asked.

"Not as bad as I thought it would be," said Rick. "We're still here, aren't we?"

He turned around to Alexis and McKenzie. "The mountain erupted, but it's okay. It was only a small crack, and all it did was let out a small ash plume. See?"

Rick pointed out the windshield. Chad had just turned on the windshield wipers, but it wasn't raining. Tiny flakes of gray ash were sprinkling the truck.

"Mom was right," said McKenzie. "It's just like gray snow!"

"We'll go into town anyway," said Chad. "I'm sure they want us to evacuate, right, Rick?"

"Yep," said Rick. "My boss said everyone should be gone by tomorrow morning."

"Where will everyone go?" asked Alexis.

"To family or friends," said Kellie. "My dad lives in Olympia. That's not too far away. Chad and I will stay with him a bit until it's okay to come back. When we get to town, I'll call and make reservations for you two to fly home. Then I'll drive you all to the airport tomorrow."

"Alex, we shouldn't have any problems getting you home since you live to the south," Kellie added. "McKenzie, last time the mountain blew, the clouds of ash went to the east, so if we have strong plumes of ash and they go to the east, we may have a challenge getting you home right away."

"You can't take us to the airport!" said Alexis. "Not right before all the action!"

"She's right!" said McKenzie. "We don't want to leave yet!"

"You may not have a choice," said Chad. "I doubt that your parents will like you hanging around this close to a volcano that could really blow any moment."

Alexis frowned out the window. She knew they were right. Her mom worried all the time anyway. She would not want to let Alexis stay this close to St. Helens. Alexis would call her when they got to town. Maybe her mom would let her stay in Olympia with Kellie, just until she was supposed to come home. She really didn't want to leave early.

As they pulled into the town, Alexis noticed that everything was closed up tight. But fortunately, warm lights from the diner shined into the street.

Chad pulled the truck into a parking space in front of the diner.

"We left our lunch on the table back at Kellie's," he said. "Anybody up for a burger?"

"I'm famished!" Kellie said.

"I'm so hungry I could eat a bear," Chad announced. "Or something of that magnitude. Just not anything as big as Bigfoot."

All five of them went in and got a table. Alexis shook the ash from her dark hair and looked around. Rosa was their server today. She dropped off their menus and spoke to Kellie.

"Good timing, Kellie, honey," she said. "I'm glad you came to town. There's going to be a town meeting tomorrow. I guess they're going to tell us to get out of here."

"Thanks, Rosa," said Kellie. "We'll just hang out here until things settle down."

"How worried did your boss sound, Rick?" said Chad.

"Oh, he's going nuts. He says if the mountain blows again like it did in 1980, there won't be much of it left."

"That would be awful!" said McKenzie.

"Yeah," said Alexis. "They'd have to start calling it Crater St. Helens."

This made everyone smile. Even Kellie, who seemed really nervous, chuckled.

"If that happens," said Rick, "I'll make sure you get the credit for coming up with the name! But I don't think he really believes it's going to blow like that. I don't think anyone is predicting that this will be a major eruption. We'll have a better idea in a couple of hours."

Rosa came back with their drinks. She gave Alexis her Dr Pepper and asked, "Are you all ready to order?" They nodded.

"I'll have the avocado burger, please," Alexis said. She handed her menu to the waitress and looked around. "Why is the restaurant so empty? I thought there would be people everywhere, with the eruption and all."

"Well," said Rosa, "most of the tourists are already gone."

"That was fast!" said McKenzie. "The eruption was only half an hour ago!"

"That's true, but Mr. Randall ran into town about an hour ago with some crazy news. He was ranting and raving about a man-eating Bigfoot. That scared people out of their socks, and most of the tourists were gone before the eruption even happened."

"Man-eating Bigfoot?" said Alexis.

"That's what he said," said Rosa. "There was something about new evidence too. Can't blame the tourists for leaving. Between an erupting volcano and a man-eating monster, who would stay? I was nervous myself, coming into work today. But you know Sam." She turned to the girls. "He's the owner," she told them.

Chad laughed. "He's not about to miss out on the potential of last-minute money coming in, is he?"

"Nope. He won't close the diner if there's a chance that one little ol' customer might walk in. Shoot, he'd serve Bigfoot himself if Bigfoot held out a quarter," she announced. "I think he figures all the scientists on the mountain and the news crews and all those people are gonna need something to eat, and he's planning on providing it. They're not the types to tote their lunch boxes up the hill with them."

"He's not worried about getting caught in a major eruption?" McKenzie asked.

"Shoot no, honey," Rosa said. "He says he's lived here all his life, and he made it through the 1980 eruption, so he can survive anything."

"Besides, he's too mean for anything to happen to him," Chad announced loudly.

"I heard that, Smith!" A loud voice came from the office. "You'd better watch it, or I'll be mean enough to tell my chef to put hot pepper in your burger!"

Rosa laughed. She turned around and took their orders to the chef in the kitchen.

"Better watch it. The walls have ears around here," she said as she walked away.

"Speaking of walls having ears, if Randall has spread the word about the hiker, it sounds like he *did* hear us," said Chad. "Kellie, are you okay?"

Alexis saw that Kellie's hands had begun to shake.

"It's okay, Kellie," said McKenzie. "We're all afraid for that poor missing girl."

Kellie nodded, but Alexis thought she knew what was wrong. Sure, Kellie was worried about the hiker, but she was also worried about Bigfoot. What if the animal her father had searched for his whole life—the animal she loved—ended up being a monster? It wasn't fun to think about.

While they waited for their food, Alex went to a private corner of the restaurant and called her mother. She explained the situation and told her mother that they'd know within a couple of hours if the eruption was expected to be serious.

"If we have to evacuate, can we at least go on to Olympia with Kellie?" she begged Mrs. Howell.

Mrs. Howell paused. "Well, okay. But you keep in touch with me and keep me informed on what's going on," she directed.

"I promise, Mom," Alexis said. "You're so cool! This is one of the reasons I love you so much!"

"My goodness, talk like that and you can have anything you want!" Mrs. Howell said with a laugh.

Alex motioned for McKenzie to join her.

"Mom said it was okay," Alexis reported.

"Well, if your mom agreed to it, it should be a cinch for my mom to say yes," McKenzie reasoned. And sure enough when she filled her mom in on the details and told her Mrs. Howell felt comfortable, McKenzie's mom agreed too.

When the girls returned to the table, they found their hot food waiting.

Surprisingly, it was a quiet meal. Kellie had apparently mentioned the Camp Club Girls and their mysteries to Chad and Rick. The men were surprised to hear about all the cases the girls had solved and all the adventures they'd enjoyed.

"So will this trip end up in the Camp Club Girls' annals?" Chad asked.

"Maybe. . .what are annals?" McKenzie asked.

"Basically a record of events," Rick explained.

"Oh, probably. That is, if we solve the mystery," McKenzie added.

"What mystery is that?" Rick asked. "Being so close to the eruption is quite an adventure, but I don't know if it's really a mystery."

"Oh no, not that," McKenzie said. "The mystery we're working on is about Bigfoot!"

Suddenly, Chad started choking. He coughed and coughed but couldn't dislodge the food that was causing the problem inside his throat.

"Oh no! He's starting to turn blue!" Alexis exclaimed. She knew from health class that when a person was choking on food, it blocked the air passage. Without air, a choking person could experience brain damage in moments.

"Chad, are you okay? Chad!" Kellie's distress showed not only in her face but in her voice too. "Does anyone know how to do the Heimlich maneuver?" she called out.

Alexis knew basically what the Heimlich maneuver was. You stood behind the person who was choking, and put your arms around him or her. Then you sharply put pressure on the diaphragm to hopefully push the food out. But Alexis sure couldn't remember where the diaphragm was!

"Here, I know," Rick said, jumping out of his chair and running around the table to where Chad sat, still coughing. "First let's try some back slaps."

Rick sharply pounded his palm on Chad's back.

Whack! Whack! Whack!

At about the twelfth whack, Chad suddenly was able to take a breath. He coughed something into his napkin.

The girls, Kellie, Rick, Rosa, the cook, and even Sam—who'd come out from the office—all breathed a sigh of relief together.

Chad coughed lightly a few more times and took some sips of water.

"Are you going to be okay now?" Kellie asked.

"Sure," Chad said, his voice squeaking a bit. "Sam, what are you putting in those burgers these days? Nearly killed me, man!"

But Alexis wasn't so sure it was something in the burger. She'd happened to be looking at Chad when McKenzie mentioned the Bigfoot mystery. That's when his eyes had grown big and startled. And the choking hadn't happened for a few minutes later. What about the idea of the girls solving the Bigfoot mystery had startled or upset Chad?

As the group got up to leave a few minutes later, Rick got another phone call.

"I have to stay here and meet my boss," he said. "I'll come by later to get my car."

"Okay," said Kellie. "We're going over to the ranger station before heading home."

They waved goodbye to Rick and then ran across the street. Alexis and McKenzie held napkins over their heads to keep the ash from getting in their hair, but it didn't help much. When they got inside the station, Alexis looked at McKenzie and laughed.

"You look like you have a million more freckles!" she said.

"You're not any better!" McKenzie said. She reached up and wiped Alexis's cheek and then showed Alexis her fingers. They were covered with the gray soot-like material.

"Great," said Alexis. "Now I'm all smudged."

"Reminds me of our fireplace," McKenzie said. "It's just like the ash the wood leaves behind."

"Well, I guess that's pretty accurate," Kellie said. "It is ash. But it can be really dangerous. We're only getting a few occasional flakes in the wind right now. If you'll notice, it's not steady. If it were any heavier, we would have already had to get out of here. It's not just a mess that gets in your clothes and hair. Any heavier and it might hurt our skin."

"Not only that," Chad added, "but ash can be very dangerous for breathing. It can get into lungs and really clog them up."

"Bailey wouldn't do well with her asthma, would she?" Alexis noted.

"No, it would be really dangerous for anyone with asthma or any kind of breathing problems," Chad told them.

●—●—●

Kellie was at the front desk trying to get someone's attention. Everyone in the ranger station was running around like they were in a hurry but had no idea where they were going.

"Excuse me!" Kellie finally yelled. "Can someone please tell me where Ranger Davis is?"

"No need to shout, Kellie." Ranger Davis waltzed out of his back office with a smile on his face.

"You always did like catastrophes, didn't you?" said Kellie.

"Shame on you, Kellie! Of course I don't like catastrophes. But it is nice to have some action around here, that's for sure." He winked at Alexis. "So what brings you down here?"

"I was just checking in. Do you need any help? You know, with the evacuation and all?"

"Not really," said Ranger Davis. "I know it looks crazy around here, but we've done this before. I'm about to ride out and make sure the campgrounds are evacuated. You just make sure you're out of that shop of yours by tomorrow morning. Noon at the latest, understand?"

"Yes, sir," said Kellie. "Oh, and we found something you might need to see."

"The hair? I know. Randall's already been in here."

"So do you want it, sir?" asked Alexis.

"No. You keep it for now. The police might want it when things settle down. If you see the sheriff, you can give it to him."

"Randall isn't giving you a bad time about this Bigfoot thing anymore?" said Kellie.

"Randall's giving me an evil time about it. He swears Bigfoot ate that missing camper. He says he's the only one who can track it down. I told him to calm down. That hair could be a man's hair for all we know."

"What did he say about that?" said Chad.

"He yelled that men don't have long blond hair." The group busted out laughing. All of them were looking at Chad, who had shoulder-length blond hair that most girls would kill for.

He wasn't laughing.

"Oh don't get mad!" said Ranger Davis, smacking Chad on the shoulder. "It's just Randall. He didn't mean anything by it."

"So you don't think he'll do anything about Bigfoot?" asked Kellie.

"Kellie, we don't even know this *is* Bigfoot," said Ranger Davis. "But no, I don't think Randall will break the law and hunt in a national park. Why don't you go on home and start packing. Hopefully, the mountain will calm back down, and everything will be back to normal in a week."

Ranger Davis nodded to each of them and disappeared back into his office.

• — • — •

When they got back to the house, Kellie and Chad started packing the statues that hadn't sold yet, as well as any other valuables in Kellie's house and shop.

Alex and McKenzie helped cover Kellie's kiln. "It's too heavy to move," Kellie said with a sigh. "So if we cover it well, even if the area ends up getting coated with ash and lava, it should be okay. After all, it's built to withstand heat.

"I don't think they're expecting the eruption to affect this area too much, even if it's strong," she added. "But even if the forest falls around us and destroys the building, the kiln would probably survive. It's an old, heavy-duty one!"

After helping Kellie, Alexis and McKenzie ran to their cabin and threw on their pajamas before firing up the computer. McKenzie logged into the Camp Club Girls site while Alexis got them each a Coke from the mini-fridge. She found a bag of mini Reese's Peanut Butter Cups in the fridge too. She opened it and grabbed a handful before deciding to just take the whole bag. They were so good when they were cold!

Sydney was already waiting online. As the girls greeted her, she opened her mouth in a massive yawn.

"What's up?" she said. "You *do* know it's eleven o'clock at night here, right? I had softball practice for *four hours* this afternoon."

"Thanks for coming even if you're tired," said McKenzie. "We really need you guys!"

Elizabeth's face was next to pop up onto the screen.

"Hey, girls!" she said. "Can you hear me?"

"Yes, ma'am!" said Alexis, imitating Elizabeth's Texas twang.

"Don't you start with me, girlfriend!" Elizabeth sassed back with a laugh.

"And don't start without me!" said Kate as her face popped up next to Elizabeth's.

"Haven't said anything important yet, Kate," said McKenzie. "We're still waiting on Bailey anyway."

"No, you're not, Ale-gator!" Bailey chirped. Now all six Camp Club Girls were talking face to face.

"Technology is so great!" said Kate. "Years ago, this never would have happened. We would have been paying mega money to even talk on the phone long-distance. Can you believe they used to charge for that? I mean, there's not a difference in the technology that—"

"Thanks, Kate!" said Alexis. "I'm sure Sydney would like us to get to the point. She looks about to fall asleep in her chair."

Sydney didn't say a word. She just gave a thumbs-up and yawned again.

"Okay," said McKenzie. "I'll make this quick. We're here doing research on Mount St. Helens, which is about to erupt. . . . Actually, it erupted today, but it was a tiny eruption. And we think we found Bigfoot, and there's a missing hiker, and this hunter wants to track down Bigfoot and kill him. And there's going to be a big eruption, and we have to evacuate, but we really want to solve this case before we go!"

All four of the faces on the computer screen stared at McKenzie open-mouthed.

"Um, let's make it a little more simple," said Alexis.

"Thank you!" said Elizabeth. "Why don't we start slowly? What's your main mystery here? Is it the mountain or the. . .um, Bigfoot?"

"Bigfoot," said Alexis. "The mountain isn't really a mystery. Either it's going to blow or it isn't. What we're really trying to figure out is if Bigfoot exists, and if he does, is it him that we're seeing evidence of?"

"That's what I said!" said McKenzie. The rest of the girls laughed.

"So what makes you think Bigfoot is walking around Mount St. Helens?" asked Kate. She took off her glasses and began cleaning them on her pajama shirt.

"First of all, we've been finding these weird footprints

everywhere," said McKenzie. "Here. . .I'll upload the pictures so you can see them."

Across the country, the pictures Alexis had been taking jumped onto the screens of each Camp Club Girl.

"You can't tell, but those things are huge," said Alexis. "Here, let me upload one that has McKenzie's foot next to it so you can see how big the feet are."

"Well, they do call him Bigfoot!" Elizabeth joked.

"They look like human feet," said Bailey.

"Yes, but who would be walking around in the woods barefoot?" asked Elizabeth. "That's really irresponsible. Even the toughest feet would get cut and bruised and hurt."

"Animals survive," Kate pointed out.

"Yes, but they have hooves or pads on their feet, or other protection," Sydney said. "They don't have feet like humans. Human feet are less protected."

"Well, obviously Bigfoot doesn't wear shoes," said Bailey.

"Or does he?" Kate said.

"What do you mean?" McKenzie asked. But no one seemed to be paying attention, and McKenzie was immediately swept away in the main conversation.

"What else do you have, girls?" asked Elizabeth. "Are the footprints what make you think Bigfoot is on the loose?"

"Not entirely," said Alexis. "We've also found a couple of gobs of brown animal fur. One was right next to the footprints. The other was on the doorframe after the shop here got broken into this morning. The door was torn completely off the hinges."

"Don't forget all the sightings," said Bailey.

"What are you talking about, Bailey?" asked Kate.

"It's been all over the internet. There have been a ton of Bigfoot sightings in St. Helens National Park this spring."

"She's right," said McKenzie. "A school bus of kids saw him *dancing* in a parking lot."

"And I think my taxi almost hit him on my first day here," said Alexis. "I thought it was a bear, but it was a lot bigger and was running on two legs."

"Bears definitely don't run on two legs," said Sydney.

"And they don't dance either," said Bailey.

"What's this about the shop being broken into?" Elizabeth asked.

"We came home from being at Spirit Lake, and the door had been ripped off its hinges," McKenzie said.

"It could have been easily broken into by smashing the window," Alex said. "But whoever—"

"Or whatever," McKenzie interrupted.

"Whoever or whatever broke in tore the door off the hinges instead," Alexis continued. "The person or thing had to be really strong to tear off the hinges!"

"And the lady across the street said she saw Bigfoot break into the shop," McKenzie added.

"I saw that on the internet news!" Bailey said. "When I was reading some of these online news reports, I saw the video of that! But I didn't know it was Kellie's shop."

"Well, it was," Alex said. "The news report, was done while we were gone."

"The reporter seemed really smug," Bailey said. "He reminded me of that reporter guy you had to deal with in one of our first mysteries—the Sacramento one. He was really repulsive."

"This is tough," Sydney said. "You have a lot of clues pointing to Bigfoot, but there's no way to be sure. I mean, it could just be someone running around in a suit, couldn't it?"

"Who would be doing that?" said Elizabeth. "Can you girls think of anyone who would have a reason to dress up like Bigfoot?"

"Not really," said McKenzie. "Anyone could be doing it to attract tourists. That's how most of the people here make their money."

"That's true," said Alexis. "The reporter could be doing it to play a mean joke on Kellie, but we haven't found any evidence supporting that idea."

"He doesn't seem to like Kellie much," McKenzie said. "They went to college together, but he's been around a couple of times and is really rude to her."

"Another strange thing," Alexis said. "Husky, Kellie's Siberian husky and German Shepherd, was loose in the shop."

"Wow, a husky/shepherd mix," said Sydney. "That would be one good watchdog."

"Yeah. Kellie says he doesn't let anyone in he doesn't know. But it looks like he did," McKenzie added. "The police had to tie him up when they got there because he wouldn't let them around the place."

"The Bible talks about the fierceness of dogs," Elizabeth said. "In Proverbs 26:17. 'Like one who grabs a stray dog by the ears is someone who rushes into a quarrel not their own.' Messing with other people's dogs is just not smart to do."

"Does Husky like that Jeremy Jones guy?" Bailey asked.

"No. The other day when Jones was here, Husky was not happy," Alex replied.

"So it probably couldn't have been him then," Bailey said a bit sadly.

"I don't think so," Alex replied. "So I guess maybe we're back to Bigfoot."

"So, like I said," said Sydney, "there's no way to be sure if this is Bigfoot."

"Well, there is one way," said Kate.

"What's that?" asked Alexis.

"You could find him, of course."

It was Alexis's turn to look surprised. What were they supposed to do? Run around on an active volcano looking for a wild animal that might not even exist? There were miles of forest here! He could be anywhere. . .or he could be nowhere at all.

Late that night, Alexis stared at the dark ceiling above her bunk. She couldn't stop thinking about Kellie's worried face. This was all happening so fast! If there was a Bigfoot, how could they keep him safe from the hunters? And what if he really *was* attacking humans? Was he worth protecting then? And if they had to evacuate, did they even have time to do anything at all?

Another lonely howl sounded from deep in the forest.

Alexis looked over at McKenzie. She was already asleep, so Alexis didn't say anything to her about the sound. She turned and looked at Husky lying in his spot on the floor.

The lonely howl sounded again—this time a little closer. Husky just raised his head and sniffed. He thumped his tail briefly. Then he yawned, showing his big white teeth, and put his head back on his paws.

Husky was clearly not concerned.

Dog Gone It

Alexis and McKenzie were still trying to figure out what to do with their investigation the next morning. They were running out of time. If they had to evacuate, they might never find Bigfoot.

They walked into Kellie's house for breakfast. To their surprise, Jeremy Jones was leaning against the kitchen counter. Kellie was doing her best to ignore him as she scrambled eggs, and Chad was staring angrily at his newspaper. Alexis noticed he was holding it upside-down.

Grrrr. Grroooowwwrrr. Rrrrrrrwwwwllll.

Husky was clearly stating his opinion of Jones once again.

"Husky, hush and sit," Kellie commanded, a bit impatiently.

"Good dog, Husky," Chad whispered. He quietly reached out to pat the dog on the head.

"Dogs know when people are trustworthy. . .and when they aren't!" he told the girls grimly.

Kellie smiled at the girls. "I hope you slept well," she said. "We'll have some food here in a few minutes. Chad already set the table, so feel free to sit down."

"Come on, Kell," Jeremy said, as if no one else were in the room or had interrupted the conversation they'd apparently been having. "You can't really be happy here!"

"You know I am, Jeremy," said Kellie. "And you know I hate it when you call me Kell."

"Just come back to Seattle," said Jeremy. "This place is so lame! You could make a fortune with your sculpting up there! Especially if you stop making so many dumb Bigfoots and concentrate on more sophisticated subjects."

"What's *sophisticated* mean?" McKenzie whispered to Alexis.

Chad lowered his paper enough to whisper back, "Worldly. Important. Grown-up. He thinks her figures are too childlike."

Alexis frowned. "I think her Bigfoots are wonderful," she announced, not caring if Jeremy Jones *did* hear.

"So do I," Chad said, his smile finally returning.

"I don't care about making a fortune, Jeremy. You know that too. And I don't care about sculpting more sophisticated things."

"Well then, come back for me," he said.

Alexis and McKenzie stared. They looked at each other and then looked back and forth from Jeremy to Kellie again.

So that was why Jeremy Jones was hanging around St. Helens. It wasn't just his news story. He was trying to win Kellie back!

Alexis saw Chad's grip tighten on his coffee cup.

"Jeremy, I'm not marrying you. I made that decision years ago, and I haven't changed my mind."

Chad's grip loosened. Alexis thought he still might throw his coffee cup at Jeremy's head any minute. Jeremy looked around, as if he suddenly realized how crowded the room had become. He changed the subject.

"I'm so sick of being out here in the sticks. I hope this stupid mountain really blows soon so I can get my story and go home," he said.

"You might get your wish!" said Rick from the doorway. He scooped up a fist full of bacon and plopped down at the table. "It looks like the mountain is really going to erupt. Should be a good one too."

"Do you know when?" asked McKenzie.

"Sometime tomorrow or the next day," said Rick. "We don't need to rush, but we should definitely be gone by this evening."

"How much more packing do you have to do, Kellie?" asked McKenzie. "We can help you."

"Thanks, McKenzie," said Kellie. "We have everything that's really important. Now I'm just packing things I would like to take."

"Kellie?" said Rick. "If you don't need the girls right away, I was going to take them up to the mountain to get one last look before she blows. St. Helens will probably never look the same again. These shots would be great for Alexis's report."

"How long would you be up there?" asked Kellie. "I have to be sure the girls are safe. McKenzie, your mom would kill me if anything happened to you, no matter how good of friends we are. I don't know your mom, Alexis, but I'm guessing she wouldn't be happy with me either."

"We'll only be up there for about fifteen minutes," said Rick.

The girls looked pleadingly at Kellie. She smiled and nodded her head.

"Okay," she said. "But be careful!"

"Yes!" McKenzie and Alexis exclaimed together. They jumped up from the table and ran toward their cabin to get Alexis's camera. Kellie called after them.

"Fifteen minutes!" she said.

The girls jumped into Rick's van, and the three of them headed up toward the visitors' center. Alexis looked behind them and noticed Jeremy Jones's news van was following them.

"Are they letting news crews back through the road block?" asked Alexis.

"Nope," said Rick. He grinned from ear to ear. "While you two ladies were getting your things, I talked about how famous the person who got the last shots of St. Helens would be. I made sure to make it sound *very* enticing."

"You *wanted* him to follow us?" asked McKenzie.

"Yeah," said Rick. "It looked like he was getting on Kellie's nerves, so I thought I'd lure him away from the shop. You two still have the name tags I gave you, right?"

Alexis and McKenzie pulled the name tags over their heads and let them hang outside of their jackets. In minutes Rick stopped at the roadblock, and all three of them flashed their tags. The policeman checking them stepped aside and let them through. McKenzie and Alexis turned around and watched as the policeman told Jeremy Jones that he couldn't get through.

Jeremy had jumped out of the van and was still yelling at the policeman when they lost sight of him behind a bend in the road.

"He'd better be careful," said Rick. "These policemen aren't in the mood to play around."

Rick stopped the van near a clump of other scientists. Most of them were packing up their gear to evacuate along with the rest of the town.

"You guys are leaving too?" said Alexis.

"Yep," said Rick. "We'll stay another hour or two, but then we'll hit the road. Many of the victims of the eruptions in 1980 were photographers and scientists who stayed just a little too long. Some thought they were at a safe distance, but no one could have guessed what the heat wave from that first blast was going to do to this area."

"Nature is powerful," said Alexis. "When I visit the ocean with my family, the strength of the waves always freaks me out a little."

"I know," said Rick. "If nature is this powerful, think of how strong the Creator of it all must be!"

Alexis and McKenzie stared at Rick for a moment. Alexis finally asked what they were both thinking.

"You believe in God?" she said.

"Sure do," said Rick. "And Jesus too."

He winked at them both.

"But you're a scientist," said Alexis. "I thought—"

"That we all believed in evolution and the Big Bang theory of creation?" said Rick.

"Well, yeah," said Alexis.

Rick laughed. "A lot of people do, but if we're really honest with ourselves, we know that there had to be a beginning and a designer. Even the Big Bang theory needed particles of matter to exist before it could happen. Something much bigger and more powerful had to put things into motion."

"I never thought of it that way," said McKenzie. "I should remember that for science class next year."

Rick took about ten minutes to show the girls around. He showed them the small cracks some of the recent earthquakes had created. He also showed them a small machine that measured gases that the volcano released into the air.

"What is that smell?" said Alexis.

"Yeah," said McKenzie. "It smells like Easter eggs that have been left out in the sun too long!"

"That's sulfur dioxide," said Rick. "Active volcanoes release the gas into the air through cracks in the surface called vents."

"That's right!" said Alexis. "When my family went to Hawaii, we went to Volcanoes National Park. They had signs everywhere telling you to keep your windows rolled up because of the gas. There was one crater where we could see steam coming out of the cracks. That steam smelled just like this!"

"Yep," said Rick. "And it'll give us a headache if we're up here too long. Why don't you girls shoot some video, and then we'll get you back to the shop."

McKenzie held the camera while Alexis walked in front of it. She made sure to mention the sulfur dioxide and told all about the evacuation. She even got some shots of the smoking mountain and the thin layer of ash that covered most of the parking lot.

When the girls climbed back into the truck, Rick told them he'd called Kellie while they were gone. "Chad is going to meet us at the roadblock and take you back to Kellie's from there," he explained. "I think I need to stay behind and help the other scientists pack everything up."

Jeremy's news van was still parked on the side of the road, but they couldn't see the news man anywhere.

"I hope he gets buried under a field of ash," Chad mumbled as they climbed in his truck.

The girls looked at each other with surprise. It didn't seem like Chad to be grouchy about someone. In the few days they'd known him, he had always been so chipper and nice.

As the girls walked back to their cabin a short time later, McKenzie asked, "So what do you think about Chad being in a bad mood?"

"I don't know that he was really in a bad mood, but he certainly wasn't happy about Jeremy, was he?" Alex said.

"He looked like a thundercloud around Jeremy this morning at breakfast too," McKenzie added.

"Yeah, for a few minutes there, I thought he was going to throw his coffee on Jeremy," Alexis said.

"Alex, do you think he wants a closer relationship with Kellie than just being her employee?"

"I don't know," Alexis replied thoughtfully. "I'm beginning to wonder. Maybe we should tell the rest of the Camp Club Girls in case it factors in somehow."

Alexis booted up her computer quickly and went onto the Camp Club Girls website chat room. None of the girls were online at the moment, so Alexis started to type a message to leave for when the girls checked in.

> Alexis: *Only have a sec, but guess what? At breakfast this morning, Jeremy, the TV guy, was trying to get Kellie to marry him. From what she said, he's asked before. A lot.*

Suddenly Kate's icon showed up.

> Kate: *What did Kellie say?*
> Alexis: *She told him she decided a long time ago that she'd never marry him. Or something like that.*
> Kate: *What did Chad say?*
> Alexis: *Chad? Do you mean Jeremy? He wasn't very happy.*
> Kate: *No, I mean Chad.*
> Alexis: *Well, he didn't seem to be too happy either. We thought he was going to throw coffee on Jeremy. And he was grouchy later when we drove by Jeremy's van. Chad's usually happy.*
> Elizabeth: *Hi, girls! Just checked in. Are things getting a little heated up in the northern woods there? Is Chad jealous?*
> Kate: *Is anyone else around the shop a lot?*
> Alexis: *Hi, Beth. No, Kate. It's usually just Chad and Kellie—besides the tourists and customers.*
> Kate: *Hmm. That sounds suspicious to me. Just what lengths do you think Chad would go to if he wanted to help Kellie?*
> Alexis: *I'm not sure what you mean, but I think he'd do about anything for her.*

Elizabeth: *Check out Proverbs 27:4–5. It says, "Anger is cruel and fury overwhelming, but who can stand before jealousy? Better is open rebuke than hidden love."*

Bailey: *I'm here now! I've been reading that they're evacuating the mountain. Will you guys have to go?*

Alexis: *Yes, we're supposed to be leaving now. So we'd better sign off.*

Kate: *Alex, what does McKenzie think of all this—of Chad and Kellie and Jeremy? You know she's the one of us who UNDERSTANDS people best. She tends to figure out what people are thinking and why they do the things they do.*

Alexis: *She and I will go talk about it as soon as we can get some more private moments. Oops. Kellie calling.*

Kate: *I've gotta go too. Biscuit is pitching a fit, and I'd better go check into it. You know Biscuit. He raises a racket anytime anyone strange comes around.*

Alexis: *Give that Wonder Dog a hug from us and a doggy bone for being a good watchdog! L8r!*

While McKenzie went outside to let Kellie know they heard her and were coming, Alex shut down her computer. The girls hurried and put their luggage in Kellie's car. Then they went into the shop and started helping Kellie and Chad pack up the last of the figurines.

"You know, I meant to buy one of these before I left," said Alexis. She was holding a small slug sculpture.

"You don't have to buy one!" said Kellie. "Just pick one out! I would love for you to take one home!"

"I like this one," said Alexis, holding up the slug.

"Gross, Alexis!" said McKenzie. "Out of all of these cute animals, you pick the *slug*?"

"It's a perfect choice," said Chad. "Slugs outnumber everything up here because of the rain. If the Pacific Northwest had a mascot, it would be the slug."

As they were laughing, Kellie's phone rang and went onto the answering machine. After the beep, Alexis, who was standing nearby, could hear Ranger Davis's voice on the other end.

"Kellie?" he said.

"Yes, Ranger Davis, I'm here. What do you need?"

"I need you to get into town right away. I was running the town evacuation meeting, and it's all blown out of control! Randall's going crazy!"

"The hunter?" asked Alexis. Kellie nodded.

"What's Randall's problem this time?" asked Kellie.

"His dog's missing," said Ranger Davis. "He thinks Bigfoot's responsible!"

Fighting and a Furry Visitor

Kellie and the girls got to the ranger station just in time. Ranger Davis had only been telling part of the truth. Mr. Randall wasn't the only one going crazy.

Everyone was talking at once, and most of the people were shouting. Ranger Davis stood at the front of the room. He was yelling too, but Alexis couldn't hear a word he was saying. He looked up when they walked in and sagged with relief. He grabbed Kellie by the hand and pulled her through the crowd to the front.

"Everyone, just calm down!" Ranger Davis yelled. For some reason the people listened this time, and the room went quiet. Alexis took a look around. What was it about Kellie that made everyone stop and listen?

Most of the room was full of citizens. They had probably only come to hear the instructions for evacuating their homes. Up front, however, there were two groups glaring at each other.

On the left stood the hunters. Leading the pack was Mr. Randall. He stood with his arms crossed over his chest and his rifle leaning against his hip.

On the right stood a group Alexis recognized as some of the scientists who had been watching the mountain. They were glaring at the hunters and writing like crazy in little notebooks. Alexis thought that a fight might break out if someone didn't settle things down.

"Okay, everyone," said Ranger Davis. "Let's all take a deep breath. The purpose of this meeting was to help people evacuate.

We don't know if Bigfoot even exists. If he does, that's something to take care of later. Right now we all need to just get out of town."

"Not without my dog!" cried Randall. "That dog's been with me for eight years! He would never go anywhere without me. I *know* that monster's behind this, just like he's behind the other missing pets *and* that poor missing hiker!"

The other hunters roared in agreement.

"Yeah!"

"He's right!"

"Let's go get him!"

"No way!" yelled one of the scientists. "You can't just run into the forest waving your guns around! If this is Bigfoot, then he's a *discovery*! We're the ones who need to find him. He needs to be captured and evaluated not killed."

"But he's dangerous!" said Randall.

"So are mountain lions!" said the scientist. "But I don't see you running out to exterminate them!"

"Mountain lions didn't take my dog!"

"They would if the dog went near them!"

"Calm down, everyone!" said Kellie. She looked at Randall. "We can't just run out and shoot this thing, Randall. What if he's the only one of his kind?"

"Good!" said Randall. "Then we'll only have to get rid of him once!"

Suddenly, Chad stepped up beside the ranger and spoke.

"Look, I can guarantee that Bigfoot isn't doing anything to anyone's animals!" he exclaimed.

"And how can you be so sure about that?" Randall said.

"Trust me. I just know," Chad insisted. "You're going to have to start figuring out what else might have happened. It's not any kind of Bigfoot!"

"Well, we'll just go hunt down that Bigfoot animal and then see if the problems stop," Randall countered.

Alexis couldn't take it anymore. Weren't adults supposed to be rational?

"Everyone, stop!" she cried at the top of her lungs. The entire room turned to look at her. She swallowed hard. She had no idea what she was going to say. McKenzie helped her out.

"This thing can't be dangerous," McKenzie said. "So many people have seen him up close, and he hasn't attacked any of them."

"Yeah," said Alexis. "There was a busload of fourth graders, and you know what he did when he saw them? He *danced*! He didn't even attack defenseless children!"

"I'd be afraid of a bus full of fourth graders too," said a voice from the back of the room. Everyone except the hunters laughed.

"The girls are right," said Kellie. "We think it was this. . .uh. . . *animal* that somehow got into my house. It didn't hurt anything while it was inside. Don't you think that's strange? Bill! Remember that elk that got into your house last spring? He demolished your kitchen before you finally got him to leave."

"What do you mean, it didn't hurt anything?" said Randall. "Didn't it break down the door to get in?"

This time the hunters laughed.

"What she means is that Bigfoot seems like more than just some dumb animal," said Alexis. "We found his cave in the forest, and he had built a fire! What other animal do you know that can do that? He's more human than we think!"

The room filled with grumbling. Doubt began to appear on some of the hunters' faces, but Alexis couldn't hear what anyone was saying.

"Well," said Ranger Davis, "I have one thing I know we can all agree on!" Again, everyone stopped to listen.

"The mountain is about to blow, and we're all in danger if we stay here," said Ranger Davis.

And just like that, people stopped yelling at each other and began asking if anyone needed help getting ready to leave. The townspeople drifted out of the station. Soon the only people left were the hunters and the scientists. They still stood glaring at each other across the room.

"We do agree on that, right?" asked Ranger Davis. "St. Helens is getting ready to erupt, and it doesn't really matter what animals are or aren't out there right now."

Ranger Davis turned to face the hunters.

"You guys need to evacuate, just like everyone else. Remember what happened to the people who stuck around in 1980? They were vaporized."

Next he turned to the scientists.

"And *you* need to finish up your work and get on out as well. You're more than welcome to search the mountain for Bigfoot *after* the evacuation has been lifted and we are sure it is safe."

Ranger Davis pulled on his jacket and turned to face everyone again.

"The thought of a dangerous animal on the loose is scary, but it's not nearly as scary as the thought of the rest of this mountain blowing us all to smithereens. Get out of town. When things get back to normal, we'll figure out what to do about Bigfoot."

With that, Ranger Davis simply walked out of the station and climbed into his Jeep. The hunters and the scientists stared after him dumbfounded. No one had expected the meeting to end so suddenly.

"You heard him," Alexis said. "We can't do anything about it right now. We'd better get ready to leave."

The ranger station emptied, and Kellie began driving the girls back to the shop. They were going to load up the car and then drive to Olympia. Kellie parked the car and was fumbling for the house key when another car pulled into the parking lot. It was the neighbor—the one who had told Jeremy Jones she had seen Bigfoot break in to the shop the day before. Alexis realized that her car was loaded with old suitcases and about twenty-five cats.

"Hello, Ms. Anne," said Kellie. "Is there anything I can do for you?"

"No, honey," said Ms. Anne as a caramel-colored cat leaped onto her head. "I'm on my way to stay with my sister, Mabel, but I thought you might want to know that I just saw Bigfoot walk into your shop."

Kellie's jaw dropped.

"Bigfoot?" said Alexis. "The same one you saw yesterday?"

"Of course, child! I don't think there is more than one!" Ms. Anne pushed the caramel-colored cat off of her head, and Alexis heard it hit the floorboard. Then Ms. Anne looked back at Kellie and said, "I wouldn't go in there if I were you."

CHAPTER 11

Running for His Life

Alexis and McKenzie followed Kellie up the front porch steps. Sure enough, giant, muddy footprints led to the front door. Kellie tried the door, but it was locked.

"Maybe he came up the steps and didn't get inside," said Alexis.

"Maybe," said Kellie.

"At least he didn't break down the door this time," said McKenzie.

Kellie jiggled the key in the lock, and the door swung inward. She and McKenzie tiptoed inside.

"He was definitely in here," said McKenzie. "There are muddy prints here too. They don't look as heavy, though, Alexis."

"I know why," said Alexis. She knelt on the porch and looked closely at the doormat. There were two big smudges of mud across the top of it.

"No way!" said McKenzie. "Bigfoot wiped his feet?"

Alexis raised her eyebrows. "And apparently he had a key to get in. This is getting so weird!"

The girls went into the shop. Alexis almost closed the door, but she decided to leave it open instead. If Bigfoot really was inside, they might need to get out quickly. She wished Kellie had left the car running just in case.

Kellie came in from the kitchen. She was carrying a baseball bat.

"He's not here," Kellie said. "I checked the whole house. It's empty, but there are a few more prints leading out the back door.

I guess he's gone."

"I thought you weren't afraid of Bigfoot, Kellie," said McKenzie, pointing to the bat.

"I'm not," said Kellie.

"Then what's with the bat?" asked Alexis. Kellie laughed and put the bat down behind the cash register.

"No animal is pleasant when you sneak up on it. What if I had found Bigfoot in my closet? Who knows what he would do if he were cornered."

"Well, he wiped his feet," said McKenzie. "If he was in your closet, he was probably trying on your high heels."

Alex snickered. She couldn't help herself.

Alexis began loading the last of Kellie's boxes in the trunk of the car. She was happy. They may not be able to solve the Bigfoot case, but at least the animal would be safe. No one was going to be hunting for it today.

But what will happen after things settle down again? Alexis thought. *Will the hunters stray into the national park? Will the scientists capture Bigfoot and do all kinds of experiments?*

She was worrying again, and she knew she needed to stop. There was no reason to worry about something she had no control over.

McKenzie kneeled to help Alexis tape one last box, and there was a knock on the front door. Kellie unlocked it, and Rick peeked his head in. He was sweating like crazy and breathing hard.

"I saw that your car was still here, so I thought I'd make sure you were ready to leave," he said.

"We're getting there," said Kellie. "What's wrong?"

"The mountain's getting a little unstable. It's closed to everyone now, even me."

"But there's nothing to worry about, right?" said McKenzie. "It's not supposed to erupt until some time tomorrow."

"Remember when I told you that forecasting volcanoes is a lot like forecasting the weather?" said Rick.

"Yeah," said Alexis.

"Well, sometimes the weather man is off, and the rain comes early."

The girls looked at each other and then back to Rick.

"Forget the tape!" said Kellie to Alexis. "Just throw the box in the car, and get in!"

They all ran outside. Kellie tried calling Chad's cell phone, but it went straight to voicemail.

"He must already be in town," she said. "But that's odd. I would have thought he would have let me know. I thought he was planning on taking one more load of boxes."

"It must be crazy down there," said Rick. He was helping load the last box into Kellie's car.

"What makes you say that?" asked Alexis.

"Well, I heard about the fight at the town meeting," said Rick. "My boss was there. Then that group of hunters almost hit my van on my way here. They drove their trucks right through the roadblock! Can you imagine? I have no idea what they think they're doing!"

Kellie's face turned white.

"I do," she said. "Rick, take the girls down to the safety zone. I'll be right behind you." She turned and ran toward the woods.

"What are you doing?" Alexis yelled.

"I can't let those hunters do this!" Kellie yelled. "I have to find Bigfoot before they do!"

Kellie disappeared into the trees.

"She's crazy!" said Rick. "Has everyone gone mad?"

Alexis looked at McKenzie. They both shrugged their shoulders and got out of the car.

"Wait a minute!" said Rick. "Not you too! Where are you going?"

"We have to help her!" said Alexis. "The sooner we find Bigfoot, the sooner Kellie can get off the mountain. You know she won't go while the hunters are out there looking for him. She can't stand the thought of him getting shot!"

"Yes, I know, but she's an adult," said Rick. "She's made her choice, now it's my job to keep you two safe."

"Come on, Dr. Rick!" said McKenzie. "Don't you want to find him? You could be the scientist to save Bigfoot!"

Rick looked into the woods. He reached back into his van

and grabbed a compass.

"Okay," he said. "But when I say it's time to turn around, you two *will* listen, alright?"

"Alright," said Alexis and McKenzie together.

Alexis led the other two to the back door. Husky trotted along with them. Kellie had run off in a random direction, but Alexis thought she had a better idea. It had rained a little this morning, and the dusty ground had become muddy. Just as Alexis had hoped, there was a set of tracks leading from the back door into the woods.

"Come on!" said Alexis. "If we can follow these, we should be able to catch up with him. He couldn't have gone very far!"

"Alex, what's that over there? It almost looks like a truck hidden in the bushes," McKenzie said. "It looks kind of like the color of Chad's truck. . . . "

"We'll have to look at it and see what it is when we get back," Alex said.

The three of them took off through the forest with Husky following. Rick kept checking his compass so he knew how to get back to the shop and his van. Alexis was thankful he was with them. She could run faster and focus on following the tracks since she didn't have to think about getting lost.

Suddenly, Alexis stopped. McKenzie slammed into her from behind.

"Why are you stopping?" she asked. Alexis pulled her video camera out of her backpack. She turned it on and searched the ground again for the tracks.

"We might as well get this all on tape!" said Alexis. "If we find him, I'll be glad I turned this thing on!"

"Shh!" said McKenzie. "Listen!"

The sound of barking dogs echoed through the forest.

"The hunters," said Rick. "We'll have to be careful. We don't want to be caught in the crossfire."

"Look at the tracks here," said Alexis. "They are farther apart, and deeper, like Bigfoot is running."

"He knows he's being chased," said McKenzie.

"The poor guy!" said Alexis. "He must be terrified!"

A tremor rocked the forest floor and made the three of them grab a tree for support.

"We'd better make this quick, ladies," said Rick. "We can't stay much longer."

Alexis took off through the forest, her camera at her side. The whole time she was following the prints, she prayed that they would find Bigfoot and that it wouldn't be too late. . .for any of them. He was running straight toward the volcano, and the farther they followed him, the farther they were from safety.

All of a sudden, Alexis heard a low rumble from somewhere behind them.

"It's a car engine," said Rick. "Might be the hunters."

"Then we have to run faster!"

Why were the hunters behind them? Weren't their dogs up ahead? Alexis was getting confused. She shook her head and decided not to think about the hunters anymore. She just had to find Bigfoot.

Alexis could still see the tracks. Now and then there were flattened ferns where Bigfoot had stepped on them. They had to jump a couple of fallen logs too.

The barking of the dogs got louder, and so did the rumbling of the truck. They were still coming from two different directions.

All of a sudden they broke into a clearing. The trees disappeared, and the three of them were standing in a ring of short grass spotted here and there with old stumps and mushrooms. Alexis saw movement across the clearing. She squinted and stopped in her tracks. There, standing on the other side of the clearing, was Bigfoot.

He was shorter than Alexis had expected—about six feet. His hair was long and shaggy, and it got in the way, so Alexis couldn't really see his face. Something about his build looked familiar to Alexis.

It looked like he was going to start running again, so Alexis called out.

"Wait!" she cried. "You're in trouble! Come back!"

The animal looked around frantically, like he didn't know what to do. The dogs were barking on one side, and the roaring of a vehicle seemed to be coming from all around.

"Come here!" shouted McKenzie. "We have to get you out of here!"

"We may not be able to do that," said Rick. "Ladies, I think my compass is broken."

They didn't hear him. Alexis took off running across the field, just as a vehicle broke through the trees behind her.

"Don't! Don't shoot! It's not an animal!" Alex hysterically cried.

Bigfoot turned around to look at her.

"Don't shoot!" she repeated as she saw the muzzle of a gun in the corner of her eye. "It's not Bigfoot! It's—"

BANG!

Alexis started to sob.

"It's Chad!" she whispered.

CHAPTER
12

An Explosive Ending

Alexis turned around to see Ranger Davis holding a smoking rifle.

"You?" she said. "But I thought you didn't want him shot!"

"I didn't," he said. "But if someone was going to shoot him, it needed to be me. I use tranquilizers not bullets. He's only sleeping."

That's when Alexis noticed the two Jeeps parked behind them. That must have been the noise she had heard. Two other rangers were dragging the Bigfoot toward their Jeep. She took a step toward him, but Rick held her back.

"We have to go!" he yelled. "I know I said my compass was broken, but it looks like it's spinning now!"

"But we can't go! It's not Bigfoot. It's—"

"Now!" Rick demanded.

"What did you mean?" McKenzie asked Alexis, but before Alex could answer, Rick grabbed her and thrust her into Ranger Davis's Jeep.

Ranger Davis pushed McKenzie into his Jeep too. A huge tremor rocked the earth just as Ranger Davis started the engine. The Jeep jumped a foot off the ground before slamming back to earth. Ranger Davis hit his head on the roof and then hit the gas, spraying dirt everywhere. He spun the Jeep around and tore through the forest with the other rangers right behind them.

"What about Kellie?" yelled Alexis. "She's still out there!"

"No, she didn't get far," said Ranger Davis. "She got turned around and ended up back at the shop. When she saw that the van was still there, she knew you three had gone after Bigfoot, so she called me."

"I have to tell you something!" Alexis shouted to be heard over the noise. "Ranger Davis, that wasn't Bigfoot—"

"What?" He yelled. "Bigfoot? The boys back there will take Bigfoot with them. Look, I can't talk right now. We gotta drive! We'll talk later."

As if to emphasize his words, the Jeep took another leap.

The Jeep bounced fiercely. Alexis thought it was just the roughness of the forest floor, but then she saw the trees swaying. Something much bigger was going on. Bigfoot completely slipped her mind. She kept her video camera going, but Alexis couldn't help but wonder if she or the camera would ever make it back to civilization.

They were almost out of the woods when it happened. A deafening *boom* rocked the air and made Alexis's ears pop. A moment later, it felt like the Jeep had been picked up and dropped by a giant. Then everything was still.

The sky was black, and ash drifted down on them like colorless rose petals.

Back at the ranger station, Alexis couldn't believe all that had happened. She was sitting in a plastic chair in the waiting room with Rick and McKenzie. All three of them were still in shock. Husky was lying at her feet.

"But you said it wasn't going to blow until tomorrow," said Alexis.

"I told you that we're not always right," said Rick. "We were really lucky that it wasn't a mega eruption."

"Is it really over?" asked McKenzie.

"Yep," said Rick. "My boss says the mountain is quiet again. There's a huge crack in the bowl where the ash plume escaped, but that's it. There's no lava flow, and no one is going to be vaporized."

Alexis couldn't help but smile.

"I guess that's a good thing," she said. "Aw, man! My mom's never going to let me go anywhere again!"

"Mine either!" said McKenzie. "We seem to attract dangerous situations."

Just then Kellie came out of Ranger Davis's office. She gave bottled water to each of them and sat down. Rick's phone rang, and he stepped outside to answer it.

"Have you seen what the rangers caught this morning?" Kellie asked the girls.

"Bigfoot?" said Alexis. "Yeah, we were there. But it's not Bigfoot, it's—"

"Yeah, there the wild man is," Kellie said. "Over there."

She pointed to a large cage in the corner. It was usually used for large animals that were hurt and waiting to be returned to the wild. Now, however, there was a person curled up in it asleep. Alexis couldn't see his face, but she recognized the spiked black hair.

"Jeremy Jones? No way!" Alexis said.

"Yep!" said Kellie. She was smiling ear to ear. "I guess he made the rangers at the road block pretty angry. They said he got upset when they wouldn't let him through. They handcuffed him and brought him down here so he could settle down. Ranger Davis said they would have put him in a human-sized cell, but they don't have one."

By the time she finished explaining, Kellie was laughing so hard, she was crying.

Alexis waited a moment until Kellie calmed down.

"But Kellie, where's—"

Bang!

The door to the ranger station flew open. Mr. Randall stood there covered in ash. His gun was nowhere to be seen, but he was carrying what looked like a very dirty young woman. His Alaskan malamute stood near him, whining.

Roof! Husky barked a quick greeting and wagged his tail. Randall's dog wagged its tail in reply.

"Oh, my goodness, Randall," said Kellie. "What happened?"

Kellie jumped up and ran to Randall. She helped him lower the girl onto a couch in the waiting room.

"Well," said Randall, "we were using the dogs to try and find that monster when I heard a familiar howl. I knew it was my dog, and it sounded like he was hurt. I stopped chasing Bigfoot and started looking for him instead."

Randall reached down and rubbed his dog between the ears.

"When I found him, he wasn't hurt," said Mr. Randall. "He was curled up next to this girl, keeping her warm. I think it's the missing hiker. I guess the monster didn't get him after all. My dog probably found her and didn't want to leave her. That's why he didn't come home."

Kellie used her cell phone to call the town's only doctor.

"He'll be here in five minutes," she said. "If she wakes up before then, we can try to give her some water. She looks healthy, except her ankle is swollen and looks like it may be broken."

Alexis and McKenzie walked over to Randall.

"Can I pet your dog, sir?" McKenzie asked. "He's a hero, you know."

"Go ahead," said Randall. "I've heard the two of you girls are good at solving mysteries. You and my pup here have something in common now!"

"Speaking of solving mysteries," said Kellie, "would the three of you like to meet Bigfoot?"

Alexis had almost forgotten that they had caught Bigfoot. There was so much happening!

"Grab your camera, Alexis, and follow me," said Kellie. "You're going to want to get this on film."

"But I already know—"

"You'll never believe what's going on," Kellie interrupted. Alexis was getting really tired of people not listening to her! "Bigfoot is actually—"

"Chad!" Alex exclaimed. "Bigfoot is Chad. I know!"

McKenzie looked at her in surprise. "That's what I thought you said back in the woods, but I decided I must be mistaken," she said. "I'd wondered. . . We just hadn't had a chance to put our clues together yet."

Kellie just stared at them with her mouth open.

"That's what I was going to go show you," she said, dropping to the chair. "How did you know?"

"Well, there were a lot of things," Alex said. "As one of our Camp Club Girl friends pointed out, a human-type of creature— no matter how tough his feet—couldn't have made it through the woods without some serious injury and scars on the footprints."

"And then Kate, our friend, made a remark about shoes,"

McKenzie said. "That made me start thinking."

"Me too," Alexis said. "Who's to say someone creative couldn't make Bigfoot boots? And walk around in them."

"And then there was the fact that an animal like Bigfoot certainly wouldn't wipe his feet on the rug before going inside," McKenzie said.

"Or use a key," Alex added.

"Then I thought I saw Chad's truck hidden in the bushes," McKenzie said. "And you said he wasn't answering his phone and was probably in town, Kellie. If that was his truck, that meant he was somewhere nearby. But why would he hide his truck?"

"And then when I saw him standing in his costume in the woods, well, he stood like Chad stands, and he was about the same height as Chad," Alex finished. "Is he okay?"

"Yes, the ranger thinks he's alright. I can't believe you two figured this out!" Kellie exclaimed.

"Well, we had help," Alexis said. "All the Camp Club Girls really had a part of it. They said things that made us think."

"Even the Camp Club Girls' dog, Biscuit, gave us a clue," McKenzie explained. "He barked at whoever was at Kate's door because he always barks at strangers and threatens to bite them. Like Husky. Only Husky apparently let whoever it was in your house."

"And it must have been Chad outside our cabin at night making the noises to make us believe in Bigfoot. If it hadn't been a scent or person Husky was familiar with, he would have gone crazy," Alex added.

"Well, that's true," Kellie said.

"And even in the forest," Alex said. "Husky wasn't barking at Bigfoot. I saw his tail wag, so he apparently knew it was Chad in that costume. Actually, it was just like Sherlock Holmes's story *Silver Blaze*. Some people call it the case of the barking dog."

"What barking dog?" McKenzie asked.

"Exactly," Alexis said. "The prize racehorse was stolen in the night, but the watchdog in the stable didn't send up an alarm. The dog *didn't* bark, and it normally would have. So Holmes figured out that the thief was one of the people who worked in the stable—someone the dog knew."

"You girls are amazing!" Kellie exclaimed, looking at them with awe.

"I want to see Chad," McKenzie said. "Is he awake?"

Kellie motioned for them to follow her into Ranger Davis's office.

Two fury legs stuck out from behind the ranger's desk.

The girls walked slowly around the desk. There, lying on the floor, was Chad. A mask had been removed and was lying beside him. Everything except his face was covered in a hairy costume, complete with rubbery bare feet. Alexis started the video camera.

"This is *so* Scooby Doo!" Alexis said with a big grin. Husky walked over and licked Chad fully across the face.

"But why in the world would Chad be running around pretending to be Bigfoot?" Kellie asked, looking at her shop assistant.

Alex smiled. "I think you can ask McKenzie that question. She's the one who's best at figuring out what makes people do the things they do."

"Kellie, have you had some low business in the past couple of years?" McKenzie asked.

"Well, yes, it was starting to slip, but then the Bigfoot sightings started increasing sales and tourists," Kellie answered. "I was a little worried for a while that I might have to let Chad go find another job, so I was really glad when business picked up."

Kellie was looking at Chad, her forehead wrinkled in a puzzled glance. Her head suddenly shot up, and she looked at the girls. "Do you mean that was it? Chad was trying to keep from losing his job by pretending to be Bigfoot and getting some publicity out there?"

"Well, that might have been a little bit of it, but I don't think that was all of it," McKenzie said. "I think it's a little more obvious—"

"Oh, you do, do you?" Chad interrupted.

Everyone looked down. Chad's eyes were wide open, and his glance met theirs.

"Man, what hit me?" he said, looking at Ranger Davis.

Ranger Davis grinned at him. "Tranquilizer dart. Better be glad I only used a little one. You dropped so fast I didn't think it was necessary. If you didn't have that thick costume on, you'd probably be out a lot longer as it is."

Chad tried to sit up. He groaned and fell back onto the floor again.

"I would stay put for a while if I were you," said Ranger Davis.

Garoror, Husky vocalized happily as he curled up next to Chad with his head on Chad's legs.

"Here, have a drink," Kellie said as she opened a bottle of water. She squatted down by Chad and raised his shoulders. Then she put the top of the water bottle against his lips.

"You don't know how close you got to being shot by a bullet!" Randall exclaimed. "That would have killed you. And if I'd done it, I would've been guilty of murder!"

"You wouldn't have if you hadn't been hunting in the national park," said Kellie.

"It's alright, Kellie," said Chad. "I was being dumb. I shouldn't have been out there today, but I wanted to give the scientists one last glimpse of Bigfoot before they left."

"All the clues make sense now," said McKenzie. "The blond hair in the cave was yours, wasn't it?"

Chad nodded and then grabbed his head. "Wow, this tranquilizer's given me an awful headache," he moaned.

"And *you* broke into the shop?" said Alexis. "But why? Why would you steal one of Kellie's statues?"

"I didn't steal it," said Chad. "I was going to put it back after everything settled down. It was my favorite too, and everyone was buying everything! I didn't want it to get taken by someone who wouldn't fully appreciate it, so I hid it."

"Why didn't you just buy it or tell me you wanted it?" asked Kellie. "And why did you break the door off the hinges?"

"Well, I didn't quite mean to," he explained. "But it's a really old door, and when I was wiggling it to try to get it loose. . ."

"It came off the hinges!" Alex guessed.

"Yeah. Since you'd need a new door anyway, I banged it around a bit to make it look like Bigfoot had been there."

"I was afraid you would know why I wanted it," mumbled Chad. He wouldn't look Kellie in the eyes.

"But why dress up like Bigfoot at all?" asked Kellie. "You didn't have to go to that extreme to keep your job! We would have figured out something. . . . "

"But I'd been trying to figure out something, and that seemed to be the best thing I could figure," Chad said.

"But *why?*" Kellie insisted.

"Well. . ." Chad paused and blushed.

"Oh, Kellie, don't you know by now? Chad didn't just want to keep his job. He wanted to help your business. He wanted to make you a success," said McKenzie.

"I think I hear the L word in there somewhere," said Alexis with a grin.

"Elizabeth was right," McKenzie said. "Or the verses in Proverbs were anyway. As Proverbs 27 says, 'Who can stand before jealousy? Better is open rebuke than hidden love.'"

"The L word? You mean. . ." Kellie looked at Alexis and then at Chad.

"Yeah, I did it for you," Chad said. "You've spent so long searching for this animal, and I know you were about to give up. I was worried about you. I hated seeing you so sad, so I made the suit and started letting people see me in it. I wanted you to have hope again, even if it wasn't real. And I figured it would help with the sales at the shop."

"I should be mad," said Kellie. "After all, now I *know* there is no Bigfoot. But you were really that worried about me?"

Chad nodded.

"After a while I really began to enjoy it," Chad said. "It was fun to make people stare and run after their cameras. Then the next day I would be in the paper or on the news. I got carried away."

Alexis stopped recording, and she and McKenzie left Chad and Kellie to talk. The Camp Club Girls had done it again.

The girls walked back into the waiting area just as Rick came back inside.

"Dr. Rick," Alexis said, "you're not going to believe this."

●—●—●

Two weeks later, Alexis got a pleasant surprise when she checked her email.

Hey, Alexis! Dr. Rick Porter, here!

I thought I would give you an update. Things in Washington have settled down a bit. Kellie's shop was damaged in the eruption, but it wasn't very bad. She says she's always wanted to remodel anyway, so she and Chad are fixing things up. Chad set up a website for her, and she's selling a ton of sculptures. I guess it's because of the eruption. People are curious. They're also developing a new line of business taking people on more Bigfoot sighting tours. As part of it, I hear Chad makes an appearance in his costume.

I've been asked to be the best man for the wedding, by the way. That is, unless the two of them find the real Bigfoot between now and then.

I got a job at the university! I'm going to be a professor. Can you believe it?

By the way, how did your documentary turn out? Keep me posted! Let me know when you make your debut on the Discovery Channel! Ha ha!

And if you or McKenzie ever want to do a summer internship in the Pacific Northwest, you just let me know. I know talent when I see it!

Later!
Rick

Alexis typed her response right away. She knew that she owed a lot of her success to Dr. Rick. Without him, she wouldn't have had much film to work with.

Dr. Rick,

It's good to hear from you! Thanks again for all of your help while we were visiting. I wouldn't have been able to make my documentary without you! It would have been really boring with only one shot of the mountain.

My show loved it! It's funny that you mentioned the Discovery Channel, because the TV station is actually talking to them about airing it! Can you believe it!?

Again, thank you for all of your help, and thank you for believing in the Camp Club Girls too. We wouldn't have found Chad. . .I mean, Bigfoot. . .without you! ☺

I hear Husky's going to be the ring bearer at the big event!

By the way, congratulations on the job! You'll be a great teacher. Who knows, I might see you in five years. I hear the University of Washington has a great journalism program!

Later, Gator!
Alexis

Alexis knew it was too early to think about college, but who knew? Maybe she *would* end up in Washington! For now, she would focus on finishing middle school. Besides, summer was just around the corner, and that meant summer camp and the reunion of all six of the Camp Club Girls! Alexis smiled at the thought.

There were sure to be plenty of mysteries to solve in the next five years.

More Camp Club Girls!

Camp Club Girls: Elizabeth
The Camp Club Girls are uncovering a decades-old mystery at Camp Discovery Lake, investigating a bag of mysterious marbles in Amarillo, untangling a strange string of events in San Antonio, and solving the case of a missing guitar in Music City!
Paperback / 978-1-68322-767-0 / $9.99

Camp Club Girls: Bailey
The Camp Club Girls are investigating the whereabouts of eccentric millionaire Marshall Gonzalez, encountering out-of-control elk stampedes in Estes Park, uncovering the rightful ownership to a valuable mine, and solving the case of frightening events in Mermaid Park!
Paperback / 978-1-68322-828-8 / $9.99

Camp Club Girls: Kate
The Camp Club Girls are saving the day for a Philadelphia Phillies baseball player, investigating the sabotage of a Vermont cheese factory, going on a quest to uncover phony fossils in Wyoming, and solving the case of twisted treats in Hershey, Pennsylvania!
Paperback / 978-1-68322-854-7 / $9.99

Camp Club Girls: McKenzie
The Camp Club Girls are in the middle of a Wild West who-dun it, investigating a mysterious case of missing sea lion pups, uncovering the whereabouts of a teen girl's missing family member, and unearthing clues in an Iowa history mystery!
Paperback / 978-1-68322-879-0 / $9.99

Camp Club Girls: Sydney
The Camp Club Girls are unraveling confusing clues that lead them through Washington, DC, and up to Fort McHenry, investigating peculiar tracks in sand of the Outer Banks, uncovering the source of menacing sounds in the Wisconsin woods, and helping a young girl search for clues about her Cherokee heritage in North Carolina!
Paperback / 978-1-68322-942-1 / $9.99